THE LEGEND OF
FIRE HORSE WOMAN

THE LEGEND OF
FIRE HORSE WOMAN

JEANNE WAKATSUKI HOUSTON

KENSINGTON BOOKS
http://www.kensingtonbooks.com

For Jim

ACKNOWLEDGMENTS

Among the many who contributed to the making of this novel I want first to offer a much belated word of thanks to Patricia Holt, Anita Walker Scott and Ernest Scott for their early belief in *Farewell to manzanar.* Their publication of that book enabled me to write this one.

Thanks, too, to George Diskant, who encouraged me when I needed it most; to George Ow Jr., whose spiritual support and generosity allowed me to complete the first draft; and to Richard Stewart for his helpful input on the history of the Paiute Indians in Owens Valley.

I will always be grateful to these dear friends, whose responses to the manuscript have been invaluable: Linda Craighead, Diane Devine, Marta and Heather Gaines, Maxine Hong Kingston, Mary Laporte, Kristin O'Shee, Judy Phillips, Marion Stegner, and Jane Yamashiro.

I'm especially grateful for a fellowship from the Sourisseau Academy of San José, California, which gave me the chance to interview Japanese picture brides; for a U.S.–Japan Creative Artists Exchange Fellowship, which sent me to Japan; and a Rockefeller Foundation Residency at Bellagio, Italy.

And finally, my deepest thanks to my agent, Linda Allen, and editor, John Scognamiglio, whose guidance has brought this book to fruition.

Prologue

In late spring of 1942, the biting wind of California's high desert blew harder than anyone could remember. Howling and tearing up sagebrush, it sent skeletal tumbleweeds cartwheeling like drunken clowns over the sandy flatlands. Churned-up dust gathered in clouds so thick they blotted the noon sun, causing speculation of an unscheduled eclipse. Some explained that dark spring as the time when the Great Wind Gods of the Four Directions had met to display their wrath—or perhaps sorrow—at some mysterious event.

Were the gods speaking to the ghosts of desert Indians who once populated the land? The Owens Valley Paiutes, driven out long before the Los Angeles Water District stole the river's water, were now scattered throughout the nation. Like windblown smoke, their villages disappeared from this elevated land so close to the sky, a land once alive with wild geese, deer, and elk, a rich land nurtured by light of a constant sun—brilliant even in winter—and pure waters from the Sierra Nevada Mountains.

The Paiutes might have explained that the balance of power between Grandfather Mountain and Grandmother Valley had been corrupted when Los Angeles engineers carved canals in the earth, lined them with cement, and channeled life-giving waters to the south. They might have explained how Grandfather drew snow to the granite peaks of his shoulders and sent it as liquid crystal down his body, directing it to the valley floor, where Grandmother received it into her breasts. Trickling rivulets and gurgling creeks fanned out from her bosom, feeding the surrounding land.

What caused the wind gods to converge that spring? Was it exasperation at the condition of the ravaged land? Sorrow for the disappearance of its stewards, the Paiutes? Or could it have been a warning? An omen of things to come?

Coincidentally, at that exact time, something strange was happening in the Owens Valley. Between the towns of Independence and Lone Pine, a hurriedly constructed compound of black tar-papered barracks arose in the parched desert. Surrounded by barbed-wire fencing, a square-mile area teemed with thousands of dark-headed bodies people dressed in somber clothes, huddling in groups for protection from the raging wind. Soldiers with rifles marched around the perimeter. The American flag fluttered its colors at the camp's entrance. What was this mysterious encampment that had sprouted up so suddenly in the barren valley?

Roaming aimlessly amid piles of suitcases, bundles, and boxes, the people waited to greet newcomers arriving in buses. Their faces were Asiatic, with complexions of ruddy brown, warm tan, and pale ivory. Almond-shaped eyes, some almost round and others thin and narrow, watered and turned red from stinging sand. They looked Indian. Could these be the scattered Paiutes now returning to the homeland? Was the droning *"Namu amida butsu"* chanted by Buddhist devotees in truth an Indian incantation?

No. These were not Indians—although some genetic particle of the blood running through their veins may have coursed through those of Mongolian nomads who, eons ago, crossed the Aleutians from Asia and later migrated down the frozen tundra to the lush North American continent. These were Japanese-Americans—immigrants and their children and grandchildren. And Japan was at war with America.

Dressed in a dark green kimono, salt-and-pepper gray hair swept up into a pompadour, a striking older woman stood alone, apart from the milling crowd. She faced west, toward Mount Williamson, black onyx eyes glittering with a liquid light that may have come from tears—or perhaps inspiration. Those steep peaks soaring toward Heaven could have drawn from her the undisguised strength that set her apart from others. Or possibly, her eyes simply were looking west over the mountains past the Central Valley, to the Coastlands, and beyond them, to the Pacific Ocean and Japan, where she had been born and raised until coming to America at the turn of the century.

Matsubara Sayo wondered if her life was to end in this desert. Years of surviving in America had given her an invincibility and a wisdom that allowed her to accept hardship, tragedy, and betrayal and see them simply as the underbelly of freedom. Was this prison camp another "underbelly"? Or was her journey in *Bii Koku* (the beautiful land), begun in Hiroshima thirty-nine years before, to end in this wasteland? Was she to ascend to the River of Souls in the Clouds humiliated and defeated, cast out of the country by "white ghosts" who saw all persons with Japanese blood as the enemy?

Matsubara Sayo refused that sentence. She, after all, was a Fire Horse Woman. Hadn't she defied the portents surrounding this birth sign, transforming morbid omens into qualities of courage, imagination and splendor? Her history would not end here though she knew a history would begin here for those born within the barbed-wire fence. As with the Kabuki stories she had learned in Japan—tales rivaling American soap operas—she knew legends would arise from this insult.

Let the winds rave, the sun scorch, frost and snow congeal. She would persevere, as she had for many years before. She would harness their *kami* power and transmute it into compassion and beauty.

Thus, this proud woman welcomed the darkened sky and gritty sand blown in her ears and mouth. She stood tall and alone and imagined the sounds of clacking wood in the wind. They were the sounds of wood blocks striking against each other, the brittle clacks that heralded the beginning of a drama. A legend was being born. A history begun across the ocean on a volcanic island chain called Japan had arrived at a concentration camp in California's high desert country.

ACT I

The Worlds of Sayo, Hana, and Terri

Matchmakers

Hiroshima, Japan, 1902

Go-Between sat in the small hut of the Seamstress, sipping tea with polite slurps. Flattered to be acting as matchmaker for the prominent Matsubara, he was more than curious to glimpse the beautiful Sayo, whose comeliness sparked both lust and envy in the hearts of villagers throughout the countryside.

"As you know, Matsubara Tadanoshin is looking for a wife for his son Hiroshi in America. He is the second son. But Matsubara is treating him like the eldest, because he feels he is starting a new family line across the ocean." Go-Between was letting Seamstress know Matsubara was not following the tradition where the oldest son inherited everything. The second son would be a good catch, too.

Purposefully sitting so she faced the family shrine on the tokonoma, *Seamstress poured another cup of tea for her guest.*

"Hai. I know about Matsubara's quest. Everyone in this village and miles around knows."

"Then you must be aware why I am here to see you."

"Hai. I am, in fact, honored and pleased for my niece Sayo."

Her directness opened the way for discussion, prompting Go-Between to proudly report the Matsubara background, their samurai lineage, and impressive holdings. His feigned humility did not escape Seamstress's keen eye. She could use to her advantage his need to vicariously identify with the Matsubara.

"Hiroshi is doing quite well in America. He hopes to start a shoyu *manufacturing business there someday." He produced a pic-*

ture of a serious-faced young man. Clean-shaven, with thick black hair slicked down on a narrow head, Hiroshi stared out from the photograph, large oval eyes fixed on Seamstress's face. An uneasiness swept over her. She felt sadness emanating from those eyes, pleading with her, for what she knew not.

Unnerved, she glanced over at the shrine. Did she catch a glint of light flickering off the gold filigree?

"He is thirty-two years old, born in the second year of the Meiji," Go-Between said.

Again Seamstress looked at the shrine, the only ornate fixture in the small bare hut. Where was a sign? She needed a sign, an omen to guide her next move. Should she go forward with the carefully made-up background for Sayo?

Go-Between smiled, gapped yellow teeth glistening from the tea. He coughed lightly. Seamstress could see he was trying to fill the moment of silence with sound, any sound.

A brisk wind rushed through the open partition of the front porch, knocking over a small vase on the tokonoma. *She drew in a deep breath, trembling with the knowledge her dead brother's spirit had spoken. Veiling eyes with politeness, she began to recite Sayo's history.*

"Aha! What good coincidence! He was born in the year of the Snake, no? Sayo is twenty-two, born in the eleventh year of the Meiji. Makes her ten years younger than Hiroshi . . . a good age span, don't you think?"

Go-Between's face did not register any questions upon hearing Sayo's age. He had heard rumors she was older—that she was twenty-four, even twenty-six. Gossip abounded about this beauty, but nothing negative had been uncovered from his early investigation. The peasants' logic was that since she was unmarried, she must be unmarriageable, and although no one remembered any attempts or failures in setting up a match, stories flew that secret inquiries had uncovered serious flaws—insanity tainted her family; she was the mistress of a high-placed official; she suffered from the dreaded inheritable tuberculosis.

Encouraged by Go-Between's attentive gaze, Seamstress continued, "As you know, my niece is an orphan, the only daughter of my older brother. He was a fisherman who was lost at sea. His wife died soon after—from grief." She forced a tear and let it slide down her cheek before wiping it away with a kimono sleeve. This second lie came more easily. After all, an accidental death while working was more honorable than having been the victim of a catastrophe caused by carelessness. It was respectable for the sea gods to have claimed her brother, not the raging inferno sparked by a glowing cinder left undampered in a kitchen fire and fanned by a turbulent wind sweeping down the mountains. A smoking ash heap was all that remained of her brother, his wife and son, and their small hut in the northern snow country. Sayo was the only survivor. Protected by the gods, she was visiting Seamstress when tragedy struck.

Go-Between need not know about the fire. People would wonder why the family deserved such ill fate. Sayo's past must not be tainted with any bad karma.

"My niece is adept at sewing. I am a seamstress, and she has been with me since she was a child. I have tried to raise her as my own daughter. She is quiet, but not timid. Does Hiroshi-san have a forceful nature?"

Blinking, Go-Between hesitated for one telling moment. He realized he knew nothing of Hiroshi's personality. Why hadn't he asked Matsubara? Biding for time to think of some profound and distinctive quality, he slurped his tea noisily, then studied the leaves at the cup's bottom, as if modesty prevented him from exalting Hiroshi too profusely.

He cleared his throat. "Yes, Hiroshi-san is very strong. In fact, he is quite a leader, would have become some military officer had he remained in Japan. Unlike most second-born sons, he has a mind of his own and is independent." He guessed she wanted to hear that. Who cared if it was not true? They would be far away in America. No one to blame, especially Go-Between, humble salt-maker, chosen by the illustrious Matsubara to acquire a wife for his son. Enjoying the thought of not being held accountable, he began to elaborate.

"He is also quite poetic and scholarly. And a very able painter. I understand he is learning the gaijin's language and even knows how to drive those machines."

She nodded, allowing eyes to widen in amazement. "Ah, so . . . they will get along. Sayo writes poetry and even knows how to read and write." She didn't have to make this up about her niece. Even as a small child, Sayo had shown a curiosity for literary things, begging to learn how to read. It was fortunate her friend, the old retired geisha from Kyoto, had taken an interest in the lively orphan, teaching her to read and write, enchanting her with Kabuki stories, even instructing her to play the shamisen *and to sing.*

"As for her health, my niece is in excellent condition—no insanity or T.B. in the family, and no history of barrenness."

Relieved by the agreeable way in which the discussion was progressing, the matchmakers relaxed and let their imaginations and tongues run wild with fabricated backgrounds for the young couple. They indulged themselves with fanciful talk, realizing there would be no checking up or further investigation. Free to create the perfect match, they projected upon the principals all those attributes and talents they wished had been their own.

When Go-Between stood up to leave, the atmosphere was jovial and light. The emptied teapot might just as well have been a spent cask of sake.

"Now, what did you say Sayo-chan's sign is?" He was already referring to the bride-elect in a familiar way."

"I believe she is a Rabbit," Seamstress lied. "The Snake and Rabbit are a good match. This union must be blessed by the gods." She was beginning to believe the new background she had created for her niece. "Please convey to Matsubara-san my delight in uniting our families with this marriage. I know my brother and his wife, who now look down on us from the River of Souls in the Clouds, are truly honored."

Go-Between bowed deeply, trying to imitate Matsuhara's authoritative style. "Excellent," he said and stepped outside the tiny hut. He hesitated for one moment, wishing Sayo would arrive so he might glimpse the famed beauty at close range. But his wish was not to be granted that day. He took leave of Seamstress, his disappointment soon replaced with the anticipation of attending the wedding, which surely would be the most talked-about event for years to come.

Teruko

Terri waits in line for the typhoid shot. She never has had an injection and dreads the needle, silk-thread thin, poised to penetrate upper arms of internees before her. The mysterious fluid forces screams from children and causes adults to squint their eyes. She leans back against Obachan, finding comfort in the incense smell always emanating from her grandmother's kimono. Obachan's musky smell. Pine forests, mushrooms, ancient moss. A damp smell that cools the dust-laden desert air.

"Don't look at the needle," Obachan says in Japanese. "Turn your face away and think of its bite as an insect's kiss." Her arms drape around Terri's neck, long cotton sleeves flowing down over her granddaughter's thin chest where developing breasts raise the kimono's circular pattern into two small mounds.

"Why do we need to get these shots?" asks Terri in English. "I heard they make you sick."

Sayo understands the American language but rarely speaks it. What she does not do well she refuses to do at all. She would rather appear mute than foolish, and thus refrains from speaking pidgin, the singsong half-English most elders in camp speak. Terri honors this. Even though she hated learning the language when she was younger, she is now grateful for the closeness to her grandmother that comes with understanding Japanese. Like the silky sound of water trickling over worn rocks, Obachan's voice smoothes the barbed edges of the unknown.

"We won't get sick," says Obachan. "I have some good herbs I brought from home."

As the line inches forward, Terri keeps her face averted from the white cloth-covered table where two young internee volunteers are jabbing waiting arms. Exposed and vulnerable, the naked flesh surrenders to the needle's swift violation. Swab. Prick, swab.

Terri smells alcohol wafting up from the cotton and needle trays. She chances a glance at her torturer and sees lidless snake eyes gleaming from a smooth, impassive face, unlined as a *mochi* moon cake, thin lips creased in a downward curve. With horror, she watches the needle approach, unable to look away from its piercing attack. Ping! Surprised, she feels no pain, only a strange tickle, as if a feather has gently brushed against her. Only when cotton is pressed against the puncture does she feel a slight burning.

"Next," the volunteer says, thin lips cracking open.

She watches Obachan roll up her kimono sleeve, slowly and deliberately, undaunted by the young woman's coldness. Obachan turns, lowering her eyes. With one arm extended and face tilted, she looks like a dancer in the musical stories she teaches. Terri imagines her grandmother fluttering a gold-gilt fan against her cheek, and hears *shamisen* music plinking in the background. With a stamp of the foot, Obachan commands flower petals to shower down from the yellow sky. Like purple snow, blossoms float over them, overcoming the sharp medicinal smell with a sweet plum fragrance.

They leave the mess-hall area. Terri's arm now aches, and she holds it tightly with her other hand. The afternoon wind has begun to blow, churning up gusts of sand that prickle her face as they walk toward their barrack. Obachan glides beside her, wooden *getas* skimming over the gravelly dirt road. She is slim and willowy, pliantly bending like a marsh reed in the wind. It is hard to believe she is sixty-four, a fact that gives Terri great pleasure whenever she has the chance to reveal it and witness the widened eyes of disbelief.

Obachan is tall for a Japanese woman, with skin the color and texture of unblemished ivory. Always erect, her back as strong and straight as a temple spire, she looks taller than she is and commands respect wherever she goes. Terri has seen even the haughtiest of persons, such as the block manager, shrivel in deference before her.

Terri is sometimes embarrassed watching reactions to her grand-mother, such as suspicious glances from women, especially wives of the issei, the first-generation immigrants who had avoided the federal prisons and were interned in camps with their families. Issei men seemed to like Obachan and treated her differently than other women, even their own wives.

Terri remembers the incident with Mr. and Mrs. Tani, who live in the barracks next door, when they first came to camp. Arriving earlier, Terri's family eagerly had awaited the new neighbors, hoping they would be from Los Angeles and would bring some word from the outside. But they came from Bainbridge, near Seattle, and had no news except to say the train trip was very long and their daughters threw up continuously from Washington State to California.

A few days later Mrs. Tani—who looks about Obachan's age but is probably younger—was struggling to lift a roll of linoleum given by the authorities for covering the splintery wooden floors. Old man Tani, in his shiny black boots, stood and watched with gnarled hands on hips. Obachan, who had been observing discreetly from her small cubicle, floated over, kimono sleeves flapping like sails. Passing Tani-san without a glance, she offered help to Mrs. Tani. Rubber Boots, unaware he had been spied on, seemed shaken by her appearance. He began berating his wife, shouting, "Baka! You are such a slow-witted donkey!" while she and Obachan stood holding the heavy linoleum roll between them. Tears welled in Mrs. Tani's eyes and her face turned as red as the crimson lacquered bowl Obachan keeps before her shrine.

Still Rubber Boots refrained from offering a hand. Then, just as Terri began walking over to help, she saw her grandmother swing her end of the roll like a giant baseball bat and smash it down with great force on Tani-san's oversized boot!

She wheeled around, grabbing Terri's hand, and pulled her back to their barracks. Terri knew her grandmother was furious, slamming the door and causing plank walls to shake as if an earthquake had struck. She noticed her grandmother's face was pale and her hand trembled as she brushed a gray wisp of hair from her forehead.

Remaining silent, Terri sat on the floor. She knew better than to draw attention to herself until her grandmother had recovered her poise. She sat with legs folded beneath the buttocks, as she had been taught to do, to sit in calm repose for hours until her legs turned to wood.

Finally, Obachan spoke. "Teruko-chan, you must promise something." The Japanese words tinkled like wind chimes. But Terri knew the chimes could change in an instant into clashing steel gongs, ringing with a resonance that could topple temples. She had witnessed enough of her grandmother's unpredictable explosions to know the unruffled exterior was an illusion—not so much deception as powerful strategy. Dazed, some of Obachan's challengers never knew what hit them.

"Yes, I promise."

"Never . . . never allow a man to speak to you like that."

Allowing the words to float between them, Terri had not answered immediately. She knew Obachan considered silence between words more important than the words themselves.

"Why was old Rubber Boots cursing his wife?" she finally asked. "What made him so mad?"

"I humiliated him. But he couldn't attack me, so he cursed his wife!" She smiled slyly. "I don't think he expected some smashed toes!"

"How come Mrs. Tani lets him talk to her like that? She was acting like *she* did something wrong."

"She did! She allowed him to treat her like a dog!"

Then Terri felt her grandmother's intense eyes, jet black, piercing, drawing out some reflection from her own, a reflection she herself had not known was there. Pulled by surging currents into this mysterious and bottomless underwater world, Terri tried to enter Obachan's vision. But she only perceived two shiny abalone pendants where her grandmother's eyes should have been.

"Remember, Rubber Boots is not a man . . . a *big* man," Obachan said. "He needs those boots to hold him up." She began to chuckle. "He needs those boots because his feet are so small they would poke holes in the ground when he walks!" No longer able to hold back laughter, she fell over on her side, covering her face with a kimono sleeve.

Terri laughed uproariously, imagining Tani-san sinking into the ground with each step, two rubber peg legs stabbing and thrusting as he waded through the earth.

Terri learned early that Obachan's lessons—especially the serious ones—end with images so crazily humorous they seem to make no sense. But she long since has given up trying to interpret her grandmother's visions. Listening with open mind, she anticipates the endings as if they were punchlines of good jokes, not deep admonitions carved in stone. And almost always, they both end up laughing, laughing so hard that Terri rarely forgets what Obachan really is teaching in her own unusual way.

Walking over the sandy firebreak between Block 16—where their barrack is—and Block 17's mess hall, they meet Hana. Terri noticed her earlier, a lone figure approaching from a distance, wavering in heat lines rising up from the dusty firebreak. Terri knows it is her mother. Not just because of her height—she is taller than Obachan—it is her bearing, the way she slumps forward, curving the upper back into a tortoiseshell that encircles the chest, enclosing and safeguarding a heart, Terri views, as heavy and sinking. She wishes her mother's stance were more like the erect, challenging one of Obachan.

Hana's head is covered with a navy-and-white polka-dotted kerchief, knotted under her chin like a babushka. She wears tan-colored slacks, full-legged with a pleat, and a white short-sleeved blouse. Tucked under a slim arm, she carries a thick crocheted purse with wooden clasps. Terri wonders why her mother always carries a purse when there is no use for money in camp.

"Where's everyone else?" Terri asks, showing Hana the injection on her arm.

Hana inspects it silently. Terri doesn't expect any torrent of talk. Her mother always dispenses words rather stingily, as if she were measuring crumbs from a leftover cake.

"No mark," Hana says, more to Obachan than to Terri.

Obachan asks, "Why are you alone? Aren't Tadao and the rest getting shots?"

"Getting them at Block Twenty-two. Fewer people there. I came looking for you two." she speaks English, crisp and clean.

Terri thinks her mother should have been a nurse or doctor instead of a seamstress. She has seen movies with Claudette Colbert and Carol Lombard playing nurses, and they spoke just like her.

"Well, we're finished." Obachan asks, "Do you want us to go back and keep you company?"

"Oh no. I'll go home with you now and get my shot tomorrow," Hana answers in Japanese, turning around to join them in their walk back to their barrack. "They're doing it again at Block Twenty-two."

As they saunter across the firebreak, a whirlwind twists toward them. The funnel of stinging sand whistles ominously, wildly spinning dried sagebrush and twigs like debris from a huge explosion. Terri never had known, nor ever imagined, before coming to camp, wind of such ferocity and fickleness. A windstorm could materialize in seconds, blowing sheets of sand that turned day into night. In the few weeks since the family's uprooting from their home on the coast, Terri already has encountered at least a dozen whirlwinds, the first one frightening her so badly she remained inside the barrack for one whole day, refusing to leave even for meals at the mess hall.

The three figures run from the approaching funnel. Terri, grasping her aching arm, flails long, thin legs that jut from red shorts. She is in front of Obachan, who clatters in *getas*, one hand holding down her flapping kimono, the other hanging onto Hana, who is now bent over like a sickle, pant legs fluttering. They lurch against the wind, unable to escape its wrath. It whistles by, flinging tiny stones and bits of wood like a jilted lover spitting out bitter accusations. But as suddenly as it appeared, it dissipates. The silence is heavy, more like the pall before a storm than the aftermath of a spent whirlwind. Trudging toward their not-yet-familiar barrack-home, the three stride together, each with her own thoughts.

Terri does not fully understand why her family now lives in this foreign land, this glaring, naked expanse of sand surrounded by barbed wire and rattlesnakes and Indian ghosts. She remembers a different kind of sand, the yellow, grainy sand of the beach in front of their home in Venice where she, her older sister Carmen and her brother Mac spent hours lolling in its warmth. How much she misses that beach and ocean, seaweed smells and the clatter of waves on hard, wet sand. Mac and Carmen were adept body-surfers, catching the curls, riding the foamy white froth like seals. She wishes she had learned to ride the waves before coming to this camp. Who knows if she will ever see the ocean again?

She and Obachan had shared a large room, actually the enclosed front porch of a rambling frame house on the promenade lining the beach. All her friends, mostly Portuguese and Italian kids whose fathers, like hers, were fishermen—also lived along the promenade. Carmen ran with the Jewish crowd, who lived in the neighboring Ocean Park and Santa Monica, some whose parents were in the movie business. At sundown on Fridays, Carmen would light candles at the Jewish temple, and when the word came that the Japanese had to move away, it was the rabbi and some temple members who came to the house offering condolences.

"Why must we leave Venice?" she'd asked Obachan, who averted her face, mumbling about a war with Japan.

"But we're Americans!"

Obachan didn't answer, seeming so preoccupied Terri knew better than to bother her with more questions.

After that day the whole house was in an uproar, with her father yelling at everyone and talking about selling his boat, the car, even their furniture. If they'd owned the house, instead of renting it, they probably would have had to sell that too.

Then came the peddlers, who descended upon them like vultures, offering pittances for her mom's silver and crystal. Obachan stunned everyone, especially the stubble-faced peddler, when she broke every piece of the china set, smashing them on the porch, rather than sell for the insulting prices he'd offered. But time caught up with them, and her dad had to leave their furniture and almost all their belongings in the cellar, hoping the landlord would honor his word to safekeep them until the family returned. Her dad gave his car to a Portuguese friend. The bank repossessed his boat, since he'd no longer be able to make his payments.

When she heard they were going to "camp," Terri had not been too scared, thinking it might be some kind of vacation camp like the rich kids from school went to, where they rode horses, swam in rivers, and hiked. What a shock when the bus arrived at windswept Manzanar, bleak and dusty, plunked in the middle of an empty desert.

Marriage

Hiroshima, 1902

A week before Go-Between called on Seamstress, Sayo had a dream. She was climbing a steep mountain, rocky and narrow. On her back she carried a saddle. The leather was slick and shiny, burnished mahogany from many years of use. The path seemed endless as she trudged upward, weighted by the ungainly load. When she reached a ledge that stretched back into the mountain's side, a huge mansion loomed at the end of an open space that looked like a meadow. Carved jade dragons and snakes writhed on massive doors locked at the entrance. It began to storm, thunder booming and lightning illuminating a black sky with jagged lights. She pounded on the doors. The moment the heavy panels parted, the storm abated and a hazy golden light glimmered from within. Surrounded by this radiance, a figure approached. She strained to recognize it. A tall male, deeply tanned, with long black hair adorned with feathers beckoned, inviting her in. When Sayo stepped past the doors, the figure disappeared, but left a simple wooden box. She opened it gingerly. Inside glinted a slim gold ring.

Mentor, trusted friend and teacher, gave Sayo her opinion of the dream. "You tell me that you think this dream is boring, that you are silly even to talk about it." Her wrinkled face was impassive. "Do you think every moment in your waking life is thrilling, or catastrophic? There is no such thing as a boring dream . . . or boring life. Only your interpretation of it determines its liveliness."

Sayo answered, "But you know how weary I am of this village.

That is why my dreams seem so meaningless, isn't it? How can you say there is no such thing as a dull life?"

Mentor said, "You create your life, my child. Besides, your dream is not uninteresting. It is actually prophetic—and promising. A ring is a promise, you see." Her small eyes flashed, a sign that encouraged Sayo. "Perhaps a promise to wed."

"To marry? Who? There's no man worth talking to in Hiroshima!"

Mentor closed her eyes and seemed to fall asleep. Sayo knew she had just sunk into a reverie that could last for a few moments or several hours, having learned at an early age that Mentor often fell into this strange state where she appeared frozen in one position, almost always with a faded yellow silk fan, painted with pink peonies, resting against her cheek. She had thought a secret code was hidden among the peonies, words Mentor read to enter into trance, but one day had slyly studied the fan and found nothing.

That was many years ago. Mentor grew old and no longer fluttered the fan. Sayo noticed lately her beloved teacher fell into this pseudo-sleep more often, which caused her to worry she may have suffered a stroke and was actually unconscious.

Seeming to sense Sayo's concern, Mentor awakened and smiled mischievously. "You will not marry someone who is here, but he will be from Hiroshima." She ignored Sayo's questioning look. "I cannot tell you anything more . . . except"—she leaned closer—"you must prepare yourself to leave this place soon."

From the tone of her voice, Sayo knew she was being dismissed and would not learn anything more that day about her impending marriage. She bowed respectfully and lit some incense in front of the household shrine. Her prayers were for Mentor's well-being. The aging geisha seemed to be fading away, slipping into a dream world Sayo could not enter. The possibility Mentor would remain there indefinitely filled her with anxiety.

As she opened the sliding door, Sayo heard Mentor call after her in a surprisingly strong voice. "Sayo-chan, be certain you dance at the festival next week. Wear your purple yukata *and peach-colored* obi. *And come see me before you go."*

Sweet incense smell trailed behind Sayo as she made her way home. It was already dusk, and the crickets were chirping. Her heart beat lightly. She felt buoyant, her slippered feet seeming to float over the pebbled walkway. Dare she believe what Mentor said? Was she truly going to leave this village?

Seamstress chattered as she hemmed a kimono. "You should see all the girls getting their hopes up. Catching a Matsubara is no small thing . . . even if it does mean going to America."

Sayo sat across from her aunt. Nodding respectfully, she pretended to be interested in this gossip. She stitched a wide sash patterned with white chrysanthemums to be worn with the green kimono.

Seamstress continued. "Both the Kato daughters are hoping he will pick one of them. Even the widows are hopeful. Remember Hisa? You know—she was the one who refused to stay with her husband's family after he died. She has her mind set on marrying a nari-ken."

The nari-ken, those who had been to America and returned to Japan, intrigued Sayo. The Nishi and Okubo families from the neighboring village had reappeared after six years away, wealthy, and, to many villagers, insufferably arrogant. It was not just their wealth that piqued, it was their new demeanor. They seemed to know—or have seen—something so miraculous their very souls had been transformed, an experience that could not be conveyed to normal Japanese. Sayo had heard they wore strange foreign clothes when they traveled to Tokyo and Osaka.

"These modern times . . . In the old days, who would dare to even think of leaving a dead husband's home. I wonder if these rich Japanese from America are a good influence." Seamstress shook her gray head, looking sympathetically at her niece, who, she realized, was destined to lead a spinster's life, even though possessing such great beauty. Raising her like a daughter, dutifully and with as much love as she could impart after seeing to her own four children, Seamstress wanted a fulfilled life for Sayo. It vexed her that such potential was cursed by the tragic Fire Horse sign, the ruinous birth date that occurred once every sixty years. Who would marry

a Fire Horse Woman? If I were a man, *she thought,* I would take a chance, even if it meant dying before she did. *There were many more widows than widowers, anyway. Men usually died before their wives—why such fear of the Fire Horse Woman?*

But, then, would she have allowed her sons, Teiji and Susumu, to marry one? She thought of the stories, terrible tragedies wrought upon families where Fire Horse Women were brought in as wives. They devoured the husbands. They were so powerful and cunning, they acted independently from the family and could not be controlled by men. Always beautiful, with elegant tastes, tall and willowy with a sensual exterior that cloaked an explosive nature, they were too strong as females, and thus to be avoided as wives at all cost. Recalling the ominous superstitions surrounding the Fire Horse sign, Seamstress's heart sank deeper. What was she to do with Sayo? She was past the marrying age. When she was young, she had thought of sending her to Kyoto, to train in one of the better geisha houses. But blood ran thick. Kamisama *had bestowed upon women the most precious gift of motherhood. Geisha could never marry. She could not do that to her brother's child. And Mentor had advised against it. Perhaps a miracle would happen, or the gods would intervene in some way. Seamstress could only keep praying to* Kamisama *and hope her brother's spirit heard her pleas.*

The women danced in a circle, offering homage to the wind gods. Not since the last hurricane, when all the crops were destroyed and sea water had polluted the coastlands, had the village engaged in such festivity. Pulsing drumbeats and wailing flutes filled the summer air, urging young maidens to swirl and bend, kimono sleeves ruffling a breeze in the hot stillness.

As Mentor had instructed, Sayo had worn a purple yukata. *Before coming to the festival, she had visited the old geisha, who studied her with approval and gave her a carved ivory ornament for her hair and an old silk fan.*

"Watch for Matsubara," she had said. "Do not be afraid to look him straight in the eyes. You may keep the comb, but return the fan to me after the festival."

*   *   *

Matsubara Tadanoshin, the patriarch of his clan, was not pre-pared for the directness of her gaze. Through bamboo slats of the fan hiding her face, Sayo's black eyes, luminous as glass, met his. Yes, she was as beautiful as he had heard. But there seemed more to her than mere physical perfection. Surprising himself, he had held his breath when those onyx eyes cut into his. How could one bold look— not even coyly seductive at that—take his breath away? Beautiful women were no rarity in his life. He had enjoyed a great share of mistresses, geisha, and even the young widow of his de-ceased friend Imuta. Was he getting old? Too easily excited by a promising look?

He watched the willowy figure. Like a stately iris, the purple ki-mono stood out against the pale pink and green lightness of the oth-ers. Narrow hands, fingers long, undulated to the bamboo flute's whine. Feeling hypnotized by the snakelike movements, he forced himself to look away.

Was she appropriate for Hiroshi? He knew nothing of her back-ground except she was the niece of old widow Seamstress. It did not matter that she was an orphan. In fact, he thought it wise to choose someone not too attached to family in Japan. America was far away. Homesickness could become a problem.

He wondered what her age was. Why had this ripe plum not been plucked earlier? Although tart, slightly green fruit had its ad-vantages—the ripening process could be controlled, the immature fruit protected from bruises and discolorations, resulting in a flaw-less product that was a reflection of the caretaker's good taste. He also knew, though, fruit allowed to ripen on the tree was sweeter, more succulent, and certainly unique—having been allowed to shape its own unpredictable form.

His eyes found her again. A rush in his loins, a tingling, familiar heat. A grandfather of three, he was virile and still easily awakened to lust. His appetite stimulated, he contemplated acquiring her for himself. After all, he was wealthy enough to consider this. Why couldn't he bring her into the family as his wife's maid, not uncom-mon for a man of his position. But he was wise enough also to know this would cause problems, the kind he was too old to deal with.

The covetous thoughts left. He would seek out Go-Between. As wife to his second son Hiroshi in America, she would be safely unavailable.

After the festival, Sayo reported to Mentor the day's events. She returned the fan, which she wrapped in a green cotton handkerchief she had received as a gift from cousin Ichiko.

"So," asked Mentor, "you did see him observing you?"

"Oh yes. In fact, he stared at me, almost rudely. He doesn't hide his feelings."

"My dear, he doesn't have to. He is a powerful man—rich and powerful. His father was, too." Mentor's eyes glazed over, and for a moment, Sayo was afraid she was going into reverie. She wanted to know more about Matsubara.

Quickly she asked, "Do you know his age? He looks so young to have grown sons."

Mentor's eyes penetrated hers. "He is not the one you should be interested in." But she added, after seeing her protégée's stricken look, "However, since he is going to be your father-in-law, I can understand your query. I would guess he is in his mid-fifties."

"And do you really think he has chosen me?"

"It is true. You will be living in America at this time next year."

Sayo's belly fluttered with excitement. She quelled the feeling, still accustomed to repressing any hope of good things happening to her. Protecting herself from disappointment, she had learned early it was best not to have expectations, or even desire. Still, she trusted Mentor. Dare she believe her?

Reading her mind, Mentor said, "I have never said anything more true to you, Sayo-chan. You will marry Hiroshi, second son of the Matsubara. It is destined." She hesitated. "It will, in some way, complete the purpose of our relationship . . . you and me."

"What do you mean?" Sayo asked. "Our relationship?"

Mentor fanned herself, slowly and deliberately, lifting wisps of hair from her face. She did this for some moments.

"I will tell you a well-kept secret. Well, maybe not everything, but part of it."

Sayo waited silently, with mounting excitement. Mentor rarely prefaced an imparting of knowledge with such a lure. She usually used tactics of surprise, shocking one with sudden pronounce-ments, sometimes accompanied by loud noises, slapping a hand on the floor or striking a gong. Once she broke a vase. The lesson she taught Sayo was etched in memory, quickly drawn up by the sight of a vase or the sound of breaking china.

"I was the mistress of Matsubara Junzaemon, Tadanoshin's fa-ther. That is the only reason why I returned to this miserable village . . . to be with him in his waning years." Tears gathered at the corners of Mentor's narrow eyes, two glistening splinters of silver. "You must marry Hiroshi. Perhaps you can have what I could not with Junzae-mon." She paused. "You can be a wife and have children."

Astounded, Sayo could not find words to comfort grieving Mentor. She knew her ancient teacher had been a geisha, a highly trained and sought-after courtesan. But she had not imagined a forbidden love for which a successful profession had been sacrificed. Somehow she had never thought of Mentor as being in love. So strong and wise, so emotionally invulnerable, never speaking of matters of the heart except with precise practicality. Although it saddened her to see Mentor weep, Sayo felt some happiness in knowing her teacher had experienced such passion. She herself had not known passion. A longing flickered within, a dull ember barely lit that might some-day explode into an ardor she could not even imagine now.

Mentor closed her eyes and fell into deep reverie. Wanting to hear more, Sayo almost shook her awake. But she knew the conver-sation was ended. She impulsively hugged her and slipped out of the hut.

The wedding by proxy was elegantly simple. The couple stood be-fore the white-robed Shinto priest, whose tall conical hat shook and waved like an obelisk in the wind as he chanted and bowed, reciting sacred marriage vows. Sayo's breath squeezed from her tightly bound chest, enwrapped by a gold brocaded obi, *lent by the Matsubara. She looked the immaculate* yamato *bride, smooth and unblemished as a fresh calla lily. Seamstress and Mentor had dressed her, adjust-ing and pinning, folding and smoothing the black silk kimono—also borrowed—while hovering about like dragonflies around a light. With hushed intensity the old women whispered last-minute advice and warnings.*

"Remember, your birth date is in the year of the Rabbit . . . the eleventh year of the Meiji."

"Mind yourself around the old man. He is no fool."

"Ingratiate yourself to the lady of the house. I hear she is gentle, and Hiroshi is her favorite."

In proxy for his son, Matsubara stood beside Sayo. She wished she could look him fully in the face, scrutinize his features to find some likeness of Hiroshi, whose photograph had revealed a soft, almost effeminate countenance. From a distance they did not look like father and son. But heeding Mentor's words, she hid her thoughts by gazing downward under the shade of the large white headdress covering her pompadoured hair. Mentor had said Matsubara was cagey and could read faces. She must remember to keep her mind still, eyes opaque, and mouth demure. Except for the telltale pulse beating in her neck like wings of a frightened bird, she appeared calm, as if marrying the father of her husband was quite an ordinary thing.

Matsubara himself was pleased, even smug about the match for Hiroshi. Although her face was now hidden beneath the wedding headdress, he knew its translucent beauty. For weeks after the festival, desire had festered in his loins, later replaced by a low-grade sadness, regret that his time was passing—perhaps his power, too. But the sake brewer was not one to give up easily. So what if she was his son's wife? Who knows what could transpire once she was within the Matsubara fold?

The moment had arrived for the san-san kudo, *"thrice three, nine times" rice wine drinking ritual, which created the deepest and most solemn of bonds between persons. Matsubara had provided the premium sake from his cellar. Three lacquered bowls, black with red interiors, were filled to the brim with deep yellow wine, shimmering liquid gold. He sipped three times from each. Sayo followed, chaste lips drawing up the warm sake noiselessly. He tried to catch her eye, see a glimpse of the fire that had burned him weeks before. But she kept her eyes modestly lowered.* This woman is no fool, *he thought. He felt envious of his son.*

Then, very slowly, without moving her head, she lifted her lids and looked at him. The movement was so deliberate, so subtle, no one else could have noticed it, not even the priest who stood before them, hands clasped and eyes narrowed as he chanted the blessings. Matsubara felt his hara *suck in involuntarily. For one moment he felt panic. Unmistakable power gleamed from those eyes. Matsubara recognized power, having been born to it and being adept at wielding it throughout his life. But to be challenged at his age—and by a woman—was not what he had envisioned when he arranged this marriage. Could he have chosen wrongly?*

Perhaps reading his thoughts, Sayo dropped her lids. She felt herself blushing, warmth spreading up her pale ivory neck. He was more handsome than she remembered. Dark-complexioned, narrow face with high cheekbones, thick black eyebrows like crows' wings jutting over fierce eyes. An aristocratic face with an unusual nose. High-bridged and hooked, a falcon nose.

She knew Seamstress had lied about her background, her age. She felt no guilt. Believing Mentor wholeheartedly, she accepted that the marriage was destined, that she was fated to live out the old geisha's dream. She was now a Matsubara. A new life awaited her in the Matsubara compound—and later in America!

The priest shook a wand of white paper strips around the couple, purifying their bonding, shaking away evil spirits. The ceremony was complete. As Sayo descended from the platform of the Shinto shrine, she was overcome with gratitude. She thanked the gods for ingenious Seamstress, for wise Mentor . . . and for Matsubara, her father-in-law, whom she saw as the deliverer and guide of her predestined karma.

Hana

Manzanar, Summer 1942

Today is Hana's thirty-sixth birthday. She sits in the shaggy planked room, alone, wondering if the family has remembered. She doesn't expect them to. After all, this internment has been a shock. Who has the calm and wit to think of such frivolous things as birthdays? Even after two months, she still is disoriented. Never comfortable with intimacy, she finds the close quarters with the whole family living together in one room the same size as their living room back home too stifling. At home she had the sewing studio where she could sometimes isolate herself and pretend to be tailoring outfits for customers.

Living near the beach had been a godsend, too. The kids spent much of their time outdoors, and Tad fished every day, often gone a week or more. Obachan, who kept herself in her porch-room, frequently visited friends in L.A.'s Japantown.

For a while Hana kept a garden in a large backyard area once overflowing with boxes, rusty pipe and tools from the boat. She hadn't known how to get Tad to clean up such a tangled mess. It was Obachan, in her smoothly diplomatic way, who convinced him to sell the stuff or haul it off. Then Mac helped Hana plow up the hard earth for planting. She filled the space with flowers and vegetables, orange and yellow marigolds, chard and napa cabbage, but soon found that neat squares of robust color and lush foliage could overwhelm her senses. Sometimes her face warmed as if she were blushing. She wasn't used to such vibrancy, preferring colors more subdued.

Now she is relieved to have the barrack to herself . . . for a few hours. Although the room is stuffy and hot, she declines to open the door. It's known that everyone is curious to see how others have arranged their space, and when doors are left open, it is an invitation to view the inside, even to enter and exchange polite pleasantries, something Hana hates to do.

Savoring the solitude, she prefers to sweat. The air reeks of vomit. Who would have thought the shots given at Block 22 would make the kids sick? She hears rumors the injections were too strong, giving them a slight case of typhoid. Terri and Obachan escaped because they received shots at Block 17, where the medical team was more experienced. She nursed Mac and Carmen as best she could, with no ice to cool, no pails or basins to catch the bile they retched up for days. She had to borrow pans from the mess hall, since so many were sick and other families had no receptacles to lend.

She thinks of her children. Mac, eighteen, and big, bigger than most *nihon-jin*. The only son, he is restless, bored, feeling their confinement more deeply than the rest. On the straw mattress, he was a vulnerable child again, allowing her to sponge his steaming body with cool wet cloths. Carmen, the middle one, suffers in silence. She reminds Hana of herself, somewhat covert, secretive, so in control of her exterior. Yet, beneath the stillness, Hana knows turbulence rumbles, threatening to crack that smooth surface. She sees it in her daughter's eyes, the way the black shimmering pools suddenly turn opaque, frozen, as if an icy wind has passed through her mind. Hana has felt her own eyes freeze, and knows it is fear, fear of revealing true feelings—especially desire—that deadens the eyes.

Terri is the youngest, the long-legged brown nymph whose wild imagination often gives Hana cause to wonder if she suffers from mental illness. She knows there is no history of insanity on her mother's side. Sayo is the most intelligent person she has ever known. If there is an abnormality, she is sure it comes from her husband's family. Terri's open, inquisitive nature, her lack of inhibition, make Hana uncomfortable. She does not admit to anyone, hardly to herself, she is relieved Sayo chose Terri as a young child to be her favorite. Even now, she feels guilty that Terri lives next door with Obachan, in a small cubicle her mother managed to wrangle from the block leader. Like everyone else, they had been assigned one room for the whole family. Sayo, who always had her own room—even when she lived with Hana—convinced Manager the compartment next to theirs was too small for any family and thus should be used for tea ceremony.

"The people will need *Ocha-ya* to transcend the humility of this place," she had advised Manager, who, wanting to appear worthy of his appointment and compassionate to the needs of his block's internees, agreed with her. He then graciously allowed her the use of the space after she informed him that she herself taught the ancient art.

"But you must live there too," he said. "The authorities would not like having an empty room used for something other than living in. They might get suspicious the space was being used for ritual . . . you know 'Shinto.' And you know 'Shinto' worship is forbidden."

Hana sits on the straw-stuffed mattress bed. It crackles and hisses as she shifts her sweating buttocks. Her cotton skirt is damp. A circle of perspiration has darkened the blanket under her. Blankets hang from ropes stretched across the room, providing partitions between sleeping spaces. Mushy walls. Wool walls, swollen and heavy, absorb the day's heat like sponges. At night they release their weight in sweltering waves, undulating as if fanned by a wind. She hates the steamy nights, the feel of wool beneath her. How she yearns for smooth cool sheets. To slide her thighs and calves against their silkiness.

Suddenly she lurches toward the closed door. Flinging it open, she steps outside, squinting in the afternoon brilliance. The sun is now high in a cloudless sky. Another scorching day. The door to the Tani compartment across from theirs is open. She sees a silhouette sitting back away from the opening, a slumped figure gently fanning herself. She knows it is Mrs. Tani. Sad Mrs. Tani. Hana feels sorry for her, even though everyone sees her husband as the culprit and she the long-suffering good wife, the block victim, perhaps a symbol of their own impotence against uncontrollable forces. And Old Rubber Boots struts around the block yelling at his wife and daughters, glaring disdainfully at other internees. Except Sayo. Around her he is meek, almost obsequious. Rumors fly that he has a crush on her, that perhaps the two might even be having an affair. Hana laughs at this. She knows her mother despises the old man, but wonders if she does not know the true reason why. Her mother would never act impolitely to anyone unless there was good cause, and she has seen Sayo snub him very pointedly.

Before Hana can reenter the compartment, she sees her husband round the corner, approaching with hurried steps. He seems preoccupied but manages a smile, revealing straight white teeth. He is handsome in a Japanese movie-star way, with refined features and thick curly hair. Unlike his short and stocky mother, he is lean, of medium height, resembling his father, who immigrated from Kumamoto. His mother, Kashi-san, came from Kagoshima, the southernmost province of Kyushu Island, and spoke a dialect even Sayo found difficult to understand. Her husband's people were strangers to Hana, more unknowable than the white Americans she had grown up with in Watsonville. Most of the time she feels her husband is a stranger, too.

"Hi, Tad," she says, forcing a smile. "Aren't you helping roof the new barracks in Block 32?"

"I am, but forgot my hat. This sun burns you bald-headed, it's so damned strong."

He steps inside. Hana follows, disappointed her time alone has been disrupted.

"Jesus! This place is stuffy!" His handsome face is scowling. "Did you close the door again, Hana?"

"No," she lies. "It's been open since lunch, since you all left."

"It stinks like puke. I can't figure out why you always keep the goddamned door shut." His voice is loud. "Keep the door open and air this fucking place out!"

She remains silent, sensing he is irritated about something else and has chosen to take it out on her. After twenty years of marriage, she has learned to make herself small and unnoticed when he is frustrated. He is the oldest son, and as Kashi-san and tradition had decreed, the firstborn male can do no wrong. He must be indulged, placated, and praised. Then harmony prevails in the home. It was up to her to see that his needs were met, and it was her duty to know without his having to tell what those needs were.

He rummages in the closet, which is basically a stack of large boxes constructed from packing crates he collected earlier when the camp hospital was being built. Finding a heavy canvas brimmed hat, he seems to relax and sits on their bed, the double-sized one they have created by pushing two cots together. He motions for her to join him. Obediently, she sits down, almost wishing he was still angry, instead of amorous. She knows he wants to make love. It's too hot, and she had been hoping for this time by herself. Privacy in camp is almost nonexistent. The olive-drab blankets provide slim partitions between sleeping spaces and hardly cloak the sounds of constrained lovemaking, confined to the middle of the night when others sleep— or during a chance time in the day when the compartment is empty.

He strokes her arm. She is perspiring, and his palm glides over the hairless skin.

"What if someone comes home?" she says, feeling only the debilitating heat that makes her body soggy.

"I'll lock the door." He jumps up and latches it.

"Don't you think it's too hot . . . on these wool blankets?" she murmurs lamely, smoothing the blanket-covered mattress.

"We'll do it on the floor." He is now fully aroused and has begun to shed his clothes. "Hurry, take off your dress."

She removes her blouse and skirt. She wears no brassiere.

"Here . . . on this cool spot on the floor." He has removed his shorts and now lies naked on the linoleum, his penis taut and pointing upward like a giant shaking finger reminding Hana of her duty.

She takes off her underpants and lies beside him. The linoleum is slick and cool.

"See, it's not so hot down here." His hands explore her body.

Surprised, she feels herself aroused by the linoleum's oily slipperiness under her buttocks and thighs, more sensually stimulating than Tad's stroking hands. He is sweating now, emitting a familiar salty smell.

Sayo's voice booms outside. "Would you care to have tea with me, Tani-san?" She is talking to their neighbor.

Tad mounts Hana immediately. Disquieted by her mother's voice she can barely respond to his furtiveness. But he is determined not to be denied this moment. His excitement builds to its explosive peak. Hana feels his pounding heart against her breasts, relieved he has climaxed so swiftly.

They get dressed. Tad's mood is now cheerful as he puts on the canvas hat, adjusting the brim before the small round mirror on the plank wall.

"Not so bad, this hat. The other guys wear baseball caps. But this looks a little more dressy, don't you think?" He tries to be funny, pulling the brim down over his ears.

Hana unlatches the door, hoping her mother and Mrs. Tani are gone. The sandy space between barracks is empty, and the shadowy figure has disappeared from the Tani apartment, whose doorway remains open. Tad shouts back to Hana as he heads for Block 32. "See you at mess hall for dinner."

Her spirits lift. If none of the kids return, she will have at least three hours to herself. She reenters the compartment, air now thick with a sweaty pungency, and closes the door.

Ghosts

It's a full-moon night. Yellow light illuminates the tar-papered barracks, streaming through windows, glinting off doorsteps fashioned from rocks. Except for an occasional cricket's chirp, the camp is quiet.

Inside her compartment, the appointed "tea ceremony" hut for the block, Terri lies awake on the cot. Her face sweats, not so much from the June-night heat, but from terror that closes her throat with an iron vise. She stares unblinkingly at the snake swaying above her head. Next to the open window, it writhes and twists, as if teasing, daring her to slap it away or smash its triangular head. It seems she has lain there for hours, too terrified to move or even cry out to Obachan, asleep on the floor on her futon.

She had been dreaming about snakes when she was awakened by the need to urinate. When she opened her eyes, she saw the snake above her, weaving rhythmically, as if dancing to an unheard flute. Paralyzed, she continues to gape, hoping her stare will prevent its slithering down onto her pillow.

She hears a "whooshing," the sound of wind spraying sand against tar paper. The snake disappears. Quick as a blink, it vanishes. Terri sits up and examines the window. Cotton curtains undulate, gracefully billowing as the breeze flows through. She realizes the snake was imagined, an illusion created by the swaying curtains. Relieved, she jumps off the bed to make the trip to the block latrine. Outside the barracks door she slides her feet into cool wooden *getas*, clogs her father has carved from leftover building lumber. She is glad the moon is full, giving off so much light, there are no shadows. Clattering to the small building in the center of the block, she rushes through its doorless entry. Behind a partition that prevents viewing from the outside, are two rows of six toilet stools, back to back, with no walls between.

Terri prefers to visit the latrine at night, when there is more privacy. When they first arrived, everyone was horrified to learn they would have to use the toilet with strangers sitting beside or behind them. The family all became constipated. In the beginning, someone from the family would scout when the building was empty and rush back to let the others know. But one latrine serving over a hundred and fifty people did not leave much unused time.

With her limitless ingenuity, Obachan had solved the problem. She found a large empty cardboard carton that had contained laundry soap, Oxydol. Cutting one side off, she fashioned a three-sided screen which could be placed around the toilet stool—like a "shoji-screen." Everyone in the block caught on to the invention and there was a scramble for empty cartons. After Obachan painted birds and flowers on hers, everyone copied that, too. Soon the latrine looked like a museum with painted shoji-screens of gaily colored flowers, pine trees, waterfalls, and cranes camouflaging the rows of white porcelain stools.

Tonight Terri doesn't lug the screen. Chances are no one will be there. After using the toilet, she washes at the long troughlike galvanized-steel sink, the cold mountain water almost icy to her hot palms. She wipes her hands on the thin cotton nightgown and runs out into the moonlight.

The cubicle she shares with Obachan is six buildings away. Illuminated, the black pine striped barracks look like toy models, each exact and clearly outlined in the stark landscape. She slows in her tracks, suddenly struck by the stillness, the absence of movement or sound, except for her *getas* clacking on the sand. Even the wind has ceased to blow.

Surprised at herself for not feeling afraid, she nevertheless stares straight ahead, not allowing her eyes to glimpse any peripheral motion. She knows her own imagination, how it creates dragons out of trees, one-eyed monsters from rocks, and snakes from cotton curtains. But now, for some strange reason, she feels safe. Perhaps the terror of the imagined snake had used up her allotment of fear for the night. Perhaps it is the moon's brightness that destroys all shadows.

Kata-kata. Kata-kata. Her *getas* scrape against hard-packed sand. She passes the Horimoto barrack, thinking how clannish the family is, how some internees are offended by their "high-toned" attitude— just because they owned a vegetable-packing shed in Brawley. Occupying the whole barrack, they are a powerful presence, and show their high opinion of themselves by hanging above the door-way of each of their four compartments a polished driftwood slab with their name carved into it.

In the open space between Horimoto's and the next barrack, she notices a tall, narrow rock erected in the center. Light gray, about six feet in height, it gleams silvery white. She gingerly steps closer, drawn by a strange warmth seeming to emanate from it. As she approaches, the monolith's sharp outline turns hazy, begins to quaver and shim-mer. When she is close enough to reach out and touch the wavering lines, a shape begins to materialize. She feels a tremendous heat. Still unafraid, she stares at a strange form taking shape before her.

More astonished by her own bravery than by the apparition, she whispers, "Are you a ghost?" Her breathing and heartbeat are calm.

He wears a loincloth and a shell necklace so full and large it covers his chest like a bib. His copper skin gleams. Long black braids hang below wide shoulders. The moonlight illuminates his face. He is smiling, eyes crinkling at the edges.

"I am no more a ghost than your imagination is not a real part of you." In a deep voice, he speaks a language she has never heard but, strangely, understands.

Terri says, "Well, if you are a ghost, I'm not afraid of you. I know you won't hurt me."

"Why would I hurt someone of my own tribe?"

Terri is surprised. "Tribe?" she asks. "What tribe?"

He doesn't answer. She studies his face. He is handsome, high-cheekboned, with a large hooked nose. Eyes that resemble her own, almond-shaped, black, and deep set, glow as they hold on her face. She feels a vague sense of familiarity, a tender tugging between her undeveloped breasts.

He raises his hand, then disappears. Terri is disappointed his de-parture is so swift. She walks over to the obelisk and touches it. Under her hands, the granite is warm, smooth, the hairless chest of a muscled man. From within, she thinks she discerns a pulsating; a strong, even pulse, a determined beat on a warrior's drum. Stroking the rock, she hopes to conjure up the vision again, and she smooths her palms across its sleekness, over and over, imagining sinew, veins, and bone.

Suddenly she hears the clatter of *getas*. Two robed figures walk hurriedly toward the women's latrine. It is their neighbor, old lady Tani, and her daughter. Terri moves away from the rock and circles to the back of the barrack. Her white nightgown flaps around her legs as she flies across the sand. *Anyone seeing me will think I'm a ghost,* she thinks. This thought amuses her and she is laughing aloud when she reaches the cubicle and rushes inside.

The next day at lunch Terri meets up with Mitzi, a new friend she has made from Block 15. Mitzi has heard food is better at Block 16 and joins Terri in the long queue at the mess hall. They wait for the signal that lunch is ready: Mrs. Goto beating on a pan with a large metal spoon. One of the cooks, Mrs. Goto was previously a seamstress back in Little Tokyo, Los Angeles. She takes great pride in her responsibility as gatekeeper of the food line. After years of working alone in her small, dark sewing studio, she suddenly is in command of hundreds who wait impatiently—but outwardly polite—for her appearance. She never has experienced such attention and takes her task very seriously, beating on the aluminum pan as if it were a taiko drum announcing the arrival of the president of the United States.

"I heard someone say a ghost appeared last night," says Mitzi between chomps of cucumber and rice, "right in the middle of the block near the latrine."

"Really? Did they say what it looked like? Who told you?"

"Sailor told me. He said Tani-san and her daughter . . . what's her name . . . Naomi . . . is that a Japanese name? They saw it when they were going to the latrine."

"Did Sailor describe the ghost?" Terri doesn't know Sailor very well, except that his real name is Hideo and he always wears a navy cap. That's why they call him Sailor.

"Not really." Mitzi is glad she has brought up the subject, enjoying

Terri's rapt attention. "Just that it was white and flew very fast—right over the top of the laundry room."

Terri giggles, realizing the Tanis had seen her running back to her cubicle. A warmth rushes through her as she remembers the vision. She's relieved the ghost witnessed last night was herself and not the warrior.

Obachan, sitting on Terri's other side, overhears Mitzi's last words about a ghost. She says in Japanese, "You know that this camp is built over Indian burial grounds, don't you?"

Mitzi turns, "What did she say? I never learned Japanese."

Terri tells her and lets the words sink in, savoring Mitzi's frightened look.

Obachan continues, "It's no wonder their spirits are appearing. We will be seeing lots of ghosts."

As Terri translates her grandmother's words, Mitzi's face pales. "I'm never going out after dark. I'm afraid of spirits."

"I am too," says Terri, though she was not afraid last night. She knows Mitzi would not understand if she told her about the incident.

The two girls gobble rice, Spam, and cucumber salad and gulp down milk from heavy white coffee mugs. Scrambling from their seats, a long wooden bench upon which Obachan still sits, they are about to leave when they are stopped by her voice, tinged with a sharpness Terri rarely hears. "Haven't you forgotten something?"

The girls freeze, lunch dishes in their hands.

"Just because we are not eating in our home does not mean we are not thankful for food."

Embarrassed, Terri sits down again. At home meals were always preceded by "Ita-da-kimasu," and followed by, "Go-chiso-sama." Weeks of eating at long rectangle tables, seated on backless benches surrounded by the din of chattering voices and banging pots had muffled her memory of intimate family meals and the accompanying rituals. She clasps her hands and with bowed head recites aloud, "Go-chiso-sama."

Obachan smiles forgivingly. "That's better. Because we are forced to live like animals does not mean we act like them."

*   *   *

Outside the girls are at loose ends, wondering what to do until dinnertime. Mitzi suggests watching the baseball game between the Red Sox from Block 11 and the EMANONs of Block 3. Both teams are teenage males, with one Red Sox player reportedly very good-looking, resembling Tyrone Power. This isn't Terri's main interest for going to the game. But Mitzi has a crush on Baby Taniguchi—called "Baby" because he looks so young for his age—and he plays third base for the EMANONs.

"What does EMANON mean anyway?" asks Terri.

"It's NO NAME spelled backwards."

Baby is up to bat. Terri can't see why she is attracted to him. He's small and wears those baggy corduroy pants with dirt caked on the knees and grime streaked down the legs. All the guys wear dirty cords. It's the style. But somehow, on Baby it doesn't look cool. Probably because his face is so clean-cut, pink-cheeked, and light-complected like her mother's Japanese dolls.

He hits a grounder that gets him to first base. The next batter pops a fly into center field, giving Baby a chance to show off his sprinting talent, which he generously displays by churning up clouds of sand with pistonlike legs as he races to second base. He slides on his back just before the ball is caught by the waiting second baseman.

Instead of jumping to his feet and dusting himself off with manly satisfaction, Baby lies in the dirt, grasping the back of his leg and moaning. The other players run from their positions, converging around his writhing figure. Terri and Mitzi join them, breathless, afraid he has broken something.

"My leg's cut," Baby groans. Blood seeps around his hand holding the back of his lower thigh.

"Cut?" says one of the players. "How can it get cut here in the sand?" Baby rolls over, revealing a long, red-stained slit in his pants. Where his leg had lain, a glinting black knife-edged stone protrudes. The second baseman digs out a perfectly shaped triangle with a short stem jutting from the bottom rim. Jet black obsidian glitters in the sun as the baseman holds it up for all to see.

"Wow!" says the pitcher. "This is a perfect arrowhead!"

Relieved to know what caused his injury, Baby stops moaning and gets to his feet. Someone wraps a bandana around his thigh, and he limps back to the sidelines, leaning on the pitcher's shoulder.

Terri approaches the second baseman. "Can I have the arrowhead?"

"What do you want it for? You're a girl." His voice is not unfriendly. "Only guys collect arrowheads here."

She thinks for a moment how Obachan would get him to turn over the relic. "Well, you wouldn't want to have something that is such bad luck, would you? There's probably bad spirits attached to it."

Quiet floats between them. "Why would you want it, then?"

"I'm a girl. Weapon karma doesn't affect me."

Mentioning the word "karma" seems to affect him. He looks at her questioningly. She is certain he doesn't know the meaning of the word any more than she does. But hearing elders speak it always fills her with apprehension, with anxiety, sometimes with dread. She sees it is the same for him.

He hands her the stone. "Aw, sure. Have it. I can find plenty more."

After dinner, Terri watches Sayo praying before the shrine in the compartment. Light from a flickering candle reflects off pale glistening skin, still free of wrinkles. Incense burns in a brass bowl, sending smoke curls into the air, filling the room with pungent clouds.

In the past Terri has not been interested in her meditative practices. But since meeting the warrior and acquiring the shiny arrowhead, she wonders if she, too, should pay homage to the spirit world. Obachan says there are no coincidences, only signs. One has to contemplate the meaning of signs, the portents from the spirit world, to unravel the outlandish in everyday life.

Sayo finishes her prayers and asks, "What is your interest in my meditation? Has something happened that scares you?"

Terri is not surprised at her grandmother's intuition.

She blurts, "I saw an Indian last night . . . between the Horimoto barrack and Yamamoto's."

Sayo is calm, does not blink. "Were you frightened?"

"I wasn't scared at all. Really, in fact I didn't want him to go away. He talked to me."

Sayo's eyes are now intense, fixed on Terri's face. "What did this ghost look like?"

"He was a warrior. Not too old. And very nice-looking. You know, brown, smooth skin and black eyes, just like our eyes."

Sayo is quiet, seeming to reflect on this. "It is true we are living over burial grounds. Bones disintegrate beneath us. It's no wonder their spirits come to see what all the noise is about. Imagine how we disturb them with our wooden clogs, flushing toilets, and baseball games!"

Terri laughs at the image of Indians sleeping beneath the earth, jolted awake by crashing sounds above, water gurgling, screaming and shouting baseball fans! She imagines them pounding on their earth ceiling. "Hey, quiet up there!"

"It is wrong the government has imprisoned us," Sayo continues, "wrong to treat us as if we are the enemy. They also are bringing very bad karma upon themselves by desecrating the ancestral grounds of the ancient peoples who were here many, many years before the white ghosts arrived." She shakes her head somberly.

Her grandmother never before has spoken about this. "Obachan, how do you know about these things?"

No answer. She rises to her feet and begins to unfold the futon upon which she will sleep. Terri understands the conversation is closed. Her grandmother doesn't like to explain herself until she is ready.

Terri had wanted to show her the arrowhead, but decides to wait. She clasps it so tightly the sharp edges sting her palm.

Crossing

Spring was late in coming to the rough port city. Winter began its thaw with warm drizzle bathing the frozen metal ships, sending gray clouds steaming into an already overcast sky. At the Ryodan Inn, charcoal fires burned continuously, an expensive proposition for Sugimoto Masao, the proprietor who generously had supplied this extra service for the dozen female boarders overflowing the small hotel.

For the past three weeks, the shashin kekkon *had trickled in. Sugimoto was surprised at the increase in numbers, having boarded only six in recent months. He heard several other inns were filled, housing the young brides while they awaited government approval for emigration. With consternation, he viewed this exodus of so many females from Japan. These were the* nadeshiko—*the wild carnations native to the land—pure and fresh and of the hardiest stock from the* inaka. *Why was Japan sending her most vital blood across the ocean?*

But if he were young again, wouldn't he too sail for the new land? America! "Bii-Koko"—the Beautiful Country. Sighing, he scratched his grizzled head, feeling as ancient and spent as the depressed countrysides from which the brides had come—Hiroshima, Kagoshima, Kumamoto, Yamaguchi. Perhaps this sacrifice would impress the gods and better times would fall upon the ailing country.

A peal of laughter rang through the inn. Sugimoto's old heart quickened its beat. For one moment he felt young and could almost smell the scent of late-to-bloom cherry blossoms.

Sayo lay on her futon, listening with slight envy to the giggles and lighthearted banter of the other brides. They all had passed the examination for ju-nishi-jo-chu, *the test for worms. Worm eggs deposited on the flesh of raw fish, consumed as* sashimi, *hatched and grew in intestines. Before leaving Japan, all emigrants had their stools examined for the parasites. Since Sayo's arrival three days before, she had been unable to move her bowels. She was certain her belly harbored no worms, but it was swollen and hard, mostly from gas. She had not eaten since coming to Yokohama.*

She rubbed her taut belly, wondering what to do. Inspector was expected to collect samples that day. Feeling slightly nauseous from anxiety and lack of food, she sat up and began combing her long black hair. Footsteps beside the futon-bed hesitated, and a young girl's voice asked, "Are you ill? I've noticed you've been staying in bed the past two days. Can I help you?" The voice was warm and strong.

Sayo hastened to stand up and return the inquirer's bow, but dizziness forced her to sit down again. "Oh, I'm so sorry to be so impolite. Thank you for your inquiry. I'm not ill, just tired from the long journey here."

The girl was tall and large-boned, dusky-complected, with an angular face. Sayo was struck by her eyes, almost round and a light brown. She exuded warmth and friendliness, like a healthy young colt.

"Yes, the trip was very tiring for me, too. I'm from Kumamoto ken. My name is Ishida Chiba . . . I mean Kimura . . . Kimura Chiba." Her face turned red. "I'm sorry. I keep forgetting I am married now." She laughed, displaying straight white teeth.

Sayo liked the gangly girl from Kumamoto, her openness and genuine friendliness. "I am Matsubara Sayo. I come from Hiroshima."

"I know." This comment slipped from Chiba. Her face reddened again. How could she explain, without offending the beautiful newcomer, how the brides gossiped, how word had circulated that Sayo was from Hiroshima and had married into a wealthy family.

And, of course, Sayo's extraordinary comeliness did not help to still tongues.

"Sugimoto-san told us before you came," Chiba fibbed. Then she changed the subject. "Most of us have been waiting two weeks already. The Morinaga Maru, *our ship, is preparing for departure, within the week, I think. But we must pass the worm test before we can leave. Isn't it humiliating?*

Grateful for Chiba's fellowship, Sayo invited her to sit down on the futon. Moving aside, she winced from a sharp gas pain.

"You haven't taken the worm test yet, have you?"

"No . . . not yet." Embarrassed, she confessed, "I seem to be constipated. The trip was long and I didn't feel like eating."

Chiba nodded sympathetically. "It's very distressing. But I guess it must be done. The officials are strict here in Yokohama, and they say the gaijin *in America are more strict. Why are they so worried about a few worms? Only three women have flunked the test, and they are taking medicine now and must be tested again before they can go."*

The thought of producing a sample for Inspector depressed Sayo. "Tell me about yourself," she said, hoping to lift her spirits with lighter talk.

Chiba chattered on, "I am the youngest bride here. I'm sixteen." Although she would have liked to ask Sayo her age, she refrained politely. "My family are farmers—there are six of us—I am the only girl. There were seven, but my older sister, Chiyo, is dead." Mentioning her sister, Chiba became somber and her exuberance faltered.

"I'm very sorry about your sister. You must miss her."

"Yes, I do." Her voice was heavy. "The truth is, I would not be going to America as a shashin kekkon *if it were not for her death."*

Sayo remained quiet, not certain Chiba wanted her to ask about the sister.

Chiba said, "Someday I will tell you the story, but we have just met, and it is a very sad story."

"Everyone has stories, especially the brides here at this inn," said Sayo. "If we all told our tales, we would be talking continuously from here across the ocean to San Francisco!"

These words amused Chiba, and her demeanor brightened. "Do

*you mind if I move my futon next to yours, Matsubara-san? You are
so wise, and I can tell you are kind, too."*

"Of course. Do move your futon next to mine. And please call me
Sayo. May I call you Chiba?"

Chiba ran happily across the long room where all the brides
slept. She pulled a steamer trunk and big basket from her spot to the
wall behind Sayo, where she lined them next to Sayo's velvet lug-
gage. The trunk was old and worn, its wooden moldings chipped
and cracked. Beside the opulence of Sayo's new trunk and bags,
her belongings looked more bedraggled than they were. But this did
not seem to bother Chiba, who plopped herself down on the floor,
gazing at Sayo with adoring puppy eyes. Carefully, she reached inside her kimono sleeve and brought out a photograph.

With shyness she said, "This is my husband, Kimura Yoshio."

Sayo looked at the sepia-toned picture. A square-jawed man
with single-lidded eyes gleamed impersonally back. His eyebrows
were bushy, and thick black hair swept from his forehead into a
pompadour. Almost coarse-looking, he was not handsome.

"He looks very intelligent," said Sayo, trying to think of something nice to say. "I'm sure he will be a good provider. And he is
kind. The bones in his face show that."

Chiba smiled broadly, cheered that Sayo saw some virtues there.
She had been honest with herself and saw he was not physically appealing, but she hoped his character would make up for that. She
was grateful for Sayo's kindness and could see this elegant lady had
a generous spirit, was not afraid to give compliments, even unde-
served ones.

"How old is he?" asked Sayo.

"The baishakunin says he is around thirty. That makes him more
than a dozen years older than myself, but they say the perfect age
span between husband and wife is ten years . . . so, I guess it is all
right."

Sayo got up from the futon and opened her suitcase. Next to
Chiba's shabby trunk, her bags looked too new and showy. Embarrassed by the contrast, she rummaged quickly and produced a
photograph.

"This is Hiroshi, my husband."

Chiba studied the photograph, the long, narrow, almost effeminate face, straining for the right words. Although handsome in a genteel way, he did not impress her. There was a sadness about his eyes, a hollow look that caused her chest to ache.

"He looks aristocratic, like a lord . . . and gentle." Chiba hoped her words were appropriate. "He is going to be so happy to see you!"

"Actually, he is supposed to be very gentle. His mother told me that. She said he was quite sensitive and artistic, too." Sayo didn't mention he was the second son. Nor did she confide her lack of feeling, how she was neither anxious nor enthusiastic about meeting him and beginning a life together. Yes, she looked forward to going to America. That would be a great adventure, and as Mentor had prophesied, a life of excitement and even passion. It was her karma. Her only regret was that it was the second son and not the father with whom she would travel this journey in the new land, a journey Mentor had warned could be perilous. Before she left Hiroshima, Mentor said, "In America you will be tested. You must use your wits to survive, be creative and unafraid to try out new ideas. There you can do it. Not like here, where women of your strength are feared and destroyed." Sayo was not sure she understood Mentor. But she knew Mentor's wisdom would become clear in time.

"You are a Fire Horse Woman, a very special sign. I, too, am a Fire Horse Woman. It has been my secret. Now it is yours, too." Mentor had revealed this just before Sayo left the village for Yokohama, before she climbed into the carriage to join the driver, Kenichi, one of the Matsubara hired hands. Those were Mentor's last words to her. During the long ride from Hiroshima, Sayo thought about the implications of being a Fire Horse Woman. Why was there such dread of the sign? What was this power, this mysterious potency that was so evil women had to disown it? She, herself, did not feel any power—in fact, she felt less strong than she imagined other women felt. Perhaps, as Mentor had said, she would discover it in America.

Worm Inspector didn't come to the hotel that day. Still, Sayo could not move her bowels, even after Chiba had coaxed her to eat some miso soup and rice, plying her with green tea and umeboshi.

*She felt mortified by her condition, the near helplessness and de-
pendence on her new friend, so much younger than herself.*

*After dinner, when kerosene lamps were lit and futons laid out
for sleeping, the two sat and sewed, exchanging information about
themselves, their hopes and disappointments. Chiba said, with such
sincerity her voice trembled, "I have known you only for a day. Yet I
feel as close to you as to my sister, Chiyo, bless her soul. I want you
to know how grateful I am for your friendship. The others have not
shown me the respect you have. They've only tolerated me . . . like a
pet."*

*"I'm sure they truly like you, Chiba-san. They must wish they
were as young and energetic as you, that's all. You appear so carefree. They are frightened of the unknown future. That's why they appear so unapproachable.*

"Perhaps," answered Chiba, "but you made me feel welcome."

*"I'm pleased to have you as a friend, like a sister. I have no sisters . . .
or brothers. You see, I am an orphan."*

*"Oh, I'm so sorry." To be an orphan was almost as bad as having
leprosy or T.B. What could Chiba say to lighten that stroke of ill fate?
"But you are married now and will soon have your own family,
many many children!"*

*Sayo laughed, appreciating Chiba's goodwill and winced from
gas pains in her belly brought on by the laughter.*

*"Worm Inspector will be coming tomorrow morning. Do you
think you'll be able to give him a sample?"*

*"I don't know." Sayo rubbed her stomach. "It's hard as stone.
Perhaps the doctor can give me something to make me go." Her face
looked pale, small beads of perspiration glistening on her forehead.*

*Chiba's round brown eyes turned dark. They glowed, reflecting
light from the kerosene lamp. She grabbed Sayo's hand.*

*"Don't worry," she whispered. "I will give my stool for your sam-
ple. Tomorrow morning! I already have passed the test! They'll
never know!" She sat back on her heels, grinning with mischief.*

*At first not comprehending Chiba's offer, Sayo only stared. When
she saw the brilliance of this strategy, she burst into a laugh so loud
she had to cover her face with a kimono sleeve. Chiba, meanwhile,*

*was rolling on her futon, convulsed. "You are a genius! Thank you
so much!" Sayo managed to whisper. "How can I ever repay you?"
Silence. "Well, I assure you, you needn't repay in kind!"
They kicked their feet and pounded the futon with curled-up
fists, stifling giggles with their faces buried in blankets.*

As the Morinaga Maru *plunged through high seas, howling winds
blew foam off waves, spraying the deck with a veil of white lace.
They were six days out of Yokohama. The brides were all sick. Even
the crew was sick. When they had steamed out of the calm bay into
wind and rain, the captain had announced the storm would pass
in a day or so. His ability to read weather was considered to be uncanny. He could look up at the sky and clouds, watch the formations of flying gulls, and predict when and where a storm would hit.
Some said he could smell weather. The crew believed in his powers
and were shaken by the length and ferocity of this storm.*

*Sayo and Chiba remained below in the sleeping quarters they
shared with two other brides. Overcome with relentless nausea that
swept through the boat like a plague, they lay on the wooden beds,
barely able to keep blankets dry and wiped of vomit that flew from
their mouths before they could lift their heads. The room reeked.
Floors remained slimy with their sickness despite feeble attempts to
clean them.*

*Except for lurching figures of the crew on deck, the ship was life-
less, a phantom ghost abandoned by its captain, left to the winds
and currents and will of an angry sea god. All the brides remained
below. As each lunge of the ship widened the distance between
themselves and Japan, they felt the separation from their families
with growing intensity. The novelty of an unknown husband and a
new land—perhaps riches beyond their wildest imagination—
began to fade.*

*On the ninth day at sea Sayo awakened to stillness. No longer
plunging and rocking, the ship appeared to be motionless, stuck in
a frozen sea. Grateful for this respite, she thought of last night's
dream.*

She had been riding in a slender reed boat with her father-in-law, who was paddling and guiding them over a placid lake she never had seen before. The oars dipped softly, lulling her into a deep repose, deeper than sleep. Neither spoke. In silence they glided, hearts beating in rhythm with each paddle's stroke.

In the distance she saw a waterfall, a river cascading from a high cliff, ending its turbulent descent in a foamy explosion. As they drew closer, she heard muffled thunder, felt the booms shaking her body. Matsubara continued to paddle calmly toward the mushrooming clouds. She sensed danger, but remained quiet, tense, watching thrusting oars carry them closer. His back muscles bulged and rippled beneath his kimono, and wet patches of sweat darkened its geometric pattern of hexagons.

He paddled faster, with deeper strokes. The roar of the waterfall became deafening. Strangely, her fear disappeared. Yearning to be engulfed by the falls, she wished for the battering water to tumble her in its billows. She wanted to feel her kimono disintegrating into shreds, torn away like the rice-paper wrapping of a long anticipated gift! She wanted to cry out . . . to break the silence between them and direct him faster to an unknown crescendo! But her jaws were paralyzed. She couldn't speak. The words remained imprisoned in her throat. Sadness swept over her as the waterfall receded in the distance. Matsubara had disappeared, and she was alone, drifting in the long reed boat.

Disquieted by the dream's forlorn ending, Sayo lay motionless on the futon, feigning sleep, reliving in her mind the last intimate moments with her father-in-law. After the wedding-by-proxy and consequent move into the Matsubara compound, her greatest desire was to learn their ways, make herself acceptable—even noteworthy—to be Hiroshi's bride. Thus, she had avoided Tadanoshin. Although inexperienced with men, other than what Mentor had taught, she knew the energy directed at her during the nuptials was not the benign cordiality of a father-in-law. Yet, when their eyes first met, had she not felt her own heart rapidly tapping, her throat warming? She was drawn to him, excited by his commanding presence and handsome features.

But being foremost a survivor, an orphan taking first steps up the *pinnacle to acceptability, she was cautious. Instinctively, she knew her greatest ally in winning over Hiroshi would be his mother, another woman, who could teach what pleased the second son. She could not afford to alienate the Lady Matsubara, although Sayo had heard the once beautiful wife, grown used to her husband's sexual liaisons with other women, turned her head the other way, concerning herself with art, music, and writing poetry.*

She had been successful in keeping a distance from Tadanoshin. Still, only a glimpse of him evoked a stirring in her heart, and, hidden from view, she often watched while he rode across meadows, cape flying, a falcon on his arm. If they chanced to meet in the courtyard, she kept her face downcast, ignoring his insistent looks, eyes that penetrated her very soul. At dinner she purposely directed conversation to Lady Matsubara, chatting politely about house matters, excusing herself often to fetch tea or more tsukemono.

But the day arrived when she no longer could dismiss him nor deny the yearning in her heart. A week before she was to leave for America, Lady Matsubara was in Osaka, visiting and shopping. Tadanoshin had traveled there with her but returned early, bringing an armload of brown-paper-wrapped parcels, which, after seeking out Sayo in her room, he excitedly presented to her.

"These are gaijin *clothes," he said gallantly. "I bought them for you myself. You will need them in America."*

Speechless, Sayo bowed very low, hiding her hot face. Finally, she uttered "Domo arigato-gozaimasu," and sat back on her heels, liquid eyes meeting his for the first time since she moved into the household. She allowed her longing to radiate from her now languid body.

Unable to constrain himself further from the prized fruit he had chosen but had refrained from tasting, he fell to his knees and embraced her, lips seeking the back of her long slender neck. She shuddered, skin tingling with new sensations. At first paralyzed by the onslaught of his passion and her own inexperience, she soon yielded, relinquishing any pretense of chasteness, and responded with quickening breath and soft cries.

Afterward, she wept uncontrollably, fearing her chances with Hiroshi were ruined. She was no longer a virgin! Deflowered by her husband's father! Would Tadanoshin now cast her out? A damaged woman too easily seduced to be a son's wife?

But Matsubara was of Samurai lineage, and although women to him—especially a son's match-marriage wife—did not deserve the same respect bequeathed to men, he treated Sayo with honor.

"Do not worry, Sayo-san." It was the first time she heard him use her name. "No one will know of this. I promise to keep it secret." He paused. "Fate can be so cruel. For the first time I think I have met a woman who can match me. But too late. At least my son can have what I cannot."

Still weeping, she could not speak. Before he left, he said, "You will always be taken care of—as long as I am alive. Remember that." And just before he closed the sliding door, "My son Hiroshi is quite different from me, but he is a Matsubara. I hope your marriage succeeds."

It was the last time she saw him. He left for Tokyo immediately, only returning after she had left Hiroshima to join Hiroshi in America.

Chiba's voice broke the reverie. "Sayo-san, we are still moving, but the storm has left us." Returned to her exuberant self, she bustled about the room, folding scattered clothing. "I have just seen Kenji, and he says the ocean is as calm and flat as Lake Biwa."

Sayo rose slowly, reluctant to leave the warm bed, but the other two roommates were now straightening up with Chiba, and she felt ashamed not to join them. The days of queasiness already had receded in their memories like an unwelcome nightmare, and they sang and chattered as they folded beds and washed floors.

Promenading on deck, Sayo and Chiba walked arm in arm, breathing in the fresh ocean breeze. They joined their roommates, who sat on a long wooden bench, sunning themselves. Deprived of conversation for so long, the four chitchatted on mindlessly, as if by talking they could fill their stomachs left so empty from seasickness.

The days passed, and Honolulu drew nearer. The air grew soft, and when the breeze picked up in the late afternoon, the scent of wild ginger teased their senses. Restless for the sight of land, the passengers eagerly searched the horizon. In Honolulu three brides and a dozen men would be disembarking. Huge sugar plantations needed laborers. After conscripting workers from China for years, the white landowners had found another rich manpower supply in depression-struck Japan. But unlike the Chinese, who mostly married women in the islands or returned to their villages for wives, the Japanese sent for brides to join them.

When the Morinaga Maru *sailed into the port of Honolulu, it was a glorious sunny morning. Lining the rails, passengers strained to catch the first view of a western outpost. Bride One, who would be joining her husband, stood with the roommates, baggage piled neatly beside her. Dressed in a formal black kimono with hair arranged by Sayo in upswept pompadours, she looked overdressed and hot. Unused to the humidity, she was perspiring profusely, swabbing her neck with a damp handkerchief.*

Sayo stood next to her and studied the waiting crowd on the dock, mostly men in light cotton shirts and straw hats. Chiba and Bride Two nervously fussed over Bride One, patting her rice-starched hair, wiping beads of sweat from her horselike face, powdered snowy white. In her hand Bride One held a photograph, which she checked as she scanned the dock with anxious eyes.

Chiba spotted the husband and tugged at her kimono sleeve, whispering, "There he is!" She shook the long sleeve like a flag.

The man held a photograph in his hand and was craning his neck to see over the crowd. He moved his head from side to side, finally stopping at the three brides waiting at the gangplank.

Quietly Bride One gathered up her belongings with shaking hands. She minced down the gangplank, barely acknowledging the roommates' farewells.

"When you get rich," shouted Chiba, "come visit us in America!"

Bride Two added, "On my way back to Japan for vacations, I will stop here to see you!"

They waved white handkerchiefs as their former roommate descended from the ship. Sayo watched the overdressed women bowing very low on the dock while the grooms simultaneously returned the greeting. In the hot blinding light, they shimmered like actors on a stage.

* * *

In the cabin that night, the three remaining roommates were quiet, sobered by the sight of brides meeting husbands for the first time. Someplace in America a man waited for each of them, a man who would be a mate for life, the father of her children. Thousands of miles away from their own kin, their destiny was now entrusted to a stranger in a foreign land. Gone were the fantasies of love. Uppermost was the hope for an able-bodied, stable, good man. Except for Sayo.

In many ways Sayo's husband was no stranger. Having lived with the Matsubara for months, she had been successful in winning her mother-in-law's approval, and thus learned some intimate facts about the son, including what the mother considered "questionable qualities."

"He is the soft one," she had said. "He will give you no problem. You must feed him well, preparing his tray very aesthetically, as he has strong opinions about beauty. But beauty is the only thing about which he shows strong feelings." The mother was gentle, speaking in a low, cultured way. "He is not demanding or aggressive . . . thank the gods." Sayo had wondered if she was comparing Hiroshi to the older son, Ichiro, or to the father. But Sayo had decided in her heart that to be a Matsubara meant power, however defined by the bearer of that name. Softness was strength, too. Didn't the slender, pliant bamboo survive the fiercest of winds, while thick, rigid poles were torn out of the soil by their roots? She would "listen to his poetry," as her mother-in-law advised, "rub his back and feet, pour him premium sake."

Chiba hoped for a tender, sensitive man. Gazing at Yoshio's picture, she willed that he be kind. Her father was gruff and hot-tempered, treating her like a boy, a "good-for-nothing," as he would call her. He had not been kind to Chiyo, either. When she thought of her older sister, tears filled her eyes. Poor Chiyo. She would have been better off as a shashin kekkon. *Chiba missed her mother, her strong and cunning mother who secretly had arranged this marriage for her only living daughter. For the first time since they left Japan, she recited some mantras on Buddhist beads. Her fingers caressed each satin-slick orb of the worn ivory bracelet, and she chanted, "Namu amida butsu." Lips moving silently, hardly disturbing the flat planes of her jaws, she prayed for wealth and many children and promised to share these gifts with her destitute family in Kumamoto.*

A full moon shone that night. Sleep was fitful, and dreams were disrupted by restless turning as the Morinaga Maru *steamed across the glassy mirror of the vast Pacific. If trees had grown upon its decks, owls surely would have settled on the branches, filling the night with hoots, speaking wisdom to the moon's luminous face.*

Volunteers

Manzanar

Hana welcomes the change in weather. Six months have passed since their arrival, and summer's golden days have ended. Mornings are cool, the air transparent, no longer clouded by haze and shimmering mirages. She was tempted to taste the first signs of autumn, a thin layer of frost glistening on the boulder outside the barracks' entrance. This morning, on the way to the latrine, she had noticed the ground and rocks shiny with a sugary glaze, and she thought of malasadas, round donuts without holes, delicious, and sticky with sugar, baked by Filipino friends in Los Angeles. She was tempted to lean down and sample the boulder's sweetness with her tongue. But she didn't, knowing if anyone saw her licking a rock, they surely would think her crazy. She suspects people think their family strange, anyway. Of course, if Sayo had felt the whim, she would have indulged it, not caring what others think. That's what confounds people about her mother. She doesn't give a damn about anyone's opinions.

Sitting in the laundry room, Hana waits for other volunteers and Block Manager, who will be bringing military uniforms to be altered into wearable clothing. She wishes she hadn't volunteered when Shimizu-san announced at the mess hall the need for seamstresses and tailors to remake jackets and coats from government surplus uniforms. She was, at first, insulted. Why wear uniforms? Isn't it bad enough their lives are already like soldiers on a military base? How demeaning to wander around in khaki men's clothes! But she remained silent, dutifully signing the roster for volunteers.

Talking herself into it, she reasons that the weather has turned cold, that winters in the high desert are frigid, and most internees come from the southland, where woolens, gloves, and hats have no place in their wardrobes. They all would need warm clothing, no matter what color or source of origin.

She sits on one of the long benches procured, with two tables, from the mess hall. The tables have been set up end to end, forming one long working space down the laundry room's center. Four washtubs line the rugged bare walls. The cement floor is grainy and dank, cool through Hana's cloth slippers, newly made rag "zoris." The slippers are the rage in camp, and she and Carmen spent several days braiding rag ropes from old clothes that they later coiled and sewed into soles for the slippers. Covering the top with a solid piece of material, they attached a braid thong to one end which fitted between the big and second toe of the wearer. Hana prefers the rag slippers— spongy beneath her feet—to the sleek hardness of wooden *getas*.

Across the room, someone has installed a long mirror. Hana sees herself reflected, a lean figure dressed in a crisp white blouse and wide-legged slacks. She appreciates her looks now, but there was a time when she didn't like her body. As a child she hated being tall and thin, gangly limbs sprouting from a root body. Looking different from other Japanese children, she was teased and called "Gobo" (burdock root) and "Crane-girl." Her complexion is darker than her mother's, with peach and apricot tones. Thick eyebrows arch above deep-set eyes, amber colored when light turns them liquid, and the bridge of her nose is high, thin nostrils flaring above full lips She knows she is beautiful—not in the classic tradition like her mother— but striking and intense, a face that immediately commands attention.

As she grew older, she began appreciating her body, even grateful she didn't need to diet like other *nisei* women friends who worried about getting plump on too much rice. Her one regret, though, is the slumping habit she developed as a child to make herself less tall and noticeable. She sometimes rationalizes that her bones grew too fast for the tendons and muscles to support them, causing her shoulders to sag and bend the upper torso into a bow. For whatever reasons her upper body curved over, the hunched back is now frozen,

and no amount of stretching and pounding straightens it. So she remains crescent-shaped, a posture she has found not totally without
merit, as some Japanese find this stance comely for women, reflecting an appropriately submissive and self-effacing nature. She turns
sideways to study her body's profile. She hears footsteps and moves
away from the mirror.

Block Manager, followed by three women and two men, lug in
huge cartons, which they set on the tables. Hana recognizes the
women. Except for Block Manager Shimizu, the men are strangers.
They open the cardboard boxes and quickly toss onto the tables
heavy jackets and pants of khaki and dark navy blue, vintage World
War I.

The men leave and return with three sewing machines, older models
operated by heavy iron treadles. Hana helps the women sort the uniforms, a hodgepodge of woolen jodhpur-style pants, high-collared jackets, navy peacoats, canvas leggings, knit caps, thick gloves. Smelling
of mold and mothballs, the clothes are mostly too large to fit the smaller
Japanese physique. They will require extensive altering, especially for
the many youngsters in the block.

Out of the corner of her eye, Hana studies the men setting up the
machines. Two are middle-aged, slightly built, with graying hair. The
third is younger, Hana guesses in his early thirties. Through lowered
lids, she watches him brush dust from the machine and then attempt
to thread it. There is a familiarity about him that pulls her attention,
prevents her looking away. He is quite tall, with thick shoulders and
chest, unlike the more delicate physiques she associates with tailors,
which she assumes he is. He doesn't seem to be aware of the others,
focused only on readying the machine.

Goto-san, ceremonial pot-banging announcer of mealtimes, calls
out to the young man, "Why don't you bachelor boys come eat at our
kitchen sometime? Good food, our place. Better than Block Seventeen."
She acts the gracious hostess, maitre-d' for Block 16's mess hall, which
now enjoys a four-star reputation for good food—not delicious, but
palatable, making it distinctly superior to other dining halls manned
by gardeners, fishermen, and farmers.

Hana notes he is a bachelor and lives in Block 17, across the firebreak. She watches him successfully thread the machine. He walks

over to where she is sorting uniforms. Hoping to hide her curiosity, she slumps farther over the pile.

He says, "Why don't we try and redo one of these jackets into a cape?"

Barely able to respond, she keeps her head lowered. Why has he chosen her to work with? She had noticed there was no hesitancy in his steps toward her. "That's a good idea," she manages to answer, still not looking up. *It must be my age,* she thinks. *I'm younger than the other women.*

"I've brought my shears and pins," she says. "This navy peacoat would make a nice cape." She shakes out a rumpled coat. Facing him now, she holds up the blue jacket, riveting eyes on its back, studying the seams as though it were a map. She would like to look him full in the face. For some reason, she is paralyzed, unable to soften into friendliness. But he is nonchalant, seeming not to notice the cold reception.

"I think we could make a nice cape for a young girl . . . just tear out the sleeves, add a panel from the shoulder and cut slits in front for the hands. You tear out the sleeves, and I'll cut some panels." He holds up another coat.

Hana is impressed by his takeover way. His manner is forceful, but not in the way she is accustomed to. It is gentle, jovial, and undemanding, yet with no questioning of his own authority. She thinks he must be a successful tailor.

Finally she allows herself to look at him. His face is craggy, square-jawed, thick brows jutting over narrow eyes. His complexion is warm brown. Displaying straight white teeth, he smiles. "I hope you don't mind my being so bossy, but no one is really in charge here, and we could go on all day doing nothing. If we start, they'll get the idea of what to do."

"Oh, you aren't bossy at all. I agree someone has to begin, and I don't think Shimizu-san knows anything about sewing."

"By the way, my name is Shimizu, too—Lincoln Shimizu, but I'm not related to your block manager. Everyone calls me 'Shimmy.' " He has started cutting buttons off the peacoat. His hands are large, fingers long and square-tipped, agile yet sturdy as they wield the scissors and smooth the woolen material.

Put at ease by his casualness, she begins tearing out the sleeves. "I'm Hana Murakami. Lived in Venice before coming to camp." She wants to ask where he's from but hesitates.

As if reading her mind, he says, "I guess you could say I'm from L.A.—Boyle Heights, actually. I was raised as a child at the Maryknoll Orphanage there." He is upbeat, seemingly unabashed about his background. Hana has heard of the Maryknoll home. His outgoing personality and cheerful disposition are not traits she would expect from someone raised in such a place.

Hana catches herself from blurting, "I'm sorry." Instead says, "Are you Catholic? I understand the only Caucasian living among us is a priest. He and two nuns, who are *nihonjin,* have a whole barrack next to the church. Block Twenty-five."

"Yes, I know about the church, but don't attend. I gave up Catholicism years ago. Are you Christian?"

"No. I guess we're Buddhist, although we never went to temple except for funerals. You know, of course, Buddhist services are forbidden in camp."

How quickly their conversation has turned intimate! Already she knows he is an orphan and a renounced Catholic. When they first came to camp, she learned the internees—most of whom were strangers to one another—were extremely careful about revealing much about themselves, especially their religion. A low-grade paranoia prevails even now, with rumors flying that informants to the administration lurk among them. Religion is a touchy matter. When the war broke out most Buddhist priests were picked up by the FBI and imprisoned in federal jails—North Dakota, Texas, New Mexico.

"Yes, I know. It's ridiculous. This whole camp is ridiculous." He is not so jovial anymore. "But we're here and can't fight the government, so might as well make the best of it."

"Now you sound like a Buddhist." says Hana, astonishing herself by laughing.

She is further astonished by his reply, "Hey, I knew you would be fun to work with!"

Within three hours Hana and Shimmy complete one cape, except for its collar, which they plan to fashion into a high-necked mandarin style. She feels a camaraderie never experienced before, even though the conversation touches only on superficial tidbits such as the unusual ways to sew buttonholes and hem with invisible stitches. She wants to ask, "Have you ever been married? How old are you? Why are you—someone so outgoing and physically imposing—a tailor?" But she swallows the words, embarrassed and somewhat frightened by the unaccustomed intensity of her curiosity.

Goto-san leaves to discharge her duty as Pot-Banger, inviting Shimmy for lunch as she shuffles past in her rag zoris.

"Number one, our mess hall," she clucks. "We treat you bachelor boys good. Come." She pulls playfully on his shirt sleeve. Just as she reaches the laundry room's open doorway, Hana's mother and Terri appear. The two older women bow deeply and exchange pleasantries.

"*Ohaiyo-gozaimasu.* Please excuse me as I now must see to it that lunch runs smoothly."

"Please do what you have to and forgive my intrusion."

More bows, as Goto-san finally leaves.

Spotting the new cape spread on the table, Terri rushes over. "Wow! That's beautiful! Who's it for?"

"Looks like it's custom-made just for you." Shimmy says, deducing who Terri is.

Flustered by their arrival, Hana bends, pretending to pick pins off the concrete floor.

"Really!" says Terri, beaming. "Did you and my mom make it for me?" Hana straightens up, feeling obliged to introduce the newcomers. "This is my mother, Sayo . . . and my daughter, Terri."

Shimmy smiles broadly, bowing to Sayo. "I'm very pleased to make your acquaintance. My name is Lincoln Shimizu. I am a tailor, and as you can see, am working with Hana to make winter jackets." He speaks eloquent Japanese, which pleases Sayo. She studies his face, her eyes soft and accepting.

"Your Japanese is excellent. I haven't heard good Japanese in a long time. It truly is a pleasure to meet you."

Terri interrupts, "Obachan, isn't this cape something? I've always wanted a cape."

Eager to befriend, Shimmy sweeps it up and motions for Terri to stand before him. He fits it over her shoulders, adjusting the neckline.

"See, this will work just fine," he says to Hana, who has moved apart from them, refolding uniforms stacked on the table. "We'll just need to add a button here and a loop." He points to Terri's chin.

Hana forces a smile, a slight upturning of the lips. She is embarrassed, not knowing why. She feels a vague sense of guilt, as though she was committing some crime and has been apprehended. She often wonders why she reacts this way whenever she is enjoying herself.

Shimmy has noticed the change in Hana's demeanor. He removes the cape and continues talking to Terri. "Yes, a perfect fit. Your mom really knows your size. We can finish this later."

Sayo asks, "Will you join us at our mess hall?"

The invitation is simple. Yet the intonation is so impeccably gracious, the prison meal seems already transformed into an elegant repast.

Hana is surprised at his polite decline. Few men are able to resist Sayo's charm. "Thank you, Sayo-san, but I have business to tend to at Block Seventeen. Perhaps tomorrow?"

Sayo's face is courteous. "Of course. And please come to our 'Ocha-ya' someday and enjoy tea. It is one way to escape the harshness of this place."

Observing the exchange between her mother and Shimmy, Hana feels herself fading, a once vibrant orange paling to dull beige, the color of parched earth. Growing up in a teahouse, she was familiar with the elaborate facade over simple rituals and tasks. She had resisted—even rebelled against in her own way—the lure of sensual power. And Sayo never had thrust that training upon her. In fact, she knew in her heart the reason the marriage had been arranged with Tad was to ensure she never would need to earn a livelihood in a teahouse. But any display of courtly sensibility still causes her to shrink into herself, to become invisible.

A loud clanging erupts from the mess hall located a few barracks away from the laundry room. Goto-san's pot-banging heralds the opening of doors for lunch. Scrupulously punctual for the day's three meals, her banging pot is as effective as a town clock, chiming at seven in the morning; twelve noon; six in the evening.

"I'll see you tomorrow morning, Hana," Shimmy calls cheerfully as he leaves the laundry room. "I can't come this afternoon, but save the cape for me to finish."

The three line up outside at the mess hall, relieved the queue is so short. Sayo remarks, "Now that is a nice young man. He doesn't look like a tailor, does he? He seems so sturdy and big. Did he tell you much about himself?"

"Not much."

"I don't think he's married," says Sayo. "He's old enough to have a family, but my guess is he's alone."

"I really don't know," Hana lies.

"Well, it's good you have such a fine partner to work with. I would almost volunteer myself . . . just to hear his excellent Japanese."

Hana's throat constricts. The thought of her mother joining the sewing group sends her into a coughing fit.

Terri pats her mother's back, concern furrowing her brow. "Are you okay, Mom? Maybe it's too damp in that laundry room."

Inside the dining barrack, Tad and Mac, already seated, wave for the three to join them. After filling heavy white plates with rice and a strange stew of wieners and squash mixed with sauerkraut, they sit with the men.

"How do you like the 'goulash'?" Mac says. "Goto-san calls it 'Hungarian goo-rashu.'"

"Yuk." Terri grimaces. "Smells weird. Looks like garbage to me."

"It's probably a secret weapon the administration is trying out on us," says Mac.

"Well, it's better than the mutton slop we had the other night," says Tad, strictly a rice and fish man who cannot abide the smell of mutton.

"Where's Carmen?" asks Sayo.

"Trying out Block Thirty's kitchen," Mac says. "She's met a new friend, someone from Pasadena."

Sayo waits a beat, then says, "I think we should eat together as a family, not run around this camp like tourists trying out restaurants."

Terri blurts, "What about Shimmy? Can't he eat here? You invited him."

"Who's Shimmy?" asks Tad.

"A tailor working with Mom. They made me a beautiful cape out of a navy peacoat."

Quietly pushing food around her plate with the large army fork, Hana remains silent, studying the mishmash as if it were a pattern of tea leaves foretelling the future. The family—used to her nonparticipation—continue talking among themselves, taking no notice of her distance. She begins to think of Shimmy growing up without parents. It makes her sad. Not knowing her own real father, she sympathizes with him, even though she was fond of Yoshio, who came into her life when she was a child. She remembers him being kind and quietly strong, much older than the other adults surrounding her at the teahouse. With his balding gray head, he was more a grandfather than stepfather, pampering her and giving the attention and affection she missed from her busy mother. And even with Night Jasmine and Jade Young Moon, her constant companions, she often wished for a brother or sister. The two young women were more like fun-loving "aunties" than entertainers.

It was not until many years later that Hana realized what roles the two Chinese women played at the Heavenly Cloud Inn—along with her mother. They were geishas. Not stylish courtesans like those of Kyoto, but a homespun, countrified version—simple entertainers fulfilling simple needs of lonely Japanese bachelors, farmers, and laborers who yearned to talk and sing, play cards and dance with women from the homeland.

Hana never has talked with Sayo about that part of the past. Not that she thinks her mother is ashamed of running a teahouse, or should be. But somehow she always has sensed a secret, a dark mystery surrounding Sayo's early life. There are no precise incidents that Hana remembers. Only vague impressions of her mother crying quietly as she looked at her hand mirror, an unfinished walnut piece she still keeps on her *tokonoma* today. She used to think her mother was crying at the reflection of herself growing older, too old to carry on the geisha profession. She was studying the back and handle, stroking them gently, an expression on her face so tender, Hana knew she suffered a sadness she wished to bear only by herself.

Those were the only times Hana saw her mother cry. Sayo was always stoic and dry-eyed, even at the death of Yoshio. Besides, Hana knows the *issei*, the first generation, do not talk about their lives in Japan or when they first arrived in America. For one thing, it would mean talking about themselves, and decent Japanese do not draw attention to their individuality. Sayo has said many times, "In Japan, the lone nail sticking up is struck down, hammered back into the wood so that the surface remains smooth and uniform."

What a shock it had been to move from the Heavenly Cloud Inn, a sensual realm of feminine tenderness, to the noisy, boisterous Murakami household, thundering with demands from four males and the fiery Kashi-san, proprietress of the Rising Sun Café. Hana wonders often if Sayo would have allowed the match-marriage to Tad had she known the hardships her daughter would endure, that even in America, the mother-in-law vented her fury at her own mistreatment upon the wife of the eldest son, who traditionally moves in with the family. After meeting Tad and being unduly impressed by the matchmaker's telling of the Murakami background, Hana had been eager to leave Watsonville's farm country for a Southern California fishing town. How was she to have known her role as the "yomei-san" would mean serving two brothers and father-in-law besides her own husband?

Kashi-san was no comfort. She was the queen bee in a hive of clamoring drones, unaware of Hana's existence except as another worker fulfilling the queen's needs. Hana knew she was as invisible as air and water to the family—and like those elements so necessary for existence, she too was indispensable. Yet she was taken for granted. Ever accommodating as the household cook, laundress, nurse, and housekeeper—never thanked or even acknowledged as being alive—she might just as well have been a ghost. Only eighteen when she married Tad, she was innocent of traditional roles in Japanese families, never having lived in a conventional home nor having close acquaintanceship with those who lived the life of rural Japan. She was raised in a teahouse, after all.

She had been terrified of her mother-in-law, whose short, squat body and loud voice filled the house like a vibrating tractor. Fortunately, Kashi-san spent the days and evenings at the café, where her boisterous personality gained respect from the fishermen who spent hours drinking beer in the small booths and later at night in the gambling room in the back. Hana was left to run the household. She was happiest when the men left for weeks at a time to fish tuna off the Mexican coast.

Hana's reverie is jolted by Goto-san banging her pot to draw attention to Block Manager, who stands in the middle of the hall preparing to make an announcement. Watching Goto-san's round figure, her short arm flailing away at the pan, Hana realizes how much she looks like Kashi-san, her long dead mother-in-law.

"I have good news for any of you who like to leave camp for a while and make some money, too." Block Manager speaks in English as Japanese is forbidden at meetings. "Because of the war, there is a shortage of labor—especially on farms. Up north the sugar beets and potatoes need to be harvested, and they are asking for workers from camp to help."

"Where would we live?" asks one young man. "Would they put us in prison up there, too?"

"There are boardinghouses and labor camps available, and you'll be paid enough to provide for your own board and room."

Tad asks, "How much do we get paid?"

"You'll get paid a certain amount for picking a potato field or chopping sugar beets. It's not by the hour. But transportation will be taken care of."

"Who says who goes, and how long is the stint?"

Hana is surprised to hear Tad asking questions. She would not have guessed he would be interested in an adventure that involved such demeaning labor—chopping sugar beets and digging up potatoes.

"The administration will determine who goes on furlough . . . I'll turn in names. But you should sign up today, because they need workers immediately. You'll leave in four days and return before Thanksgiving."

Six weeks! Hana looks over at Tad, who is speaking earnestly with Mac, hunched over, eyes darting around the room. They look like conspirators planning a great escape. For Mac this would, after all, be a chance to know life outside the barbed-wire fence.

Hana remains quiet.

Sayo says softly, "This is a good idea, I think. But isn't Mac too young?"

Mac answers, almost petulantly, which is unusual since he respects his grandmother greatly, "Obachan, I'm old enough to join the army. This will be good for me. . . . At least I can get the hell out of here for a while. I've got 'rock' fever."

A small crowd gathers around Block Manager. Hana notices several young wives among them. She wonders if she is expected to volunteer, too. But Tad's question to Sayo dispels that possibility.

"You women will be okay while we're gone, won't you?"

"Of course," replies Sayo. "What could happen to us in here?"

Accustomed to being invisible around the family, Hana doesn't expect him to direct any remarks to her, and is surprised when he says, "Is that all right with you, Hana? We won't be gone for too long."

She nods her head, feeling a strange sense of gratitude.

"Let's just look at it this way," Mac says. "We're doing our duty for the war effort. They do call it 'furlough,' you know." He laughs. "Heck, we're volunteers, all of us." He holds up two fingers making a "V" sign. "This doesn't mean 'V' for victory—it's 'V' for Volunteer!"

1903

Three weeks to the day since sailing out of Yokohama harbor, the passengers lined the rails. Dressed in heavy clothes, they huddled together for warmth, anticipating land for the first time since Honolulu. It was a gray day, clouds obscuring the horizon where the California coastline edged the Pacific. Watching for a break in the fog blanket, they patiently waited to glimpse the "mountain of gold," eyes glittering with expectation, to be dazzled by light that would send them staggering through San Francisco's fabled gold-cobbled streets.

Sayo and Chiba pressed close, arms entwined. "When do you think we should dress in our kimonos?" asked Chiba.

"It will take a while before we can get off the boat, I'm sure. I think we should wait until we are given notice to disembark. It could be days."

"Days? Oh no, Sayo-san, so you think we will have to wait in this stinking boat for days?" Chiba's voice edged on whining. Sayo attributed this to anxiety. Until now, she had not heard any form of complaint from her young friend.

"Well, maybe not days. But the authorities are much stricter here than in Hawaii—and more efficient. So we probably will be allowed to leave the boat quite quickly."

"I understand we have to take the worm test again, and Steward says we must also have an eye examination.."

"Yes, for pink eye."

"Pink eye?"

"Don't worry about it, Chiba. Ours are fine." Sayo looked at her bright eyes, the bluish-white sclera surrounding large brown pupils. No sign of inflammation. Like a young deer, Chiba looked up at her trustingly. Feeling the burden of this adoration, Sayo's heart twinged. She hoped Chiba's unknown husband would deserve the total loyalty she knew Chiba would give him. In many ways she worried more about Chiba's meeting with her spouse than meeting her own.

A cry from the crowd.

"Land!"

"Land!"

"America!"

A cloud bank had lifted to reveal jutting headlands of dark rusts and brown. Flushed with excitement, Chiba jumped up and down, clapping her hands. Sayo was subdued, a strange heaviness crushing any joy the sight of land might command. She wished she was thrilled, breathless with anticipation. Was she not starting a new life—and with a Matsubara? Why did she feel such foreboding?

The ship steamed past a fort and entered the bay's protected mouth. After the rhythmic rolling of open sea, the harbor was a placid lake, dark green, glinting gold reflections of a brilliant yellow sky. The air smelled of seaweed, salty and pungent. Sayo's eyes followed the shoreline on the north side of the bay. Empty of buildings or any man-made structures, it was a spectacular expanse of open space, backdropped by smooth rolling mounds of green and brown. This was a landscape both familiar and strange—familiar for its rich, clean earth, and like Japan, bordered by the sea. But there was a rawness, an immaturity that contrasted with Japan's sculpted terrain of experienced land, ancient land, impregnated with centuries-old memories of wars, famine, liaisons, and birth. This new land seemed fresh and young—perhaps even innocent.

She and Chiba walked to the ship's south side, where they viewed an astonishing vista of wood and brick buildings lining the shore and set in steep hillsides. The populated city contrasted with the open land across the bay but was not unfamiliar, resembling Yokohama without high hills. Sayo turned and looked out to sea. Would she ever see Japan again? A strange large bird flew low over the water. Its bill was long and baggy. It dove cleanly into the ocean and surfaced with a fish in its odd mouth. With graceful sweeps of its huge wings, it flew toward the open sea, shrinking to a waving dot before it disappeared.

Sayo scanned the docks. The mass of people blurred into a wavering blob of dark coats that changed shape with each surge of the anchored ship. She couldn't recognize Hiroshi among them. She watched the other brides searching the wharf, clutching photographs that they periodically drew from their long, black kimono sleeves. Their arrival at Honolulu had been so different, free of the chaos and urgent restlessness that stirred the crowd below. The three brides there had left the ship with dignity. Would she be able to remain calm and composed amidst this nervous seeking?

She looked for Chiba. Spotting her close to the gangplank, she made her way through the brides to her side.

"Do you see your husband?" Chiba asked.

"I don't see him yet," said Sayo.

Chiba turned and looked down. A squarely built man of medium height was gazing up. His face was featureless, but she felt his piercing eyes. He wore a black suit and a gray fedora hat that shaded his face.

She whispered to Sayo, breathless, "There he is. There is Yoshio-san." She could not bring herself to say, "my husband."

Sayo slowly turned her head, careful not to move abruptly or with apprehension. Like a wilting flower, she seemed almost to droop, inspecting Yoshio with heavily lidded eyes. She turned to Chiba and said quietly, "He is a bull."

Chiba raised her eyebrows. "A bull?"

Sayo smiled and patted Chiba's hand. "Don't be dismayed by my words. What I mean is he seems to have great physical strength. But then, so have you."

Sayo's eyes swept over the crowd, searching for Hiroshi. She began to feel panic, suddenly realizing he might not be there to meet her. She had heard of brides arriving at ports only to discover their husbands nowhere to be found. Fortunately, other bachelors—those not able to afford passage for brides—lurked in the sidelines, hoping to acquire an abandoned and frightened wife by default. These were rumors, of course. Still, Sayo became increasingly agitated as she scrutinized the men below.

Then she saw him. Taller than most, a slender Hiroshi, hatless and dressed in a black suit, waved to her. Even from afar she could tell he was quite handsome. Uncertain if it was from relief or from excitement, she felt heat creep up her neck into her cheeks. She waved back with the silk fan Mentor had given her before leaving Hiroshima.

The brides began filing down the gangplank, stepping gingerly in their slim kimonos, white-powdered faces somber and appropriately unfathomable. No spontaneous greetings, cries of recognition, or tearful outbursts. Like a well-ordered line of black calla lilies slipping down from Heaven's Flowerbeds to fallow earth, they quietly and slowly descended to meet their mates.

The men stood in a row waiting, and as each bride met her partner, she bowed very low several times. The men returned the salutations.

During the three bowings to Hiroshi, Sayo was able to discern his nature as Madame Matsubara had claimed—gentle and nonresistant. His black eyes were warm, open, and readable as they scanned her face and figure. She could see he was pleased with what he viewed.

"Welcome to America, Sayo-san," he said. His voice was surprisingly deep, and his Japanese quite elegant, still edged with its Hiroshima accent. She had expected a higher pitch to his speech, perhaps due to what she viewed as a somewhat effeminate look.

"Thank you kindly, sir. I am more than pleased to be here and to meet you. Your family sends their heartfelt greetings."

"Thank you. I know you must be tired from your long voyage. So, I hope we can retrieve your baggage quickly and be on our way to San Jose."

"Oh yes, that would be most welcomed. Should I go with you to the baggage area?"

"No." His voice sounded kind. "My friend who has come with me can help. Please remain here."

* * *

Sayo was standing alone on the wharf when Chiba reappeared, running toward her, crying. She grabbed Sayo's hands. "Sayo-san, we must keep in touch. We will not be too far from each other, will we? Let us vow we will meet before the next year."

She was gratified to see Chiba, having thought she already had left. There was such confusion on the dock—strangers meeting for the first time, wagons and horses lining the streets waiting to whisk couples away to new homes. "Don't cry, Chiba, I know we will meet again soon." She patted her hand. "I know it in my heart."

"Please write me, Sayo-san. I will learn how to write and send you letters. I promise."

"Of course. I will write you once a month. Does your husband have an address now?" Sayo looked over at Yoshio, approaching with Chiba's basket and bag hanging from his short arms.

He bowed as Chiba introduced him. "This is my husband, Kimura Yoshio."

While bowing low the third time, his fedora fell from his head. Chiba already had noticed his gray sideburns, and was somewhat prepared for the glistening bald head. But Sayo was not. Shocked, she stepped back involuntarily, eyes flying to Chiba's. For the first time she could not read her young friend, whose face was impassive. Sayo composed herself, still inwardly unsettled. He was so much older than his picture! She felt betrayed for Chiba.

Chiba retrieved Yoshio's gray hat and dusted it off with her kimono sleeve. Observing the gentleness and care of this gesture, Sayo understood that her friend had accepted the situation.

Yoshio smiled and said thanks, his voice sincerely appreciative, his smile warm and forthright. Sayo's alarm subsided. He looked fierce, but she sensed an earnestness that made him appear younger. He would be good to Chiba. She was sure of that.

Compared with Yoshio, her own husband seemed delicate, a young bamboo reed, slender and pliant, easy to bend with the slightest breeze. His new suit and shoes dazzled beside Yoshio's faded and worn clothes. Still, Hiroshi did not emanate the strength that seemed to radiate from Yoshio and his old tattered suit. Sayo felt satisfied Chiba's future with him would be bright.

Chiba and Yoshio left on a wagon to Marysville, after which

Hiroshi returned to lead her toward their transportation, hidden from view. Following slightly behind him, Sayo was pleased to see he walked very much like his father, Tadanoshin. Were there other features and qualities he had inherited from the older Matsubara? She hoped time would reveal them.

As they rounded a building, she saw a large wagon with two chestnut-colored horses. Even from a distance, she could see the cart was new, with large wooden wheels, polished and gleaming, and sideboards of deep red mahogany. It looked like a well-kept schooner without sails.

Next to the horses, a tall man stood, adjusting a bridle, his back to the approaching couple. Hiroshi called out in the American language, "Cloud! We finally ready to go!"

The words sounded strange and guttural. Nevertheless, she was impressed Hiroshi could speak the foreigner's tongue. Except for some conversations between officials when they disembarked, she had never heard English. Would she have to learn this strange speech?

"My wife, Sayo. Please to meet," said Hiroshi as the man turned around.

She never had seen such an unusual face—dark copper skin, thick feathery eyebrows, like those of Samurai warriors. His cheekbones and jawline were finely chiseled, lending an aristocratic look. Black and thick, his hair was collar length. But it was his eyes that intrigued her. Almond-shaped like those of Japanese, they gleamed a green hue, the color of a clear, tranquil sea. Impolitely, she stared, allowing her eyes to meet his without any pretense of modesty.

Adding to her astonishment, he spoke in Japanese—not well, but clearly. "I'm very pleased to make your acquaintance." He bowed rather awkwardly, but with a dignity that did not escape her attention.

Hiroshi said, "Cloud is my best friend here in America. He works and lives with the bachelors at the compound. You will find him a loyal and good friend, too."

Since Cloud spoke the language, Sayo almost asked if he was Japanese.

"Well, let's get going," said Cloud in English.

Hiroshi clambered onto the wagon seat and was already seated when Sayo attempted to follow suit, straining to climb aboard in her narrow-skirted kimono. To her surprise, she felt herself lifted bodily by Cloud, his large hands encircling her obi-wrapped waist. Astounded by this unfamiliar assistance from a male, she was unable to thank him. Meanwhile, Hiroshi sat jauntily on the wide seat, seeming to ignore his friend's gentlemanly conduct. Although having lived in America for several years, he refused to relinquish those manners from Japan that still gave him some sense of power. He also knew Cloud would not judge him for seeming uncouth.

Cloud jumped up to the driver's seat and took the reins. He shouted some strange words to the horses, and the wagon began its journey out of the city. With Hiroshi seated between herself and Cloud, Sayo was unable to observe him any further.

As they climbed hills, Hiroshi pointed out houses and stores lining the dirt roads.

"That is Rosie O'Day's Saloon. And there is a barbershop. That brown house belongs to a famous painter."

"Do you visit San Francisco often?" she asked.

He was quiet for a moment. "Not too often. But I like the city and come here when I can. How do you like it?"

She was uncertain whether she could be candid. She decided to speak with honesty.

"Of course, I have seen so little. But what I have viewed in these few hours is not staggering. Somehow I expected the buildings to be more opulent. I guess more like castles and temples."

Hiroshi laughed. She also heard the driver chuckle. "Yes, and I'm sure you thought the streets would be paved in gold!" Apparently he understood the Japanese language, too.

"No, I realized those tales were exaggerations. It's just that these buildings compared to Japan are strange—so tall and narrow, like towers."

"You will find San Jose's countryside more like Japan. There is much for you to learn. Just be prepared to find life very different here."

Sayo leaned against the wooden seat's back, feeling her eyes droop and shoulders sag as the rhythmic clatter of hooves and gentle jostling soothed her. She was relieved Hiroshi had turned out as she expected, not a shock as Yoshio had turned out for Chiba. But in some ways, she did feel shaken, disconnected from her body, as if she had suffered a great jarring that had caused her soul to flee, leaving her numb and without feelings. She tried to relax. The tension of finally arriving and meeting Hiroshi had knotted her shoulders. The wide-belted kimono constricted her already tight chest. She wondered how long the trip would take to San Jose.

Before sleep overcame her, Sayo's last thoughts were of her father-in-law. She saw him galloping on his favorite horse, a falcon gripping his forearm. With gray cape fluttering behind, he raced across the fields, then released the falcon into the air. It circled the misty sky, growing larger instead of smaller as it climbed higher. Suddenly it swooped back down, now with a wingspan of about eight feet. It had transformed into an eagle and began shedding its feathers. Like autumn leaves they fell, floating softly, brushing against her cheeks, the dry edges stinging. She heard whispers. "America, America."

Fall 1942

At loose ends, Terri walks on the oiled road toward the camp's perimeter. She crosses over a firebreak where a hill of books decay in the sun. Some philanthropic organization had donated truckloads of books to camp, but not able to spare a barrack in which to stack them, the authorities simply dumped them in the break. Terri remembers her astonishment when she and Mitzi first came upon this huge mountain of bound books, pages fluttering like flags in the wind. Baby and Sailor were climbing the hillock as if it were Mount Everest, slipping and sliding between slick pages. Unable to resist this new mode of entertainment, Mitzi and Terri joined the boys. They clambered up the mound, jamming legs in crevices, tearing pages. They dug holes in the sides and built edifices and temples. They even played war, throwing books at the boys, who designated themselves as the axis . . . Tojo and Hitler. Sailor threw an extra-large book that hit Terri's face, bloodying her nose. Interpreting this as a sign to stop the game, she and Mitzi surrendered, but before descending down the unusual mountain, Terri retrieved the missile that had wounded her. It was *Gone With the Wind*. The next day it rained, a sudden summer storm that drenched the paper hill. Water-soaked, the books disintegrated, and what pages remained intact, faded in the brilliant heat that followed the rain. She never returned to retrieve more books, although she read *Gone With the Wind*. Now when she passes by the book mound, worn down to a gentle knoll, she sees internees scavenging through the parched volumes, as if rescuing flesh-and-blood survivors from a graveyard of bones.

* * *

Terri gazes up at the soldier in the guard tower. Obachan had warned about meandering too close to the barbed-wire fence, especially where soldiers watch from thirty-foot-high sentry posts strategically placed around the camp's boundaries. Today she feels brave. She has worked herself up to this moment, observing the soldiers from afar for weeks, observing how they smoke too many cigarettes, tossing used matches and half-smoked butts from the wooden platforms, how eager they seem to change guards, joking and laughing, anxious for conversation. She figures they are as bored as she is.

What finally bolsters her courage to venture out into the open space separating the barracks from the fence is the red-headed soldier's pleasant face, which, after so many days of scrutiny, she has grown to like. When he takes off his helmet she can almost make out the color of his eyes, and she imagines a splattering of rusty freckles across his cheeks and nose. His hair is deep auburn, the color Terri wishes her own hair could be—long shiny strands of copper cascading down her back like a horse's mane. But what she likes most is his habit of singing and whistling, which he seems to do when he isn't talking to himself.

She wears wooden *getas* and thick socks that stretch between her big and second toe to accommodate the strap holding her feet onto the slippery clogs. Her legs are bare up to the knees, where the navy peacoat cape falls in a straight line, an armless tube. Nonchalantly she saunters onto the sandy strip. Beyond this forty-yard buffer zone between camp and the barbed-wire boundary, a grayish-green sagebrushed desert stretches for miles and miles, out to the surrounding foothills and the Sierra Nevada Mountains.

Terri sometimes views camp as a kind of oasis, a strange tar-papered wallow plunked in the center of a snake-infested no-man's land.

Noticing her appearance, the soldier comes out of the tower's enclosure onto the deck. He still carries a rifle.

"Can you speak English?" He talks down to her slowly in a friendly tone.

"Of course," she answers flippantly, shouting up at him. "Probably better than you."

He laughs, displaying large white teeth. He throws down some objects he has withdrawn from his pocket. She stands still, noticing from the corner of her eye, wrapped candy and chewing gum scattered in the sand. She doesn't move.

"Don't be afraid." His voice is youthful, not yet deep or booming. "It's all right for you to have it."

She knows Obachan would disapprove of her taking anything from the soldiers, and she feels no yearning for the candy. But she has not tasted chewing gum in months, and the thought of chomping on the mint-flavored rubbery globs causes saliva to gather in her mouth. She is tempted to pick up the green-paper-wrapped sticks but remains frozen.

"Heck, it's not poisoned. Go on. Have some. See, I'm chewing on the same stuff." He opens and shuts his mouth, chewing exaggeratedly.

She surrenders to her hankering and picks up the gum.

"Thank you," she says, unwrapping a thin rectangle.

"You're very welcome." He is now seated on the platform, boot-clad feet dangling over the edge. The rifle lies out of sight. "What's your name?"

"Teresa." She doesn't need to tell her real name, "Teruko." "But everyone calls me Terri. What's yours?"

"My name's William. Some call me Will, others Billy."

"I like Billy. Is it all right to call you Billy?"

"Sure. How old are you, Terri?"

"Thirteen."

"Thirteen! Wow. I thought you were younger—maybe ten."

She doesn't know if she should feel insulted or complimented, or if he is teasing.

"How old are you?" she asks.

"I'm eighteen, soon to be nineteen."

She notices an accent, the way he slurs words together and says "ah" instead of "I."

"That's a fine cape you got on there. Looks something like a navy peacoat."

"It is. My mom sewed it out of a peacoat."

"Well, that is impressive. You people seem to be making out all right in there. Where you from?"

"Venice, near L.A. Where are you from?"

"A long ways from here. North Carolina. Ever heard of North Carolina?"

She can see Billy perceives her as someone either very foreign or very ignorant—or both.

"Of course I've heard of North Carolina. In fact, I know its capital: Charleston. And South Carolina's is Columbia." She is suddenly grateful to Mrs. Henderson, her fifth grade teacher in Venice.

"I know all the states and capitals," she adds.

"Now ain't that something." He seems genuinely impressed. "Now tell me somethin'. You are the first person from the camp who's willing to talk to me—or any of the soldiers. Aren't you afraid?"

"No, I'm not afraid. The others don't cross the sand barrier because we're told not to. That's why. Besides you've got guns. One could go off accidentally."

Billy laughs, shaking his red head. "What if I told you the guns aren't even loaded."

"They're not? Wouldn't you be afraid of us, then? There are thousands in here . . . and people are getting pretty bored. The food's bad, too."

"You know, you're pretty smart for a thirteen-year-old. If you're told not to talk to the soldiers, why are you talking to me?" His voice is serious.

Terri doesn't answer immediately. She fidgets, decides to be honest. "I've been watching you for a while now, and I trust you. My grandmother would not like it if she knew what I'm doing." She chews hard on the wad of gum, savoring the peppermint sweetness. "She would be especially upset because you have red hair."

"What?" Billy laughs. "What about my red hair? Lots of Americans have red hair—you know, the Irish and the Scots."

"My grandmother thinks anyone with red hair is a demon. They think violent thoughts. That's why their hair's on fire."

"Do you think I'm a demon?" Teasing.

"Of course not. Jeanne Crain, the movie star, has red hair. She's my favorite actress. I like red hair. I also like it that you sing so much. My sister Carmen can really sing, too—"

"You have a sister named Carmen?"

"Well, Carmen's not her real name. She named herself after Carmen Miranda. Her name is Keiko. And I have a brother named Mac."

"Now that's a nice Scottish name." Billy roars, throwing back his red head, mouth open like a yawning lion. "You know what, Terri? I like talking to you. Come here any time I'm on duty. . . . I'll bring some more gum, too."

"Will the other soldiers be mad at you?"

"Hell, no. What for? It's pretty damn boring in these towers. We know none of you plan on escaping into the desert, anyway."

She begins to feel nervous, realizing their voices have been loud enough to be heard in the nearest block. Great fodder for gossip. She wonders why she hasn't seen any internees, then realizes it is the noon lunch hour.

This lifts her spirits. Now she can continue visiting Billy as long as it is during mealtimes! No one around to eavesdrop, and more importantly, to report to Obachan.

"Hey, cat got your tongue?"

Recovering her courage, she answers, "Will you be coming to this tower tomorrow . . . and every day?"

"As far as I know, I will be. But you never know with the army. Why?"

"I just thought I'd come again. If you're here, anyway."

"I told you I'd bring some more gum."

She's worried lunch is about finished and the internees will be returning to barracks. "I have to go now. Thanks a lot for the gum. See you tomorrow. Same time."

Billy now stands, rifle on his shoulder. The sight of the gun fills her with some dismay. Its appearance changes his demeanor. But she is relieved when he speaks. "Sure enough, girl. Now I'm going to eat my lunch. I hope your meals aren't as shitty as the sandwiches our cooks make for the guards!" He's laughing, a lion roaring across the sand barrier.

She cannot contain herself and laughs loudly, too. "Hey, I have news for you. It's shittier!"

*　　*　　*

Secret meetings with the red-haired soldier give Terri a new purpose. She looks forward to the noon lunch hour, wishing it started earlier and lasted longer. Sitting in the sand at the tower's foot, in rapt attention, she ogles his seated figure, as if the platform is his throne, and he a flame-haired god descended from the burnt orange sky. They laugh a lot. He tells her silly "Kilroy" jokes, which delight her, not so much for their contents, but for the soft singsong accent she grows to love. Sometimes she doesn't even comprehend the words. She listens only to the music of his voice, mesmerized, imagining white-columned mansions surrounded by green lawns, magnolia trees; shiny, sequined peacocks with widespread fantails of purple, gold, chartreuse, magenta.

One day she asks, "Billy, do you live on a plantation in North Carolina?"

"What?" he says, surprised. "I wish I did. Closest I've ever come to a plantation is a tobacco farm . . . my uncle had one. No, we ain't gentlemen farmers. Why'd you ask?"

"Oh, I just thought that coming from North Carolina, you probably lived in one of those big houses, like in *Gone With the Wind*."

"You mean to say you've read *Gone With the Wind*? Where'd you get that book?"

"I found it." She doesn't feel like explaining where or how. Obviously Billy doesn't know about the gigantic mound of books mummifying in the firebreak between Blocks 12 and 13.

"Well, that book's about the South a long time ago. It's not like that now."

"Really? I liked the stuff about the balls, gowns, and food."

Changing the subject, Billy asks, "You say you have a sister. How old is she?"

Terri doesn't know how to receive this question. She's glad he has remembered something she told him several weeks earlier, but his interest bothers her.

"Carmen? Oh, she's sixteen." She swallows jealousy.

"Hey, now," his silky voice seems to coo, "Why don't you invite her here, too? I'll bring some movie magazines, ones with Carmen Miranda. Tell her that."

She is sure Carmen will not be interested in meeting a tower guard, especially one with red hair. Carmen's a lot like their mother and wouldn't dare break any rules. "My sister has a digestion problem," she lies, "and has to eat every meal. She couldn't come at this time—you know, while everyone's at the mess halls."

"That's too bad. I figure any sister of yours would be great to meet."

Flustered by this compliment, heart squeezing with pleasure, she cannot answer.

"Uh oh, cat got your tongue again."

She tries desperately to think of something clever, but remains silent, too moved by his flattery.

"Listen, Terri, you've been so much fun, I'm going to do something I shouldn't."

She panics for a moment. "Oh, please don't do anything that will get you in trouble."

"I won't get into trouble . . . and neither will you, if we're careful."

She stares up at him, eyes wide with innocence.

"Over in that grove of apple and poplar trees," he points to a green clump of trees about a mile from the tower, "there's a beautiful pool fed by a creek. Some of us guards have swam there when we're off duty."

"A real swimming hole?"

"Sure enough. And it's not too deep." He hangs his head over the platform's edge. "Would you like to visit it?"

"Wow! Yeah! But it's outside the fence. And it's too cold to swim now anyway."

"What I'm saying is I will look the other way, and you can slip under the barbed wire and go see the pool. It's really a magic place. They say the Indians went there for healing."

"Really?" Overwhelmed by his offer, she scarcely feels any fear about committing such a grave offense. She had heard that in another camp one fifteen-year-old boy was shot by a guard because he had wandered outside the fence looking for driftwood.

"Not today. But one of these days, you can do it if you want. I'll keep watch up here, and if someone catches you, I'll say I sent you there for something. Okay?"

"Okay. But we should do it pretty soon before it gets too cold. How about next Thursday?" His silhouetted figure is surrounded by yellow sunlight. She never has had a date and imagines this planned rendezvous to be her first.

"Good. I won't be here for a few days . . . off on a three-day pass. So next Thursday will be fine." His shadowy shape seems to shimmer. "Now, don't tell anyone. And I'll bring you back something, too. Anything special you'd like?"

She thinks for a moment. "I'd like any movie magazine with Jeanne Crain or Lon McAllister . . . Betty Grable, too."

Walking back to her barrack cubicle, she dares to imagine what the pool is like. Would it be crystal clear, bordered by lush plants with vines dangling from the trees, just like the hidden pools in her favorite movie, *Jungle Girl.* She thinks of the neighborhood theatre, the Saturday matinees that cost ten cents and were worth every penny, especially the love stories. She had cried watching *The Brave Nurse,* even though she didn't quite understand the plot.

She wishes there were movies in camp, but knows that's silly dreaming. They don't even have a school yet, something Terri never thought she'd miss. Yes, school and books. Who would've guessed that? Most of the kids are bored like her, roaming around camp in groups, seeking baseball and volleyball games played by older teenagers they can watch and cheer on. That no longer interests Terri. Now, instead of being a watcher, she prefers to be the player!

Hugging the peacoat close, she scrapes her wooden clogs over the tarred toad and soon arrives at her block. She skips up the rock entry way to the barrack door whistling "Chatanooga Choo-Choo," and feels a happiness she hasn't known since leaving home.

On Thursday, she arrives earlier than the usual noon hour. Until now the thought of exploring beyond the barbed wire never entered her mind. Like the other interneess, she accepted the boundaries without question, assuming the world outside it was wild, poisonous and haunted. And, after all, freedom did not even exist out there for them. She had heard about the hate that supposedly flourished in the towns and cities beyond the mountains surrounding the desert. How could they escape that?

Her heart hammers as she approaches Billy's tower. She sees him sitting on the platform's edge, dangling legs swinging in rhythm to some song she knows he is singing to himself. She slows down, noticing several people sauntering toward the mess hall. It's still too early. She decides to sit on a bench made of two large rocks set up outside the laundry room. Pretending she is basking in the sun, eyes closed, she sits quietly until the mess-hall gong stops clanging.

Emptiness. The block is deserted. She runs to the tower. Billy holds up two magazines, waving them as she nears. She can see his white teeth sparkling.

"Hi!" he calls cheerfully. "What took you so long?" He tosses down the magazines. They're both *Silver Screen,* with pictures of Jeanne Crain and Betty Grable on the covers. She picks them up lovingly, imagining they are fragile flowers, a corsage for their first date.

"Oh, thank you so much," she says, her voice muffled by emotion.

"You're welcome, sure enough. Now you better get going. The sagebrush is taller along there." He points to a strand of darker green. "And here's my wristwatch." He tosses down a leather-banded watch. "Now, keep track of the time and be back within an hour. Okay?"

He seems nervous, which scares her. But she has decided to risk herself for this, and shakes off the feeling of alarm. Quickly she scoots under the barbed wire and heads for the taller bushes, bending over to hide herself behind the brush that thickly borders the fence like a hedge. She's glad she has worn shoes instead of *getas*. Thorns protrude from tumbleweeds and pepper the sandy dirt. They could cut into her feet like nails.

She straightens up when she reaches the taller strand of brush. A trickling creek, narrow and shallow, winds between the foliage, explaining the greenness. She follows the water, intrigued by the sharp smells of sage and other plants she has never seen. Feeling stifled by the overhanging bushes, she realizes she has grown accustomed to bareness, to dry, brown open space. There are no trees within the compound, and only recently have some internees begun creating gardens, but mostly of rocks and driftwood. She imagines herself in a jungle, perhaps in Africa or South America, trekking deeper into darkness. She begins to savor the green closeness, feeling safe and protected.

After about fifteen minutes, she sees the creek has widened. The gurgling water lapping over rocks grows louder. Almost abruptly, she finds herself in a clearing, brilliant sun lighting an area as large as a basketball court. A placid pool reflects the sky's marshmallow clouds and glitters from the sun's rays. Another larger creek, flowing next to the one she has followed, tumbles into the pool, and at the opposite end, a creek of similar size drains it.

Awed by the secluded oasis, she sits down at the pool's edge. Pungent smells sting her nostrils. Feeling a chill in the fall air, she pulls her peacoat cape closer around her body. In her hand she holds Billy's wristwatch. She studies its worn leather band, the black numbers etched in the round silver-rimmed face.

She dips her other hand into the pool, shocked by the iciness that sends pangs up her arm. She wonders what the Indians did to heal themselves in this special place. Did they bathe in the water? Drink it?

A sudden wind ruffles the leaves. They whisper a language similar to the one the handsome brave spoke that night in the Horimoto compound. The granite rock still stands between the barracks, a lonely sentinel. Terri figures the brave is not there to guard the Horimotos, but a secret site.

The leaves stir, murmurs growing louder. She hears footsteps crashing through brush. Straining to capture sight of the intruders, she stands up, staring at the moving brush across the pool. Two birds fly out of the thicket. They chirp nervously, flapping wings wildly, and soar up into the sky.

Stillness. No movement or sound. She sits again, immersed in silence. She shuts her eyes and lifts her face toward the sun, savoring the electric patterns playing against the lids. Relaxed, and feeling truly free of others' looks, smells, and opinions for the first time in months, she falls asleep.

A loud rustling awakens her. Not knowing how long she has slept, she is overcome with panic and jumps to her feet. Clumsily she runs down the brush-hidden path toward camp, soaking her shoes as she splashes in the small creek. She glances at Billy's watch. She has about seven minutes to make it to the tower. She takes off the cape, allowing herself to run faster.

From afar she sees his shiny red head. He is looking away from camp, out to the desert. "Oh, God! I hope he isn't mad," She is angry at herself for falling asleep. "He'll never trust me again."

Crouching low as she leaves the tall greenery and hurries behind the sagebrush hedge surrounding the barbed wire, she wonders what to tell him. She reaches the fence and slides under it. Billy sits on the deck now, shiny boots glinting. Her stomach stops quivering when she sees his friendly face.

"Ain't that a pretty place?" No sign of agitation in his voice or manner.

"Oh yes! It is the most beautiful pool I've ever seen." She is almost tearful with relief. "I'm sorry I'm so late."

"You aren't late." His face turns serious. "But I admit the thought entered my head you could drown. I should have told you not to wade or swim in the pool."

She laughs, "Are you kidding? That water's so cold I couldn't put my hand in it!" But she is elated he was worried about her safety.

She retrieves the two magazines she left under the tower.

"Thanks so much for the watch," she says as she tosses it up to him. "And for letting me out."

"Anytime. If you promise not to get in the water." He straps the watch to his wrist.

As she gazes up at her flame-haired god, adoring his gray eyes and big white teeth, she decides she will try to persuade Carmen to meet him. It is the best way she can reciprocate his kindness, and who knows? Carmen might even like him. Then she'd be nicer to Terri, at least.

San Jose

"We are just about there," Hiroshi said. It was the second day since they had left San Francisco. Cloud still drove the wagon, with Hiroshi next to him and Sayo on the outer edge of the wooden seat. She was now dressed in a long gray skirt and jacket over a white ruffled blouse. Shiny black boots, ankle high and laced tightly, hugged her feet. Shading her rice-powdered face, a large-brimmed straw hat sat jauntily atop her upswept hair. Uncomfortable as she was in the strange attire, she was nevertheless relieved to be free of the kimono and tightly wrapped obi. It would have been tortorous traveling for two days in Japanese dress. She felt grateful to Tadanoshin for wisely providing the Western-style clothing.

They had stopped overnight at an inn in San Mateo. A couple from Japan, the wife herself a picture bride from Fukuoka, were proprietors of the small hotel, which was like a boardinghouse, housing a number of Japanese bachelors as well as providing rest for travelers passing through. Hiroshi had rented a room for Sayo alone so she could rest while he and Cloud slept in the bachelor dormitory. Exhausted and feeling slightly ill, she welcomed the time apart. Since leaving the Matsubara household, where she had enjoyed a room by herself, she had not been alone for any time. And she knew from that night on she would be sharing Hiroshi's bed. She had not dwelled on that thought, dismissing it, too tired even to feel apprehension or excitement.

The next morning, after folding up the futon bed, she dressed slowly, savoring the time alone. She wondered how Chiba was faring. She hoped Yoshio was as considerate as Hiroshi and had given her time to adjust to the new surroundings before claiming his *rights. As she painstakingly buttoned the unfamiliar blouse, fumbling with small pearl buttons, she thought of the elder Matsubara, tenderly remembering his thoughtfulness in purchasing the clothes for her. But quickly she brushed the memory away, reminding herself she had vowed never to think of him after being united with Hiroshi. With tightened lips, she continued dressing. The shoes were especially difficult. Tight-fitting and stiff, they embraced her feet like parched tabi (stockings), suffocating the toes. The straw hat perched on top of her head resembled the basket she had used in Hiroshima to gather fruit.*

After a breakfast of miso soup, rice, and eggs, the three boarded the wagon again and headed south for San Jose. During the meal, she had the opportunity to study both Hiroshi and Cloud, who had changed into more informal clothing. Hiroshi wore a dark brown shirt and pants. Thick-heeled leather boots that reached to his knees caused him to appear taller. Somehow the rough-looking clothes did not match his refined looks. Cloud, on the other hand, dressed in red-checkered shirt with leather vest and pants of dark blue heavy material, looked at ease. She was intrigued by him and had to constrain herself from staring. He didn't eat with chopsticks like the others, but seemed to enjoy the food, consuming several bowls of miso and rice.

Cloud said, "When you begin to smell pear blossoms, you'll know we have arrived." He had been quiet the whole way from San Mateo. No one had spoken much, perhaps still too tired from the wagon ride the day before. Out of the city, the landscape had softened. Lush greenery and sturdy trees pluming with abundant foliage dotted the low hillsides. She was pleased the land seemed similar to Hiroshima. They passed some houses, odd-looking wooden buildings, mostly painted white, some with white-painted sticks circling them. These were different from the houses in San Francisco, which were tall and narrow, and painted many colors.

As the sky began to turn orange, pink, and lavender, clouds formed over mountains to the south. The light cast a warm glow on their faces, giving them an eerie iridescence, like demon masks in a Kabuki play. A sweet smell filled the air, reminding her of plum buds and peach blossoms bursting open in Japan's spring country-

side. Cloud leaned forward, speaking around Hiroshi, "Do you smell it?" His green eyes were friendly.

"Hai," she answered. She knew this man was strong and masculine and also had a sensitive nature. To be aware of nature's beauty and sensual gifts was extraordinary even among Japanese men, and they had to be trained to appreciate them.

They passed a big house and turned down a narrow road. Hiroshi said, "The hakujin *boss lives there."*

"Boss?" She somehow had not thought Hiroshi was working for anyone. The family understood he was attempting to start a shoyu manufacturing business. "What is he boss of?"

"He owns this land." Hiroshi swept his arm in an arc. "We live in his houses . . . workers on his farms." Noticing the questioning look, he explained, "Cloud is a foreman. He's worked for Mr. Daley a few years. I don't work in the fields . . . I help Cloud."

Hoping not to appear too inquisitive, Sayo asked, "And how do you help him?"

"I speak the hakujin *language, so I translate to the workers. I also teach Cloud Japanese. That's why we are such good friends."*

"You have taught him well. How long have you worked together?"

Cloud answered her question, obviously eavesdropping. "Five years. Yes, he's a fine teacher."

"Does your boss speak Japanese?"

Both Cloud and Hiroshi burst into laughter. "Of course not. He's a white devil and hardly speaks his own language well. Besides, hakujin *don't want to learn our language."*

Ahead in the distance, she could make out buildings—a barn, several small unpainted wood cabins, and a long, low bungalow with many windows from which soft lights glimmered. After jostling over some deep ruts, they turned into a large yard. Two dogs bounded out of the barn, yelping and jumping at the wagon.

"Down, Sanjo! Down, Kiko!" Cloud scolded.

The door to the low building burst open, and several men appeared. They ran to the wagon. Hiroshi and Cloud had alighted and were unloading baggage, leaving Sayo sitting alone. In the dim evening light,. their features vague, the men shyly shuffled around the horses. There were four. She couldn't discern their ages or faces, but because of their spritely figures and unabashed staring, guessed them to be quite young. She kept her eyes demurely downcast.

Cloud helped her from the seat. Already she had accepted that Hiroshi would not lend her any assistance, allowing—or perhaps even expecting—his friend to act the American gentleman.

"This is Sayo, my wife," said Hiroshi to the men.

She bowed low to each one as he introduced him. They gawked, some bowing without lowering their heads, eyes riveted on her. She was accustomed to male attention, her beauty attracting it wherever she went. But the raw hunger she felt from these men was disturbing. Their eyes seemed to devour her.

Hiroshi led the way to the bungalow, followed by Sayo and the four. Cloud had disappeared with the baggage. They entered a large room lit by two kerosene lamps set on each end of a long wooden table. Three seated men were eating dinner. Familiar odors of fish and pickled vegetables wafted up from the table, where ribbons of steam also curled from a pot of cooked rice. Sayo was too tired from the day's journey to feel hunger.

The three men stood up and bowed when introduced by Hiroshi. Obviously older and more mature than the other four, they bowed with dignity and kept their discreet eyes unaffected by her presence.

"Will you join us for dinner?" said one of the older men, slim, with refined features and pale skin. He wore a blue-and-white yukata.

"Are you hungry?" asked Hiroshi. "Would you like some food now?"

The four young ones, who had scrambled back to their seats, ogled her hopefully.

"Thank you so much, but I am quite weary from traveling." She hoped her answer would not be considered rude, but in Hiroshi's voice heard permission to refuse.

"Tomorrow night we will celebrate," Hiroshi said quickly. He beckoned to Sayo, and they left the dining area.

Outside the air felt cool. The door led into a large open space enclosed by a wooden fence. Next to the dining room, an outdoor cooking area, sheltered by a tin roof, contained a stone fireplace stove, wooden sink, and shelves stocked with foodstuffs. Pots and pans hung from nails jutting from the roof's eaves. Set apart from the building and surrounded by a bamboo wall, a gazebo rooftop was outlined against the darkening lavender sky. Cloud emerged from behind the bamboo.

"I'm heating your bath."

"Thank you, good friend. We need a soak. Shall we save the water for you?"

In the darkness she barely could make out his lean silhouette standing in front of the bamboo fence. Her breath caught. For one moment she saw the elder Matsubara's eyes studying her, but they were now luminous green, no longer consuming, only observing like a wise wolf measuring a prize from afar.

"Not tonight, thanks."

She followed Hiroshi down a narrow pathway alongside the building. Numb with surprise at his living situation—now hers—she walked as if in a trance. Weren't there any women in the compound? Were they all bachelors? Where was the shoyu factory?

Before they came to the end of the long bungalow, he pointed out two sheds. He opened a heavy wooden door. Soft candlelight lit a small room whose floors were covered by tatami mat. Sitting on a stool near the door, she unlaced her shoes. Hiroshi, without removing his boots, stepped onto the straw matting. She was shocked. Had he forgotten Japanese manners?

Noticing her eyes on his boot-clad feet, Hiroshi explained, "Usually I remove my shoes, but tonight I'm forgetful. This is the only room in the compound with tatami matting . . . and you may have seen the men did not remove their boots at the dinner table. We need women to remind us."

"I observed there were no women," she said, glad he had provided an opening for her question. "Am I the only one?"

"Yes."

"And these men are all bachelors who work for the hakujin *boss?"*

"Yes."

She wanted to ask, "But why are you living here when your family thinks you are busy developing a shoyu factory in San Jose town?" She refrained, not wanting to appear too questioning or perhaps dissatisfied. She would let matters reveal themselves. Tonight was not the time for interrogation.

She looked around the room. It was spare and clean, with bare wood walls and two small windows hung with cotton panels of indigo blue cloth. A futon of similar material was spread out on the floor. Her bags were piled in one corner. She presumed Cloud had brought them there, as well as lit the candles, which were set on a high wooden tantsu *chest and long* tokonoma. *Paintings, indecipherable in the pale light, hung on all walls. She could see Hiroshi's mother was right. Her favorite son had good taste.*

He stepped behind a curtain, which hung across an alcove. Sayo surmised it was a closet. In stockings, she walked over to the futon bed, relishing the feel of tatami against her liberated feet. She sat down, wondering what to do next. He soon emerged from the alcove, dressed in a dark blue yukata.

"Let's bathe. You can change into kimono in here." He motioned to the space behind the curtain. In one hand he carried a wooden pair of getas. *Handing them to her, he said, "These are for you. Ito-san made them. The wood is from the mountains where we go to gather mushrooms."*

Moved by the gift so beautifully crafted, she tried to remember who Ito was. Then recalled he was the refined-looking older man, the only one dressed in yukata *at the dinner table.*

"How kind of him," she said. "I must thank him tomorrow."

"That would please him very much. He has been in this country longer than any of us and misses Japan. He tries to remain Japanese as much as possible."

Inside the alcove, she slipped out of her clothes and donned a red-and-white cotton kimono retrieved from her baggage. When she emerged, Hiroshi looked pleased. "I think kimono suits you better than hakujin *clothes."*

The air had turned cooler, even biting. She slid into the smooth clogs, appreciating the familiar satiny feel of flesh against wood. Hiroshi led the way, his getas *clacking on the gravelly path.*

Inside the bamboo wall, a fire burned under a large tin tub where water bubbled, boiling like soup in a cauldron. Next to it, a half-filled wooden tub of cold water sat on gravel. Hiroshi removed his yukata, hanging it on one of the pegs lined along the gazebo roof's eaves. Inside the gazebo, he sat down on a short stool and began washing himself with soap, retrieving water from the boiling tub and a cold water faucet nearby.

With a washcloth Sayo found hanging from one of the nails, she began rubbing his back.

"Thank you," he said.

She didn't answer. She soaped the back of his neck, studying his smooth-muscled shoulders, skin as white as her own. Oddly, she felt calm, as if washing a man's back was as common for her as washing her face. She had never seen a man naked before. But Mentor had prepared her for this night, telling her what to expect, teaching secrets learned only in high-class geisha houses. On the ship, the brides had shared Sei Shonagon's Pillow Book, *exciting themselves with the erotic drawings. She remembered how her belly tingled, the moistness gathering between her legs, dampening the dark moss of her nest. But her thoughts then were not of the face of Hiroshi, imprinted on a photograph, but of his father, Tadanoshin.*

Now Hiroshi was no longer just a print on a piece of paper. He was warm flesh and blood, sitting before her, responding politely to her back-scrub. She filled a basin with some hot water cooled by faucet water and rinsed his body. He stood up, his back to her, and began scooping boiling hot water and emptying it into the wooden tub, already half-filled and cold. Steam hissed and rose, enveloping him in mist.

She washed the rice powder from her face with a strong-smelling yellow soap and rinsed with cold water. Her teeth chattered. Was she so cold? Turning her back to Hiroshi, now sitting in the tub, she removed her kimono, hanging it neatly next to his yukata. She sat on the stool and washed her body, continually holding a cotton cloth over her pubis, hiding the mound of black hair. Mentor had said, "Do not reveal everything fully at first. Only a glimpse."

She rinsed off. Slowly, and with studied grace, she walked to the tub. She was glad the moon was only a thin crescent, giving off little light. She barely could see him, immersed in water amid rising columns of steam. Slipping into the tub, she sat facing him, knees bent and pressed against his. Water spilled over the sides onto gravel.

Neither spoke. They both sat, eyes closed, perspiration glistening on forehead and cheekbones, rolling off chin into the heated ocean between them. Keenly aware of the hairless legs pressed against hers, she wondered if he felt excitement. The legs remained smooth and relaxed, his arms and hands still by his side. Suddenly sadness swept over her. She wished desperately it was Tadanoshin sharing this tub. Through the mist, she evoked his face. Even in the hot water, she felt cold, so cold the nipples of her breasts prickled into erect raspberries. Her inner thighs tingled. She felt a pulsating in her lower belly, rhythmic and rapid. She wondered if Hiroshi could feel its throbbing through the water.

Children's Village

Manzanar

Hana perspires as she walks toward the laundry room. After a period of cool days, the weather turned hot again. "Indian Summer" she has heard others call it. She feels giddiness in her belly, excitement she tries to quell. The sewing crew hasn't met for two weeks, waiting for a new shipment of uniforms to renovate.

She enters the cool laundry room, and he is there, with Goto-san the Pot-Banger, already sorting through mounds of khaki and navy blue wool heaped on the table.

"Hi, Hana," he calls. His smile sparkles. He seems truly happy to see her. "Wondered when you were coming. Goto-san says we're the only ones sewing today."

"What happened to the others?"

"I think they're helping at Block Twenty-five. There aren't as many sewing professionals in camp as I thought."

Her spirits lift, knowing only Shimmy, Goto-san, and herself will be working together. She begins to sort through the coats and pants, tossing them into piles according to size and color.

Goto-san sings in her high crackling voice, "We make numba one coat. Our block best block everything. Best food. Best 'benjo.' "

She is referring to the painted cardboard screens for the latrines. The colorful partitions caused a great commotion throughout camp, drawing crowds to view the artistic ingenuity.

"Yeah, you folks are really getting it together in your block," says Shimmy. "How is it going with so many of the guys gone to harvest potatoes in Idaho?"

"Well, most were away working in other parts of camp, anyway. You know, building the hospital and new barracks. They weren't around much." She hoped she didn't sound critical. She wonders why he did not volunteer and asks before losing courage, "Why didn't you go? It would be a chance to get away for a while."

He is pensive, brown forehead smooth. "Well, you know, I considered it. But there's still lots to do here. And there aren't that many men left. Most of the *issei* were taken away earlier, remember. If you look around, it's mostly women and children."

She hadn't thought of that. She realizes he speaks the truth and feels ashamed for not having noticed the imbalance herself. She had been absorbed in her own world, reveling in the absence of the family males.

Tad and Mac have been on furlough in Idaho for two weeks. Accustomed to their absence, Hana now savors the extra space and quiet she at first found strange. Their male presence had always been an anchor, holding her to schedules, purpose, duty. It is odd to not have to think of their needs, to be able to float around the compartment like a boat without moorings, free to think only of herself. Carmen and Terri also react to their absence. Like butterflies they flutter between the wool partitions, Carmen singing softly, Terri sometimes twirling and spinning, mimicking a ballet dancer.

But after two weeks, Hana finds herself looking forward to the sewing sessions scheduled to resume today. A few weeks earlier, after completing Terri's cape, Block Manager announced the rest of the uniforms were to be distributed among other blocks until a new shipment arrived. Shimmy returned for one day to help finish Terri's cape, and Hana has not seen him since.

The trio work quietly throughout the morning, stopping once when the sewing machine breaks down, resuming soon again after Shimmy's fixing it. Hana admires his competence. She has not known any man like him, a male who takes swift action without shouting and ordering around to draw attention to his feat. She thinks of Tad and his brothers, the loud joking and commands, especially if what they do does not benefit them directly. They have to let you know their sacrifice.

At one point Shimmy says, "Actually, I've been working over at the Children's Village."

"What's that?"

"It's the orphanage."

"I didn't know we had any orphans here . . . I mean, where do they come from?" Again, she feels embarrassed at her ignorance.

Shimmy doesn't seem to judge her. He even seems pleased, as if he were a teacher introducing a student to a world of new facts and outrageous ideas.

"They come from California, Oregon, Washington, and Alaska. At least one hundred kids—from toddlers to teenagers. Haven't you noticed those buildings between Block Twenty-two and Twenty-eight in the old apple and pear orchards?"

Words stick in Hana's throat. How can she tell him she never leaves the compartment except to eat at the mess hall, visit the latrine, and sew with him in the laundry room! The olive-drab lined cell has become a hermit's cave, a wool cocoon where she can safely bask in solitude, where only thoughts can disturb her. She remains silent, carefully snipping buttons off a jacket as if that simple task demanded her full concentration.

Shimmy is gentle. "You know, a lot of people don't see the Village. It's pretty much hidden in those trees." He seems to hesitate. "But there are those who do purposefully ignore it. Some Japanese think orphans are 'bad luck.' "

Hana stops snipping the buttons. Could he be thinking she is like the others? Has she hurt his feelings? She quickly blurts, "I really haven't seen the Village, Shimmy. Honestly. I don't have anything against orphans. My mother Sayo is an orphan, raised by her aunt in Hiroshima."

Shimmy chuckles. "I know you don't have anything against 'us orphans.' Don't take what I say so personally. I'll be afraid to say what I think." He pauses. "I also know you hardly leave your compartment. How could you know what goes on in camp?"

Hana is relieved she has not offended him and surprised he knows this much about her.

"Would you like to visit the Village? They need help."

What kind of help?" She envisions changing diapers, washing clothes, cleaning barracks. As much as she enjoys being with Shimmy, taking over household chores does not enchant her.

Shimmy smiles at her lack of enthusiasm. "They're building a garden area around the dormitories . . . with a teahouse. I'm helping there. It's peaceful. The only place with trees."

She smoothes her dirndl skirt, rubbing her belly and thighs as if wiping wet hands. She looks over at Goto-san, cutting off sleeves at another table. She whispers, "Do you think it's all right?"

His scissors fall silent. "What do you mean?"

"Aren't we supposed to be sewing?" She glances again at Goto-san.

Shimmy's voice seems to boom, "Hey, we may be in prison, but we aren't slaves. We can sew today and go to the Village tomorrow. Give us some variety. We can do both."

The confidence in his voice lifts her. The certainty soothes her doubting heart like a warm wind. "Of course," she hears herself say, "we can do both! And be of help to everyone!" Delighted, Shimmy throws his head back, laughing loudly, mouth open. She can see inside his pink and glistening mouth.

Goto-san looks up from her chore. "What joke you say? Me laugh, too!"

"No joke," says Shimmy, still chuckling. "Hana just broke out of prison."

"What?"

"I'm kidding. It's just that I've never seen you so . . . so . . . free . . . with words, that is."

She is not sure how to take his remark. He is younger than she. Yet he seems so much wiser. Or perhaps, it is just herself. Perhaps she is too immature.

"Well, let's get on with some sewing here," Shimmy says in a business-as-usual tone. "I figure we can alter three more coats by tonight."

The next morning she waits at the firebreak between Blocks 22 and 28. They agreed to visit the orphanage after breakfast. They fibbed to Goto-san, telling her they were needed at the Children's

Village to alter jackets. Pot-Banger was not too happy being left alone, especially having to forfeit the camp's best tailors to the orphanage where some of the children were not even pure-blooded Japanese. She had heard some were not true orphans, but children whose parents were in other camps. She had heard a few internees complaining how much nicer the dormitories were, with running water, baths, and inside toilets. And now they were confiscating her block's most reliable helpers. Goto-san wondered about the authorities and their strange attitude toward orphans. Didn't they realize there was surely a cosmic reason the children had no families? Fate had its lessons. One should not interfere with karma by rewarding those born with bad luck. Compromising with her two star tailors, she said, "Okay. But only two days. Remember, we best block. Don't bring bad luck."

Hana was stunned by Goto-san's cruel remark but realized she did not know Shimmy's background, nor her mother's. Of course, no one knew much about Sayo. Even Hana only guessed, and filled in what her mother omitted whenever she was asked about her past.

It is still early, yet as hot as high noon. Hana is perspiring, not sure if it is from heat or from nervousness. She feels awkward waiting at the edge of Block 22 where the oiled road snakes across the firebreak, the only road crisscrossing the open spaces between blocks. She wonders what people will think seeing her standing there, as if demented by the sun, hallucinating, perhaps imagining the sticky road is a highway to freedom outside the fence and she awaits a nonexistent bus.

She hears running footsteps. Shimmy appears beside her. "Sorry I'm late," he says, out of breath. His face glistens from sweat. "One of my roommates is sick, so I took him some breakfast. Phew! It's hot already."

"Oh, that's all right. Is he okay? What's the matter?"

"I don't know. Some kind of dysentery. Could be food poisoning."

She remembers the sickness from the typhoid shots and feels sympathy for the roommate. The four other men living with Shimmy in the bachelor's quarters are lucky. He is much younger and energetic and has a helpful disposition.

"I'm worried about him. He's pretty old, one of the older *issei* in camp."

"And he's never married? I mean, is he a widower?"

"No, he's a real bachelor, said he never could afford a picture bride."

Already, the road's oil, cooked by the sun, sends a greasy smell into the atmosphere.

"This road is too wet to walk on," Shimmy says. "We'll cross over to those clumps through the firebreak." He points to some trees about a hundred yards away. He looks down at her feet, clad in saddle shoes she has borrowed from Carmen.

"Good. No zoris."

Their feet sink in the hot grainy sand as they trudge to a row of scraggly pear trees, remnants of an old orchard left twenty years before by farmers who settled in the Owens Valley. She notices irrigation furrows circling each tree, attempts to revive them from their long dry sleep.

"Isn't it amazing these trees are still alive?" says Shimmy. "They've been abandoned for at least thirty years. There's water stored under the earth here, even when it's parched on top. It seeps down from the mountains."

She studies the gnarled branches, peeling bark, scrawny leaves straining to remain green and tender. They are tough survivors, she thinks, like some of the old *issei* in camp, lean and weathered but not yet completely dried up.

Beyond the trees stand two large buildings, one with a covered porch at its entrance. The ground is bare around them. A few yards away from the larger building are signs of landscaping—several mounds of dirt, a pile of boulders.

"That's the Japanese garden I'm trying to design." He steers her toward the site. "I could use some help here. You know not many internees are going to want to come to the orphanage to beautify it." He jumps down into the excavation. "But I knew you would."

She is speechless with pleasure. *Does he really know me? He seems to think I am a good person.* She doesn't reply, but follows him into the shallow figure-eight pit.

"This is going to be a pool. Since I can't get any cement, I'm lining it with rocks," he points to the larger loop, "and I need to build a mound in the center. So, you can see, I've lots to do."

"How can I help?" she asks, eager to prove her worthiness.

"Are these rocks too heavy for you to line the sides?" He is hesitant.

"Oh no." She is already pushing a large, smooth stone into the dirt lining.

Shimmy laughs. "Take it easy. We don't have to finish today. Besides, it's too hot and you might get sunstroke."

She is suddenly aware of the sun beating down on her bare head. Sweat drips into her ears, the cotton blouse sticks to her back and midriff. With each setting, the rocks become heavier and her breath shorter. She glances at Shimmy scurrying up and down the pit, retrieving them from a pile. He is tireless.

"You're very strong, Hana. I really didn't expect such dedicated help."

Gratified he has noticed, she works more arduously beside him, enjoying the same camaraderie she felt as his sewing partner. After they line one side, he suggests quitting for the day, filling her with relief.

Faces streaked with dirt and sweating, they stand above the half-finished pond and admire the improvised masonry. Stones of varied hues—gray, black, rust, deep purple, tan—glisten from a wall both sturdy and aesthetically pleasing.

"Just think of those poor slaves building the Great Wall of China," Shimmy says, laughing. "Sure glad we're only doing a pond."

"Me too!" She brushes off Carmen's brown-and-white saddle shoes.

"Would you like to visit the orphanage?"

She is not particularly interested in seeing the orphans' quarters, but feigns enthusiasm, wanting to please him. "Oh yes," she says and gives a rare wide smile.

They enter a large reception room, which also acts as the recreation center. Seated around two long rectangular tables, newly made and still smelling of sweet pine, several children work puzzles and draw with stubby crayons. She thinks of Shimmy's past, how as an orphan he must have entertained himself like these children, drawing cars and animals on the backs of used office memos. They are hand-some children. The boys seem to be full-blooded Japanese, but she discerns a "hapa" look in the three girls also drawing at the table. Light brown hair, thin skin—rosy and translucent. Their eyes remain downcast as Shimmy and Hana approach, and not until Shimmy sits down with them and begins drawing do they come to life.

One of the girls glances up at Hana shyly. Her eyes are hazel, round, and fringed with long black lashes. She looks about five years old.

"What's your name?" Hana asks.

"Mary." The voice is barely audible.

"What are you drawing?"

The gray-green eyes gaze at her with a steadfastness that is un-nerving.

"Are you my mother?"

Shocked by the unexpected question, she cannot reply and is res-cued by Shimmy.

"No, Mary." His voice is gentle. "Hana is my coworker and friend."

"Oh, she's nice. I thought she might be my mother." Her pink lips tremble.

Later Shimmy tells her that Mary was left at the orphanage in Los Angeles when she was an infant, born out of wedlock to a Japanese woman. Because the father was Caucasian, and probably married, it was impossible for the woman to keep the child, and she had aban-doned her at the orphanage.

"She keeps hoping her mother will come and claim her. I remem-ber that feeling well. For years I hoped my parents would come for me, even though I was told they were dead. I made up it was a mis-take, that they really had survived and had amnesia or something like that."

"Were your parents in an accident?"

"My dad was a fisherman. One day my mom went out with him and his partner, and the boat exploded from leaking gas. They all were killed."

"I'm so sorry." She wonders if he knows Tad's family were fisher-men. She would have guessed his family were gardeners or even merchants, but not of the sea. Tad's father and brothers fished out of

San Pedro, rough, crude men shouting gruffly, never merely speaking, in a harsh dialect. She can't imagine Shimmy in such a setting.

"How old were you?"

"Nine. I was an only child with no living relatives. So I was placed in the orphanage."

Her eyes sting with tears. "It's good there are places like the home. Were they nice to you?"

"Yes, they were. I owe a lot to them. That's why I'm here helping."

At noon they leave for lunch at their respective mess halls. The children eat at the orphanage, a kitchen and dining area providing a homelike atmosphere in the larger building. She notices their quarters are indeed more comfortable than the regular barracks, with toilets and a large dormitory of beds with cotton instead of straw-filled mattresses. She doesn't begrudge this, as some other internees do. After all, they are parentless and without family. They deserve some kindness to offset their ill fate. Her attitude differs from others, but she has learned from Sayo—and is now more aware of it than ever since meeting Shimmy—that having a different opinion is not a sickness of the mind. It can even be a strength.

In the mess hall, Sayo asks where she has been all morning.

"I've been at the Children's Village." She wonders if her mother knows about the orphanage. Her question is answered with the reply.

"Were you sewing jackets for the orphans?"

"No."

"Didn't Shimmy go too?"

She should have known better than to think Sayo would not have surmised she had been with Shimmy. Still, it galls her that her movements are such public knowledge. Had Pot-Banger said anything?

"Yes, we were going to sew, but we worked on another project instead."

Sayo accepts this explanation with graciousness. "Ah so. I'm sure it is a fine project. That Shimmy-san is smart . . . and talented."

Sayo doesn't ask what the project is, but Hana figures she already knows. They finish the lunch of bologna sandwiches and iced tea, talking little, except to comment on how uncrowded it is without the men.

The girls rarely remain in the barracks. Terri, who sleeps in the tearoom with Sayo, even has stopped eating lunch at the mess hall, and Carmen has found a friend at Block 15 with whom she practices singing and jitterbugging, leaving the room empty for most of the day. Hana is resigned to the fact that Carmen eats with her friend at another block and Terri has been conspicuously absent for the past weeks.

"Have you noticed how thin Terri is?" asks Sayo.

Feeling guilty that she has not, Hana lies. "I think she's on a diet. You know girls that age. They look at the movie magazines and want to be like those movie stars."

"Well, it's not a good idea. I'll have to talk to her."

When it comes to Terri, Hana leaves any problem or question to Sayo. She isn't sure why she never bonded closely to her youngest child. Perhaps it was because Sayo took Terri under her wing when she was young. After she married Tad, she learned from his family it was customary in Japan for grandparents to select a grandchild who would be favored and groomed to care for them when they grew old. Thank God, neither of the Murakamis followed that tradition. While she lived with them they more or less ignored the children.

But after Tad's parents died and Sayo closed the teahouse in Watson-ville, Hana was quick to invite her to live with them. Obligation to a parent was stronger than that for siblings, which meant Tad's two bachelor brothers, who still lived with them, would have to seek another living situation. She was tired of caring for them. Tad even found another house in Venice, far from the Japanese fishing ghetto in Terminal Island where they had lived with his family.

After Sayo moved in, she began favoring the youngest child. At first, Hana tried to stop this unfair treatment by her mother, having just been freed from her mother-in-law's domination for the past years. But already burdened with two other children and a demanding husband, it was easy to allow Sayo to take over Terri. Besides, she truly didn't know how to assert herself against her charismatic mother, whose strength and wisdom had piloted her "teahouse family" through many storms. How could she dare to question her actions? Thus, she accepted it as Sayo's return to some semblance of tradition in her own family. Hadn't she matched her marriage to Tad?

Disastrous as that marriage turned out to be for Hana, she knew it had been her mother's way of protecting her. Although she didn't like to admit it, accepting this favoritism as tradition also alleviated the guilt she felt for not having more possessive feelings toward the child.

In the years that followed, Hana often has envied the intimate relationship between Terri and Sayo. She finds it difficult to be close with her mother, or with anyone, for that matter. Perhaps it is because of growing up in a teahouse where personal consideration was directed to patrons and not to a youngster often underfoot. The Chinese girls had been the most attentive adults in her childhood, while Sayo had seemed unreachable, devoted only to running the inn.

Though she's never imagined living in Japan, Hana sometimes yearns for those grandparents she never had who might have given her the second home Terri has found with Sayo.

For the rest of the day, she remains in the compartment. Cleaning the linoleum floor with oil, she kneels on her hands and knees, rubbing the smooth surface with an old towel. Her mind is full of the morning's events. As she remembers every word spoken by Shimmy, every expression on his face, she is stung by an urge to rearrange the room. She doesn't know why she feels so compelled to move around what little furnishings there are—blankets hanging from ropes as partitions, stacked boxes making up closets, a table and three chairs.

First she changes the sleeping spaces by rehanging the army blankets. She restacks the boxes, creating one long cupboard that provides a low partition and illusion of a sitting room. She separates the double bed made up of two cots, and sets one of them in the sitting room to serve as a couch during the day.

Feeling exhilarated, she sits on the olive-drab couch and contemplates the changed room. She feels herself smiling. Embarrassed by this new feeling, she jumps up from the cot and resumes polishing the floors.

ACT II

Fighting Warriors

Billy

When Terri tells Carmen about Billy, halfheartedly hoping to set up a meeting between the two, she is not surprised at her sister's response. Carmen's large black eyes turn to stone—deep liquid pools suddenly filling with cement.

"What in goddamn hell are you doing fooling around with soldiers? Do you know how much trouble you could get into? The whole family could be punished!"

Terri knows her sister is really upset, using swear words and bringing up family obligation.

"Hey, I'm not doing anything wrong." Terri hasn't told her about the previous outing to the pool. "It's not a crime to talk to them, is it?"

"But he gave you magazines and gum. How come?"

"Because he's a nice guy, that's why! He's lonely in that guard tower and wanted to meet you when I said I had an older sister."

Light flickers in Carmen's eyes, but is quickly extinguished.

"No. I won't do it. Everyone will gossip. And what would Obachan think?"

"You better not tell her, Carmen. Promise me you won't."

Carmen's eyes remain steely, but begin to soften when Terri offers to keep bringing movie magazines from Billy.

"Well, okay. I won't tell anyone. But be careful." Light has returned to her eyes. Terri notices how pretty her sister is when she relaxes, how her full lips, magenta-colored naturally, unfold like a flower, a dark-petaled peony. Her skin is tawny and free of blemishes, unlike Patty from Pasadena, whose face is peppered with blackheads and acne scars. Admiring her sister's loveliness, she feels disappointed for Billy. In spite of her envy imagining them together, she wishes Carmen were more adventurous and would meet with him just once.

She delivers the news to Billy, lying a bit to protect his feelings. She says Carmen would like to meet him, but has joined the glee club that gathers at the other side of camp during lunch hour, and that she thanks him for the magazines.

Billy doesn't seem too disappointed. He sits on the platform edge and lights a cigarette. "Can't much blame her, I guess. Not many people would want to talk to a guard"—he sucks on the cigarette—"except you." He winks and removes the helmet.

His red hair glows. He has taken off his jacket, and she notices circles of perspiration staining his shirt under his arms. Terri is back in her shorts and wooden *getas*. She thinks of the forbidden pool outside the wire fence with wistfulness. How pleasantly cool it would be.

As if reading her mind, Billy says, "Wish I could be swimmin' at the pool right now. This Indian Summer sure has snuck up on us."

"Do you know much about the Indians who lived here before?" She wonders if he would think she was crazy if she told him about the warrior ghost she saw that night at the Horimoto barracks.

"I just know some tribe lived in the valley many years ago. There's still some living in towns around here." He flings his arm in a sweeping arc.

"Really? Have you ever seen one?"

"Sure. I've seen a couple in Big Pine. Hell, I'm part Indian myself."

Incredulous, Terri stares. She imagines his red hair grown long and flowing, bare arms and chest rippling with muscle, eyes intense as he scans the desert horizon. He transforms easily into an Indian warrior, much more appealing to Terri than the khaki-clad soldier who sweats in the afternoon heat.

"Yeah," he continues, "My granddaddy was half Cherokee . . . from Georgia. 'Course, they didn't brag on it. They were ashamed, I guess."

"Ashamed? Why? They were the first Americans, weren't they?"

"With some people that don't matter. They're just scared of 'em."

"Like they are of us here in camp?"

He pauses and pulls a cigarette out of its pack. He lights it and takes in a long drag. After exhaling a stream of white smoke, he chuckles. "You are smart, you know that? Someday I bet you go to college."

"You mean in here? There's no college here. There isn't even a real school."

"You ain't going to be here forever, Terri." His voice is serious, unfamiliarly grown-up sounding. "This war will be over, and you'll go out in the world."

"But what if the war goes on for years and years?"

"It ain't going to, so forget about that."

"Have you ever been to college?"

"No. But I plan to after I get out of the army. On one of those G.I. scholarships."

Hearing Billy talk about the future bothers her. At home no one dares to talk about it. She wonders what her family will do after the war ends. What will she do? She can't imagine ever being in the outside world again. Having heard talk about the hatred toward Japanese out there, she thinks of her Caucasian friends in Venice. Do they hate her now? Well, if they do, they can go to hell, she thinks. Yet Billy is Caucasian, and he's nice, nicer to her than her brother Mac. And he also wants to meet Carmen.

This serious talk is too disconcerting. Terri changes the subject. "Hey, have you been to the secret pool lately?"

"It's been too cold, but now that it's hot, I plan to." He sucks on his cigarette. "Why? Do you want to go again?"

"Yes, I do. I won't fall asleep. Promise."

"How about day after tomorrow? It'll still be hot. And tell your sister I'm sorry she can't come."

She is peeved at Carmen for being such a goody-goody. She would like to see Billy happy, even if it meant sharing him. But she knows Carmen would be too scared, especially sneaking past the barbed wire. And then there was the possibility she would double-cross Terri and tell Obachan. That thought makes her shudder, erasing any desire she has for Billy and Carmen to get together.

"I'll see you soon," she shouts as she backs away from the tower. "Day after tomorrow, okay?"

He flashes a smile and points past the fence. He flicks his cigarette butt toward the barbed wire and stands up. For the first time, she notices how tall he is. From the ground, he looms even larger, a fiery-headed giant, maybe even a king, surveying his domain of parched desert and tar-papered shacks, his subjects a race of tiny people with dark hair and narrow eyes. She would like to be his queen—or maybe his princess—or even a lady-in-waiting.

Two days later she sits by the pool, studying the glints bouncing off the silver water. It is not quite high noon. She had taken a chance and left camp before lunch, scurrying under the barbed wire while no internees were in sight, still inside their compartments, probably escaping the blistering heat. Billy was at the tower and had waved her through, grinning like a coach for a winning team. Retracing her steps to the pool was easy.

Running her fingers through the cool water, she imagines herself back on the California coast basking at a beach where waves gently roll onto shore and the sand is grainy and yellow. She dangles her bare feet in the pool. It feels icy, and she wonders how Billy can swim in it. In her mind's eye, she sees him stroking toward her; long, muscled arms glistening with golden hair, slicing the water. Around his head float tendrils of red seaweed. She enjoys the daydream and lies down, under the shade of a small tree whose translucent leaves filter the sun's rays dancing on her face. She squints at the cloudless sky, now a brilliant azure.

Suddenly she hears the hard steps of booted feet. She sits up and crawls behind a thick bush, crouching low, heart hammering. Until that moment she had not given a thought to what the consequences could be for someone caught outside the barbed wire. Now she is terrified. They even could shoot her on sight! She remembers the teenager shot to death in another camp.

She hears voices. With great relief she recognizes the lilting accent. But who is he talking to? She peers around the bush and sees Billy and another soldier, helmetless but in uniform. Billy is chewing gum and laughing, and the other soldier, who she recognizes as his friend who guards the next tower, wears the dark glasses that distinguish him from other guards. They are silver-rimmed, shaped like aviator goggles, giving him a somewhat sad look.

As they arrive at the water's edge. Billy's soft voice calls out, "Hey, Terri, where are you?"

She emerges from behind the thick brush, slightly embarrassed by her fearful reaction.

"There you are! Thought for a moment you had hightailed it out of here, headed for them Alabama Hills."

Recovered from her shock, Terri quips, "I was thinking about it, but forgot my cape. Gets pretty cold at night, you know. How come you guys are here? Did something happen?"

"Hell no," Billy laughs. "We're both off for the afternoon and thought we'd join you for a swim." He gestures to his friend, "This is my buddy Skip."

"Hi," Terri says shyly. "Nice to meet you." She stares at the opaque glasses, wishing he would take them off. His lips turn upward in a narrow smile, but appear stiff, like the mannequin's mouth she used to see in the JCPenney department store window in downtown Los Angeles.

Skip removes the glasses. His face comes alive, and Terri sees blue eyes, viewing her with friendliness. His smile now looks soft. "Happy to finally meet you, too," he answers in a deep voice, devoid of any accent. "I've seen you visiting Bill."

"Yeah. I've noticed you, too. Your glasses really make you stand out."

He laughs, a deep rumbling sound. She admires Billy's easy laughter, and had thought it was his personality. Now she wonders if this spontaneous reaction to everything is simply a Caucasian trait. Obachan often has said the White Ghosts were easy to read because they displayed their emotions so readily, leaving no reserves from which to draw when a momentous or weighty occasion demanded it. "They leak their strength frivolously," she would say, "laughing out loud so much."

"Well, Bill says you're smart and speak what you think."

She is flattered thinking Billy has talked about her. For the moment she is wordless. The guards begin unbuttoning their shirts, eager to take a dip. Realizing they are undressing in front of her, she panics. She wonders if she should cover her face, or just head back to camp. Frozen, she sits down and stares into the water, dipping her hands into it like a ladle. She is holding her breath.

From the corner of her eye, she sees the whiteness of their chests and backs. Skip is removing his trousers. Terri wants to avert her eyes, but is paralyzed. Were they actually going to swim naked?

Skip's khaki pants are off, and Terri releases her breath. He is wearing bathing trunks, dark navy blue shorts of some shiny material. Billy also has undressed, and she sees a flash of red as his buttocks and legs disappear after he dives in headfirst. She feels light, elated, as if she has escaped a near tragic accident.

Billy's red head pops up in front of her. "Come on in," he gasps. "It's mighty cold, but great!" Skip's dark head also emerges.

"I can't swim . . . and I'm not wearing a bathing suit."

"That's okay . . . jump in with what you have on. I'll teach you to swim."

Actually, Terri does know how to dog-paddle and isn't afraid of deep water. It doesn't take much cajoling before she jumps into the icy pool, holding her nose and breath as she first sinks below the surface. She feels Billy's hands at her armpits lifting. When her face breaks water, she gasps, the cold had tightened her chest and throat. Exhilarated, she opens her mouth and laughs loudly. Billy is holding her up, kicking his legs.

"Now, that's what I like to hear . . . you're downright pretty when you laugh. Now, kick your legs." He is breathless. Skip is swimming across the pool with slow, graceful strokes.

"I can dog-paddle. Why don't you just go on and swim with Skip."

"No way," he says, almost sternly. "It's bad enough us letting you out of camp. I ain't going to have a drowning on my hands, too!"

She feels his legs brush against hers. They feel smooth and hairless. Obachan says Caucasians are hairy. She wonders why his legs are not.

The water's iciness soon forces them out of the pool. They lie on a small clearing carpeted with pebbles and surrounded by pungent reeds. The sun, now high in the sky, warms their bodies and soon dries Terri's shorts and sleeveless top. They lie quietly, comfortable in silence and with each other.

Terri breaks the stillness. "Skip, where are you from?"

Almost asleep, he mutters, "Rhode Island. Now don't ask me where that is. No one knows about Rhode Island here in California."

"I do. And I know the capital is Providence."

Billy chuckles. "I told you she'd put you in your place."

Skip sits up and puts on his aviator glasses. "You know, I've never seen an Oriental before I came here. You people are just like any American . . . speaking English, dressing like us."

Terri stares at his now inscrutable, dark eye-glassed face. "Well, what kind of people live in Rhode Island? What do they look like?"

He thinks for some moments. "I guess lots of white people from England and Scotland, and then there's some colored, and some Portuguese and Italians. I'm half Portuguese."

Billy pipes in, "Well, what d'ya know, you learn something every day. I thought you were Black-Irish."

"Well, you want to know something?" Terri says, "I've never known many Caucasians, either."

Skip says, "What do you mean, 'Caucasians?' Is that a fancy word for 'American?' "

"I'm an American. I was born here," Terri says somewhat defensively. " 'Caucasian' seems more polite than 'white,' that's all. It's the word we use for 'white people' in camp." She didn't want to tell them about the other not-so-nice names like *ketto*, the most derogatory, which meant "white ass" and *obake*—"white ghosts."

"Let's explore around this place," says Billy, putting on his boots.

Terri and Skip follow as he pushes through thick brush edging the pool to the small fall of outflowing water. The waterfall splashes over rocks into another small pool partially hidden by overhanging foliage. They climb down a steep slope next to the fall, and when they reach bottom find themselves in a mini canyon about twenty feet deep and twelve feet wide, cool and shaded by a bower of leafage above them. A narrow creek, deep and smooth-bottomed, glides from the small pool. Looking up they can see a thin strip of blue sky framed by greenery.

"Jesus," says Billy, "no one'd ever guess this spot was here. You can't see it from the top."

"Goddamn! It's even got a climate all its own," exclaims Skip. "Feel how cool it is."

Entranced by the hidden canyon, lulled by the creek's soft gurgling, Terri walks carefully on the moss-covered earth. She feels slightly dizzy.

"Man, this is a strange place," says Skip. "Do you think it's haunted?"

Golden light, streaming through the overhead foliage, casts an iridescent glow over the plant-covered canyon walls. The atmosphere is moist, and the smells are woody and sweet. Terri walks along the creek's edge until she comes upon a large, smooth boulder that seems strangely out of place in the junglelike terrain.

Billy's voice calls out from behind it, "Hey, there's a cave back here!"

A dark hole has been cut into the canyon wall. The entrance is about five feet high. Once inside, they find themselves in a space the size of a large closet or small kitchen, barely over six feet in height. The air is damp and smells musty.

"Goddamn," Billy exclaims. "This is not a natural cave. Someone dug it out."

"Might've been Indians," says Skip.

"Of course it was," says Terri, almost arrogantly. "It sure isn't one of us internees!"

Her eyes have become accustomed to the dim light, and she now can make out a long shelf carved into the wall. Scattered on it are rocks, some strangely shaped driftwood, bones, and two flat baskets. A thin gauze of spiderwebs veil the artifacts like a shroud.

"I don't think we should touch those things. They've been here a real long time. It could be bad luck."

She can feel a mysterious presence, similar to what she had felt emanating from the granite obelisk in the Horimoto compound. She remembers Obachan's words: "People leave things at special places not because they want to get rid of them, but because the things mean something. Good feelings . . . especially feelings of love, remain forever and give a place special power, and you can benefit from that power when you visit. But if you take things away, the place will lose its love and will no longer be special."

Obachan had told her those words when she was ten, while they were walking on the beach and had come upon an elaborate shrine carved into a cliff. Pieces of colored glassware were imbedded in the alcove walls. Laid neatly at the bottom were feathers, shells, pebbles, several beaded necklaces, coins, a pack of Camel cigarettes, and a silver-backed mirror. Obachan had said, "Can you feel the love the person has put into this shrine?" Terri was more interested in the shiny mirror and had reached over to confiscate it when Obachan stopped her. "Bad luck!" she had said, her eyes no longer black, but fiery lava. Then she gave Terri the lecture on the power of a place.

"Damn right," says Billy softly. "We ain't touching anything. Look at them carvings in the wall." Despite the dimness, it is possible to make out drawings of deer, rabbits, and some ducks in flight etched into the earth walls and filled with an ocher color. The drawings seem to speak to Terri, almost chanting in the strange language she'd never had heard before but could understand when the warrior spoke.

"Do you hear it?" Terri asks.

"What?" says Skip.

She closes her eyes and begins to sway.

Billy comes close and peers at her. She opens her eyes, barely making out the color of his eyes, but notes thick, dark red eyebrows and a faint spattering of freckles across his forehead. She feels his quick breathing, a soft warm wind on her face.

"Are you all right?" Billy asks. "Let's get out of here. Maybe the air is too close."

Skip is already out of the cave. Billy grabs her hand and leads her through the opening, stopping before the large boulder. On the side facing the cave, it is decorated with symbols drawn with some substance that once could have been colored red. The circles, stripes, and wavy lines are a deep henna, still discernible despite the passage of time.

"Wow," exclaims Billy. "These are old, but probably have been preserved 'cause of protection in this canyon from the sun and weather."

Skip is nervous. "Let's go. We better get Terri back to camp."

Snapped back to the present by fear she hears in Skip's voice, Terri squeezes Billy's hand and laughs, a light lilting tinkle. "I'm sorry. I was just fooling around . . . trying to scare myself, that's all. My folks think I'm weird. Except my grandma."

"Just don't want you faintin' or getting sick on us." Billy sounds serious. "We better get back."

They scramble out of the canyon, into blinding sunlight. Terry looks back at the ravine, now innocuous, hidden by brush and treetops, indistinguishable from the many clusters of greenery dotting the desert.

They take another route back to the fence, choosing a path where shrubs hide Terri but not the soldiers.

"There's an unguarded stretch between towers where you can crawl under the wire real easy," says Billy. "No one's around there . . . not even your people. In fact, you could get out anytime from there."

"No, thank you!" says Terri "I don't want to get shot!"

"Hey, no one's going to shoot anyone. Most of the guys in the squad here are like us . . . Skip and me. We're all mostly teenagers, little older than you." Billy talks earnestly, and without his cigarette, looks younger, more like a boy than a man.

They finally come to the isolated spot. It's at the western end of camp where the hospital and new blocks are under construction.

Skip and Billy hold up the wire as Terri crawls through.

"Thanks so much," she says, scampering to her feet and searching for another close look at Billy's face. He's smiling, his gray eyes crinkling.

"Anytime," he says. "And tell Carmen she missed a good time." He winks.

She backs away from the fence and watches them disappear into the brush, probably to their quarters outside the southern edge of camp. The sun is still high. She wonders how long they were at the pool, amazed how it seems it was for hours, even days. She is sure it is a magical spot, a spirit place, as Obachan would call it. Almost dancing back to the barracks, unmindful of the sun beating down on her bare head, she plans her next pilgrimage into the desert.

The Compound

*I*t was four o'clock in the morning. Sayo fanned embers under the rice pot, coaxing them into flames. After several minutes, she set bubbling rice on another stone stove where it could simmer until the grains grew plump and soft. Over the hotter stove she set a pot of water to boil for miso soup.

For several weeks now she had been fixing breakfast for the bachelors and Hiroshi. In the first days after her arrival she had noticed the men took turns cooking meals. Not knowing what role she should assume as Hiroshi's wife and the only woman in the compound, she had stayed away from the outdoor kitchen, remaining in her room most of the time, recuperating from the long journey, writing letters to Mentor and the Matsubara, still not sure what she should tell the family about Hiroshi's strange circumstances. She elected not to say anything, even to Mentor, until she learned more.

Finally, bored with being treated as if she were some rare artifact, she asked Hiroshi if she might help with the cooking. He seemed surprised—not unpleasantly so—and said he would talk with Cloud. That night she asked what Cloud had said.

"He was at first skeptical because it is hard work and he does not want to take advantage of you. But I told him you wanted to help. So, he said all right, as long as the bachelors pay you."

Sayo had been touched by Cloud's protectiveness, as she had not thought of being paid. She knew Hiroshi received money from home and earned some from Mr. Daley. But she trusted Cloud, knowing he understood the hakujin ways . . . and the minds of the men. So, it *had been agreed Sayo would cook breakfast and dinner for two dollars a week paid by each, and the men would clean up after the night meal. On days they were not working, she did not cook. She was satisfied with the arrangement, pleased to make some money, which Hiroshi urged her to keep for herself.*

She dropped dried seaweed into the boiling water. The sky was beginning to lighten from its blackness, erasing the stars as it turned gray. She blew out the kerosene lantern and added more kindling to the embers glowing under the pot.

Inside the dining room she began setting the table with chopsticks and bowls that she noticed were chipped and cracked. She must remember to buy new ones. Hiroshi had mentioned he would take her to San Jose's Japanese section to shop as soon as they had a free day.

The clatter of getas *announced the men were getting up.*

"Good morning. Another fine day." It was Ito-san, clad in his yukata. *Sayo looked forward to his polite morning greeting. He always was the first one up and made it a point to visit the outdoor kitchen on his way to the bath area where the men brushed their teeth and washed up before breakfast.*

Cloud usually arrived at the table while the men were eating, lingering until Hiroshi joined him after the others had finished. Sayo felt her spirits lift whenever he appeared. She was especially impressed by his authority, his leadership among the men, and had noticed even Hiroshi's willingness to let Cloud make decisions regarding her. With each passing day her admiration grew, and she was cautious to dampen her enthusiasm upon seeing him.

"Good morning, Sayo-san," Cloud greeted as she served him rice and miso soup. "I hope you are not working too hard. You don't have to do this, you know. You can stop whenever you wish."

She loved hearing him speak Japanese. His voice was deep, yet had a softness, like that of Buddhist priests chanting mantras. "Good morning, Cloud-san. Thank you for your concern, but I am enjoying myself, really. It gives me something to do while you all work."

She refilled the men's bowls, replenishing plates of pickled vegetables placed in the table's center. Accustomed to the bachelors' ogling, she no longer was embarrassed by their childlike attentiveness, and even joked with them, which delighted them immensely. Although she was not that much older than the four young ones, she felt motherly toward them. They had begun calling her onesan— *"Older Sister."*

When the men were finished, Hiroshi came in and sat next to Cloud. "Good morning, good friend. So today we pick cherry orchard number seven." He sounded cheerful.

"Daley would like us to finish today, too."

"That's a lot to ask. Will he pay overtime?"

"Don't think so. That's why I'm concerned. Daley's been strange lately." Cloud seemed worried. "But we'll find out soon enough."

After they departed and she was alone in the compound, she cleaned up the dining room and outdoor cooking area, boiling water in a large pot for washing dishes, a task she noticed the men did not practice. Cold water did not clean the dishes and chopsticks adequately, and she feared the spread of germs. Not surprising, though, was the personal cleanliness of the men. They bathed often in o furo, *spending many hours after work chopping wood for the fires.*

She still did not fully understand the relationship between the bachelors and the hakujin *boss. Hiroshi said Daley-san allowed the men to live in the compound for a very low rent if they worked for him exclusively during the growing and harvesting seasons. In the winter months, they still could live on his farm, but for higher rent.*

"How long have you been with Daley-san?" she had asked Hiroshi.

He mumbled some words that sounded like "six months."

"But you've known Cloud for five years. Where did you meet him?"

Hiroshi had seemed hesitant. "In San Francisco."

Somehow she knew not to ask any further questions. Besides, she had not wanted to appear too curious about his past . . . or Cloud.

Finished with the chores, she returned to her bedroom at the end of the long bungalow, relishing the clean morning air. It was still early, the crowing cocks welcoming the rising sun only a short time before. With smells of wood fires and abundance of greenery, espe-

*cially the bamboo the men had planted, she easily could imagine
herself back in Hiroshima. She had not grown homesick for Japan
yet, and this surprised her. She attributed this to the fact there was so
much to learn. She simply was too busy to indulge in nostalgia.*

*She folded up the futon bed and swept the tatami mat. She dusted
the six paintings that hung on the wood walls, wondering what kind
of material produced the shiny, thick glaze. She had never seen such
artwork, although her experience in artistic things was limited, being
exposed at the Matsubara compound only to Chinese scrolls of calli-
graphy and landscapes. She wondered who was the painter, and
who were the people depicted in the strange paintings, especially
the nude* hakujin *woman reclining on a sofa, light brown curls
piled on top of her head, black ribbon encircling her throat, a
folded fan in one hand. She had not found a way to ask Hiroshi
about the paintings, and actually was embarrassed to seem curious about the nude woman.*

*The truth was, she was intrigued. She never had seen such volup-
tuous breasts with nipples so tiny and pink, like* mochi *cakes dusted
with rice powder and topped with rosebuds. The woman's eyes were
a startling blue, clear as a summer sky, and when Sayo gazed back
at them as she dusted the golden frame, she felt odd, as if the woman
knew her, could see into her soul.*

*There was much to discover about Hiroshi. She found him more
handsome than she had expected, and his manners impeccable.
There was no question he had been raised well as a Matsubara. Yet
she felt a barrier between them—not so much a solid wall, but
something elusive, a veil that floated, and retreated, camouflaging
the true nature of their alliance.*

She remembered their first night together after taking o furo.
*Mentor had coached her many times about the act of love, how to
excite, how to calm if excitement was too great. But that night all
the teaching had flown with the wind. Although she no longer was a
virgin, she was nervous. Her initiation into the realm of the senses
by Tadanoshin had been quick, quick enough that if her feelings
about him had not been so strong, she easily could have dismissed
the act and considered herself still untouched. But despite her vow*

to forget the elder Matsubara, her will weakened and she found herself wishing it were he and not his son sharing the futon that first night.

After bath, Hiroshi had lit candles instead of the kerosene lamp, filling their room with a shimmering orange light. He lay down on the futon, his yukata still loosely wrapped around him and beckoned. She slid her feet on the cool tatami, gliding instead of walking, as if dancing in a Kabuki play. Loosening the tie around her yukata, but not undoing it, she lay down beside him.

Gently he pulled her against him, opening the front of his yukata so that she felt warm flesh and the hardness of his rigid penis. Sliding his hand inside her robe, he pulled away its folds. She almost cried out, shocked by the rawness of his body as he pressed its length against hers. His hand stroked adeptly, smoothly caressing her breasts and buttocks. Sayo had not thought about Hiroshi's sexual life in America. His mother had intimated her favorite son was sensitive and naive, perhaps innocent of women and the so-called floating world of flesh and sex.

Each was silent, still strangers to each other. Yet there seemed to be an understanding between them, an unspoken pact that they would fulfill their duties to the Matsubara despite their own desires. She felt in her heart Hiroshi had no great passion for her, and she understood this. Did she not yearn for the elder Matsubara's love? Thus, she respected Hiroshi, even admired his sense of honor. Yes, he was honorable. And with this judgment came a willingness to surrender. She was able to relinquish her body to him completely— yielding, pliable—so that when the moment of final openness occurred, his entry seemed more her giving than his conquest.

Hiroshi quickly fell asleep. She remained awake, contemplating the night's scene, wondering why the act of love possessed such power to cause men and women to kill others and themselves over it.

True to his promise, Hiroshi took her into San Jose to nihonmachi, the Asian section of town. Loaded with four of the young bachelors and Ito-san, the shiny wooden wagon rumbled over the dusty street with Cloud at the reins. Attentive to Hiroshi's remark that Japanese dress, rather than Western, was more becoming, she wore a laven-der kimono of light silk with maroon obi. *She carried a pale yellow parasol to shade herself from the afternoon sun.*

As they drove through nihonmachi, *she noticed people gawking, stopped in their tracks on the wooden walkways that ran along the building fronts. She was not surprised. It must have presented a queer sight, a wagonload of young men and one kimono-clad woman. Among the dozen or so Asian men, she saw two women. They, too, seemed to stare in disbelief, as if the entourage was a strange mi-rage brought on by the sun's heat.*

Cloud parked the wagon on a back street. The bachelors clam-bered out, and with Ito-san went their own way—to the pool hall she later learned. The trio sauntered on the boardwalk to the gro-cery store, passing a barbershop, tofu factory, clothing store, and café. There were two hotels, which Hiroshi explained were boarding-houses for bachelors and some families. "These boardinghouses are good places for nihonjin *to live when they first arrive from Japan," he said. "It's a meeting place. There's a bulletin board for messages, for people trying to contact relatives or someone from their vil-lage." They peeked into the lobby of one hotel, which consisted of a counter and large message board tacked on one wall. Wooden chairs lined another. The small room was empty and devoid of dec-oration, not even a vase of flowers.*

At the end of the boardwalk, they entered a grocery store with a large sign, LEE'S STORE, *hung over the door. Inside, it was cool and dark, smelling pungently of salted, fermented foods. Sayo's getas clacked on the wooden floors, along with Cloud's and Hiroshi's boot thuds. They were the only customers. The proprietor seemed to materialize out of nowhere, a dark-clad figure with a shaved head.*

"Hello, Mr. Lee," said Cloud. "We bring Hiroshi's wife to shop at your store. She has just arrived from Japan."

Lee bowed his bald head, revealing the start of a long braided queue that hung down his back. Sayo enjoyed the formality of deep bowing, something she had not had the opportunity to do since her arrival.

"Yes, I know this lady Hiroshi missee." Lee spoke the hakujin *lan-*

guage in a singsong way. "Velly nice." His round face was smooth and shiny, his smile discreetly unimposing.

She surveyed the store, surprised at the abundance of fruit and vegetables stacked in boxes. Sacks of rice and large bottles of soy sauce, oil, and sake lined one wall. Shelves displayed chinaware, pots and pans, dishcloths made of flour sacks, utensils, knives, baskets, soap, matches, and kerosene lamps.

"Get anything you think we need," said Hiroshi.

Excited to think she could buy without restraint, Sayo pointed out items to the men. Even with the Matsubara, whose wealth was substantial, she was never privy to their shopping habits, never allowed to spend money. And, of course with her aunt, they were very poor. Thus, with great fervor, and to Mr. Lee's delight, she filled their sacks with produce, oil, soap, dried fish, salt, and some new bowls and plates. On their next visit they would buy sacks of rice.

After shopping, Hiroshi announced he would get a haircut and asked Cloud to chaperone Sayo. Accommodating in his gentlemanly way, Cloud guided her down a side street, lightly holding her elbow.

"I'd like to show you a special place," Cloud said as they walked away from the wagon, where they left their provisions. After several blocks, they came upon a thick fence of tall bamboo with a slatted wooden gate. It opened easily. Inside the walls of bamboo leaves appeared a miniature park, moss-covered rocks, a small pond.

For a moment she thought she was back in Japan. Grass carpeted the ground. Orange-gold carp glided in the clear pool, over which arched a weathered wooden bridge with two tiny stone lanterns at each end. In one corner, a small octagonal gazebo with a table inside stood off by itself. She easily could have been in Hiroshima, in the Matsubara compound where ancient gardens, covered in velvet moss and gray-green lichen gave refuge to generations of sake-masters.

She murmured, "How exquisite! Who is responsible for such a beautiful garden?"

Cloud seemed pleased, smiling in a way she had not seen before, with mouth open, displaying even white teeth. "I knew you would appreciate it. It is a very special place. Not many people come to enjoy it. It's a shame."

"Really? Who does it belong to?"

They sat down on the grass.

"No one knows. Mr. Fujita, who owns the nursery, takes care of it. The story is that about thirty years ago many Chinese lived around here. They had come to work on the railroads. This corner was their communal garden where they grew vegetables. Then there was a big fire in nihonmachi *and two men perished."*

Sayo gasped, "How sad! Did they have families?"

"No," Cloud replied. "They were bachelors, as are most immigrants from Asia today. They say the two men are buried here because the white eyes wouldn't let them be buried in their graveyard."

"Here in this garden?"

"Yes." He surveyed the small park. "But I don't know where. There aren't any stone markers. It could just be a story."

She closed her eyes, feeling the cool grass through her light kimono. It had been very still and hot, but at that moment, a soft breeze rustled the bamboo and stirred the pond's water. She smelled sweet jasmine. Opening her eyes, she noticed two pine trees that, intertwined with the bamboo leaves, seemed part of the wall, and except for their graying trunks, were nearly invisible.

"The story is true," she said. "I can feel their spirits. They are buried under those two pine trees."

"What pine trees?" Cloud viewed the park again.

Sayo pointed to the wall. Astonished, Cloud jumped up to inspect the trees. She joined him, kneeling down to brush away fallen leaves.

"You are right. I feel their spirits, too." He looked down at her in an odd way. "There are spirits in everything, don't you think? . . . the rocks, the fish, the plants."

"Japanese believe that kami, *gods, reside in all things, too."*

"Well, I guess that is another thing we have in common."

She wanted to ask what were the other things, but he was looking up at the sky, measuring the sun's light. "Time has flown. We should get back to the wagon. I can see we have much to talk about." He helped her stand up, large hands seeming to lift her bodily. She felt his hands lingering around hers, firm fingers stroking her palms. It was a novelty to be concerned for in such a physical way. She couldn't imagine Hiroshi or Ito-san or even the elder Matsubara helping a woman get to her feet.

As they walked the boardwalk back to the wagon, she thought of the Chinese bachelors and Cloud's story about the white ghosts' refusal to allow them to be buried in the cemetery.

"Do the hakujin *hate men of Asia?" she asked.*

"Not all do. There are bad and good in all races. In Japan, clans fight other clans. The white eyes from across the other ocean have come to conquer by stealing the land. They think the land can belong to humans." He spoke haltingly, his jaws tense.

She was surprised by the undercurrent of anger in his answer. She remained silent, uncertain what to say. Ito-san and the four bachelors were waiting at the wagon, and within a short time, Hiroshi arrived, looking dapper with freshly cut hair and clean-shaven face.

As they rumbled past a two-story house on one of the side streets, Sayo overheard the young bachelors referring to it as a brothel. She craned her neck, hoping to catch sight of the women. But there was no sign of life around the house. Dark drapes covered the windows, and the front yard consisted simply of a cement square. On the front porch, two wooden rocking chairs guarded the door, which was cream colored with a lace-curtained oval window.

Noticing her interest, Cloud explained. "You know there are many more nihonjin *men than women here. So, the 'water-world' has become a necessity."*

"You mean the women in the brothel are nihonjin?*"*

"Yes. I hear the women are Japanese and Chinese."

"Where do they come from? I mean—how did they get to America?"

"Some were shashin kekkon*—picture brides—I have heard. I don't know about the Chinese."*

She was stunned by this information. What could have happened that would drive a woman from the security of marriage to prostitution in a foreign land! Should she be wary of her own situation? Who in her village in Hiroshima would imagine she was the lone woman in a compound of nine men, one her husband! She thought of Chiba, only sixteen years old and fooled into a marriage with a man old enough to be her father. And Hiroshi still had not mentioned his plans for the shoyu factory that his family thought he had been constructing. She rode the rest of the way home in deep thought, oblivious to Cloud's questioning glances and Hiroshi's sleeping head on her shoulder.

Two weeks later, some of her questions were answered. It all began the day she decided to take lunch to the men working in the last unpicked cherry orchard, not too far from the compound. In the morning she announced she would be bringing bento, *relieving them from the chore of making it themselves. Ito came back early to help her carry the baskets and large kettle of hot tea.*

As usual, it was hot. She wore a big straw hat over her pompadoured hair and a cool blue-and-white cotton yukata. *Ito carried one basket and the teakettle. "The men have been looking forward to lunch today. It's a special treat to have you with us. Since your arrival the days seem shorter and the work less arduous."*

His comment was polite, in cultured language. She knew his words were respectful and not intended to convey any hidden meaning. She always felt comfortable with Ito-san, perhaps because his gentle nature was similar to Hiroshi's. But there was a sad quality about him, a sense of disappointment. He had been in America longer than any of the bachelors. Who knows what he had seen and experienced.

"I hope you understand the young men and their enthusiasm. Some of us have not seen a Japanese woman for months—especially someone like you. We all are grateful to Hiroshi for bringing you here . . . and sharing you."

Embarrassed by the flattering words, she felt heat rush to her cheeks. "I'm beginning to understand, Ito-san, but I confess the situation is not what I expected." She sensed she could trust him, that she could confide in him, and perhaps even find out more about Hiroshi.

"I realize that. You are in a very vulnerable position, and I admire your dignity in handling it. I want you to know I am your friend."

Before she could answer, they rounded the road's corner and came upon the men seated under a large tree, branches drooping from the weight of glistening red cherries. She noticed Cloud and Hiroshi were absent. Two large blankets were spread on the ground, where the bachelors lounged, hats off, some wiping their perspiring faces with cotton towels.

Two of the young ones jumped up to help carry the baskets. "How good of you, onesan, just like a picnic in Japan."

The bento *consisted of rice balls, cold grilled fish, and* tsuke-mono—*pickled vegetables—simple fare, which the men ate with gusto, slurping green tea between bites. Sayo surveyed the orchard, awed by the profusion of plump cherries clustered so high on the huge trees. She was used to smaller trees in Japan. Ladders and buckets were scattered about, and boxes filled with cherries were stacked in the shade. She could see many more trees were ready for picking.*

After lunch, as she and Ito walked back to the compound, a man on horseback came riding toward them. Heat shimmered around the figure, and dust rose in clouds from the horse's hooves. She blinked, thinking they were a mirage. As he neared, she could make out a yellow-bearded face and bright blue eyes, similar to the eyes of the woman in the painting. She was intrigued, having not yet seen a gaijin *up close. She had been whisked from the boat in San Francisco, then traveling with Cloud and Hiroshi, and stopping at the one Japanese boardinghouse before settling in the compound.*

Ito greeted him in singsong English like Mr. Lee. "Haroo, Mister Day-ree."

She noticed Ito did not bow, but she bowed low, lowering her eyes. Mr. Daley swept off his straw hat, revealing a shock of hair the color of dried hay.

"Howdy. Nice day today. This must be Matsubara's wife."

His voice was thunder, loud and deep. Ito nodded, obviously understanding but unable to answer, even in pidgin English.

"Well, she's a pretty one. Glad to see you don't have her working in the fields." His words sounded harsh and guttural to Sayo. She knew he was speaking about her, the way his eyes trailed over her. She felt uncomfortable. Just at that moment, Cloud rode up, appearing out of nowhere it seemed.

Ito greeted Cloud warmly in Japanese. "Daley-san has met Sayo-san. I'm glad you're here to interpret."

"Say, Cloud, I'm wondering if Mrs. Matsubara here would like to help the missus in our home. Glad you don't have her working with the men."

She saw Cloud's face harden. "Mrs. Matsubara is not for hire. But thank you." By the sound in his voice, she knew Cloud was angry.

"Hell, I wasn't thinking of paying her. Give her a chance to learn some English from the missus . . . clean the house . . . you know. What the hell she doing with all you men, anyway?"

As swift as a samurai sword, Cloud's fist struck Daley's face, knocking him off his horse. Ito grabbed Sayo's hand and pulled her down the road toward the compound. She could hear shouting and saw Cloud and Daley rolling on the ground, churning up dirt between the whinnying horses.

"What happened, Ito-san? Did I do something wrong?"

Ito's brow furrowed, eyes riveted on the road. "No, Sayo-san. Nothing you did. There is trouble brewing, and the white ghost is an insulting man."

"Who did he insult?"

Ito didn't answer.

"Hasn't Cloud been foreman for him a long time?"

"Only two years. Cloud is an honorable man and knows the whites better than we. I trust his judgment."

Back at the compound, Ito told her to remain in her room the rest of the afternoon or until the men returned. She locked the door, not knowing against whom or why she felt so anxious. What caused Cloud to fight Daley so ferociously? She knew he was a man of strong character, of strong feelings, cloaked under the guise of nonchalance and calmness. Watching his explosion she had thought of the elder Matsubara, of his confidence in himself and a belief that he deserved the highest respect from other men. Cloud possessed those qualities, too.

She rested for what seemed like hours, composing in her mind what she would write to Mentor about this new turn of events. A rapping on the door broke her reverie.

"Sayo-san, may I come in?"

She jumped to her feet and unlocked the door. Cloud entered, dusty hat in hand and boots already removed. A gash over one eye had dried a deep red, as if painted by a brush. Other than that, his face did not show any sign he had just been in a fistfight.

"Sorry to disturb you, Sayo-san, but I know you want to hear what happened."

"Oh yes, Cloud-san. Thank you so much. I am worried it was something I did."

He sat down on the tatami floor, crossing legs in front. "No, Sayo-san, you did nothing wrong at all. I have been angry at Daley for a while now. He's an arrogant white eye, the worst kind, and has been refusing to pay us full wages."

"How can he do that? How can he cheat you?"

"Easily. We live here during the winter when there's no work, so he credits us rent. This year he raised it without our knowing and has docked it from our wages."

Sayo nodded. "Just how the greedy lords in Japan controlled the farmers. You can refuse to pick the fruit. That's how the farmers won."

Cloud grinned, eyeing her with respect. "That's another thing we have in common. You're a fighter, too. And you're right. We're going to walk out."

She felt panic. "To where? You mean leave the compound?"

"Yes. There's another big farm several miles south of here. Hiroshi is there right now."

She realized the men probably had been planning this move for some time.

"But he'll tell you about it."

Her present life had come as a surprise indeed, and although she was not discontented, another arrangement in which she would have some say seemed more desirable. In America less than two months and already moving to another home! In Hiroshima, villagers stayed in one place for lifetimes, living in the homes of their ancestors. American life truly flowed like a river without banks, no boundaries to restrict the currents that could spread out over the land, free to change course at any time. Instead of feeling anxious, as she surely would have if this move had happened in Japan, she was excited.

Cloud stood up and began studying the paintings, his back to her. She watched him, admiring his wide shoulders and narrow haunches.

He turned around. "Hiroshi is getting very good, don't you think?"

Sayo was uncertain if she had misunderstood his Japanese. "Excuse me, what did you say?"

Quick to notice her confusion, Cloud said, "Well, I guess he just hasn't told you yet. I think he's shy about his work and doesn't let many people know he paints. But I think he's pretty good."

Recovered, Sayo said, "No, he has not mentioned it, but I have wondered who the painter was." She looked at the nude woman. Cloud followed her gaze, looking uncomfortable.

"Where does he work?" she asked.

"He has a studio on the other side of the furo."

She had seen the small shack but had surmised it was a toolshed. Not wanting to pry, she refrained from asking further questions although she yearned to know more.

"I'm sure Hiroshi will explain it all to you. As you see from today's happening, much has been going on beneath the surface."

She admired his loyalty. Without thinking, she grabbed his hand and clasped it between hers. "Thank you, Cloud-san. Thank you."

Before she could unclasp her hands, Cloud lifted them and pressed his lips against the back of her fingers, his eyes on her face, on her neck that was turning crimson. She caught her breath. She had heard from Mentor about the exotic art of kissing, called seppun when mouth touched mouth. Now here was Cloud sliding lips on her hand and fingers. What was she to think? Was this a common gesture of friendship? Or had she been too forward?

Suddenly his arms encircled her. She at first stiffened, but giving in to the attraction she had been feeling for the past weeks, she wilted, languid against his pressing body. She smelled fresh pine as his cheek brushed hers, heard the wind rush when his lips touched her ear. She felt his mouth covering hers, tasted the sweetness of his caressing tongue.

Rapid breathing the only sound between them, they faced each other. Finally, Cloud spoke. "Please forgive me, Sayo. I was impetuous. I meant no disrespect." His expression was pained, lines deep between his thick brows.

Regaining her composure, she was gently aloof, but remained warm enough to prevent his losing face. What could she say to disperse the moment's awkwardness? "There is nothing to forgive, Cloud-san. I should not have taken your hands as I did. You must forgive me." She would take the blame. After all, she was the married one, the wife of his best friend—who needed Cloud's friendship, especially at this time when they had decided to break off with Daley.

"I also have been remiss in thanking you for all your kindness, your concern for Hiroshi and the others . . . your protectiveness of myself . . ." Her voice trailed. She was speaking too much and too fast, attempting to breach the uneasy silence, to answer the questions in his hawk eyes.

"I understand," he said finally, the tone conveying he understood what could not be said—at this time, anyway. His forehead was now smooth.

She bowed, very deeply, hoping to fill the space between them with ritual. But she felt his hands on her shoulders. "Please, Sayo, you needn't ever bow to me again. I know it is your custom. But in mine, women do not bow to the men . . . or to anyone. Can that be an understanding between us? You and I?"

Cloud was, indeed, like no man she ever knew. He did not need even the semblance of submission to affirm his own sense of power. He was a true warrior. Before she could respond, he was gone. A graceful wolf, boots in hand, he noiselessly had retreated from the room.

Alone again, she rethought the day's events. The encounter with Cloud she chose to tuck away in a special corner of her mind, a delicious secret to be tasted only when the time was calm enough to savor it. She must deal with the urgent matter at hand—the move away from the compound and the revelation of Hiroshi's true character. So, he was the painter. Not surprising considering what his mother had revealed of his artistic tastes. But why the secrecy? Obviously, his family knew little of his activities in America, sending money with high expectations of his establishing some sort of business and a family branch to uphold the Matsubara name in the New World. Torn between loyalty to the grand family that had taken her in, to Tadanoshin—and to Hiroshi, of whom she had grown fond, if not protective—she wrestled with her options, pondering the most honorable course of action. Should the Matsubara be apprised of Hiroshi's true situation? Should she confront Hiroshi and ask his intentions? She realized she no longer could act and react as if she knew his desires, left unspoken or merely alluded to under the facade of civility. This was the acceptable exchange between husband and wife in Japan. But she must relinquish those instincts taught and refined where they worked so well, where society's rules were understood by all.

Here in America, the rules were different, because what was being thought in each individual's mind was different. In fact, the more different the thought, the more value it had! Could it be Hiroshi no longer thought like a Japanese? This idea stunned her, for it became clear as pure water from Mount Fuji, that in order to survive in this country, she, too, must change her way of thinking.

In the Firebreak

Manzanar

The oil stove blazes, emitting a smoky odor that overrides the sweet incense of Obachan's shrine offerings. Inside their room, now commonly known in the block as the "Ochaya," Terri sits on the floor next to the stove and reads the latest *Silver Screen* Billy has given her. Outside the wind howls. It is a week before Thanksgiving and already it seems winter has arrived.

Obachan is embroidering a large peacock pattern that she herself has created and later will frame as a picture. Terri knows when the other internees discover this new recreational activity, there will be a flurry of embroidery groups meeting in the mess hall and probably an art show to display the work. Obachan will help teach them, of course, just as she did with the painted bathroom screens.

Despite stories circulating about Sayo's obvious eccentric and unknown past, she is highly respected and even sought after for counsel. On Tuesday, Thursday, and Saturday afternoons, when their compartment is open for "tea," more and more internees have come to sit and exchange polite conversation with her. On those days Terri has begun to visit Billy at the tower, no longer confining the time to lunch hour only.

Due to the change in weather, she has not been back to the pool or cave, but she manages to chat with him, hunched at the tower's foot between windbreaks of thick sagebrush. One day he was worried about her being too cold and threw down his thick scarf. She brought it back to the barracks and hid it in her straw suitcase.

Probably because of the cold, the internees no longer mill about outside, leaving the "no-man's land" between the barracks and towers empty. But even if someone spotted Terri talking to the soldier, she no longer cares about the gossip that surely would arise. And if Obachan finds out, she will deal with that problem then. But somehow she feels her grandmother might not be appalled. Living with her so closely now, Terri sees how complex she is. She never knows what Obachan will say or do.

Just last week she was surprised again by Obachan's fiery spirit. Not too far from the "Ochaya," outside the Horimoto compound where her granite Indian warrior stands, the tailor Shimmy had been accosted by three young men from another block. Shouting in Japanese, they made such a ruckus Obachan flew out of the room and, as Terri watched from the doorway, walked very fast and determinedly toward them.

"*Yogore!*" she called in a sharp voice never heard before by Terri. The men stopped talking, astonished by this elegant woman in flapping kimono whose eyes were afire. They stared back, not sure who she was, but certain she was not just any old grandmother on the block. From a distance Terri couldn't understand Obachan's words, but she knew they must have been strong by the way the men hung their heads and lowered their voices. She stood straight-backed and tall, hands on *obi*'d hips, eyes flashing black lightning, a samurai warrior challenging them to a duel. They soon dispersed like chastised mongrels, kicking sand as they sauntered away with occasional backward glares at Shimmy.

Then Obachan invited him in for tea, again surprising Terri by her quick change of demeanor. Gracious and gentle, she welcomed him, offering a purple *zabuton* upon which to sit on the oil-polished floor. Terri left the two to talk alone, as she could see they were enjoying each other's company.

"Where do you get those movie magazines?" Obachan asks.

Jolted from her daydreaming, Terri does not answer. She wonders if she should tell her grandmother the truth, tell her about Billy.

"I've noticed you read them a lot. What's so wonderful in the magazines?"

Terri decides this is not the time. "Mitzi gets them from the canteen. I like to read about the movie stars."

Obachan nods, eyes still focused on her embroidering. "Aren't there other books to read? What happened to all the books you brought home from the pile in the firebreak?"

"I read them all, Obachan. The only thing left is the Sears and Roebuck catalog."

Obachan laughs. "Well, I don't want you to grow stupid. I wish the new school would begin. Shimmy is right. The military is very bad at administering this camp. Things must change, or I'm afraid we are going to have trouble." It's as if she is talking to herself.

"Obachan, what's a *yogore?*"

Sayo looks up, eyebrows lifted. "What makes you ask that?"

"I heard you call those guys that when they were yelling at Shimmy."

"It means 'roughneck,' uncouth types."

"Are they the trouble you're talking about?"

Sayo sighs, as if tired of thinking of them. "They're part of it . . . but not the main trouble. The real problem is that we are in a prison, and the government put us here. But when people cannot fight the true culprit, they attack each other."

Terri tries to understand. "Is that why they were yelling at Shimmy?"

Sayo looks at her, as if weighing how much more to say. "Partly so . . . yes." Then, changing the subject, she asks, "What do you and Mitzi do besides read movie magazines? You must miss going to school."

"Oh . . . we do a lot of things." She panics a moment, worried Sayo may suspect her meetings. "In fact, I'm supposed to go to her barracks right now." She jumps up from her futon.

"Dress warmly. This weather is so unpredictable we could have a blizzard anytime." She doesn't look up, intent on her embroidery.

The next day the weather remains cold and blustery. At breakfast, Terri sits with Sayo and Hana, enduring a bowl of creamed wheat cereal that tastes like paste. The two older women talk in hushed tones about trouble brewing with the discontented *kibei*. She watches Hana speak. Her mother is almost vivacious, talking in long sentences, a far cry from her usual short retorts accompanied often with a sad face. Since her father and Mac left for Idaho, she has noticed Hana has been more relaxed, even enthusiastic about camp activities. This amazes Terri, but then, her mother would be pretty shocked if she knew about her own secret meetings with Billy. And who knew what Carmen was doing, always with her friend from Pasadena, never eating with the family anymore. Thinking about her scattered family, Terri feels a strange emptiness. She has enjoyed the lack of supervision, the freedom to roam anywhere within the barbed-wire fence, to eat at any mess hall. Like a balloon let loose to dance in the sky, she sees herself floating and weightless, cut off from moorings to the earth.

"Aren't Tad and Mac coming home any day now?" asks Sayo.

"They should," says Hana. "Thanksgiving is just around the corner, and they're supposed to be back before then."

"I hope so. We need some more levelheaded thinkers besides Shimmy."

Terri interrupts. "What's all the trouble about, anyway? What are they planning to do? What's Shimmy done?"

"Nothing," Hana retorts. "He's trying to stop trouble from happening."

"Well, I can't see them doing too much against soldiers with guns," says Sayo.

At the mention of soldiers, Terri decides to withdraw from the conversation and hastily gathers her dishes. "*Go-chi-so-sama*," she remembers to say, and leaves the mess hall.

Outside it has grown dark, with ominous clouds hanging low over camp, turning morning into dusk. She considers walking to Billy's tower, but instead chooses to check out the canteen at Block 2. She heard a new shipment of chocolate candy bars had arrived, and even though she has no money, it will be a diversion to just look in the canteen, the closest thing to a real store the camp has to offer.

The wind has picked up. She notices she is alone on the oiled road that circles the camp's perimeter. She wraps her blue cape tighter, wishing she wore a hat or Billy's scarf. Pummeled by gusts of wind, she reaches the first firebreak, the wide, empty square of sand where there are no barracks to mollify the wind. She wonders if she should turn back. But what is there to do inside the barracks?

The wind has now taken on a strange sound, a high whining like a steam kettle's whistle. She looks to the firebreak's center, where it seems a crowd has suddenly formed. Where did they come from?

She peers closer and realizes they are not internees. She hears shouting, whooping, screaming! Terrified but too mesmerized to tear her eyes from the battle, she stands frozen to the road. Indians are fighting on horses, charging with bows and arrows, knives and clubs, their faces and bodies painted in stripes of white, black, and yellow.

A blinding flash and crackling thunder precede a massive downpouring of rain. Their brown skin glistening and streaked with smeared paint, the braves fight ferociously. From outside the firebreak, staccato gunshots pierce the air. The Indians fall, wounded and dead. Where have the shots come from? Terri sees a line of bearded white men in cowboy hats holding rifles. More Indians fall. An eerie silence hangs over the firebreak. The wind has ceased to blow, but rain continues to fall in sheets, washing the blood and paint from the fallen, gathering in pools of reddish brown water across the firebreak's sandy expanse.

She stares at the carnage. Then the rain stops and the sun appears. Its rays beam down over the battlefield like a searchlight, drying the stained sand and bloodied bodies.

Terri blinks. The scene disappears. The firebreak is empty and silent, except for the wind churning up sand and tearing at her cape. Shaken, she turns back toward Block 16, wondering what she has seen and if she should tell Obachan.

Allies and Adversaries

Hana sits on the wooden bench Shimmy built for the orphanage garden, eyeing with satisfaction the newly completed pond and surrounding landscape of rock formations and freshly transplanted reeds. Reflecting a deep blue sky with scatterings of clouds, the pond remains glassy until a gust of wind ruffles its calm.

She wraps her peacoat closer and stuffs her hands into the deep pockets. After days of extreme heat, the weather has turned frigid, calling for sweaters, coats, and even gloves. Remembering the first cold day, Hana is again amused. They had lined up for lunch at the mess hall, a long queue of huddled figures in navy blue and olive-drab wraps, strange woolen caps and mufflers hiding faces. Commandeering this ragtag army without weapons was Pot-Banger, who sported a pair of cut-down jodhpurs of World War I vintage and long jacket with renewed mandarin collar. Flushed with pride over her uniformed flock, Pot-Banger beat on the pan with extra flourish, striding up and down the line of shivering internees.

Hana had tied a blue bandana over her nose and mouth, bandit-style, to warm her face. Sayo, who refused to wear any uniform or remnant of one, had laughed into her kimono sleeve, shoulders shaking under the heavy shawl draped over her shoulders. Terri, who wore her cape, giggled with her grandmother. Still too reserved to laugh with them, Hana had retreated to the end of the line, gazing off into the distant mountains whose peaks were newly covered with snow. She saw how ridiculous they looked in their military costumes. But a part of her was grateful for those uniforms. Hadn't she met Shimmy because of them?

After the sewing project ended, Hana threw herself into helping

Shimmy with the orphanage garden. Today she will begin making rag dolls with the younger girls of the home. It is too early to begin class. She is hoping Shimmy will drop by and they can visit for a while, catch up on the past week's happenings. The last time she saw him, he had just returned from a meeting and seemed preoccupied, not his usual cheery self. There were rumblings of dissatisfaction with the military administration, something about sugar being stolen by soldiers and then sold on the black market. Hana doesn't quite understand what the ruckus is about and attributes much of it to rumors, of which there are many. Just yesterday she heard a baby had died from drinking a milk formula sweetened with sugar substitute because of lack of the real thing. But it turned out to be gossip. Maybe all this unrest will cease when the men return from the potato fields.

She waits, hoping Shimmy will show up. After lingering at the rock pond, she finally leaves to teach her first sewing class.

At the recreation room ten young girls wait patiently for Hana. Suzuki-san, the orphanage "house mother," has laid out scissors, thread, pins, and needles on the large rectangular table set in the middle of the room. The girls are well acquainted with Hana, having seen her working on the garden and visiting them often in the home. She is one of the few internees who come to the Village besides Shimmy, Father Stephens—the Catholic priest—some members of the medical staff, and the cook. The Suzukis, of course, live in the compound.

Hana begins by cutting a pattern out of cardboard, a large gingerbread-cookie figure. She lays it on a white sheet and cuts around it. The girls gather closely, quiet and well-behaved, showing their best manners to the kind lady willing to come to the Village and break their monotonous routine. After cutting forms for each child, Hana patiently instructs them how to sew the edges together. Later they will stuff them with bits of rags and attach yarn to the heads for hair, then create faces of button eyes and embroidered lips.

She stays with the children for the rest of the morning, concentrating on the task at hand, pushing to the back of her mind the desire to see Shimmy.

*　　*　　*

Two days later Hana hurries across the firebreak, Carmen's saddle shoes crunching over the frosty sand. She wears slacks and a wool sweater under the peacoat. A red knitted scarf covers her head and wraps around her throat. Usually wearing subdued colors—navy brown, beige, black—Hana today has brightened her appearance with the red scarf borrowed from Terri. She has started for the Children's Village earlier than usual.

As she passes the pear orchard and alder trees surrounding the compound, she sees he is waiting by the rock garden. He does not see her, and sits hunched over on the wooden bench, looking dejected.

"Good morning, Shimmy."

He breaks into a smile. "Oh . . . you're here already. I came early." His eyes sweep over her. "I like you in red. You should wear it more often." He appears cheerful, but she senses something is wrong.

She sits down. "Is everything okay?"

He is quiet for a few moments. "Actually, it's not. I was at another meeting last night and made a big mistake, I think."

She waits for him to continue.

"I guess I shouldn't have been so outspoken, but I objected to some things they plan to do."

"Like what?"

"When they started talking about protesting in front of military headquarters with banners and wearing headbands and loincloths, I stood up and told them they were crazy."

She cannot help herself and laughs. "I bet no one's ever said that to them!"

"They called me a traitor. What bullshit!"

She never has heard him swear and recognizes how stung he was by the insult.

His outburst seems to relax him, brow no longer furrowed. "I'm just worried what they'll do. Sure wish the men would come back from Idaho and Montana soon. We need someone who is respected."

Protective, Hana says, "You're respected, Shimmy. You're helpful to everyone in camp."

He shrugs his shoulders. "Oh, I don't kid myself. I know some people see me as a weird bachelor without family who sews and must be a queer."

She is shocked by this out-of-character self-criticism. *He must feel very low today,* she thinks.

He continues, "I've been called a 'do-gooder.' You know, people don't like 'do-gooders' because they make others feel guilty that they're not doing enough." He pauses. "As an orphan kid I did things for others to be accepted and liked. I guess I still do it."

Her motherly instincts reach out. "That's not true, Shimmy. You are genuinely a good person. You told me the other day that I was good. I didn't believe you, either. But I know you are."

His head is lowered. She cannot see his face. Finally, he looks up and smiles, eyes twinkling, lines creasing around his mouth. She's glad he seems to have let go of the incident.

"I shouldn't bother you with all this stuff about camp protestors and missing sugar." He studies her, as if reflecting. "You know, you really remind me of someone . . . someone I cared a lot about."

"I do?" Her heartbeat quickens.

"A woman I grew up with. You look a little like her . . . tall and slim and same coloring."

Pleased he is offering to talk about his personal life without her asking, she says simply, "Really?"

"Yeah. I haven't thought about her for a long time." He now stares at his clasped hands, as if praying. "Would you like to hear the story?" He faces her, eyebrows raised.

She encourages him with a compassionate nod.

Shimmy's Story

When both parents were killed in a boating mishap, he was placed at an orphanage in Los Angeles. Having no siblings or living relatives in America, the only recourse was the Catholic home, shelter for parentless Japanese children. The day he arrived, flanked by two large suitcases containing all his belongings, he was met by a gray-robed nun, who eased his first day with gentle words and thoughtful gestures.

"Welcome to God's home," she said softly. "God loves you and takes care of all his children. I'm going to introduce you to someone from your new family who will show you around . . . won't you like that?" She carried one of the suitcases and he the other as they walked down a dark hallway to an office.

Inside, two other nuns waited with a young girl, whose wide eyes studied the newcomer while she shifted her weight from foot to foot. "This is Sophia."

Shimmy shook the little girl's hand, recognizing her solemnity as the same he had felt since his parents died. Their eyes met and they understood each other perfectly—he, nine years old, and she, barely seven.

She held his hand the whole time Sister Emanuel showed him the dormitory where he would sleep, the dining hall, library, and recreation room. She helped him unpack, never uttering a word, scrutinizing his every move with cat's eyes.

He let her tie his socks together and arrange playing cards and his domino set on a bureau. When he showed a picture of his father and mother and himself standing in front of their oceanfront home in Santa Monica, she ogled and finally spoke. "I've never lived in a house . . . except here." Her voice sounded thin, with a slight lisp. "I've never had a mother or father, either."

Although sad from his own recent loss, he put aside his gloom and tried to comfort her. "Sister Emanuel says God takes care of all his children . . . so He's your father. Mine, too . . . now, I guess." His family never went to any church, except to attend occasional weddings and funerals at the Buddhist temple in Japantown. "God" was an unfamiliar word. Nuns in flowing robes he sometimes viewed outside the neighborhood Catholic church were mysterious figures who appeared now and then, seeming to float through the air, black and white head coverings flapping. Once, he asked his father who they were. "Witches," his father said. "Good witches."

"And I'm your new brother." She smiled when he said that and hugged him, pressing a thin little body against his. He hugged back, feeling for the first time in weeks, warmth in his heart. Now he had a sister, at least, an adoring younger sister whose total acceptance took the edge off his first day at the orphanage.

Sophia and he were inseparable. As older brother, he was her protector and teacher, showing her how to ride a bike, to roller-skate, turn cartwheels and shoot marbles. A deep bond developed from, oddly enough, an intense devotion they both shared for catechism classes and church rituals. Fascinated by stories of martyrs and saints, whose lives became models for their own aspirations, they lived a "holy childhood." Praying together, for them, was like listening to radio programs or reading comic books. Both wanted to be saints when they grew up.

But when Sophia turned fourteen, things changed. She learned about her background, that her father was Mexican and her unwed mother a Japanese woman who killed herself after leaving her baby at the home. This information affected her, and she sometimes would disappear after school, wandering in the Mexican section of L.A., not far from the orphanage.

Then, on the day of her confirmation at church, Shimmy saw her in a different way. Light streaming through stained-glass windows shimmered in colorful hues around the group waiting to be confirmed. She was dressed in a pink dress, brown hair waving to her shoulders. When she entered the vestibule to receive the ritual slap from the bishop, she stood slim and tall, and walked with sure steps toward him. Alongside the pride Shimmy felt for her, a new feeling also arose, an unfamiliar tightening in his stomach. She was now a woman, he realized, and beautiful. At that moment, he fell in love. No longer was she a younger sister, the "buddy" who tagged after him, who often fell down, scraping knees that he bandaged.

His behavior toward her remained the same. He acted the older brother, never letting on how his feelings had changed. He was sixteen, in the prime of adolescence, and she was a young fourteen-year-old who adored him with the innocence of a saint. For more than a year he maintained this status quo, although his desire increased as she grew more mature.

Then an incident happened that altered everything. Sophia asked him to take her to a festival in L.A.'s Mexican section. They sauntered by the food booths and bright-colored piñatas swaying overhead, enjoying the spicy smells of garlic and chili, amidst the sound of loud Mariachi music. Outside the crowded booth area, they came upon an old woman selling statues of the Virgin Mary among Indian carvings and artifacts. The wizened woman had piercing black eyes that seemed to see through them. A sign, FORTUNE TELLER, sat on the table with her wares. She looked like she might be a gypsy or full-blooded Indian.

Shimmy wanted to buy a Virgin Mary statue for Sophia, but when he pointed one out to the old woman, she grabbed his hand and then Sophia's and began speaking in a clear voice. "If you are to have the love that burns so strongly in each of your hearts, you must run away together now! Run away before next year's Day of the Dead!" She gave Sophia the statue and wouldn't take any money, just shook her head, looking at them with what seemed like pity.

Although haunting, the experience blew away the facade covering their true feelings for each other. They grew closer. She became his best friend, his mother, his sweetheart, and they basked in their discovered love until they were caught embracing one day.

It was an innocent hug in the study room, a hug one would share with a family member. But Sister Emanuel knew instinctively the two were wading into dangerous waters. If nothing had happened already, something surely would soon! Without any disciplinary action—or even a confrontation in the office—the two were separated. Sophia was sent immediately to a convent in Canada.

Shimmy left the home and lived as a houseboy for a Japanese diplomat and his wife, learning excellent Japanese during his five years with them. He later apprenticed as a tailor under one of the best in Los Angeles. Never again hearing from Sophia, he buried himself in a busy life, dating many women, even becoming engaged once. He still loved Sophia even though he heard she had become a nun. When he learned that, he gave up Catholicism entirely, believing she had been punished for loving him. She had never mentioned wanting to be a nun.

But his fantasies were dashed when he saw her years later. She had returned to visit the orphanage before she left for a mission in Japan. He was able to talk with her at a public event sponsored by the home. Now Sister Margaret, she was as lovely as ever. But he could see in the smooth face, her heart had changed. It belonged to the Church. The Sophia he loved was gone.

Nihonmachi

San Jose

*A*fter *the fight between Daley and Cloud, Sayo's life changed in ways she could never have imagined. First of all, it was decided she and Hiroshi would not live with the bachelors at the new farm. This meant she no longer would see Cloud as often, but she had decided to speak her mind to Hiroshi, pointing out his obligation to start a business for the Matsubara, something that would be difficult if he continued working for someone else. As his wife, she felt the burden of his responsibility. Besides, living with nine bachelors still seemed peculiar, even though she was determined to change her way of thinking.*

At first, she was apprehensive, speaking so candidly. But he had listened with openness, even a semblance of respect, and agreed to move into nihonmachi. *He was not as cooperative about taking steps to start a shoyu factory. His handsome face grew somber, furrows creasing his high forehead when she suggested San Jose would be a good place to begin.*

"I must confess something to you, Sayo-san," he said, his voice tight. "I hate building a shoyu factory. I hate the very thought of it. In fact, I hate all business!" As he said this, his face turned red and distorted, his eyes bulging like those of a balloon fish. Sayo was taken aback. His mother had not mentioned the second son also had a temper. Stroking his arm, she placated him as a mother soothes a petulant child threatening to throw a tantrum. Her mind raced. What else could he do to fulfill the Matsubara expectations?

He was obliged to carry on a family business, and, indeed, their livelihood depended on the money sent from Japan for that purpose.

Finally, she came upon an idea. Why couldn't she help him with the business? "I can work with you, Hiroshi."

"What do you mean?"

"I can look for a suitable place in nihonmachi . . . *learn about the business, help you hire workers." She spoke quickly, the words a turbulent river flowing from her mouth. "I can be your partner . . . " She faltered. "You could spend more time painting."*

Silence. His face returned to its normal handsomeness, still slightly flushed. "Then you know about my painting."

"Yes. Cloud told me. Why have you been so secretive about it?"

"I haven't been exactly secretive. I just didn't bother to tell you. Didn't think you would be interested."

"Of course I am interested in everything you do. I am your wife." Inwardly, she knew his hesitancy was more because of his family. He didn't want Tadanoshin to know he was spending time painting instead of planning a future business.

He smiled broadly, almost childlike in his relief, as if he had just escaped a terrible sentence in prison.

"I thank you for your offer to help. I've dreaded even thinking about the shoyu factory." His eyes brimmed with warmth, looking at her with a newfound interest. "I'm grateful, also, for your . . . understanding about my painting."

"Your mother told me of your artistic talent. I think it is fine for you to continue doing what you love." And to his unhidden delight, she added, "Of course, we need not mention it to the family. It will be our secret, yours and mine."

Showing his gratitude in a most un-Japanese way, he surprised her with a spontaneous bearlike hug. Other than washing his back before o furo *and during their lovemaking at night, they rarely touched teach other. This "hugging" was another raucous display of affection among Americans, she guessed. There was much to learn about Hiroshi, but for now, she was content to deal with her new role. Unlike the good wife in Japan who lived totally in the*

*country of her husband's shadow, Sayo could emerge into full sun-
light, out of the confinement of the traditional duties of kitchen
and bedroom, and take on responsibilities heretofore assigned
only to him.*

*They moved into one of the smaller boardinghouses, called the
Persimmon House because of a lone persimmon tree growing in the
small backyard. Located on one of nihonmachi's back streets, it was
a wooden building with five rooms that, except for theirs, were
rented to bachelors. It was a step up from the rough shedlike quarters of the farm. A large communal kitchen and dining room faced
the street while the bedrooms lined a long hallway on the back side,
ending with the bathroom, which consisted of a flushing toilet and
small sink. Their room was larger than the others, with an alcove
housing a kerosene cooking stove, sink, and wooden cupboards.
Although small and dark, the kitchen was a blessing for Sayo, who
was pleased to have her own cooking area, not relishing the thought
of eating with strange men again.*

*Hiroshi had covered the scruffed wooden floors with tatami,
which lightened the windowless room. After their furniture of table
and four chairs, tansu chest of drawers, tokonoma, and wicker baskets were in place, the room appeared smaller than the one at the
compound. But Sayo was not disheartened. She had made up her
mind to view her life now as an adventure. Discomforts and hardships were not acts of fate to be endured, but rather challenges she
could attempt to change. She now was at ease leaving familiar
friends and entering a new community where rules would most
likely be similar to those of her village in Hiroshima, the rules of
conformity and proper conduct that had irked Mentor so much.
Mentor had managed to remain outside the village standards yet
was accepted by all. Sayo would have to figure out her own path to
accomplish this in San Jose.*

*For the first two weeks, she spent most of the time acquainting
herself with the community. Each day she visited the grocery to pay
her respects to Mr. Lee, buying an article that she held up so he could
name it in his pidgin English. Lee joined the game and grabbed*

other items whose names he shouted in his singsong voice. "Lice!" he said, holding up a bag or rice. He pointed to apples and oranges. "Flute!"

During that time Hiroshi visited San Francisco twice. She wondered what business he had there that required his presence. But, still wanting to fulfill the role of a good "yamato" bride, she refrained from asking.

She visited the laundry, sewing shop, vegetable stand, barbershop, and herbal store. The proprietors soon knew her by name, anticipating her appearances as she made her morning rounds. Dressed in colorful cotton kimono, ivory skin glowing in the umbrella's shade, she was a rare figure floating over the boardwalk, a fragile flower amidst a field of weeds. The few wives who lived in town wore dull, dark western attire, and even they came to their open doorways to watch her pass, seeming to enjoy her comeliness without signs of envy. Perhaps she represented the sculptured beauty of the Japan they had left behind, reminding them of velvet fog, gray-green moss, pine trees, and koi-filled ponds. Stories soon arose that she was, in fact, the bastard daughter of a great lord; that she had been a nun who was banished from the temple; that Hiroshi was actually her protector, not her husband; that she had great shamanic powers and could transform into a fox, bear, or turtle at will. Despite these stories, the town members welcomed her, although with some awe. They still stared wide-eyed when she passed and kept a respectful distance—exactly what Sayo had hoped to achieve—unquestioned acceptance shrouded by mystery and intrigue.

Soon after Hiroshi and Sayo had moved to nihonmachi, *a letter finally arrived for Sayo from Mentor. The night before it came she had a dream so vivid and strange she had awakened in the middle of it, sweating and choking on cries stuck in her throat. She had looked over at Hiroshi, releasing long breaths in streams of guttural song. His snores sounded like the warbling doves in her dream.*

She had been back in Japan, sitting in her room at the Matsubara compound, attempting to write a letter, to whom, she did not know. A falcon flew into the room, its talons gleaming silver spikes. It swooped and arced through the room, flapping wings stirring the air into wind, blowing paper like the loose autumn leaves in their courtyard. Then some doves flew through the open panel door. They cooed and sang while chasing and circling the falcon as if daring it to attack them. But it did not. Instead it landed on Sayo's arm, its sharp claws preventing her from writing the letter. Deep purple eyes stared into hers, and when she returned the gaze, she saw a reflection, a clear image of Tadanoshin, her father-in-law. He was angry. His hook-nosed face was fierce, eyes glaring red below bushy black brows. She began to weep, but her throat emitted no sound. Then she awoke.

Although thrilled to finally hear from Mentor, Sayo was hesitant, because of her dream, to read the letter. It might be a premonition, a warning of bad news from Hiroshima. Would it be about Tadanoshin?

As it turned out, there was indeed some bad news. Mentor wrote that sickness had claimed many lives in the village and the surrounding countryside. Cholera. Go-Between had been taken, as well as many of her aunt's sewing friends. Fortunately, Mentor herself and the Matsubara had escaped the virulent disease. But the smell of death still saturated the air and clung to the winds churning in from the coast. What could the gods be angry about, Mentor had wondered in her letter. She ended by mentioning that the elder Matsubara had suffered a slight accident—a fall from his horse— while falconing. Only slightly injured, he had soon been back riding.

Although the news was disquieting, Sayo was elated to know Mentor, Sayo's aunt, and the Matsubara were well. She could smell the musky scent of Mentor's incense in the rice-paper letter, a special scent that filled her heart with a yearning she had not allowed herself to feel since she had arrived in the New World. Would she ever see Mentor again? And Tadanoshin? Somehow the great Matsubara's face had grown dim in her memory, only to materialize clearly in dreams. In the past few weeks when she had thought of him, had seen his strong body clad in kimono, his face would fade and be replaced by someone else, someone with deep green eyes and a hawklike nose! For a while she was dismayed, even feeling a sense of guilt as if she had betrayed her father-in-law.

Hiroshi

San Francisco, 1898

*W*hen Hiroshi first arrived at San Francisco from Japan, he was
so dazed by the city's beauty he remained there for months before venturing into the countryside where the family expected him
to buy land and establish a business. He walked the steep streets,
impressed by the ornately decorated houses, narrow and bunched
together with gargoyles and multicolored carvings jutting out from
eaves and doorways. For hours he would sit on a bench overlook-
ing the bay, contemplating his new life, savoring the exhilaration of
being free from the heavy presence of his father and older brother.

He purchased a drawing book and sketched the landscape and
street scenes, something he would not have dared to try in Japan.
He remembered as a child overhearing a conversation between his
parents. "Don't fill the child's head with your romantic fantasies,"
his father had said. "We are not degenerate nobility. You are not
Lady Murasaki and I am not Lord Asano. Better that he learn to shovel
manure than draw pictures and write silly poems."

A poetic dreamer, his mother was also a wise Japanese wife. She
had bowed deeply, touching forehead to the floor, and answered in
the most obsequious voice she could muster. "Please forgive me,
Tadanoshin-san. It is my own selfishness. I promise not to indulge
myself anymore." But when his father was gone, which was quite
often but never enough as far as Hiroshi and his mother were concerned, she continued to encourage him to paint and to appreciate
poetry and fine music.

In San Francisco he found a small hotel that catered to single

*Asian men, many like himself, who had money and an adventur-
ous spirit, eager to learn the arts of gambling, drinking, and nightlife
entertainment. Some posed as students, as diplomats, and one even
deemed himself a baron and sported a monocle over a narrow eye.
It was at the hotel that he met Cloud. With his unusual face and tall
stature, Cloud was conspicuous among the shorter, trimly dressed
bachelors.*

*After a month at the hotel, Hiroshi decided one evening to try his
luck gambling at some of the saloons near the docks. He had
learned to gamble the American way and found he not only enjoyed the game, but was quite good at it. In one of the taverns he
was startled to see Cloud sitting at a table with several white men.
Cloud recognized him and nodded, an odd expression on his face.
He seemed to be warning him. Uneasily, Hiroshi sat down at the
next table. He then noticed he was the only other nonwhite. He also
felt obtrusive in his dapper black suit. The other men, some seated
and others milling about in the gaslit room, were boisterous and
dressed in working clothes of the waterfront.*

*Before he could get up to leave, a loud talking arose from
Cloud's table.*

*"You goddamn greaser! You're a cheat! I saw you sneaking a
look at my hand!" A large man with frizzy black hair hiding most of
his face spat the words at Cloud.*

*The room became quiet. Hiroshi could see Cloud's eyes darting
around the table like green lights. Hiroshi understood the situation
and knew Cloud and he were in trouble, but for what he did not
know. Without hesitating he stood up, withdrawing all the money
from his pocket. He slapped a thick packet of bills in the middle of
the table. "Everybody wins! Everybody wins!" he shouted in
Japanese, spreading the bills toward each player.*

*Dumbfounded, the men gawked, uncertain how to react. Cloud
jumped up and grabbed Hiroshi's arm, propelling him through the
room and out the door. With furtive backward glances, he ran down
the street, pulling a shocked Hiroshi. They didn't stop running until
Cloud entered a small café in the Chinese district.*

*Cloud ordered tea. Foreheads gleaming with sweat, the two fugi-
tives faced each other for the first time. Neither spoke, unsure what*

the other could understand. Cloud said "Thank you" in English, a phrase familiar to Hiroshi, which he answered by nodding his head and smiling widely. Then, to his astonishment, Cloud said a few words in halting Japanese. "Those men were serious. They wanted to hurt us. You were very clever to thwart their intentions. I thank you again for your generosity."

Exhilarated to communicate with someone not Japanese, Hiroshi shook Cloud's hand vigorously, words racing from his mouth with such speed Cloud could only look at him. After several attempts at talking and motioning, they found a way to understand each other, a jumbled combination of Japanese, pidgin English and broad gestures.

Though Hiroshi had already guessed it, Cloud conveyed he was Indian and yearned to sail to Japan someday, and therefore worked at the waterfront to be near the ships and to learn the language from any Japanese willing to teach him—which was also the main reason he had chosen the Asian hotel. Willing teachers were few, but he found the language came easily. He also found an affinity with the Japanese and Chinese—not only because of the common prejudice directed against them all, but for the comfort he felt in their presence, as if they shared a deeper connection than simply being outcasts.

As the days passed, Hiroshi learned more about his new friend. His name was John MacCloud, and he was a California Indian whose grandfather was Scots, coming west during the Gold Rush. Called Captain John, his grandfather had never been successful in the mines and soon found his way to Cloud's tribe and to his grandmother's bed. Like so many of the white traders, miners, and soldiers who through the years sought temporary solace in the arms of native women, he had returned to the East, leaving a green-eyed son in the California wilds.

Hiroshi taught his gifted student Japanese, and Cloud showed Hiroshi San Francisco, revealing parts of life in the city that otherwise would have remained unknown. Hiroshi lost his virginity at a high-class brothel that Cloud also frequented. Lily O'Brien was a buxom, red-haired Irish woman who astounded him with her loud voice and huge jiggling breasts. When Cloud introduced him, she had trilled in a delighted Irish brogue, "Well, look who's come to see Lily! You must be the bloomin' emperor of Japan. Darlin', I swear your face is sweet as any angel in heaven, slant eyes and all!" She clasped him against her mountainous breasts and shouted non-stop, her voice booming louder as she tried to make him understand her words.

He visited Lily often. He found her opulent white body, thick red pubic hair and strong body odor strangely erotic. She perspired profusely, causing water to collect in the crinkles of her neck, moistening her limbs, which she enfolded around him like slick octopus tentacles. "Me lil' ol' emperor. How I loves to squeeze ye!"

After many visits to Lily's pink-wallpapered room and tousled four-poster bed, Hiroshi decided he was in love. Could he marry her? When he revealed his desire, Cloud had gaped with astonishment. "But she's a prostitute! Do you realize what that means? Besides, you are forbidden by law to marry a white woman."

"What do you mean the law forbids me to marry a white woman? I'm samurai. I can marry anyone."

"Not in America, my friend. Not intermarriage between races . . . that is, any dark race with Caucasian. That's you and me, the 'dark race.' "

As the two ventured deeper into city life, Hiroshi's infatuation with Lily and his dejection after learning of the prejudices that existed against him soon faded. Hiroshi refused to even think about starting any business and spent the days sketching and touring the city, the nights gambling with Cloud at taverns welcoming Asians. On occasion they visited whorehouses, but Hiroshi never met another that appealed to him as much as Lily, the buxom redhead who spoke with an Irish brogue.

After many months, the letters from Japan became more frequent and questioning. He had been putting the family off by writing of his difficulties trying to start a business in the city. He dreamed of a way to survive as an artist, a painter preserving on canvas the beauty of the wild country he was beginning to love despite its small-heartedness toward nonwhite people like himself.

He lied to his family, writing that the tofu business he had started had failed and he was thinking about a new enterprise, a shoyu brewing plant. The wealthy Matsubara, trustful that their second son was learning the foreigner's complex business ways, did not begrudge sending money—in fact, they were proud he could recover from one loss and begin planning to start another business, something unthinkable in their own country. What a miraculous land this America was! Convinced their roots now truly could be transplanted in the New World, they began thinking of acquiring a bride, an appropriate wife who would assist in his rugged journey to the pinnacle of American success. They were aware of the scarcity of Japanese women, aware that three years was too long to be without a woman's unconditional acceptance and unquestioning loyalty. Too long to be without the sensual blessings of soothing backrubs, well-cooked meals, and a warm body, smelling of incense, with whom to share food and a soft futon.

Meanwhile, Hiroshi had tried to solve this problem in another way. At an artists' group that gathered each week to sketch nude models, he met Ruby McLean. The first time he saw her, his heart was lost. When he entered the studio that day, he saw from a distance a voluptuous form reclining on a sofa. Like his former Irish love Lily, her body was ample and alabaster white, but instead of a mass of flaming red tresses, her hair was a long, straight shawl of light brown.

What ignited Hiroshi's soul was Ruby's eyes. As he drew near, she returned his stare with a look so penetrating he stopped, unable to move or tear his gaze away. She sees through my body to the bone, *he thought. Then she smiled, a slight upturning of fleshy pink lips. Never understanding what came over him, he remembers only that he had approached the sofa as if in a trance, beckoned by her dazzling sapphire eyes. Falling to his knees, he whispered in English the only words he could think of.* "I love you."

She did not scorn him by laughing or joking—as Lily surely would have. Her face did not change. The soft smile remained on her lips as if he had merely uttered, "Good afternoon."

"Thank you," she said in a slight Irish brogue.

From that day on, Hiroshi's life changed. He dropped his playboy pose and became serious about his art. Ruby entered his world—or rather, he entered hers, a community of painters, writers, and mu-

sicians. She was an Irish immigrant housemaid for a wealthy San Francisco family. An aspiring artist herself, she posed for the painting group, who paid for her services by pooling their money. In her off-duty hours, she sketched at the wharf or socialized at the cafés frequented by other would-be painters and writers.

Inexperienced with women as he was—especially those of the West—Hiroshi nevertheless recognized Ruby's eccentricity. He saw she was a renegade in her own culture, perhaps even to her own sex. Alone with him in his room at the hotel, she smoked a small, thin pipe, using a tiny silver spoon to daintily fill its bowl with tobacco. She loved to be naked, tearing off her clothes as soon as she walked in.

At first he presumed she was overcome with passion. After the first few meetings, when he matched her amazing entrance by hastily disrobing and flinging his clothes around the room, he learned differently. She coached him to understand this was not an invitation for sex, but an exuberant display of feeling free. She felt free with him, she said.

"I have to be so proper in my boss's home, like a trussed-up leg o' lamb, ready to be cooked and eaten," she said in her lilting brogue. "But I can come here and be myself . . . 'cause I know you don't judge me. That's why I love you."

She sometimes donned his clothes, which, surprisingly, fit her full body. She would strut around the room, thin pipe jutting from between plump lips, posing arrogantly like a young Irish gentleman. Hiroshi sketched portraits of her dressed in his clothes, but hid them among his practice drawings, uncomfortable about how they might be viewed by others. He never questioned the nude drawings, displaying them on his walls without reservation.

Despite Ruby's odd antics, Hiroshi's experiences with her remained frivolous and carefree—until she introduced another side of her life. She had arrived at his apartment one cold night, playful as usual, quickly doffing her long coat and wool scarf, abandoning them on the floor as she danced around the room, grabbing teasingly at his sketchbook, over which he was hunched, laboriously finishing a drawing.

"I'm bored tonight, my Oriental prince. Must you continue draw-

ing?" She pressed close, emitting a titilating scent of musk mixed with brandy. Ignoring her, he concentrated on his work. Not to be put off, she leaned against his back, breathing sweet fumes into his ear.

"I have a wonderful idea . . . a perfect thing to do this winter's night," she whispered.

Unable to resist, he put down his pen and drew her into his lap, burying his face in her ample bosom.

"Not that, silly," she laughed, pushing him away. "I mean, let's go out. I want to take you to a secret place." Pause. "Do you know what I'm saying?"

He was learning the American language quite well, understanding words, but still too proud to try speaking them. He sometimes talked Japanese, which, oddly, she seemed able to decipher; other times he attempted a few awkward sentences in English, finding the pronunciation of "L" and "R" almost impossible. But mostly he used facial expressions and body language—a far cry from the inscrutable countenance he had learned to present as a Japanese— to communicate with her.

Bundled in coats and mufflers, they walked for about an hour, ending up in a neighborhood unfamiliar to Hiroshi. Some saloons and storefronts lined a steep, empty street lit eerily by gas lamps glowing yellow amidst a sea of swirling fog rising from the bay. They turned down a narrow alley and stopped at an inconspicuous door that Hiroshi presumed opened into the back of the herbal store fronting the street.

Ruby knocked four times, slowly and deliberately. Shuffling, slippered feet sounded and the door opened slightly, barely enough to reveal one side of a smooth-skinned face.

"Chang?" whispered Ruby, eagerness in her voice.

Without answering, the man opened the door and beckoned for them to enter. Strong smells of roots and herbs permeated the dark store, crowded with glass-doored shelves containing jars and pots of various sizes and shapes. Stacked wooden cases in the room's center left little space through which to maneuver toward another door leading into a musty hallway.

Hiroshi followed Ruby, who chattered softly at Chang's long braid hanging down his back. At the end of the hall, Chang opened a door, releasing a waft of pungent fumes that accosted Hiroshi's senses. The murky interior was lit dimly by several small spirit lamps set on the floor beside figures reclining on pillows, at first glance appearing asleep. With a shock, he realized this was an opium den. Cloud had warned of such places and advised never to partake. "Highly addictive," he had said. "The devil's dreamland."

But as Hiroshi observed Ruby's zealousness, blue eyes flashing fire as they did when ignited during lovemaking, Cloud's warning waned, and when she said softly, "My darlin', you will love this . . . you will dream like the gods," all the admonitions flew to the wind. He was in America, was he not? Was he not an artist, a free spirit like Ruby? Accustomed to the dimness, he recognized the prone bodies as those of her writer friends. Perhaps the heavenly demon gave them inspiration and visions.

Chang brought a tray containing a small lamp, long thin needle, small bowl filled with brown pills the size of peas, and a long bamboo pipe with metal bowl set several inches from the bottom end. Ruby arranged some cushions, gesturing for him to lie down like the others, who he noticed had not responded to their entrance but continued to lie languorously, oblivious to the world.

Ruby pierced a waxy pill with the needle, holding it over the lamp's flame until it bubbled and grew soft. She stuffed the gummy substance into the pipe's bowl, which she then held over the lamp's flame and inhaled deeply, eyes closed. She passed it to Hiroshi, who followed suit, lying opposite her, the lamp between them.

Soon, he felt his body relax, muscles melting into bone, bone dissolving into the pillows beneath. His mind, set free from his body, reveled in vaporous clouds of pastel shades, rainbow temples, steaming vents of golden light. Detached from flesh, numb to any carnal stimulation, he wallowed in an illicit paradise of sinister beauty where time evaporated and pleasure existed only in the absence of feeling. When he became aware of bodily sensations, he inhaled the heavy smoke time and again, yearning to return to euphoric paralysis.

When he and Ruby descended from their dreams, he was surprised to find they had passed the night and next day's morning in the den. He had thought he had been under the spell for a few hours only! Realizing the power of this pastime, his survival instincts warned him the servant of pleasure could easily become the master. But Ruby's joviality and robust visage overshadowed his doubts, and he saw opium smoking as just another aspect of her eccentric personality. Visits to Chang's shop were rare, convincing Hiroshi the demon was not in control and therefore could be refused at will. Their secret bonded them closer, infusing their union with a mystical tenderness.

Unencumbered with money worries or thoughts of a shoyu business, he felt the gods had finally blessed him. He had buried his obligation to the family, basking in a fanciful world brimming with hopeful artists, wild impostors, and even some madmen. He lived a sensuous surreal dream with Ruby, until the letter arrived from Japan, addressed in his father's hand.

It was a thick brown envelope, not the usual scented letter from his mother, and contained a picture of a beautiful Japanese woman. "This is your wife," Tadanoshin had written. "I have chosen her for you myself, and your mother also agrees it is a good match. After the marriage by proxy, she will live with us to learn our ways and should join you next year."

Catastrophe! There was no escape. Smothered by the strong scent of Matsubara sake wafting over the Pacific from his father's villa in Hiroshima, unable to earn money, and fully aware he was not accomplished enough to sell his paintings, he resigned himself to his fate. He would marry the picture bride chosen by his father. But somewhere in his mind he preserved a possibility, an unformed plan that would reveal itself when the time was right.

How could he explain this to Ruby? It was not as difficult as he had thought. One night, soon after receiving the letter, he embarrassed himself by weeping while making love. His pent-up feelings exploded in a torrent of tears when she cradled his head against her pillowy breasts.

Wiser than he in matters of the heart, she asked, "What are you unhappy about, my prince? Are you not in love with Ruby anymore?"

Incapable of answering in words, he left her embrace and re-

vealed the photograph. She studied the exotic beauty gazing from the sepia-toned photo, the long sloe-eyes, dark and liquid like Hiroshi's. She knew it was his wife or fiancée. "And is she comin' to America?"

He nodded. He sat down on the bed, holding his head in his hands. Ruby got up and opened her handbag, rummaging until she found a small, thin folder covered with embroidered velvet. She sat beside him. Tucked inside its frayed satin lining was an old photo of a very young Ruby with masses of curls around her face. She sat on a high-backed chair, a small child on her lap. Next to them stood a tall light-haired man with round, soft eyes, his hand on Ruby's shoulder.

"That's my husband and son. I left them in Boston." She pointed to the east. "It's another life I once had, a life I didn't want. I would have gone back had my child not died. So, I understand your situation. Life is not simple."

Strangely relieved by the photograph, Hiroshi felt no sense of shock or betrayal. Furthermore, Ruby gave no sign their relationship should end or even change. He was grateful. He could continue to live his fanciful life. He could enjoy to the fullest this new measure of freedom, and just as he had buried his obligation to start a family business, he would repress any thought of his marriage and bride's arrival almost a year away.

In the meantime, Cloud had moved south to San Jose, a small town nestled in the luscious Santa Clara Valley, where fruit orchards and farms carpeted the earth with greenery and fragrant blossoms. Hiroshi discovered his Indian friend was well known for championing workers' causes and, indeed, had fought many battles in the Sacramento area before moving to San Francisco. Farmworkers organizing for fair wages, hearing of Cloud's talent, had recruited him to San Jose, where he lived most of the time when not visiting San Francisco.

Several months after receiving word of his marriage by proxy, Hiroshi traveled to San Jose to ask advice from Cloud. He was still involved with Ruby and knew it would be impossible to deceive the family further about supposed business plans in the city.

As usual, Cloud had an answer. "Why don't you join me here in the country? I'm working with Japanese men. You'll be at home . . . and so will she." He was studying Sayo's portrait. "You always can go to the city," he added, not mentioning Ruby, of whom Hiroshi suspected he did not approve. He had never revealed his opium smoking to Cloud but, knowing his friend's uncanny instincts, figured he had guessed.

Thus, he had relocated to San Jose's countryside, working with Cloud during the week and sojourning in San Francisco some weekends. When word came that his bride would be arriving in three weeks, he panicked, begging Cloud to meet her at the docks with him. Cloud agreed, but only if Hiroshi stopped seeing Ruby for a while, which Hiroshi surmised meant not indulging in the heavenly demon.

When Sayo descended from the boat, floating down the plank with the other brides, he was staggered by her beauty. She stood out like a rare orchid set in a bouquet of wild daisies. He could not help but congratulate his father for his good taste. Seeing the kimono-clad women with pompadoured black hair, powdered white skin, and shy decorum, he unexpectedly was overcome with homesickness for Japan. He thought of his cultured mother, the refinements surrounding his life there. But the nostalgia lasted only a few moments, for when his bride bowed low at their first meeting, eyes appropriately lowered, he was reminded of the rigid protocol between husband and wife in Japan, and how he now basked in freedom with Ruby. Yet, when Sayo looked him in the face, speaking with warmth and civility, he knew she was not usual, and, committed to Ruby as he was, he still felt an electricity radiating from his wife that caught him off guard.

He admired how gracefully she accepted and adjusted to living at the compound with bachelors, even offering to cook for them. Discreetly, she never asked of his past life in America nor questioned why he hadn't established a business yet—until she so generously offered to help him begin one. Foremost, she didn't object to his artwork. He felt fortunate. If he had to be married in order to assure money from his family, he could imagine no bride so perfect for his situation as Sayo.

Accustomed to the lusty eroticism of his Irish paramour, he was concerned about how to initiate into lovemaking a delicate Japanese woman he assumed was virginal. But during o furo that first night, when she adroitly washed his back and later disrobed slowly without shame, ivory skin glowing with its own luster, and then joined him in the tub, demure yet inviting, he knew instinctively she was not innocent. Perhaps she was innocent of the actual love act, but hands that made a simple task of washing a back an art of tenderness belonged to someone acquainted with the sensual realm. Suspicion of his father's undue involvement in choosing a wife for him flitted through his mind; he had not been blind to Tadanoshin's lusty appetite for mistresses. But the thought vanished quickly as he himself began dwelling on ways to continue the affair with his own "mistress," Ruby. Or was his mistress the harlot opium? At times, when he remembered his obligation to the family, anxiety churning his belly and souring his breath, he yearned to float on Ruby's alabaster breasts . . . or was it on opium-induced clouds, voluminous with visions? As the days passed, despite his growing affection for Sayo, Ruby and opium became inseparable in his mind, and he began thinking obsessively of ways to possess them both.

Thanksgiving, 1942

Manzanar

A few days before Thanksgiving Tad and Mac returned from Idaho, bringing tales of backbreaking labor sacking potatoes and cutting sugar beets, living in quarters hardly different from the camp barracks. The farmers were unfriendly at first, Mac said, but warmed up when they saw how fast and competent the internees were and that they spoke English.

"Amazing!" exclaimed Mac, who had lost some weight, but looked tan and fit otherwise. "They're real country bumpkins up north. They were surprised we spoke English and didn't have buck teeth and wear glasses. But after we got to know each other they were pretty nice . . . even a bit grateful."

Their six-week stint of freedom was no different from life in camp, except they were not surrounded by barbed wire. Hana had no prior notice of their return and was startled when they tumbled through the barracks door, dragging their duffel bags across the newly polished linoleum. Tad took no notice of the changed beds, and unpacked furiously, as if by reinstating his presence in the compartment, he could erase the past six weeks. He is tense, more tense than before the furlough. In contrast, Mac unpacked his bag deliberately, smoothing wrinkles from each piece of clothing. Watching him, Hana's heart wrung. She realized he was on the threshold of manhood, wanting to be an adult, but still a teenager, worried about the look of his clothes.

During the short time they were alone, Tad made love to her with a frenzy that was frightening. She knew intuitively it was not the time away nor the possibility he missed her that spurred his turbulent lovemaking. He seemed angry, frustrated. Even after his explosive release, he was not relaxed.

Though it is Thanksgiving Day, Hana knows for them in camp it will be no different from any other day. No turkey with trimmings or big table around which the family could sit and gorge on mashed potatoes and gravy, succotash, yams, and limitless varieties of pickles, olives, and relishes. She has heard from the mess-hall crew they will be eating lamb stew.

She remembers the Thanksgivings of her childhood, the cheerful, sometimes raucous festivity at the Heavenly Cloud Inn with the geisha and her mother and Yoshio. They had turkey stuffed with rice and many accompanying dishes of raw fish, pickled vegetables, and yams—all washed down with copious amounts of warm sake. Dressed in kimono, her mother and the younger geisha danced and played the *shamisen* while Yoshio and she watched, laughing uproariously when the ladies tripped and sprawled on the tatami as the evening wore on and sake took its toll.

Hana sits in the barracks, sewing a pinafore for Mary, one of the orphans at the Children's Village. Mac and Tad enter, ignoring her presence.

"Goddamn, we're gone a few weeks and the whole place is ready to explode!" Tad sounds angry. "You'd think there'd be some rational thinkers left here."

"I think the *kibei* have a point. I heard they're not all crazies. Buffalo has a cool head." Mac seems to be trying to placate his father. "And then there's that Shimizu guy—the Boy Scout tailor—he goes to the meetings, too. So they're not all *kibeis* rebelling without any thought."

Hana stops sewing. She remembers Shimmy saying he knows his reputation is that of being a "goody-goody," even a queer. It offends her that Mac, her son, is one of those who thinks in such an unfair and crude way. She listens carefully, an uneasiness dampening her Thanksgiving reverie. She realizes Tad and Mac already are becoming involved in the controversy. She wonders if they plan on attending the meetings. Her question is answered when Tad says, "I'm going to find out what's really happening. You can't believe anything you hear by the grapevine."

"I'm going, too," says Mac.

"Fine. The more sane people the better. Someone was saying at the canteen that some guys plan on marching to army headquarters—headbands, flags, and all. What the hell's the point? We should have protested earlier, when they brought us here."

Hana hears resentment in Tad's voice. She doesn't remember him being so bitter before he went on furlough. Maybe she simply hadn't noticed. Since meeting Shimmy she has become more aware of the world around her, as if she'd been hibernating in a cocoon, safely in-sulated from a dangerous and demanding life. Still not fully engaged in that life, she is not sure if she wants to join it wholeheartedly. Since the men returned she finds herself at times retiring into her former shell. But she has not seen Shimmy since the day he told her about his life, and now even the thought of him quickens her heart and overcomes any desire to retreat again into that refuge.

She thinks she, too, would like to go to the meeting, but she doesn't ask, knowing it is for men only. She will finish sewing Mary's pinafore and deliver it to the Children's Village before dinnertime. Lamb stew for Thanksgiving!

After an uneventful dinner—during which no mention was made of Thanksgiving—Hana walks with her mother to the tearoom. She notices how Sayo stands so erect, her back seamless and flat as a mil-itary officer's. Even at her age—Hana guesses she is in her middle sixties or even seventy—she is stunning. Having lived a great part of her life in the shadow of this elegant woman, Hana still feels small and insignificant next to her. But gradually the resentment has light-ened, even transforming into admiration. Now, instead of resisting her mother's power by denying it in herself, she seeks to find it.

"Where is Terri?" Hana asks. "I hardly see her anymore."

"I was just going to ask you."

"She must be with Mitzi . . . or watching the boys play baseball."

"And Carmen?" Sayo asks.

"I've given up on her. She's always with her friend Patty. They're interested in singing and dancing. The other day I told her she should move to Block Thirty with Patty."

"The family is slowly breaking up," Sayo says gravely.

Hana says, "I was just thinking about Thanksgiving in the old days at Watsonville—how fun it was with Yoshio and the girls."

Sayo smiles wanly, remembering. "And what about your Thanksgivings in Venice—the fancy china and silver like the *hakujin* pictures in magazines. . . . I never could stand that cranberry sauce you served in place of *tsukemono*!"

Her voice strong, Sayo continues, "Our tree has been cut at the root. But we can remain standing, even if blown by the greatest wind. We must hold on to the earth. Keep our feet on the ground."

Hana is not certain what her mother means, but takes the chance and asks, "Do you think the *kibei's* roots are cut, too, and they are floating around this desert?"

Sayo laughs, a soft girlish tinkling. "Absolutely!" Pause. "You know, there's a meeting tonight. I'm of the mind to go, just to shock those *yogores*. Such troublemakers."

"Did you know Tad and Mac are going?"

"Good! Bring some sense to the meeting. Our friend Shimmy has been attending, and they've given him a rough time."

Hana bravely suggests, "Why don't we go? We don't have to participate—just observe from the sidelines."

Sayo stares, studying her daughter as if seeing her for the first time. Then she laughs. "A great idea! We can at least go and watch from the back. I'm glad you are suggesting it." Her eyes are warm. Hana feels bathed in respect. The two quicken their steps back to the barracks. Hana realizes this is the first time she and her mother have contrived together to do something questionable. The thought pleases her, and she is all the more determined to continue speaking what she thinks.

It is an especially dark night, with a splinter of a moon barely visible in the clouded sky. Hana wears woolen trousers and her navy peacoat while Sayo still dresses in kimono, which she has layered with several undergarments for warmth. She has draped a woolen shawl over her shoulders and head. On her feet she wears thick socks and high wooden *getas,* clattering clogs that make the only sound in the silent camp as they cross the two firebreaks to Block 34, the one farthest away from the administration buildings.

Sayo breaks the quiet. "This night is strange. I feel something bad is going to happen. See? No moon." She points to the sky. The thin crescent has disappeared. Hana feels goose pimples rise on her neck and arms. She is used to her mother's premonitions, and although she herself does not believe in ghosts and spirits as do Sayo and Terri, she feels the eeriness of the night, can almost see apparitions forming in the misty firebreak.

They soon reach the mess hall, from which they hear loud male voices. They climb some stairs to a small porch where the double doors of the large building are closed but not locked. Sayo gently pulls one of the doors open enough so they can slide through discreetly. A few men turn with shocked looks as they enter the smoke-filled room, but soon return their attention to the speaker in front. There are close to forty men seated around the mess-hall tables.

Hana sees Tad and Mac with some men who are not wearing headbands. She surmises those wearing the white headbands, of whom there are about twenty, are the *kibei.* She looks for Shimmy and finds him at the front near the podium. The speaker is slight and pimply-faced. Sayo whispers, "He's one of the *yogores* ganging up on Shimmy that day."

Speaking rapidly in a Japanese dialect unfamiliar to Hana, the *kibei* waves his arms and begins shouting. Even from afar she can see his wild, glaring eyes, spittle flying from his mouth. "What is he saying?" she whispers to Sayo.

"He's saying nothing. Just hot air about traitors in camp."

"Traitors? Against who? America or Japan?"

"He doesn't know. They just want to blame someone for our predicament so they can have a fight, beat someone up."

To Hana's consternation, Shimmy stands up to speak. In English, he says, "We shouldn't be attacking each other. No one put us in here but the government! I say we sign a petition and protest peacefully to the administration. Remember, the army has guns."

"*Inu!*" someone shouts.

"Coward!"

"Go back to sewing with the women, queer!"

Suddenly Tad stands up, shocking Hana. She sees he is trying to stay calm, his jaws tight and speech measured. "Hey, I think you guys are being unrealistic. I've just come back from the real world outside, and let me tell you, they don't like us much out there. What makes you think the soldiers feel any different? Why give them an excuse to shoot us?"

More booing and shouts.

Just as another speaker takes the podium, the door bursts open and a huge man enters. He is dressed in kimono and wears high *getas*, elevating him well above six feet. It is Buffalo Iseri. He stands beside Hana, arms folded across his vast chest, and waits for the man to speak. After a flurry of excited whispers, the room quiets and the speaker begins a screaming rampage. Hana notices Buffalo's jaws clenching and unclenching as the voice rises in pitch and volume.

"What is he saying?" she whispers to Sayo.

"This one is talking about marching on army headquarters! He's crazy."

Buffalo yells in a booming voice, speaking English. "Hey! Talk American so everyone can understand. We're not supposed to be speaking Japanese at meetings."

Hana can tell he is baiting the speaker. She knows he could care less about what language is spoken.

Buffalo's words cause an explosion of curses and shouting as those internees not affiliated with the *kibei* and now strengthened by his presence begin voicing their opinions. The yelling mounts. Benches are turned over, and most of the men are standing, fists and feet ready to fly.

Suddenly the room becomes pitch black. Someone has turned off the lights. Buffalo grabs Hana and Sayo and propels them from the mess hall, almost carrying them bodily. After depositing them a safe distance away, he leaves without a word. Sayo calls, "Iseri-san, please come and have tea with us at our ochaya. Block Sixteen."

He calls back, "Thank you, Sayo-san, I will. I know about you and your tearoom."

As they cross the firebreak Tad and Mac catch up with them. Hana is oddly unafraid of what Tad will do or say.

"What in hell were you and Sayo doing at that fucking meeting?" As she expected, he is furious.

He is stunned when she answers back. "Sayo and I want to know what's going on. You and Mac could have gotten hurt, too."

"Fuck!" he shouts.

She braces herself.

"As if there aren't enough crazy fuckers in this fucking camp! Son of a bitch! My wife and her mother are nuts, too!"

Mac intercedes. "Okay . . . okay, Dad. Mom and Obachan are fine. No problem. Nobody cared they were there."

"I fucking care! And what about that giant asshole Buffalo? He was there right next to them. What the hell was he thinking? Probably wanted to hit on them."

Unable to contain herself, Hana blurts, "That's not true! Buffalo helped us. He ushered us out of there, practically carried us!" Why does Tad react so violently about anything to do with her?

Her passion shocks everyone. They stop in their tracks, dark shadows in the mist-shrouded firebreak. Even Sayo is shaken by the change in her daughter.

Mac says gently, "Mom, are you all right?"

The realization sweeps over Hana. Simply because she has spoken out, the family thinks she has gone mad! She begins to laugh, unable to stop giggling.

Sayo puts an arm around Hana and leads her away. She peers through the darkness at her daughter's face, studying the relaxed mouth and mirthful eyes. She sees the spasmodic fluttering of a butterfly, a newly born butterfly emerging from its cocoon. She, too, begins to laugh with Hana, and they quicken their steps toward the barracks.

Mac and Tad mutter as they follow the women. In worried tones they speculate as to whether Hana has begun an early menopause, or perhaps the shock of the internment has caught up. "It could even be the water," says Mac. "They could put anything in it to make us sick or control us. Maybe that's what's driving everybody crazy around here—the water. Look at the way they shut out the lights? Who would do that?"

Tad changes the subject. "Well, now we're really going to have trouble. Mark my words. Who do you think shut the lights?"

"It sure wasn't Buffalo. Had to be someone up front or someone sneaking in through the kitchen."

The next morning before breakfast a pounding on the barracks door awakens the Murakami household. Hana is first out of bed. It is Buffalo, worry on his unshaven face. His breath steams in smoky trails. Standing in the doorway, his shoulders bulky under a thick coat, he does resemble a buffalo.

"Come in, come in." The others are up and surround him, awaiting his message.

"Lincoln Shimizu's been beaten up bad. He's in the hospital."

Hana chokes. Buffalo goes on to explain that Shimmy had been the one to turn off the lights and break up the meeting. "It could have gotten pretty nasty, you know. They wanted to fight then and there. Shimmy wanted to avert violence. The *kibei* had been drinking . . . the rotgut they've been brewing in the barracks."

"Can we go and see him?" asks Hana, stomach sinking.

"No. He's guarded by soldiers. No one knows who did the actual beating and the *yogores* will deny everything."

Hana notices he calls them "yogores," the same term Sayo has used. "Is he badly hurt?"

"It's serious, a concussion, but the doctor says he'll survive. When he gains consciousness he can tell who attacked him."

Tad and Mac dress quickly, planning aloud their next moves. They must meet with other internees and form a coalition for protection against the *yogores*. They know this beating could set off retaliations unless they organize. Scheming and plotting, the two men ignore Hana. She is invisible again. Falling back into her usual pattern, she remains silent, softly backing away to her bed behind the partition. When Tad and Mac finally leave, she allows the tears to flow. She sobs noisily, venting her fear and frustration. She is certain Shimmy will be all right. But she now worries if alone she can be strong enough to withstand Tad's power to overwhelm her. And now that he is back, how can she continue seeing Shimmy?

Warnings

Terri visits the soldiers almost every day, braving windstorms and rain to exchange a few words or at least wave. She feels it is more or less her duty to help relieve their monotonous task of circling the wooden platform for hours without talking to anyone. After all, hadn't they disobeyed the rules and taken her on a forbidden excursion? Even now Billy and Skip still defy orders, taking her out to a sheltered gully beyond the fence where they hunker down in the deep hollow to play cards. Bordered by thick sage, the gully is invisible to anyone gazing past the barbed wire.

Today it is exceptionally cold, and her stomach has felt upset for the past week. She would like to see Billy, but the thought of bundling up and trudging the half mile to the tower makes her more tired. Obachan is puttering around the compartment, dusting bowls and saucers, polishing her wooden mirror.

"You look pale, Teru-chan. Are you feeling all right?" She knows her youngest grandchild has not begun her menses yet and suspects that this explains much of her secretive behavior of the past month. Deciding to break the ice, she says, "Do you remember what we talked about last year? About menstruation?" It seems to Sayo that Terri has reached that crucial age and, like her mother and sister Carmen, will probably enter womanhood as they did at age thirteen.

Terri only manages a nod. She remembers Obachan telling her to expect changes in her body, monthly bleedings that would purify the female organs and prepare them for carrying babies someday. But she has not been thinking about that supposedly momentous event. In fact, she hasn't looked forward to it at all. Carmen calls it "the curse." Terri has managed to suppress any thought of it, reminded only occasionally by blood-soaked pads in the latrine waste pails.

"You will probably be starting soon," continues Obachan, "so I will get some Kotex from your mother. Don't be upset. It's nothing to be afraid of. It means you are becoming a woman."

Thinking about it, Terri changes her view a bit toward crossing that threshold. Perhaps it would make her look older, and Billy would regard her in the way he regards Carmen. But she knows that along with "the curse" come other burdens—like more responsibility in the family, no more playing with boys, dressing "ladylike." She watched Carmen change from a gentle, quiet cat into a moody, sometimes sullen tiger, quick to anger, full of suspicions, afraid to have fun. Terri wants still to run around in shorts, allowing her long legs freedom from the entanglement of skirts. She doesn't want to wear those brassieres that would encase the small volcano cones she feels erupting on her chest.

Obachan puts on her shawl, reminding Terri, before she leaves, to eat lunch. "You're getting too skinny. You need fat for this cold weather."

The heaviness in her stomach seems to have subsided. Terri feels a surge of energy and dresses hurriedly into warm clothes. Thinking about Billy sparks some excitement, and she is filled with anticipation as she slams out the door.

Bundled in long woolen pants, oversized army boots, cape, and Billy's scarf, she shivers as she waits below the tower, hoping he can see her from inside. Ever since the weather turned cold, the soldiers no longer promenade around the deck but stay inside the tiny cell, occasionally glancing out a glassless window. For weeks now, she, Billy, and Skip had been meeting under the tower, then crawling under the wire to a nearby hidden gulch. When the sun was out, it was comfortably warm inside the hollow, even if the wind above was blowing with a gale's force.

She worried Billy and Skip would get in trouble for neglecting their guard duty. But they both laughed. "No one gives a rat's ass about patrolling you people. Hell, the brass never checks on us and the other GIs could care less. Shoot," said Billy, "some of them are doing the same thing as us over at the other side of camp, I bet."

"What about the internees?" Skip asked. Are they giving you trouble about talking to us?"

She was careful to meet them during mealtimes, she had explained, and now that the weather had turned cold, none of the internees loitered outside the barracks. "Besides, even if they do notice, they figure I'm too young to get into mischief with you guys."

They taught her how to play poker and blackjack, which she grasped with great facility, soon beating them soundly.

"Are you sure you're only thirteen?" Billy asked. "You are very smart, you know that?"

"I know it," she answered flippantly. "You told me that before."

Both Billy and Skip laughed hard, a reaction that always amazed her. She never meant for her remarks to draw such amused attention. Whenever she volunteered any comment while her father or Mac were speaking, they were quick to chastise her.

"Don't be a smart-ass," they'd say, or, "Girls should be seen but not heard."

She looked forward to playing cards, basking in their easy camaraderie, enjoying Billy's gray eyes studying her with what she perceived as admiration. What they were doing was forbidden, could even be dangerous. But she stopped her mind from thinking about what would happen if they were caught.

Now Billy emerges from the enclosed section. He walks across the platform and climbs down the ladder to ground level. Without saying a word, he runs to the fence and lifts the bottom wire, beckoning with gloved hand for her to crawl under. An urgency in his movements makes her uneasy. Silently obeying, she creeps under the wire, wondering what's happened to Skip.

They scamper to the nearby gully and jump into it. A thick cluster of sagebrush hangs over one side of the five-feet-deep hole, forming a canopy under which they settle, protected from the cold wind blustering overhead. The air is damp and smells pungently of earth and moss. Terri blows on her bare hands to warm them.

"Where's Skip?"

"He's at some training session." His voice sounds tense. He pulls off his gloves and offers them to Terri. "I can't for the life of me figure out why the brass here is so damned ignorant they don't provide you people with decent winter clothing."

Terri senses the underlying anger of his words is not due to lack of warm clothes. Innocently, she asks, "What's really the matter, Billy?"

She scrutinizes him, her finely chiseled child-woman's face eager. He fumbles in his pocket for a cigarette, which he finds and then lights, inhaling deeply. Exhaling a fine stream of smoke, he says, "Now, I'm goin' to tell you something you can't ever tell no one. I'm telling you 'cause I like you and 'cause I think this whole goddamned business of locking you all up is wrong." He pauses and sucks again on his cigarette. "Now, there's going to be trouble for you folks. Somebody in camp has put the finger on soldiers selling sugar and meat meant for you all . . . selling on the black market. There's probably some brass involved, too. But there's going to be trouble 'cause they'll want to cover it up."

Terri does not fully understand what Billy is telling her. In her straightforward way she asks, "Are you warning me about something?"

"Yes. Stay away from any meetings or crowds. The army will want any chance to shut up the troublemakers. We've been training for riot control."

"Riot control? What's that?"

He doesn't answer. Instead he grasps her gloved hands, holding them tightly. His hands are large with long, square-tipped fingers, ruddy and thick-skinned, holding a warmth that she feels through the knitted wool.

"I'm truly sorry, Terri. But I just wanted you to know I consider you a real friend. I want you to know that."

Terri's heart sinks. "Are you saying good-bye? Are you going away?"

He laughs his normal chuckle.

"Hell, no. At least not soon, I hope. When we leave it means we're going overseas."

He is sitting so close she can see the light spattering of freckles across his nose and cheeks, the gray eyes fringed with dark red lashes, eyes that look at her with what she feels is sadness. "Oh, I hope you don't have to go overseas. I hope this war is over soon. Please don't be sad." Unexpectedly, tears fill her eyes and she begins to cry.

Billy chuckles, "Hey now, don't go getting sentimental on me. You're the one's so sad. Why are you sad?"

She swallows her tears. What can she say? That she loves him and thinks he is more handsome than any movie star pictured in *Silver Screen*? That she's sad she is only thirteen and he's nineteen, a grown man? Unable to retort with a smart line, she turns mute.

"Wow, first time I've seen you wordless," Billy teases. Then the gravity in his voice frightens her: "But I'm not kidding. You and your folks be careful. Stay away from any crowd or meetings. Promise me, okay?"

"Thanks, Billy, for the warning. But I still don't understand. Who can hurt us?"

He looks uncomfortable. "No one wants to hurt anyone. But things can get out of control. You're my friend and I'm just warning you. Okay?"

He stands up and jumps nimbly out of the gully. Offering a hand, he pulls her to the top, where the bitter wind cuts into her face. The sky has turned dark, and gusts of sand explode intermittently as they run to the fence and under the bottom wire. Terri starts to pull off Billy's gloves.

"No, you keep them. I can get others."

"Thank you." It is so cold her teeth chatter, but she would brave any icy weather to visit a few more moments with him. She fights an urge to throw her arms around him. To her astonishment, Billy bends down and kisses her lightly on the cheek.

"Well, keep your chin up, partner. And tell your sister Carmen she's missing the chance of a lifetime." He has begun climbing the ladder to the tower and smiles down at Terri, saluting smartly.

Unable to respond, she holds the cheek he has kissed with one hand and with the other waves until he disappears into the enclave. The gloved hand smells of tobacco. She covers her nose and breathes deeply, savoring the scent. Her heart seems to float up to her throat, and the freezing temperature feels warm. She turns and runs toward the barracks, glancing back in time to see him waving from his cell in the tower.

For the next two days, she remains inside the barracks, heeding

Billy's words. She leaves only to eat and visit the latrine. Obachan is gone most of the time and when she is present, seems preoccupied with her own thoughts. Billy's warning festers, and she now worries about her grandmother.

Despite herself, she asks, "Is there trouble brewing, Obachan?"

"Why do you ask?" Sayo lights incense on the shrine. "Have you heard something?"

Not wanting to betray Billy, she mulls over what she can say. "Well, I heard you and Mom talking in the mess hall the other day. Are the *kibei* going to do something to the soldiers?"

Obachan laughs. "They'd like to, I'm sure. And there are a few kamikaze pilot types who are crazy enough to think they could. But they're stupid. Stupid." She seems exasperated.

"What would they do?" Terri imagines hordes of half-naked *kibei* brandishing knives and invading the soldiers' barracks.

"I don't know." Concern crosses Obachan's face. "Do you know that Shimmy is in the hospital?"

Terri is shocked. "No! What happened? Is he okay?"

"He was beaten up at a meeting. The doctor says he had a concussion, but it is not serious."

"Oh my God! Why would anyone want to hurt Shimmy? He's such a nice guy." Terri remembers him fitting her with the peacoat cape. "Were the soldiers there?"

"Of course not. That kind of meeting is forbidden here. Besides, some people were accusing the soldiers of stealing our sugar and meat and selling it on the black market."

Without thinking, Terri quips, "Good riddance to the mutton! They're doing Dad a favor."

Sayo laughs despite the seriousness of the situation. "But the sugar is definitely a problem. The babies' formulas need it."

After Sayo leaves, Terri becomes bored staying inside the barracks. Billy's quick kiss has occupied most of her thoughts, and she yearns to talk with him again. She decides to go to the tower, hoping he will be guarding. Just to see him.

Blown sand stings like ice particles as she hurries across the firebreak to the outer perimeter, where she sees from a distance a lone soldier in the tower. Her heart skips. She knows it is Billy.

Seeing her approach, he scrambles down the ladder with alarming speed to meet her. Without speaking, he grabs her hand and almost jerks her behind some dense sagebrush.

"Didn't I tell you not to be outside?" His gray eyes are now granite. She can't tell if he is mad or scared.

"You said not to go to any meetings or crowds," she answers defensively, surprised by his intensity. This was not the fun-loving Billy she knew.

His voice softens. "I'm sorry, Terri. But I'm real worried what's goin' on here. There's definitely going to be trouble . . . real soon." Eyes lightening to liquid gray, he studies her uplifted face.

She senses he is more afraid than angry, and smiles, wanting to comfort him. "It's not your fault, Billy. My grandma says being locked up makes people crazy. Besides, I know you guys aren't going to shoot anyone."

"Hell, I sure don't want to . . . but like your grandma says, people get crazy being locked up . . . and some of these army guys feel locked up here, too." Now relaxed, he asks gently, "What's up?"

"Oh, I just wanted to visit. I'm bored."

He laughs. Her lion prince has returned. "You know, when we leave this place I'm going to miss you. I don't suppose you know how to write."

"What do you mean?" she feigns outrage. "I'm writing a book right now!"

"Well, how about writing me when I leave?"

"I thought you said you wouldn't leave unless you went overseas. Have you received orders?"

"No. Just thinking ahead."

"I promise, Billy. I'll write."

The wind has picked up. She gathers her cape closer.

"I don't think I should stay down here. Believe me, I'd much rather be here with you . . . but the brass will be checking. They're real antsy. So, gotta go." But he makes no move to leave.

Amazing herself, she flings her arms around his torso, burying her face in his tobacco-smelling jacket. His body feels rigid at first, but softens, arms holding her close in a warm hug. They stand embraced for some long moments.

"Too bad you're so young." He pulls away.

"I'm a teenager," she retorts, hardly able to respond. She is beside herself with happiness.

"But, you're still a babe. I'm not a cradle-snatcher, either."

"Well, I can grow up, you know."

He laughs again and kisses her lightly on the cheek. "I might even wait for that to happen." His voice turns serious. "Now, I have to go, and you be careful . . . you and your family, okay?"

She nods and blows him a kiss as he scampers up the ladder to the tower.

The next day, Terri and Sayo are relaxing in their *ochaya* when suddenly the door flings open and Hana enters, breathing hard as if she had been running for miles instead of from next door.

"Soldiers have arrested Buffalo and put him in the camp jail!"

"What!" Obachan's eyes are round. "Why Buffalo? He hasn't done anything wrong!"

"Mac says everyone's upset. The soldiers are saying it is Buffalo who beat up Shimmy."

"Ridiculous! We know that's not true." Obachan has regained her composure and is now calm, her voice steely. "We must go to the authorities and tell them Buffalo was with us at the meeting. Hasn't Shimmy been able to identify his attackers?"

"Mac says he can't. He was knocked out immediately. Tad and Mac say the soldiers are scapegoating Buffalo because they know he's a *kibei,* and one of the *kibei* has accused the soldiers of black marketing. People are really mad, and a crowd is going to march on the jail!"

Terri is startled to hear her mother speak with such emotion. Observing the two older women so animated, she is struck by how much they resemble each other. Always withdrawn and unavailable to Terri, Hana had seemed worlds apart from Obachan. But now her mother emits a new strength. Even her posture is more erect, and her skin seems to glow, ruddiness in the cheeks. Steeped in her own drama with Billy, Terri had not noticed the change in her mother, how much younger she looks.

"We must get to the jail," says Obachan as she bustles about, searching for her shawl.

Terri remembers Billy's warning. "But you're not going to any big meeting where there's a crowd, are you?"

Obachan looks at her. "Why do you say that?"

"I mean there could be a riot."

"A riot? Where do you hear such things?! We're just going to the jail to clear up this matter. Buffalo is innocent."

She begins to cry. "I just don't want you and Mom to be in any crowd. It could be dangerous."

Obachan turns to Hana. "See, I told you. I think she is going to start her period—so emotional these days."

In a voice Terri has not heard since she was a child, her mother says gently, "Don't worry, Teru-chan, we'll be careful. Nothing can happen to us. I promise you."

Before Terri can respond, the two women leave. Alone and cold, she unfolds her futon-bed and lays it on the floor. She covers herself with several army blankets and tries to sleep. She lies there listening, for she knows not what.

Some time later she is awakened by a strange sound, a droning mumble of voices punctuated by sharp yells and guttural shouting, mostly in Japanese. Beneath the rumble she hears the scraping of footsteps on sand. She jumps up and peers out the window. It is now twilight and the sky has turned purple. She can make out figures running between barracks; some carry burning torches and wear white headbands. Where are Obachan and Hana?

She must find them. She grabs her cape and, without changing, runs out into the winter dusk in a short skirt and *getas*.

The air is sharp. She sees her breath stream in white puffs. Her cold hands are stiff, and she wishes she'd remembered to put on Billy's gloves. Trying to remain unseen, she slowly edges along the barracks' walls, following from a distance a knot of young men carrying torches. Now and then she hears agitated yelling from afar. Suddenly a line of about ten men, naked except for white loincloths and white headbands, run past. They chant in unison. The leader carries a banner in Japanese.

At the last firebreak before the line of administration buildings and the entrance to camp, she hangs farther back, pressing against a barrack wall. The firebreak is filled with hundreds of figures milling like restless cattle, ready to stampede at the least provocation. Burning torches throw an eerie glow over the sweaty faces and through the dust rising up from the break. The loinclothed runners now weave among the crowd, shouting roughly.

Someone has set up a large taiko drum and begins beating a fast staccato rhythm, hypnotic and stirring. With the drumming Terri's heart beats faster. She sees a contingent of soldiers guarding one of the buildings. She presumes it is the jail. Carrying rifles, and with helmets and gas masks covering their heads and faces, the soldiers look like grotesque invaders from another planet. The leader carries a bullhorn and shouts at the mob. "Go back to your quarters! Disperse immediately!"

The crowd responds with yells and curses. surging ominously toward the armed soldiers. "Free Buffalo!" "Where's our sugar?"

"Stay back! Stay back!" the leader shouts with panic. "Or we'll shoot!"

The crowd stops its surging, and the taiko ceases its pulsing. But only for a moment. Someone yells "Banzai!" and the mob moves forward again, the taiko beating militantly faster. Watching in terror, Terri strains to find her grandmother and mother in the crowd but sees few women.

"Again I'm warning you! Disperse this crowd! Stay back!"

This time the *yogores* in loincloths begin throwing rocks, breaking windows and hitting some of the soldiers. Terri knows a tragedy has begun, and she watches transfixed as the figures in the crowd become warriors. The taiko drum beats a war chant as they whoop and holler; torches turn into spears and bows. Paint stains the faces and chests and arms. Their horses neigh and rear up on hind legs. The firebreak is thick with dust and the smell of sweating horses.

Suddenly shots ring out, and the warriors fall. The crowd has disappeared, the drumming ceased. It is silent except for the wind blowing sand across the break, across the few bodies lying on the ground, their jackets ruffling in the breeze.

Terri is breathless, her heart heavy. She stares at the soldiers who stand frozen in front of the jail, their guns out of sight. One of the tall ones tears off his mask and helmet, releasing a shock of red hair. His face is chalk white, his mouth a dark, open hole.

Fighting a scream, Terri backs away. She remembers his warnings.

He was trying to help. Why would he shoot at them? The guns had fired real bullets. Hadn't Billy said the rifles weren't loaded? Her throat closes. She can't breathe. He suddenly is a stranger, an ominous red-haired demon with the power to kill. If she had been in the crowd, he could have shot her! This realization jolts her back to breathing.

She feels a heaviness in her lower belly giving way to a warm trickle that runs down her inner thighs and legs, seeping past the wooden *getas* to pool on the ground. She looks down and sees a dark stain widening in the sand. Chest heaving with sobs, thin body tottering, she runs from the death scene as fast as her wooden clogs can clatter, leaving a line of blood in the desert.

ACT III

Fateful Meetings

Fourth of July, 1903

San Jose

*T*oday was Fourth of July, a great holiday for Americans, Sayo
had learned, and nihonjin were staging a picnic in respect for
their adopted country. The festivities were planned by nihonmachi's
barber, Hori-san, who fancied himself honorary mayor. Taking
place on the Buddhist temple's grounds, entertainment would include Japanese music, taiko drumming, and even a shibaya, a dance
drama from classical Kabuki. Having had no luck so far in finding
a shoyu factory site, Sayo looked forward to spending a day without thinking about it. But secretly she hoped to see Cloud. Since the
kissing incident after the fight with Daley, she had not talked with
him except to exchange polite greetings.

True, she had been fully occupied acquainting herself with town.
But she also hoped to run into him somewhere. She missed their
conversations, and although inwardly treasuring his "American
kiss," she regretted that moment of weakness, since it seems to have
resulted in his avoiding her. Yet, she admired his honor. She decided
that if he was to remain an accessible friend, she must be the one to
cross the barrier between them.

Sayo and Hiroshi could hear taiko drumming as they neared
the temple, a large wooden building of simple design with a curved
roof and veranda-like porch. A low stone fence surrounded an
open space of grass and trees where gaily dressed people clustered,
seated on blankets under trees and large umbrellas. She recognized most of the crowd, families from town. It was not yet noon,
but the sun was already glaringly hot. Hiroshi's handsome face glis-

*tened with sweat, and she felt her armpits moistening under her silk
kimono.*

*"Hiroshi-san! Sayo-san! Come over here!" Ito's voice shouted from
across the grass where he stood waving among a group of bachelors
and kimono-clad women. She saw Cloud lounging under a nearby
tree, a Japanese woman sitting next to him. She followed Hiroshi,
who strode rapidly toward Cloud, quickening her already antici-
patory heartbeat. She wondered who the woman was.*

*Cloud spoke first, his voice reserved. "We've been waiting for
you. Didn't want you to miss the taiko." He nodded toward the
small stage set up in front of the temple, an American flag draped
around its edge.*

*"Oh yes, we heard them back in town. They are excellent." She
tried to keep her own voice neutral.*

*Ito and some other women came over, seating themselves on the
blanket with Cloud and the Japanese woman. They carried baskets
containing rice wine and picnic fare, which they opened and shared.
Discreetly, Sayo studied the women, mostly younger than herself except for Cloud's companion. She was surprised by two girls dressed
in high-collared shiny dresses, realizing they were Chinese. Cloud's
friend was older, her hair upswept in pompadours around a soft,
round face, reminding Sayo of Chiba.*

*The woman poured some wine and brought two cups to Sayo
and Hiroshi. "My name is Kiyomi. Please have some sake, and welcome to our picnic." Graciously, she handed them the wine.*

*Ito chirped, "Please let me introduce Matsubara Sayo . . . Hiroshi's
wife." He paused. "Our onesan."*

*"Of course I know who she is," retorted Kiyomi. "Everyone in ni-
honmachi and miles around have been talking about her beauty."
Smiling openly, she fondled Sayo's kimono sleeve. "But I am pleased
to meet you and see that all the rumors are true. I love your kimono. Is it silk?" Her voice held no envy.*

*Neck and face flushing, Sayo attempted to answer Kiyomi's in-
genuous words with proper grace. "Arigato gozaimasu. You are very
kind." Noticing Kiyomi's worn cotton yukata, she offered, "Yes, this is
silk . . . but I find it much too warm for this climate. Stupid of me to
wear it." She looked Kiyomi full in the face, liking her despite the*

possibility she might be a rival for Cloud. "Please borrow it anytime. In fact, I would like to give it to you."

Eyes round as her open mouth, Kiyomi exclaimed, "Oh . . . you truly are an elegant woman! So nice as well as beautiful. I hope Hiroshi-san appreciates you." She led Sayo to the other women and introduced them. Jade Young Moon and Night Jasmine, slim as bamboo flutes, giggled and hugged, eager as young pups. Sayo wondered how they came to be living in San Jose's Japantown, seeming so young to have been brides for Chinese bachelors. Both wore their hair in braids, wrapped around their heads like halos. Jade Young Moon was exceptionally beautiful, with white porcelain skin, tiny chiseled features, a petite rosebud mouth, and dainty petal nostrils flaring from a narrow nose. Night Jasmine's otherwise perfect ivory-complexioned face was marred by pockmarks.

Two other Japanese women, both older than Kiyomi and the Chinese girls, were also friendly, welcoming her like a long-lost relative. Sayo basked in their feminine warmth, reminded of how much she missed Chiba and Mentor. Since her arrival she had not befriended any women and missed the camaraderie she shared with the brides on the boat.

"Where do you live?" she asked Kiyomi.

After hesitating, looking questioningly at Cloud and Ito, she said, "We live at the New Moon Inn."

"New Moon Inn?"

"The brothel here in Japantown." Kiyomi spoke bluntly, but without crassness.

Sayo was momentarily at a loss for words but quickly recovered her composure. "I would like to visit your home sometime," she said without condescension. "I believe it is not far from the Persimmon House, where I live."

"Please do. We would love to have a female visitor." She giggled, covering her mouth with a kimono sleeve. "But only when Manzo is gone."

"Manzo?"

"He's our manager . . . or rather, pimp." She stopped smiling. "We don't like him. But he's gone a lot."

Overhearing their conversation, Cloud interrupted, speaking di-

rectly to Sayo. "Won't you sit down? I haven't seen you for a while."
He patted a spot next to him.

Grateful for the interruption and Cloud's pointed invitation, she
sat down, barely able to disguise her pleasure. Hiroshi had seated
himself amidst the Chinese girls and other women.

"How is your work with the bachelors?" she asked, gazing fully at
his face, admiring the dark features she had tried to recall as she
reminisced during the past weeks.

He sipped his wine, eyes studying her over the cup's rim. "Frankly,
pretty boring. But, things might become more challenging." He swal-
lowed, still looking at her closely. "I hear from Hiroshi you are help-
ing him with his business. Any luck?"

Gratified to know he was interested enough to talk about her
with Hiroshi, she smiled unabashedly, dissolving her last bit of re-
serve.

"I haven't found a site yet. But I plan to be more aggressive next
week."

He chuckled, "I'd like to see you be 'aggressive,' Sayo-san . . . do
you plan on carrying a sword?"

She laughed, warmed by his familiarity. "Maybe."

She began to confide. "I told Hiroshi I would assist him with his
search for a business place, and he could paint, as you know how
much he loves art. And I want him to be happy. I promised his
mother I would see to his happiness before mine."

He was silent, staring at his wine.

Unsure why he was quiet, she continued, "He is good . . . isn't
he?"

"Of course . . . of course, he's very good."

"And to be honest, it is a good feeling to be of use. I know how
much he hates business, but his family expects it. I am his wife and
obligated, so I have to help him. I've even suggested he go to San
Francisco some weekends to visit and paint with his artist friends."

Cloud dropped his cup, spilling the last dregs of wine. He coughed
slightly. "Excuse me."

She wanted to tell him she had been shocked at first to know
Hiroshi had painted a nude woman, a hakujin *woman, at that. But*
not familiar with art, she felt she could not judge his world from the

narrow perspective of hers. Besides, she liked that particular paint-
ing, the radiant blue eyes and soft round body, plump white breasts
that gleamed like mochi *moon cakes.*

"Do you know his artist friends?"

Cloud avoided her eyes. "Yes. I didn't know he's been going to
San Francisco. He hasn't said as much while working on the farm
lately."

Withdrawn now, he twisted the empty cup in his hands. What
had she said to have caused this sudden remoteness?

Kiyomi reappeared with a platter of teriyaki chicken, sold at the
temple food concession. Seating herself beside them, she served the
chicken on small plates retrieved from the picnic basket.

"Let's enjoy the food before it spoils in the heat."

Brows furrowed, Cloud ate quietly, ignoring Kiyomi, who di-
rected her conversation to him. "Cloud-san, why have we not seen
you at the New Moon lately? We miss you." She sucked on a bone,
eyeing him coyly. "Did you notice I brought your favorite wine?"

Sayo felt a twinge of jealousy, but it passed as she noticed his an-
noyance at Kiyomi. Besides, why wouldn't he frequent a brothel,
being a bachelor, and to her knowledge, leading a lonely existence
like the other men.

Abruptly, he got up and motioned to Hiroshi, who was sur-
rounded by the Chinese girls and other women from the brothel.
They stood apart from the group under a close-by tree and seemed
engrossed in intense conversation. Hiroshi stared up at Cloud in a
defensive manner. Whatever they were discussing, Sayo could tell it
was serious, with Cloud's green eyes flashing fire, noticeable even
from a distance. He looked like a tiger ready to seize a prey. She
was reminded of his swift attack on Daley, fist shooting out like
lightning. Uneasy, she watched as if her stare would prevent their
talk from accelerating into fisticuffs. What was this all about? Cloud
was such a mystery. There was so much unsaid between them, or
was she just imagining this? Perhaps she had misread his feelings,
forgetting his culture was different even from that of the white ghosts,
the American culture of which she also knew so little. Because of his
knowledge of Japanese, she may have mistakenly thought they un-
derstood each other.

"May I sit here?" It was Ito, the only male wearing Japanese dress—a brown kimono with dark belt slung low on his hips.

Somewhat relieved to be distracted from her husband's drama, she invited him to join her, remembering how kind he had been at the compound.

"We miss you, older sister. Life at the new farm is joyless without you."

"You are too kind, Ito-san. But surely you will not stay long there . . . as a bachelor, I mean." She knew he had come to America even before Hiroshi and wondered why he had not sent for a picture bride. Although not from a background as wealthy as Hiroshi's, he was well-bred and could attract a personable woman from Japan. *"Forgive me for being too inquisitive, but have you considered shashin kekkon? You have been alone much too long."*

Smiling in his gentle way, he said, "I know it must appear strange that after all this time here I haven't acquired a bride . . . or even sought solace from available women. But celibacy is not a problem for me. You see, I was a Buddhist monk before I came to America."

She was not surprised. He would have been an impeccable monk. She easily could imagine him robed in brown burlap, head shaved, meditating for days in a stark temple. Noticing Cloud and Hiroshi had disappeared, she was pleased to have his company and encouraged him to talk more. "Why did you come to America?"

"One day during meditation I experienced a vision. I saw clear running rivers filled with huge orange fish swimming against the current, leaping over rocks into the air. Purple trees lined the banks, and overhead birds of every hue flew. I even smelled the sweet scent of jasmine. Was this the vision of the Pure Land? I had wondered. For months the image recurred during meditation. I began to feel uneasy with my practice. Was this the ascetic life I wanted?

"One day a monk who had traveled in America came to the temple. He talked of an open land, virgin forests, crystal rivers flowing untouched by humans. When he spoke of salmon struggling up the river's torrents to spawn their eggs and then die, I was deeply moved, and realized what my vision meant. It was not the Pure Land I had seen. It was America, and my karma was to go there."

*Touched by his story, Sayo's lips quivered as she asked softly,
"And did you ever see the salmon swim upriver?"*

*"No, unfortunately." He poured himself some wine. "But being in
this country for as long as I have, I now know the struggle up the
river is my own journey . . . I am the fish." He made the statement
without bitterness. "Now I accept each day's unfolding without attachment. Everything works out. Life is beautiful."*

*Eyes filled with tears, she said, "I am so fortunate to know you,
Ito-san. Please accept my most loyal friendship."*

*"That is understood without saying." Pausing, he drank from his
cup. "You have the fine quality of attracting deep loyalties. I see
Cloud already is devoted to you."*

*She felt her neck flush. But she knew Ito meant no disrespect.
"Oh, how do you know that?"*

*"Cloud is an unusual man, an Indian, you know. He does not
talk much, but his spirit is deep. He knows much more about hakujin than we do—their tricks, their strengths, and their follies. He is a
leader and, I think, sees some of his own talents in you."*

"Is it obvious to others?" Worry lining her forehead.

*"No. Most of us are too concerned with our own dramas to be
aware of others'."*

"What about Hiroshi?"

"You mean, is he aware of Cloud's attraction?"

"No. What do you think of him?"

*"Hiroshi is a good man, a gentleman. But he is weak, if I may
say so. And . . . perhaps, he has been seduced by pleasures of the
senses." He waited before going on. "I think he is falling in love with
you, but he has no idea who you really are."*

*Sayo was silent, mulling over Ito's clear and revealing percep-
tions of Cloud, Hiroshi, and herself. She trusted his views, as bru-
tally honest as they were.*

"Thank you, Ito-san. You are a true friend."

*He smiled, and Sayo wondered why she never had noticed be-
fore how he looked so saintly, how his wisdom seemed to match
Mentor's.*

*"Perhaps I, too, am an orange fish swimming against the cur-
rents," she said.*

"You may swim against the currents, but unlike the orange fish, you will survive."

The picnic ended at sundown. Hiroshi had returned to the grounds without Cloud, who he reported had gone to Watsonville for a week or so and sent his "good-byes." Sayo walked with Hiroshi back to town, dejected that her talk with Cloud had been so brief. Empty basket swaying in her hand, and Hiroshi slightly drunk and stumbling, they looked like weary pilgrims on the road to Edo. She was curious about the conversation between Hiroshi and Cloud, but seeing her husband's condition, knew she would have to wait to ask.

The next day, he announced he was going to San Francisco to paint while Cloud worked in Watsonville. At first troubled at being left alone without either man nearby, she quickly regained confidence in her new role with Hiroshi and refrained from asking questions. It would give her time to continue searching for a factory site.

Before he left, she did ask what had transpired with Cloud at the picnic. Eyes round with innocence, he asked, "What talk?"

Not to be put aside, Sayo said, "When you talked privately under the tree and then you both disappeared. You seemed to be arguing."

"Oh, that . . ." he stumbled for words. "We weren't arguing, just talking about work matters. Why do you ask?"

"Cloud is your loyal friend, and I don't want to see any problem between you."

Hiroshi remained quiet, biting his underlip. "Yes, I know." Then, almost petulantly, "He's your loyal friend, too."

She felt her face grow warm. He sat on the driver's seat, gazing at her with languid, sad eyes. She noticed his face was thinner, somewhat haggard, and with a pallid complexion. He seemed to have lost the buoyant vigor of earlier days. For one moment, she saw Lady Matsubara gently urging her to nurture her favorite son. Then she thought she heard a crow caw, and coldness swept over her, cooling her face. Unable to answer, she bowed deeply. "Have a safe journey and enjoy your painting."

"Thank you," he said politely and turned his attention to the horses. He was soon wheeling up the road toward San Francisco.

A *few days later she met Kiyomi accidentally in front of the barbershop.*

"Sayo-san, I'm so happy to run into you. I was even considering coming by your boardinghouse."

"Why didn't you? Please feel free to drop by anytime."

"I understand you are looking for space to rent for a business."

"How did you know that?"

Kiyomi grinned. "I have ways of finding out things. And I hear the men running the cane furniture shop are leaving for Los Angeles. Their building might be available."

"Oh, thank you, Kiyomi-san. What good news!" Sayo felt gratitude sweep over her, erasing any residue of jealousy she had felt about Cloud. "Can you take me there to see the place?"

"With pleasure, Sayo-san. How about tomorrow afternoon? Can you come by the New Moon at two o'clock?"

"I will be there . . . and thank you so much again." Before parting she asked, "Did Cloud-san tell you I was looking for a building?"

"No. This is a small village. Word gets around very quickly. At the inn we get all the latest gossip, true and untrue." She hesitated. "I hope you will not be offended if I tell you how ridiculous the gossip is." She giggled. "One of my customers, a truly stupid man, said you were looking for space to start a geisha house!"

"That is not a bad idea! In fact, if the shoyu plans fail, that is exactly what I will do!" The thought of a Matsubara Geisha House seemed so absurd, she laughed, imagining her delicate mother-in-law and Ichiro, the eldest son, swooning with humiliation; Tadanoshin, on the other hand, might react differently. As Mentor once said, true power was the capability to accept all that life threw at one, even downfall. Her father-in-law seemed the embodiment of this power. She speculated he probably would make a success of such a venture—and enjoy himself greatly doing it.

Joining Sayo's joke, Kiyomi added, "And your inn will be the classiest Japanese teahouse in the New World!"

* * *

The next day she paid a call on the New Moon Inn. She knocked on the cream-colored door, discreetly peering through its lace-curtained window. No one in sight. She heard a light pattering of bare feet, and Kiyomi opened the door, welcoming her with contin-uous bows and smiles, then led her through the front rooms to the kitchen, where a round table with chairs took up much of the space. While Kiyomi prepared tea, Sayo sat at the table, glancing through the open doorway to the bare, clean rooms they had passed. Dark brown carpeting of blue and beige flowers covered both the living and dining room. A long wicker couch extended along one wall, above which hung a large oval mirror. In the cor-ner Sayo could see a floor lamp with fringed shade. She assumed the bedrooms were upstairs.

Pouring tea into blue-and-white china cups, Kiyomi asked, "What is Hiroshi doing in San Francisco?"

"How did you know he was in San Francisco?" Again, Sayo is surprised at how Kiyomi seems to know so much about her life.

"Like I told you, we hear everything," she chortled. "It's interest-ing how those close-mouthed stone men, so tough, fall apart when they're in bed without clothes on." Noticing Sayo's pink face, she apologized. "Forgive me. Being in this profession has hardened me, and, truthfully, it has been a long time since I have even talked with a lady such as you."

"Please . . . I am not offended." In fact, Sayo was more than slightly curious about what went on in the New Moon, and about the pasts of the women working there. "And please forgive my ask-ing, but were you a shashin kekkon?"

Kiyomi seemed pleased by her inquiry. "I am from a village out-side Nagasaki. I believe my family still lives there. We were poor . . . nine children. I was sold to a geisha house in Fukuoka, but I ran away. I met a man who told me about America, that there was much money and a need for Japanese women in my trade. So I left Japan."

"Then if you weren't a picture bride, how did you get through immigration?"

Kiyomi's black eyes glinted mischievously. "I was smuggled over

*from Mexico." Enjoying Sayo's incredulous look, she laughed and
continued. "The man who told me about America paid for my passage and four other women. We lived in Mexico for some months
and then were smuggled over the border to California in a fishing
boat. See, I still remember a few Spanish words,* Buenas dias, muchas
gracias.

*"I have lived in Brawley, Seattle, San Francisco, and now here. I
suppose I will travel south to Los Angeles next."*

"And have you always worked . . . in a brothel?"

"Not always. But I made my living serving men."

*"Again, forgive my curiosity. But is your profession similar to the
art of geisha? What is expected of you?"*

*Kiyomi laughed loudly. "We are not geisha. How wonderful if we
could be. It's very simple. Men pay to pillow with us."*

*Encouraged by Kiyomi's openness, Sayo asked questions without
reservation and soon learned that Manzo, their "pimp," was often
away, either in Sacramento or San Francisco. She also learned that
Jade Young Moon and Night Jasmine had been sold to a Chinese
man for whom Kiyomi also worked. When Kiyomi met Manzo and
joined his brothel in San Jose, she brought the two girls with her.*

*"I know life must have been hard for all of you," Sayo sympa-
thized. "I hope things are better here."*

*"Much better. We have very nice regular customers . . . bachelors
from the farms, even some* hakujin. *You'd be surprised who comes
here."*

*Despite the intimacy of their conversation, Sayo was embar-
rassed to bring up Cloud, but to her gratification, Kiyomi broke the
ice. "Cloud has been a good friend to all of us for the past two years.
I will admit I was once in love with him . . . all of us were. He is gal-
lant, such a giant among men . . . don't you think?"*

"Was he in love with you?"

*"Of course not." Kiyomi's usual high voice lowered with respect.
"Cloud-san is mysterious. It is amazing how well he speaks Japanese
and understands our ways. But he is also unknowable. He comes
and goes, quiet, like a forest animal."*

"Did you pillow with him?"

"Of course, but only to serve him physically. After all, he is a vir-

ile man, like most leaders." She paused. "Since your arrival he has not visited us." She teased Sayo, fluttering her short lashes. "I think he is in love with you."

"Really? Why do you think so?"

"I know men. I have noticed how he looks at you. Pity you're married to his best friend."

Sayo was quiet for some moments. "Nothing has happened between us, you know. He is an honorable man."

"I guessed that. But I truly don't understand why Hiroshi goes to San Francisco and leaves you here alone for all the wolves to devour you. Is he crazy? And Cloud-san, too. He should be protecting you!" With each sentence, Kiyomi became more incensed.

Attempting to justify the men's actions, Sayo explained, "I don't mind Hiroshi's trips to the city. In fact, I have encouraged him to pursue his love of painting. I promised his mother I would see to his happiness. As for Cloud, he owes me nothing."

Kiyomi studied Sayo, weighing her next words. "For such a worldly-looking woman, you are very naive. This is America, Sayo-san. Duty to family comes after *duty to oneself. Selfish as it sounds, you must think of yourself."*

Oddly, Kiyomi sounded very much like Mentor. Of course, she didn't have the old geisha's refinement, but her wisdom was refreshingly primitive and to the point.

"Thank you for your concern, Kiyomi-san. I do forget things are different in America. But, in all honesty, I think I can get more things done without Hiroshi here."

Kiyomi nodded in agreement, and the two finished sipping tea, cheeks flushed with pleasure—by their intimate talk and the satisfaction of having forged a close friendship in so short a time.

After Kiyomi changed her kimono, they walked to a section near the edge of town where several warehouse buildings lined a street. At one of the buildings they peered through a large window caked with oily dust. Bundles of cane and wood and several unfinished chairs were strewn about a debris-laden cement floor. The huge room looked cold, even in summer heat.

"Have they left already?" asked Sayo.

Kiyomi's face was troubled. "If they have, it means they left in a hurry. What decent nihonjin *would leave a place in this condition?"*

"Who were they?"

"I don't know them myself. But Night Jasmine says one is a gambler. My guess is they owe money and have flown the coop. You'll never get the rental now."

"Why not?"

"Because the owners are hakujin. *They'll never rent to* nihonjin *again if those two have swindled him. Such dog shit, they are!" Kiyomi worked herself into a rage, convinced the furniture makers were gone already to Los Angeles.*

Calming her, Sayo said, "Don't upset yourself, Kiyomi-san. There are other buildings if it is true they've left. Let's wait. We've plenty of time," she fibbed.

"I'm sorry to have let you down, Sayo-san."

"It's not your fault. And besides, we don't know what's really happened yet."

Christmas, 1942

Manzanar

To Hana, the riot had cleansed the air. After smoldering underground for weeks, powerful forces had finally collided, exploding like a volcanic eruption. But instead of gray ash filtering down from the heavens, snow began falling, blanketing the bloodstained desert in white, silencing echoes of drumbeats and shouts and gunfire. Two men were killed, four wounded. Suddenly the soldiers left camp. The military presence was gone, leaving the guard towers empty.

Hana is grateful no one in the family was hurt during the whole episode. Knowing Tad and Mac were trying to thwart the trouble-makers, she had worried there would be a fight. At the jail they had hoped to inform the military police Buffalo was not responsible for Shimmy's beating. But their purpose was foiled by the gangs milling out front. It was impossible to get through to the door.

"This is no place for us," Sayo said. "We must leave here quickly. Do you see Tad and Mac? We must warn them to leave!" Hana felt the urgency in Sayo's voice. They couldn't find the two men. "They're not here. Maybe they're inside," said Hana.

Sayo already was hurrying down the oiled road, against the current of men and a few women descending upon the firebreak. "Where are you going?"

"My God, we must get to the hospital! The mob will go after Shimmy next! We must warn them!"

Hana was out the door before Sayo. They ran across the firebreak past the Children's Village to the barracks that served as the camp infirmary. The compound was quiet. In one of the wards a few volunteer nurses' aides were ministering to patients.

But when they entered another barracks ward, they were shocked to see a group of men loitering in the aisle between rows of empty beds, Tad and Mac among them.

"What in hell . . ." sputtered Tad.

"There's a mob gathering at the jail," Sayo said. "They might come here after Shimmy."

Mac said, "That's why we're here. We know they would come for Shimmy with the word going around that he fingered Buffalo as the attacker."

"Where is he?" Hana said.

Tad answered almost coyly, "We've hidden him."

"Where?" both women asked in unison.

"Under the table in the operating room."

If the situation hadn't been so serious, Hana would have laughed. It all seemed so ludicrous. Hiding him under an operating table! But as it turned out, the ploy worked. When a renegade group from the crowd at the jail pounded on the hospital doors, the doctor reprimanded them.

"Shimmy is not here. He's been transferred to Lone Pine. You are disturbing the patients and the operation Dr. Imari is now performing! You will be held responsible if anything happens!"

After some muttering and threats to the doctor, the mob dispersed, returning to the jail, where their thirst for violence might be appeased. Inside the hospital Sayo and Hana listened to the yelling of the crowd, the military bullhorns droning orders . . . and then the rifles firing. They had congregated in the operating room, determined to protect Shimmy with their own bodies if the mob, in its helpless fury, decided to overrun the hospital. But, thank God, that did not happen. After the crackling rifle shots, an eerie silence hung over the desert valley. Even the slight breeze blowing that night ceased. It was as if time stood still so that the appalling moment could be burned into the brains of every witness.

Hana sees Shimmy's sheet-draped body under the operating table, bandaged head lightly covered with a towel. Her heart races as she remembers the gang pounding on the doors, ready to kill him or anyone protecting him. Her hands sweat. Then she looks out at the snow-covered desert, the startling contrast of tar-paper black walls and white roofs. The quietness is soothing, the air heavy and cold like a shawl muffling sighs of a child in the aftermath of a temper tantrum.

It was Sayo who gave the message from Shimmy that the orphanage needed help for a Christmas party and that the children had asked for her. "What a compliment," Sayo had said. "Even a small kindness will be remembered forever by those children. It is good that you and Shimmy are using your time in this prison so positively."

Sayo did not seem to suspect anything hidden in her relationship with Shimmy. And what was her relationship with him? Why did she feel so culpable? Shimmy had never said nor done anything that indicated he cared for her other than as a friend. He is faultless. It's all in her own mind.

With the peacoat wrapped tightly around her, she walks over the thin layer of snow in the firebreak. The leafless trees of the orchard are dark skeletons raising spiny arms to the sky. Up at the orphanage, winter has transformed the landscape, blanketing the rock garden in white and freezing the pool's water into a shiny crystal crust. Remembering helping Shimmy a few months before, she can hardly imagine being so hot and perspiring in the sun as she blows on her gloveless hands to warm them.

Inside the recreation room she finds him chatting with the home managers. He looks slightly pale, a bruise above his left eye shining purple like the skin of an eggplant. The white of the same eye is deep red. He greets her with his usual cheerfulness, "Here she is! Now we're sure to have a great fiesta for the kids." A sadness seeps through his smiling eyes. She realizes how traumatic the attack must have been, not only as a physical assault but also because of the hatred and rage he must have felt from his attackers. Shimmy, more than most, wants to be accepted, to be liked. He had told her that. How humiliating to be the target of such violence.

The managers leave. She and Shimmy are now alone, sitting at the square wooden table. She feels shy, not knowing quite what to say. Would it be embarrassing to bring up the hospital incident? Her uneasiness abates when he says, "It was pretty spooky lying there under the operating table. I kept thinking there might be an emergency and the doc would have to operate on someone right above me! I heard everything, and I never felt so grateful for friends in my life. Your mother is terrific, helping me recuperate. And I owe a lot to your husband and son. And . . . of course, to you."

Her shyness disappears with his openness. "I was so worried about you, Shimmy. I wanted to visit after you came home from the hospital, but Tad was sick, you know." She gazes at his battered face. Tears gather and, to her embarrassment, trickle down her cheeks.

Tad had come down with a bad cold and was childishly demanding, wanting her to remain inside the barracks during the whole time he was bedridden. Feeling guilty for her thoughts of Shimmy, she relapsed into her former role with Tad, quietly soothing his complaints with hot mustard plasters and backrubs, sitting by his cot, ready to jump at his command.

He grabs her hands across the table. "Hey, I'm okay. Really. I understand. I'm just so glad you treat me like family. You know I never had one."

Her heart sinks. Yes, it's all in her own mind, her fantasy. He sees her as a friend only, maybe even an "auntie."

"Guess what?" he chatters on. "The new administration is bringing a big Christmas tree for the children here. How about that? We'll need to figure out how to decorate it. I guess one way to look at the riot is that it caused a lot of changes. The soldiers are gone, and we have a civilian director who feels bad about what happened. So now they're distributing trees to the block mess halls, too."

"Really? I hadn't heard about that. Everything seems to happen so quickly. It's strange looking at those empty guard towers. The soldiers were gone so fast."

She steers away from asking personal questions and concentrates on the Christmas tree decorations.

"Let's fold paper into cranes and fans for decorations. We don't have origami, but we can use colored paper or paint them."

"Great idea! I knew you would think of something."

"We also can paint small pieces of driftwood and rocks and wrap them in colored yarns."

"Wonderful."

Shimmy still holds her hands, his brown fingers clasped around hers, firm and warm. Should she withdraw them? She sits frozen, again at a loss for words. As if reading her thoughts, he loosens his grip and releases her hands, all in a smooth natural way.

At that moment, the house managers enter with several children. She wonders if that's why he withdrew his hands. Hope kindles in her heart. Perhaps he is flirting and she is too inexperienced with men to know it. After all, she is married. He has to be covert . . . unless she makes a move, says something. That much she does know. This lifts her spirits, and she greets the children with unexpected hugs and endearing words, which they receive enthusiastically. She is aware of Shimmy watching with approval, even admiration.

That evening, back at the compartment, she sits by the oil stove folding cranes. Tad and Mac play pinochle at the table, and Carmen lounges on her cot reading some outdated *Silver Screen* magazines. Snow blows heavily in the wind, thudding against the windows like saturated cotton. The compartment is warm and cozy, and Hana thinks of the days before Christmas at Venice when the family decorated the tree together, days when they hid in their rooms to secretly wrap gifts. She remembers the Japanese meal of tempura, sukiyaki, and sushi on Christmas Eve, the turkey dinner on Christmas day. Nostalgia sweeps over her. Would the family ever be the same again? No one has even mentioned Christmas, hardly inquiring about the party at the orphanage. And Tad declined to take a tree from the mess hall where the administration had left a pile for the internees. It's like any other day . . . except for the snow, the beautiful translucent flakes that seem to soften the harsh reality of tar-papered shacks and bleak desert landscape. It's Hana's first taste of snow. Aside from the unexpected coldness, she loves the stillness and the shock of stark white, nothing she could imagine from her southern California background, or even from photographs and Christmas cards depicting winter scenes. Somehow, the muffled whiteness makes her feel safe.

*   *   *

At the orphanage recreation room she helps Shimmy drape red crepe paper ribbon from the ceiling and around the doors. The crepe paper rolls were donated by the American Friends Service Committee, he tells her, along with some presents. Even mistletoe, too, he says. The older children are hanging decorations on the large tree, Hana's cranes and their own made of colored-paper cutouts, painted driftwood, yarn-wrapped bits of cardboard. House Manager Suzuki has persuaded the cook to bake cookies, despite the sugar shortage. The children are cheerful, and for the first time, the hall is filled with laughter and chatter. Hana realizes how light the room feels, how buoyant she herself feels. Such a contrast to the suffocating dullness of the compartment where Tad and Mac and Carmen mostly brood and sulk. She admits her own moods have added to the heavy atmosphere. *We each have been living in our own worlds,* she thinks. *No longer sharing in common goals.* But she is not certain if she wants to leave her new separate world and share herself with the family.

The children begin singing Christmas carols. She notices Shimmy has disappeared. After "Jingle Bells," a loud clanging sounds from the hall and a deep voice calls "Ho, Ho, Ho."

"It's Santa Claus!" squeals one of the children.

Crashing into the room, stomps a round, white-bearded Santa banging on a pan with a large metal spoon. Has Pot-Banger joined the party? No. It is Shimmy. Following him is House Manager with a large sack filled with presents, which Santa distributes to the delighted children.

One of the older children announces they have a gift for both Santa and Hana and calls them to a spot near the entryway. She moves shyly next to Shimmy, whose smiling eyes peer at her from under heavy white cotton eyebrows. She can smell glue holding the cotton beard to his face.

"Kiss! Kiss! Kiss!" the children scream. She looks up and sees mistletoe hanging above. Before she can react, Shimmy laughingly kisses her on the mouth, a gentle, moist kiss, quick and precise.

"Merry Christmas, Hana," he says.

Too stunned to respond, she accepts from one of the children a small gift wrapped in painted paper and beribboned with bright colored yarn. She finally manages to say. "Thank you."

Walking home, she clutches in her coat pocket the painted rock given her by the children. Smooth and oblong, with a flat surface, it pictures an angel with a needle and thread in her hands. The words "To Hana, our Angel" are printed at the bottom. She had been so touched by the gift, she had wept. Santa-Shimmy had to dry her cheeks with a handkerchief, which thrilled the children even more.

With her other hand, she touches her lips and mouth, wondering if his lips felt what her fingers feel—soft, warm, pliable flesh. She still can smell the glue, taste the moistness of his mouth. Whatever his feelings are for her, Hana now knows they are not shallow or frivolous. She must think of a way and bolster courage to express her own. What has she got to lose? She knows he would never judge her if she made a fool of herself. He would never allow her to feel shame. But what would she do if he confesses he loves her? This thought is frightening, more frightening than her challenge to herself to be open and honest.

The late afternoon light is turning blue-gray. Except for a few figures moving in the landscape, the white expanse is still, a frozen tableau of a Hiroshige woodcut. She wonders if the snow truly has mollified the raging emotions that climaxed in the riot. For herself, it brings a sense of peace. Her heart lifts as it begins to snow. Cold crystals brush her face; gentle wisps soothe the fire of a breaking fever.

Aftermath

Manzanar

"Teru-chan, you must stop your brooding. Enough time has passed since the riot, if that is what's depressing you," Sayo says gently. "Or is it because you have begun your period? I am worried about your health. This mourning is abnormal."

Terri sees her grandmother's concerned face, eyes unusually penetrating. She wishes she could sleep away the day, stop the sounds of gunshots and yelling, the images of enraged men and faceless soldiers, Billy's shocked expression. She returns her grandmother's gaze with listless eyes. Why does her chest ache as though it is tightly bound by an *obi,* the way it felt when she was younger and dressed in kimono? Her breath is a sigh. She forces herself to speak. "Obachan, I'm really okay. I'm just sad." Her heart releases its bindings, tears begin to flow. The floodgate is open and she sobs loudly, rocking back and forth on the futon.

Sayo sits down and cradles her, wiping the tears with her own kimono sleeve. She remains silent, allowing Terri to vent whatever sorrow she has been carrying these past weeks. She waits patiently while Terri wails, thinking how her laments seem more like the grieving of an abandoned lover.

Finally, Terri's paroxysm is over. Spent, she hiccups and averts her face from Sayo's.

"Why don't you tell me what's really the matter."

Silence.

"Is it something I have done?"

"Oh no, Grandma. You haven't done anything. I'm the one who has."

"You can tell me. There's nothing you could do that would upset me. Really."

Terri stares down at her hands, still quiet.

"Grandma, would you think I was terrible if I told you how I broke the law?"

"What law? There are no laws in this place. Only the ones put on us by the administration. As far as I'm concerned, those laws were made only to be broken. What could you have done to break any?"

"Well . . . I went outside the barbed wire."

"Yes? But obviously no one caught you because you were not shot. Were you alone?"

"No."

"With Mitzi?"

"No."

Sayo sits quietly, pondering what Terri might be attempting to tell her. Could she have been involved with some boy?

Terri blurts, "I went with the soldiers!"

Sayo tries to hide her shock. She realizes the situation may be worse than she could have imagined. But Terri just began her period, at least she is not pregnant. She tries to be tactful. "Who were these soldiers?"

Eager to tell all, she relates how she had befriended Billy, how he had given her chewing gum and brought movie magazines.

Sayo glances over at the *Silver Screen* magazines. A smiling blond movie star beams from the cover. Betty Grable.

"He wanted to meet Carmen at first and brought the magazines for her."

While Sayo listens, showing no signs of shock or judgment, Terri babbles on, recounting how Billy and Skip became her friends, the card games in the gully and the excursions to the pool. "And Obachan, I think we discovered a holy place."

This catches Sayo's attention. "What? Tell me about this place."

"It's a cave not too far from the pool, like the shrines you told me about. There are bones, and old Indian stuff there. I know it's holy, Grandma . . . or haunted."

"Did you see any ghosts?"

"No, I didn't see any. But there are spirits. I felt them. Billy and Skip were spooked by the place. I wish you could go there, Grandma. You'd know what it is."

An impish look crosses Sayo's face. "Well, why don't we go then?"

"No kidding?" Terri is surprised, but only for a second. She knows how unpredictable her grandmother is. "But . . . it's outside the fence."

"The soldiers are gone. Who will shoot us?"

At the mention of shooting, Terri is plunged back into a dark mood. "Teru-chan, did you know any of the boys who were shot during the riot?"

She shakes her head.

"Then were your soldier friends there?"

Terri nods and begins to cry again. "Billy was there. He fired his rifle. I saw him." She sobs, shoulders heaving. "I trusted him. And he did that. Now he's gone and I'll never see him again."

"Teru-chan, he is a soldier. He was following orders. I'm sure he did not like what he had to do."

She stops crying. "Yes, he looked very shocked and unhappy. And he did warn me about going where there were crowds. He told me to warn you, too. But I didn't know how to tell you. Maybe if I had there wouldn't have been the riot." She cries again.

"The riot is not your fault! It's not any one person's fault. It's what happens when people are penned up and miserable. The *yogores* blame Shimmy, the military blames Buffalo, the people blame the black-marketing soldiers. Even if I had known, I could not have stopped it."

Terri seems appeased by Sayo's words. "Would you really like to go to the cave?"

"Of course. Anytime you would like. But you must start eating again and gain back some strength."

Quiet. "Obachan, do you think Billy is sorry about the shooting? I'll probably never see him again and will never know."

"One never knows what the purpose of tragic events are until later. . . . But, I would say he is very sorry, and you will know it."

"But how?"

"I'm not sure. But I am certain he has not disappeared from your life."

Eager to believe this, Terri accepts her grandmother's words wholeheartedly. She jumps up from the futon and rummages in a basket, retrieving the scarf and wool gloves. "He gave me these."

"They are very practical gifts."

"He gave them because I was cold." Terri looks dreamily at the scarf and gloves. "He always was so kind and funny."

"Well, wear them when we visit the holy cave. We will go when it stops snowing."

Three days later Terri awakens to a dazzling white morning, with the sun lighting a pristine blue sky. Not a cloud in sight. Obachan is gone, her futon folded in a corner. Terri rises, hoping she is not too late for mess hall. For the first time in weeks, she feels hungry.

Obachan and Hana are still seated at one of the tables. Terri joins them, her thick white army plate heaped with French toast and dripping with melted margarine and syrup.

"Good to see you eating again," says Obachan.

Hana looks at Terri as if seeing her for the first time. "I'm sorry I didn't notice you weren't eating. But you must be feeling better now."

Knowing the burden of guilt, Terri does not want her mother to carry it, too. "I'm okay, Mom. Everything was so crazy around here, how could anyone notice anything else but the trouble?" Terri sees her mother's slumped shoulders straightening. Her thin nose is no longer pinched.

Terri gobbles the too-sweet fried bread, self-conscious as her grandmother and mother scrutinize every morsel chewed and swallowed. She is unaccustomed to this hovering, and wishes they would turn their attention from her.

Hana soon leaves to help at the Children's Village.

"Obachan, can we go to the cave today?"

"Yes. I've been thinking it is perfect. Let's get ready and leave as soon as possible."

They return to the tearoom and dress warmly, Terri in long khaki pants, peacoat cape, and army boots. Sayo still wears a kimono over long wool pants and sweater, wrapping her shoulders with a thick shawl. She also wears army boots. Terri dons Billy's gloves and scarf.

At the empty guard tower, looking more forlorn than ever with its scaling wood and glassless windows, Terri feels a twinge in her belly. She half expects to hear Billy's cheerful voice, the southern drawl she grew to love. She looks up and imagines his freckled face looming in the window, red hair glinting.

"Teru-chan, where do we go through the fence?"

Terri tries to fathom where the loose wire is located under the snowpack. Guessing it is right where Sayo is standing, she begins digging. Sayo helps her, and before long they expose the tan sand beneath and are able to scramble under the wire. Terri is amazed how supple her grandmother is as she easily slides through.

With the landscape transformed by snow, Terri is disoriented until she spots the line of tree limbs that mark the stream's path. They crunch over virgin drifts up to the clump of bare-branched trees and boulders. The pool is unfrozen, with thin crusts of ice floating about like large silvery lotus pads.

They hear the trickling waterfall emptying into the mini-canyon barely visible from above.

"Obachan, the cave is down in this canyon. Can you climb down these rocks?" Terri points to boulders flanking the fall.

Without answering, Sayo climbs nimbly down. At the bottom, they both stare in awe at the still green foliage lining the canyon walls. The air is oddly warm and smells of moss and musk.

Sayo's eyes drink in the vivid green, body responding to an unseen energy circulating throughout the gorge.

"You are right, Teru-chan," she whispers. "This is a magical place."

"Wait till you see the cave."

They follow the thin stream to the large boulder jutting out from the wall. Terri disappears behind it. Sayo follows. Inside the cave, it remains as Terri remembers it. Rocks, bones, driftwood, and baskets lay in tranquil sleep, still shrouded by spiderwebs. In the summer the air had been musty and cool. But now it is warm and smells pungently of sage.

"What do you think?"

Sayo does not respond. She stands by the artifact-laden shelf, staring at the bones as if she has seen a ghost.

"Are you okay, Grandma?"

Sayo replies in a shaking voice, "Yes, Teru-chan, this is a very special place. These bones are speaking to me, but I don't know what they're saying. It is as if I have been here before."

"But it is a good place, isn't it?"

"Yes it is . . . a place where one can pray to make miracles happen."

"Billy said Indians dug this cave."

Sayo nods. Tears glisten on her cheeks. "I knew an Indian once."

"Really, Grandma? When?"

"He was a wonderful man, the greatest man I ever knew."

"Tell me about him, won't you? I see ghosts in camp all the time."

Sayo sighs. Suddenly she appears very young to Terri, her sun- and wind-battered skin now smooth as porcelain. The graying hair is thick and luxuriously black, piled atop her head in pompadours, eyes smoldering coals. The smell of sandalwood permeates the cave, and Sayo begins to dance, swaying in a deep purple kimono that has replaced the worn brown one covering the military garb. A gilded fan flutters in her hand. The darkness is now transformed by a pale light, as if moon rays have snaked in through the opening around the boulder.

A form materializes next to Sayo, a smoky figure, tall and lean, with long black hair. It is a brave. Not the one from the Horimoto compound, but an older, very handsome man. Sayo does not see him and continues dancing. Terri exclaims, "Obachan! Look!"

As the words leave her mouth, the vision disappears. Sayo stands by the shelf, looking dejected in her drab kimono and army boots. Terri's shout has shocked her from her reverie.

"Someday I will tell you about him. But not now. It makes me too sad to think about that time in my life."

Unused to seeing her grandmother so depressed, Terri changes the subject in her mind. What can she do to create a miracle, to see Billy again?

As if reading her thoughts, Sayo says, "If you would like to hear from Billy, leave something of his on the shelf."

Terri removes the gloves and places them next to the rocks, gently pushing aside sticky cobwebs. She catches a whiff of tobacco, and sees Billy grinning as he flicks down a cigarette butt from his perch on the tower.

After Sayo meditates for some moments before the artifacts and Billy's gloves, they leave the sanctuary. Terri doesn't know how much time they have spent inside the cave and is surprised to see the sun is now high in the sky. As they trudge back to camp through the snow, Obachan is so quiet, Terri is anxious she may have changed her mind about the place. But her worries are unfounded.

"Thank you very much for telling me your secrets," Sayo says. "I feel something wonderful is going to happen. Perhaps it will make sense of our humiliating imprisonment in this barren desert."

Terri's gloveless hands are now red with cold. She remembers Billy's big hands warming hers. She realizes it no longer hurts to think about him. By remembering his acts of kindness rather than the pained, shocked face at the riot, she is able to recapture the joy of the good times. She smiles, picturing him with his demon red hair, blowing cigarette smoke from his nostrils and teaching her to play poker hunkered down in a sandy ditch.

Mochi

In the laundry room, now converted to a steamy *mochi* shop, Hana stands around the long mess-hall table with Sayo and a half-dozen women shaping globules of rubbery rice into patties. The riot had delayed preparations for making the rice cakes. Usually the ceremony, which meant pulverizing cooked rice grains into a glutinous mass and allowing the shaped cakes to dry into rock-hard mounds, began before Christmas, before *shogatsu*, the New Year, when man's spirit could be renewed.

Outside, several vats of cooking rice steam over charcoal fires tended by Tad and Mac and other men from the block. Next to the vats is a large hollowed stone into which the newly cooked rice is mounded, awaiting the rhythmical pounding of heavy wooden mallets wielded by two muscular youths. Hana observes the ritual through the open double doors of the laundry room. The steady beat of the mallets, punctuated by the men's grunts and barking shouts, take her back to the festive *mochi*-making times when she was a child growing up in the Heavenly Cloud Inn. She remembers the bachelors from the surrounding countryside congregating before the holiday, assisting her mother and the women of the inn with *shogatsu* preparations—pounding *mochi*, cleaning the big house and grounds around it. She remembers later days when Ito took over the ceremonial tasks and brought a masculine authority into their lives. He was such a solid presence, yet as gentle and kind as a house cat.

Mac has now taken over one of the pounding chores. He is shirtless and wears army jodhpurs that reach to his knees, exposing his lower legs. Around his head a rolled cotton bandanna catches dripping sweat. Steam rises from his hairless muscled chest and arms as cold air hits his body. Hana realizes her son is now a man, handsome and brawny, at the prime of his physical life. She thinks of *his* situation, how frustrated and bored he must be imprisoned in this mile-square camp. She notices the determined set of his jaw as he slings the mallet down on the quivering rice, barely missing the hand of the man dancing around the bowl, who is throwing water on the mass and deftly turning it over.

Shimmy appears and takes over the other pounding position. He, too, is shirtless and wears a white headband. The bronze torsos ripple and steam as the two men beat the *mochi*, transforming individual rice grains into one inseparable lump.

Sayo's words break the magical scene. "Those are two beautiful gods, if there could be such a thing in this camp." She nudges Hana's arm. "One is your son . . . and the other, someone very special." Hana keeps her eyes lowered, still too unsure to open herself to intimacy. What does her mother know?

The men bring the sticky lump to the table, where the women dust it with rice starch, smoothing the powder over the mound until it shines with a satin sheen. With starch-covered hands, they pinch off balls and shape them into half-moon patties, constantly dusting with the white powder. It is still cold, and the ground is covered with snow. Hana is warmed by the heat from the *mochi* cakes between her palms.

They work throughout the afternoon until Pot-Banger's meal call clangs outside the laundry room. They have just completed the last batch. Rows of rice cakes set on wooden planks line the room, stacked over tubs and attached to the walls like shelves. Not every block in camp is able to pound *mochi*, so those that can, make enough to share with others. From New Year's on, for weeks after, the hard patties will be softened in boiling water and then eaten with sauces of shoyu and sugar, or roasted soy flour and sugar. On New Year's morning, it is traditional to eat the boiled *mochi* in a soup broth called *ozoni*. Hana wonders if the mess hall will be able to provide the special soup.

She volunteers to stay behind and clean up the laundry room. After the family and other internees leave for the mess hall, Shimmy joins her.

"Haven't seen you since the Christmas party."

The bruise above his eye is barely discernible, a lavender shadow.

"Yes, I've missed you." She is surprised at the sureness in her voice. She waits to see if he will respond with his usual smile and a cheery remark, tactics she has noticed he uses to dilute any deeper meaning to her words. But he is quiet, sweeping away the starch on the table with some folded paper.

"I wanted to tell you that I'll be leaving camp for a while. I didn't want to go without letting you know."

"Where are you going? Are you on furlough?"

"No. I'm not supposed to talk about it. But it's for the United States Army. Secret stuff."

"But you will come back to camp?"

"That's what they tell me. I just wanted to let you know before I leave."

"When do you?"

"Tomorrow."

"Oh my God!" Her hand flies to her face, and she holds her cheek as if she has been slapped.

"But I'll be back. I'm sorry I can't explain more."

She feels weak. All her bravado to express herself has disappeared.

Shimmy is also quiet. They finish cleaning without speaking. Outside the double doors, they stand facing each other. It is dusk, and the dark sky is heavy with clouds. It begins to snow. They stand alone in the middle of the block, still as mountain pines, their navy coats turning white.

Hana hears herself say, "Promise you will see me as soon as you get back. There is something I need to tell you." Uttering those words, she feels her heart expand—as if a door has opened in her chest, allowing a rush of light to pour into a dark, closed room.

"I promise." He does not smile. His Boy Scout facade has fallen away. He turns toward Block 17, walking crisply over the newly fallen snow. She watches his broad back grow smaller as he nears the next block and disappears into the mess hall.

The day after Shimmy leaves, Hana and Tad have an argument, the first time in their marriage that a confrontation between them could be viewed as a fight. She overheard Tad and Mac talking about the possibility of Mac joining the army. There had been rumors about *nisei* men in Hawaii volunteering to form units.

"What the hell, why waste your best years rotting in this camp?" Tad says. "You'd be in a good situation because they wouldn't send you overseas. You'd probably end up as a clerk on stateside. They couldn't send you to the Pacific or Europe, you being a Jap and looking like the enemy." He speaks matter-of-factly, a father advising his son.

"I know. I'd join up if there was a chance. I heard from the grapevine Shimmy's being looked at for some secret military stuff. Wonder how he got chosen for that."

Hana has been sitting on the bed behind the partition embroidering. Up to that moment she thought Tad and Mac were just chatting to while away a cold and cheerless afternoon. But something in Mac's voice frightens her. He often talks about joining the army. She thought it was the usual talk of restless young men, more bravado than reality. But he sounds serious, as if he has reached a decision and there is no turning back.

Tad exclaims. "Hell, he wasn't chosen. He volunteered, just what you should do! Get yourself out of this shit-hole!"

Outraged by Tad's goading voice, she jumps to her feet and lunges past the partition. Flabbergasted by her sudden appearance and the wildness in her eyes, the two men stare.

"Shimmy didn't volunteer!" she screams. "He was assigned by the army!"

After a moment of stunned silence, Tad recovers his voice. "And how in hell do you know that? Since when has the military been reporting to you?"

"Sayo told me. Shimmy confided in Sayo before he left."

Unused to Hana speaking out about anything, Tad's displeasure shows in his flushed face and clenched jaws. He glares at her. "Well, whether Shimmy volunteered or not, joining the army might be a good thing for Mac. Why should he rot in this stinking place? He should be in college, not roaming around in this prison like a caged rat! Look at all the young guys . . . the best years of their lives spent doing nothing. Why do you think the riot happened? Frustration. That's what. He should get out of this place before there's more disaster!"

She refuses to be intimidated. "But the army isn't even allowing *nisei* soldiers to serve now. He can't volunteer. You are giving him false advice. And why should he join the army and fight for a country that puts us here in this prison?!" Her voice shakes.

Mac intervenes. "Hey, you guys. Stop it." Unsettled by his mother's strange behavior, he stands up and begins inching toward the door, hoping to make a quick exit. He never has seen her stand up to his father. The last thing he wants is to be cause for an argument between his parents.

Tad holds his temper in check, a flicker of respect replacing the anger in his eyes. "Okay . . . okay. Take it easy. What the hell's bothering you, anyway?"

Assured there would be no serious fight, Mac leaves. Hana retreats back behind the partition, crying softly. Tad follows, oddly aroused by her passionate defense of Mac. Never has he felt such fire from her. On the bed, he puts his arms around her and tries to force her to lie down. She resists, pushing him away.

"No. I don't want to." It is the first time she ever has refused his overtures. Fearlessly, she stares at his incredulous face, her red-rimmed eyes smoldering. After a moment of shock, he stands up, embarrassed. Then his anger returns.

"What kind of fucking wife are you? Don't you get high-faluting with me. I'm still head of this family! Get that! I'm still the boss here."

She can see he is working himself into a fury. A cornered cat, she slithers off the bed and past the partition to the door. He does not follow.

She runs next door to Sayo's, bursting in without knocking. Her mother is alone, seated on the floor sipping tea. An empty teacup resting in front of her indicates someone has just left. Hana falls to her knees and begins sobbing.

Without a word, Sayo gently rubs her back. "My goodness, this must be the time for daughters and granddaughters to shed tears. First Terri . . . and now you."

Hana stops weeping and faces her mother. "I'm sorry, *Oka-san*, but Tad and I just had a disagreement."

"I know. I could hear you. These walls are thin, embarrassingly thin. Are you sure that's all that is bothering you?"

Her mother's voice is soft and sympathetic.

"He was encouraging Mac to join the army. I couldn't stand it and told him what I thought. Of course, it made him furious." She catches her breath. "Sometimes I hate him!" She says the words with such vehemence, she surprises herself.

Sayo takes Hana's hands in her own and looks her fully in the face. "I need to apologize to you, Hana. I should have rescued you from your bad marriage years ago." She lets the words sink in. "More than that, I should never have let you marry Tad." Hana is so astounded she cannot reply. "But I could not see you living in a geisha inn for the rest of your life. I wanted you to have a normal marriage with children. The *baishakunin* who arranged your match was very corrupt, I later found out. The Murakamis paid him good money to bring in a good wife, someone young and innocent to be the "yomeii-san" and care for all those men. I should have known better, but it was too late when I found out. You were pregnant already." Tears gather in Sayo's eyes. "Forgive me."

Hana flings herself against her mother's bosom. Smelling the kimono's musky incense takes her back to childhood, that safe and joyous time full of music and high lilting voices of happy women. As she embraces Sayo, those safe feelings return and all the bitterness and disappointments of life with the Murakamis melt away with the words, "Forgive me."

"Now tell me about Shimmy," says Sayo.

Hana did not even feign surprise at the question.

"I think I am in love with him," she answers.

"And has he declared his love for you?"

"No. He hasn't said as much. He isn't in a position to do that."

"Well, when is it ever the right time?"

"By the way, I told Tad Shimmy had confided in you about his being called by the army. I lied."

"You didn't lie. Shimmy told me."

Hana takes this in. "It seems Shimmy and you have become close friends." Before she would have resented this fact, would have been threatened by her mother's charismatic power. Now she is grateful. Sayo also has become her close friend, an ally.

"He came here because he wanted to talk about you. He also is very intuitive and knew I would understand things of the heart."

"Did he come here often? I never saw him."

"He came for tea when you or the family were not around. He's not stupid, you know."

Hana is quiet, realizing how far her involvement with Shimmy has come. Now her mother knows and has not passed judgment.

"What should I do? Leave Tad?"

Sayo laughs gently. "Don't you think that would be hard to do in this place? Where would you go? Move in with me and Terri?" She becomes serious. "One can't get away from anyone here . . . even from oneself!" Sighing, she continues, "And you have children, obligation to them."

"I know." Hana turns glum.

"But love is not turned on and off, Hana. True love never dies. It can last lifetimes—whether or not you are together." Saying those words, her mother's eyes take on a faraway look, sad and pensive. For the first time, Hana sees her mother as vulnerable. Had she ever been in love with anyone other than her father? She remembers Yoshio, who was more like a grandfather. Now, feeling closer to her mother, Hana asks the question she never has dared ask before.

"*Oka-san*, what happened to my real father? Wasn't he an artist? I only know he was from a good family in Hiroshima. I learned that during the matchmaking for my marriage to Tad. What happened to him?"

"It's understandable that you ask. You have a right to know." Her eyes lost their sadness. "Matsubara Hiroshi was a fine man, the second son in a powerful sake-brewing family. Yes, he was an excellent artist. I came to America as his *shashin kekkon* but lived with him only for a few months."

"Only a few months?"

"He didn't want to be married. Besides, he was in love with someone else, a *hakujin* woman he met in San Francisco."

"Really." Hana's voice trembles.

"So after trying to be a proper husband, he gave up and followed his heart."

"He went to San Francisco? But how could he leave you alone?"

"People often follow their hearts. Sometimes they have no choice."

Hana's mind reels. "Is that why you opened a teahouse?"

"Yes." Sayo's face now looks closed, and although Hana wants to hear more, holds her tongue. "You did not come here to talk about Hiroshi. You came to talk about Shimmy."

Hana nods.

"When he returns you must meet with him alone."

Stunned silence. "You mean . . . we should have an affair?"

"I'll have to think of the appropriate place."

"You will help arrange it?"

"Of course. Isn't that what mothers are for?" Sayo laughs. "Dealing with matters of the heart was a great part of my profession in the Heavenly Cloud Inn. I am quite expert at it. Even here in this godforsaken camp love finds a way. Most who visit and have *ocha* with me in this room really come to bare their hearts—of lost loves, forbidden love, yearnings, and memories. They trust me, as Shimmy did."

The rest of the day, until Terri comes home from visiting her friend Mitzi, Hana and Sayo reminisce about life at the geisha inn. Like two young girls sharing secrets, they giggle and laugh uproariously recalling the many absurd predicaments in which the women of the inn found themselves, all of their own making, of course. The subject matters of Tad, Shimmy, and Hana's father fade into the background.

When Hana returns to the compartment, Tad acts as if nothing has happened. He barely glances her way as she steps behind the partition. But she can tell by his relaxed manner, the earlier confrontation is forgotten, most likely attributed to some momentary "bug up her ass." In her newfound identity, it doesn't bother her one bit.

* * *

Hana walks swiftly toward the block latrine, long skirt of her cotton *yukata* flapping, wooden *getas* skimming over the icy ground. She carries a towel, soap, and shower cap. It is early morning, and she hopes at such an hour the shower room will be empty. The block is deserted and barracks dark except for the yellow lights of the latrines.

Inside, the stall lined room is empty. She shivers as she clatters to the shower room, a large cement space with twelve showerheads jutting from the walls. She turns on one of the spigots, grateful the blast of water is hot, another reason she chooses to shower early, while there is still hot water. She disrobes and lays her *yukata* and towel on a bench outside the shower room.

The room is opaque with clouds of steam. She enters and stands beneath a shower, savoring the hot, prickling rain upon her shoulders and back. Relaxed, she thinks about her encounter with Sayo several days before. She still finds it hard to believe what transpired between them. But whatever the outcome, she now feels comforted that after sharing her deepest secret, she received no condemnation, only sympathy and encouragement.

After finishing her shower, Hana sits quietly embroidering, waiting for the morning light. She can hear Tad snoring and Carmen muttering in her sleep. An oily smell wafts from the roaring stove, unpleasant, but a necessary by-product of keeping warm. She notices the three-tiered stack of *mochi* cakes on the makeshift *tokonoma* shine with an oily yellow glaze instead of their original whiteness. New Year's has come and gone with no celebration to bring in good fortune. Even the *mochi* looks drab and disappointed.

Mac has awakened. Yawning, he shuffles in his boots to the door, carrying a toothbrush, tooth powder, and towel. He dons a jacket and turns to his mother. "I hear Shimmy is back already. Came in last night."

"Oh. Word sure gets around fast here."

"We always hear from the guys who hang out at the gate. They like to be the first to know everything. You know, gives them prestige," he laughs.

She doesn't say anything, feigning complete disinterest in the news. After Mac leaves, she quickly slips over to Sayo's, knocking lightly before entering. Terri is asleep on the floor. Sayo sits before her shrine, upon which a bowl of incense burns, smoke tendrils curling up into the air.

"Oh . . . I'm sorry," whispers Hana.

Eyes remaining closed, Sayo answers, "It's all right." She lowers her voice. "He's back, isn't he? That's good. I have thought of the perfect place." She opens her eyes, glowing now. Hana never ceases to be amazed at her mother's beauty, how she never seems to age. This morning she looks exceptionally young and vibrant.

Terri awakens. Voice thick with sleep, she greets Hana with a jovial "Hi, partner." Ever since the riot, her disposition has softened toward Hana, in fact, toward everyone in the family. Hana figures it is another phase of adolescence and is prepared for the time when her youngest will be sullen and critical again. But for now, she is grateful for the reprieve.

A long army coat covers Sayo's kimono, and heavy boots have replaced the usual *getas*. She carries a scarf-wrapped parcel. They swiftly trudge over the hard snow through the block and across the firebreak, heading for the camp perimeter.

Hana guesses her mother has found an empty cubicle in one of the new barracks being built near the hospital at the camp's edge. "Is it here in one of the new blocks?" she asks.

"Of course not! That would be too dangerous—and unromantic!" Mist streams from Sayo's offended mouth.

Finally they reach the fence. Hana has never seen this part of camp, preferring to stay away from the guard towers and barbed wire. Sayo walks toward the looming sentinel. Could she be thinking of the abandoned guard tower, Hana wonders. Her heart sinks viewing the splintery beams and worn tar-papered roof. A cold wind penetrates through her wool coat to the bone.

Sayo is digging away snow near the fence. Hana helps, not knowing quite what she is digging for. They scoop out a shallow trough under the wire, and, to Hana's astonishment, Sayo slides through to the other side. She beckons for Hana to follow.

For Hana the thin barbed wire had represented more than a boundary imposed by the military. It might just as well have been a foot-thick stone rampart as high and forbidding as the Great Wall of China. Contained within, she could accept its limits, remain unchallenged to break the barrier between herself and the open space of her soul. She hesitates, uncertain. Sayo is impatient, already heading out into the snow-covered desert. Finally Hana takes a deep breath and crawls under the wire. On the other side, she jumps to her feet, ebullient, breathless, close to tears. Without glancing back at the tower or barbed fence or distant barracks, she catches up with Sayo and impulsively hugs her. Surrendering to her mother's plan—wild and outrageous as it might well be—she follows the erect figure marching with determination toward the Alabama Hills.

ACT IV

Wet Scene

Changes

Sayo was uneasy. Hiroshi and Cloud had not come back to San Jose, and it was more than a week past their scheduled return. She was disappointed Cloud had not come earlier, hoping to have some time alone with him before Hiroshi returned. She still felt their last meeting at the picnic was strained. But now both were late. What was she to think?

Since the failed attempt to acquire the cane furniture shop, she hadn't looked further for other rentals, spending most days visiting at the New Moon Inn, enjoying the company of women. Sitting with them around the kitchen table, she sipped tea while they chattered about the previous night's adventures. She felt almost envious of their lives listening to the lighthearted banter, punctuated with peals of laughter and sometimes raucous imitations of their clients. While she worried over a husband and his obligation to family, and wrestled with feelings she had toward a man whose intentions and past were mysterious, these women were able to let go of any attachment to men other than the night's afterthoughts, about which they could laugh the next day.

She did not remember Mentor's stories of life being so gay in a geisha house; she thought of her old friend's world as very sedate and fastidiously mannered, even with an undercurrent of sadness. And that sadness itself was exquisitely poignant. After Mentor confessed her lifelong affair with Tadanoshin's father, Sayo understood the tragic aura that seemed to surround her. But as in Kabuki drama, tragedy was the ultimate spice of life; the most intense was that of giving up a great love to uphold honor of one's family. For Mentor, it was honoring the Matsubara patriarch.

Sayo left the inn before dusk, when clients began arriving. As she rounded the corner to her boardinghouse, she saw Cloud's horse tethered in front. He was waiting in the lobby, seated on one of the wooden chairs. Catching sight of her, he rose up and greeted her with a warm smile, his arms carrying a filled bag. She reminded herself not to bow and remained straight-backed, slightly breathless with pleasure.

"So good you are back, Cloud-san. Was your work successful?"

"Took longer than I wanted, but returned soon as I could." He nodded toward the bag in his arms. "I brought you some apples. Watsonville is noted for them."

"You are so thoughtful. Thank you very much."

He followed her through the dark passageway, the flapping of her zoris the only sound as they walked down what seemed to her an unending path. Finally, she reached her room, which she unlocked and entered, beckoning for him to follow. She again constrained herself from bowing, honoring his request that she not ever bow to him. But a lifetime of courteous kowtowing was hard to break, and she found herself feeling awkward without the ritual to fill empty moments. It was strange to confront another so openly, exposing one's vulnerable areas of heart and belly.

Cloud set the bag of apples on the low table and removed his boots.

"Where's Hiroshi? I noticed his wagon is gone."

"He hasn't returned yet from San Francisco." The words were automatic, said without emotion, as her mind was only on Cloud and her own happiness at seeing him again.

Silence. Finally he asked in a tight voice, "I didn't know he was in San Francisco. What exactly did he tell you when he left?"

Why was he suddenly so tense? "He said he would be seeing painter friends and would be back in a week."

"Damn," he muttered.

"Do you think something bad has happened?" She felt an anxious twinge.

He began pacing back and forth in the living room, head bowed as if studying the tatami-matted floor. Was there something about Hiroshi and his life in San Francisco she should know? True, she was naive, as Kiyomi had said. But she was not dim-witted and realized Cloud would not be so upset if Hiroshi merely was late. "Is he in danger, Cloud-san?"

He stopped pacing and faced her. She noticed the sharp outline of his clenched jaw. "Yes . . . he is in danger, but not in the way you may be thinking."

His careful manner and tone of voice persuaded Sayo whatever Cloud knew about Hiroshi must involve another woman. Of course! The blue-eyed woman. But how could that be dangerous? Weren't she and Cloud teetering on the brink of an affair themselves? Daring, yes, but not perilous.

"Is Hiroshi having an affair with the hakujin *woman in the painting?" Sayo surmised the woman was married and her husband was seeking revenge on Hiroshi.*

"Yes," Cloud answered quietly, "but that is not the danger."

"Then what is?" she blurted.

"Before I left, Hiroshi promised he wouldn't be going to the city."

"He went immediately," Sayo answered, feeling oddly guilty she was betraying him.

Cloud shook his head, staring at the floor. "Then he's hooked."

"Hooked? What does that mean?"

A long silence. "I'm afraid Hiroshi is addicted to opium."

"Opium?" Sayo remembered a vague reference to the drug by Mentor, but she knew nothing more than it was something indulged in by wealthy dilettantes. "But why do you say he is addicted? Perhaps he is in love with the blue-eyed woman and cannot resist seeing her." Passion, she could understand, but not craving for a drug.

"I wish it were just that. But, unfortunately, his obsession is more for the demon drug than a woman. I'm sure of that. Besides, he told me his feelings for you had become stronger, that he was falling in love with you and wanted to break off with Ruby . . . that's her name." He spoke slowly, seeming to measure each word. "If he had gone to San Francisco to do that, he would have returned days ago. No, he couldn't resist the pipe."

Shaken, Sayo sat down on the floor. She began thinking of Hiroshi's actions in the past weeks, his listlessness upon returning from visits to the city. She had noticed a peculiar odor about him, fruity and sweet, that she had ascribed to his working on the farms. And his sexual disinterest. Inexperienced in that realm, she nevertheless knew instinctively a man of his age and virility should have been more amorously inclined. Opium! Such disaster. And Cloud? Obviously he knew of Hiroshi's habit.

"We never discussed his smoking. It was apparent to me Ruby was deeply addicted, but I hoped Hiroshi would stop if he no longer saw her. He swore it was over with her. I thought he had kept his word." He shook his head again. "But it's worse than I thought."

Sayo now realized why Cloud had been avoiding her. Respecting Hiroshi's confidence that he was falling in love with his own wife, Cloud had tried to step out of the picture. She also understood he must have been protecting her when he insisted Hiroshi break off with Ruby, which in effect would put an end to his opium smoking.

"I told Hiroshi I was in love with you and would pursue you myself if he wasn't fair with you."

She sucked in her breath. "You mean you discussed this with Hiroshi?"

"Of course. We have been good friends for years." She no longer could constrain herself and stood up to embrace him. But before she could, his arms were around her, lifting her bodily. She felt lips on her throat and neck, finally her mouth. The American kiss! Hungrily she responded.

Finally they released each other. "I must leave now for San Francisco and try to find Hiroshi. I'm worried."

Regaining some composure, Sayo offered, "Please let me go with you." She hesitated. "I'm afraid. Something could happen to you too."

He laughed. "Nothing can happen to me." He was hurriedly putting on his boots. I would love to have you with me, but this is not the time. I have to see that Hiroshi is okay. Then we can decide what to do from there."

After embracing her again, he left quickly. Weak-kneed, she sat down on the floor, mind whirling. All this happening within a mat-

ter of minutes! She at one moment felt delirious with joy knowing Cloud's feelings, then at the next was overcome with ominous sadness when she thought of Hiroshi. Fond of him, but not in love, she was nevertheless anxious for his welfare, and, in fact, like his mother, wanted his happiness. If he loved the blue-eyed ghost woman, he should be with her. But, how tragic their karma should be marred by enslavement to a drug. She knew Cloud's assessment of Hiroshi's plight was not exaggerated, that serious trouble was afoot, and if anyone could deter it, it would be Cloud.

The challenge for her now was to remain patient and calm until she heard from him—or Hiroshi. She had no thoughts on what might happen if Hiroshi returned home with Cloud. All she could do was meditate and pray their destinies would unfold and be harmonious for all concerned.

That night Sayo had a dream. She was in an ancient castle, seated on a stack of seven various-colored pillows. Kneeling before her, several women in elegant court robes of brocade and embroidered silk fluttered fans about their powdered white faces. Their hair hung long and straight, streams of dark velvet that reached the floor. A black wolf sauntered among them, tail swishing gracefully. She watched from her perch, holding Mentor's antique painted fan against her face as she had seen the old geisha do. Then an older woman, with graying hair, dressed in strange khaki-colored clothing, appeared. She held a sake cup in one hand and in the other a wood-handled mirror. Sayo was surprised how much the woman looked like herself, except older.

When she awakened she immediately wrote to Mentor telling her of the dream. She did not mention her predicament, not knowing yet how the situation would turn out. But she knew the dream held guidance, and she needed the geisha's interpretation to assist in future decisions.

Sayo calculated it would take at least another week before she would hear from Cloud—three days of travel and some days searching for Hiroshi. What could she do in the meantime? Should she tell Kiyomi? Of course, she must! During a time such as this, she

needed staunch allies, especially women. What if both men disap-
peared! She brushed the thought from her mind and readied herself
to visit the New Moon Inn.

"What! That bakatare!*" Kiyomi screamed after Sayo broke the*
news. "Doesn't he know the white ghost woman will suck his soul
out of his body? You are lucky to be rid of him, Sayo-san."

Feeling some loyalty to Hiroshi and the Matsubara, Sayo per-
suaded Kiyomi that Hiroshi's behavior was as much due to a sick-
ness for opium as a yearning for another woman. And she had not
mentioned Cloud's declaration of love for herself. It was premature
to confide that as she had no idea what Cloud had in mind if
Hiroshi could not be found. She must not depend on Cloud. She
must consider her options as if she were alone.

"I do not feel hatred toward Hiroshi. After all, he had no choice
in marrying me. And his family was good to me. So, please, let us
not talk of him from this day on."

"But what will you do, Sayo-san?" Kiyomi's voice trembled with
concern.

"What do you think I should do?"

Kiyomi's answer was immediate. "Marry another fool . . . a rich
one. There are many who would almost kill to have you. I never
told you, but the old blacksmith—the one with warts on his nose—
he's insane over you. He comes to the inn even though he's married
and boasts he would send his wife back to Japan or sell her to some
bachelor here if there was a chance he could win you from Hiroshi.
The dog-piss. What nerve. But he's rich."

Sayo laughed. "I'll never marry again."

"But what will you do for money?"

Sayo had not thought of that. Both Hiroshi and she were depen-
dent on the Matsubara allowance. What could she do to earn money?
Wash and cook for bachelors again? "I always could work in the
fields like the men."

"Oh no! Sayo-san, you mustn't ever think of doing that! Your skin
would darken and your hands would roughen and crack. You
would lose your beauty." Kiyomi spoke as if she were seeing a ghost,
shock widening her eyes. "I wouldn't let you do that . . . even if I had
to take care of you."

Touched, Sayo smiled gently at her friend and promised she would consult with her before making any decision about working. But speaking with Kiyomi was sobering, as it brought home the reality of what it would mean to be a woman abandoned alone in America without money and not speaking the language.

"I know Cloud would help you," Kiyomi offered.

"Perhaps. But, I will not depend on him."

They sat in silence. Kiyomi began fidgeting, tapping slim fingers on the tabletop.

"What are you nervous about?"

Kiyomi exhaled a long breath. "Sayo-san, please forgive me if what I say is an insult, but I have a crass suggestion. I only mention this because I can't think of anything else." She waited a moment. "You could work here in the New Moon."

As if she had been contemplating the same idea, Sayo answered matter-of-factly. "It could be a possibility." She had not thought of it and, in fact, was jarred, but did not want to offend Kiyomi.

"You could demand a very high price. They'd pay just to look at you. Really."

"Well, it still is too early to make any decision. But thank you for your suggestion."

She sipped the rest of the tea calmly, hoping to convey she was not worried. But her stomach churned. What could she do? And what would she tell the Matsubara if Hiroshi did not return? They were, after all, her only family. Depressed by these thoughts, she excused herself and returned home, promising Kiyomi she would see her the next day.

But Sayo remained a recluse for several days thereafter, refusing to unlock the door for Kiyomi, who came by daily.

"Please, at least, say something so I know you are all right," Kiyomi called anxiously, envisioning Sayo's lovely white throat slashed, her heroine lying dead in a pool of blood after committing seppuku. Realizing this, Sayo always answered with a strong voice, placating her loyal friend. "Please do not be concerned. I am meditating and praying to kamisama. Do not worry." She would fan incense smoke toward her door.

Indeed, Sayo meditated for days, just as Mentor had taught.

Ridding her mind of all thoughts, thoughts that did not help her situation but only caused anguish, she relaxed and surrendered to her destiny, to whatever the gods willed.

Finally, she dressed in the yukata she had worn at the dance festival in Hiroshima when she first saw Tadanoshin. She stepped outside, refreshed by slightly cool air. Summer was ending. Wearing Ito's hand-carved getas, she glided to the secluded garden and sat in the octagonal gazebo, facing the hidden trees that marked the gravesites. She didn't know what drew her to the sanctuary. Perhaps it was because she could be utterly alone there, without connection to anyone, even her ancestors, as were the Chinese bachelors' bones buried under the trees, isolated from their kin across the ocean in China. She remembered the ceremony for Aunt Sachiko's brother after his cremation, the long chopsticks so delicately managed by family as they sifted through ashes to withdraw the bones, the last remaining matter to be stored for eternity in a bronze urn. Who would salvage her bones someday?

She studied the undulating carp glinting silver in the oblong pool. Over and over, they flitted in the water, never losing their eagerness in searching the same small territory for food. She realized she must survive like the carp, like the salmon swimming upriver that Ito had talked about. She must be courageous, unafraid to swim against the current, eager for life even in the smallest and seemingly most insignificant world.

Contemplating rustling leaves, welcoming a fresh breeze rippling the pond and stirring the bamboo wall, she sat for a long while, losing track of time. Just as she stood up to leave, she heard the wooden gate open. Cloud strode to her side. His face was lined with fatigue, looking as if he hadn't slept for days. Whatever the news, she knew it wasn't good.

She felt tension in his body when he embraced her without saying a word. Her face against his chest, she felt the strong beat of his heart, smelled leather and grass.

"Hiroshi did not come back with you."

"No." He released her, and they sat down on the gazebo bench. Pain darkened his eyes as he continued. "It took a while to find him . . . and Ruby. They both had been smoking for many days. By the time

I got there, they were in a stupor, unconscious. It took several days to restore them back to the living." He shook his head. "I'm afraid it's too late."

"Could he understand his situation? I mean, was he coherent enough to know what he is doing to himself . . . and the Matsubara?"

"He was. But unfortunately, he no longer is in control of his life. Opium is." Cloud took her hand and said gently, "Hiroshi can die from this."

"Does he intend ever to come back to San Jose?" Somehow she knew, perhaps even wished, Hiroshi would not return. Still, there were so many questions yet to be answered—such as, what was to become of her; what was she to tell his family?

Cloud reached inside his shirt pocket and withdrew an envelope. "He wrote a letter. I think he explains everything in it."

Relief softened her voice, which she realized had been growing shrill. "Thank you, Cloud-san. Did Hiroshi tell you what he wrote?'

"No."

"Will you excuse me if I read it now?"

"Of course." He stood up and walked to the pool.

Hurriedly she opened the envelope and retrieved some calligraphy-inked pages. She noted how the characters were scraggly, unlike Hiroshi's usually elegant script.

> *Dear Sayo-san,*
>
> *By now you have become aware of my situation. Please forgive my cowardice in betraying your trust this way. I have no excuse other than my weak nature, which, as you must know, displeased my father greatly. I have asked Cloud to inform you of my condition. I am too ashamed to write it, as I have grown very fond of you. I know you will be concerned about my family and what to tell them. You need tell them nothing. The money they send is yours. Perhaps you can set up the shoyu business yourself, as you showed great talent for getting things done. I, also, personally dissolve the marriage contract between us. You are free to pursue your happiness as an*

independent woman. My family need not know anything of our arrangement.

I will not be returning to San Jose. I leave everything there to you, except for the wagon, which I have given to Cloud. Our destinies appear to follow separate paths, which, too late, I regret. You are truly an admirable woman, loyal and strong, much stronger than myself. Please forgive my act of selfishness.

Sayo slowly folded the letter and returned it to the envelope, aware of Cloud watching by the pool. Nothing in the letter was surprising, except for his seeming affection for her. The days of contemplation had prepared her to receive any news with calmness. Now, at least, she could plan what to do.

Cloud steered her toward the gate. "Are you satisfied by the letter?" he asked.

"Yes. But it is a sad letter. Is he very ill, Cloud-san?"

"He is. But if they rehabilitate themselves somewhat they might survive."

"But, he has no money if he doesn't take it from his family. What will he do?"

"He was talking of moving to Seattle, where Ruby has friends."

They approached the Persimmon Inn, where Sayo saw the mahogany wagon with Cloud's horse leashed to it. "Will you come in?" she asked, feeling numb.

Strain deepened the fatigue in his face. She saw how tired he was, how much the turn of events saddened him. After all, he and Hiroshi were best friends, knowing each other much longer than either knew her. Now he probably would not see his friend again. Compassion compelled her to suggest they meet another time after both had rested and contemplated a course of action. Standing in public view outside the inn, they shook hands instead of embracing and planned to see each other soon.

She was glad to have some days by herself, to think calmly what her course of action should be. She immediately wrote a letter to

Mentor, telling her what had happened, relating Hiroshi's addiction. As for the Matsubaras, she decided not to tell them of Hiroshi's downfall, but inform them the marriage contract between Hiroshi and herself was dissolved and they need not send money to San Jose any longer. She knew their distress would be great, causing them to call on Mentor, who she was certain would appease their anxiety with a proper story. As she wrote to Tadanoshin and the Lady Matsubara, it seemed they were not only in a land far away, but in another world, a place fading like an old scroll painting. Somehow her father-in-law's power also seemed dimmer, as she tried to envision his reaction. She could see his frustrated face, aristocratic nostrils flaring with impotence, not able even to insult and rail at his son or order his daughter-in-law to return to Japan. She felt sorry for them. They were ambitious parents who wanted a good and prosperous life for the second son and had been more than generous, as well-bred samurai families could be. She would save Hiroshi's face and not expose his weakness, but merely say she was discontent in the marriage. Remembering Tadanoshin's vow to take care of her as long as he was alive, she purposefully mentioned she needed no money nor anyone's concern for herself. If she chose to be with Cloud, they would soon hear of it through the trans-Pacific grapevine anyway.

After writing to Japan, Sayo's thoughts turned to her future. What could she do? There was some money left from the Matsubara's last installment, but it would not last forever. Should she consider working at the New Moon Inn? No. That was out of the question. She was certain Cloud wanted her—perhaps as a wife. But having tasted some freedom, she was reluctant to be totally dependent on a man again.

A week passed before Cloud came to see her. When she let him in the apartment there was a moment of awkwardness, each of them not knowing how to cross over the barrier of Hiroshi's tragedy. Cloud's face looked rested, copper skin smooth as honed leather. His ebony hair was gathered at the back of his head, similar to a samurai warrior's knot. Finally, they embraced, more like commiserating friends than lovers.

"Will you come with me to Watsonville? There's a special place I'd like you to see," he said.

"Will you be working?"

"No." His hand now caressed her back. "I want to show you a very beautiful place. I promise, you will like it."

"When shall we go?" Her spirits lifted as she realized she could leave this room and San Jose for a while.

"I'll come by tomorrow morning, very early. Let's say four o'clock. It will take a long day to get there." He kissed her hands. "We'll have plenty of time to talk."

The beach was like nothing she ever had seen before—in Japan or in her imagination. From atop sandstone cliffs, they could see a long shoreline, a glorious expanse of white sand edging the dark green waters of the bay, sweeping in a curve to Monterey. Pine trees grew along the soaring cliffs, and where creeks emptied into the ocean, dense foliage formed clumps of green.

After a long day's wagon ride from San Jose, they finally had arrived at Cloud's surprise. It was nearing sunset, the sun setting to the west casting a golden glow over the water and over Cloud, who stood beside her. During the journey, they had talked at long length about the situation, mostly about Sayo's options.

Sayo had confessed, "I do not want to take money from the Matsubara, even though I need only ask my father-in-law for help. But that is out of the question."

"I respect your integrity," Cloud had said. "So will you live with me? I can take care of you."

"But I am still married to Hiroshi."

"The hell you are. Most couples in California are just living together anyway. That's what marriage really is. Loyalty to each other.

She laughed, hearing humor in his voice. "Please give me a few weeks to think about our living together." She paused. "But surely you know I love you and have been attracted to you from the beginning."

"I hoped that. I fell in love with you from the moment I saw your picture from Japan. I knew our lives were destined to be together."

"Really?" Her heart soared. Still, she didn't know how to tell him

how important it was for her to try to survive somehow on her own. She wanted to seize that opportunity to test her courage.

But Cloud seemed to understand what she couldn't say. He didn't press her. Time would reveal the form their relationship would take. Until then they must enjoy the moment.

In awe of such untouched natural beauty, Sayo could not speak.

"Do you like it?" Cloud said softly.

Regaining her voice, she answered, "I have never seen such a beautiful place. Thank you so much for bringing me here, Cloud-san. Do you come often?"

"As much as possible when I'm in Watsonville."

"Does anyone own this beach?"

"Not yet." He scoffed: "As if man can own the earth." He turned back to the wagon, the mahogany wagon Hiroshi had given him.

Seeing him unhitch the horses, she asked, "Are we staying here for a while?"

"Of course," he said and laughed. "Did you think we would ride so far just to look? We'll camp here for the night." He began unloading boxes.

"Camp?"

"We're going to sleep on the beach, under the stars. Have you ever done that?"

"No, but it sounds so wonderful . . . very American!" Delighted, she ran to the wagon to help.

Again, he laughed. "Not American. Indian. This is how my people lived for years, sleeping under the stars, next to the earth."

"Where was that? In San Jose?" She often wondered where Cloud came from.

"No, no. Far from San Jose. I would like to take you there someday."

Embarrassed by her ignorance, she nevertheless asked, "You have told me you are Indian. Is that another race? Do you come from another country?"

"Indians lived in America long before the white eyes came." He stopped unloading and sat on the ground. "There were many tribes with different names, and we spoke different tongues. We have been here many, many years."

She was fascinated. She had no idea America was populated by anyone other than the hakujin. *"Then your different tribes were something like the clans who lived and fought in Japan years ago."*

"Not quite. But I guess you could say there was some similarity."

"So the white eyes fought you, too."

He nodded and rose up to carry some boxes down the cliff. She followed with several blankets loaded in her arms. Close to the path, they stopped at a cove sheltered by a pile of washed-up logs and scattered boulders. He spread out one of the blankets for her to sit on and announced he was going to fish for their supper. He had brought a fishing pole.

Waiting on the shore, she watched his silhouette against an orange sky. The memory of Hiroshi's plight dimmed to a shadow, she was at peace and could not remember a happier moment in her life. Japan, Seamstress, the Matsubara, even Tadanoshin, were a lifetime away, memories to be stored like gems in a jewelry chest, opened perhaps on special occasions. The riches of her new life began now with Cloud. In the present. She realized she had let go of her attachment to the powerful father-in-law whose imagined invincibility mirrored only her own desire for such potency within herself.

"Look. Here's our dinner." Cloud dangled three silvery perch. "They were waiting to be caught."

While he gutted the fish, she gathered firewood, an easy task as the beach was littered with bits of timber. Over a small circle of rocks with burning wood in the center, he set a frying pan, which soon held the fish, sputtering deliciously in hot oil.

"You have thought of everything!" she exclaimed, discovering in one of the boxes he had brought cooked rice and some fruit.

"That's right. I even put some vinegar and sugar on the rice so it wouldn't spoil during the long ride here."

Facing the ocean, turned a deep purple with glints of orange where the last vestiges of the sun colored the horizon, they quietly ate dinner. The air was hot and the sand still held the day's heat.

"Is the water warm enough to bathe in?" asked Sayo.

"I think so. Warm enough for me. Would you like to go in?"

"Oh yes! My first bath in the American ocean!" Already she had risen and began loosening her kimono.

With consternation, he warned, *"You mustn't go in alone! It's too dark, and these currents can be dangerous."* He began to undress also. *"Don't go in without me. We'll stay in the shallow part."*

She had taken off her obi, flinging it down in the sand. With the freed kimono wrapped around her, flapping gently in the breeze, she strode down to the water's edge. Cloud followed, naked except for a towel draped around hips. She tested the water with her foot, surprised at the tepid temperature. She took off the kimono. It had grown dark, but she could make him out standing at the waterline.

Before she could wade deeper, she felt him beside her, his hand grasping hers. *"Stay next to me."*

Shallow waves broke farther out, folding over in gentle foam that bubbled around them as the water surged toward the beach. He turned to face her and held her against him as the water receded, gently tugging at their bodies. She pressed her cheek against his chest, smooth and hairless, tasting of salt when she kissed the shapely muscles and nipples. She smelled seaweed as he pressed his hardness against her. A large wave broke, sending a surge of water that knocked them off their feet. She rolled on the wet sand, Cloud still hanging on to her, water filling her mouth and ears. Coughing, she sat up, long hair loose, caked with sand, falling over shoulders and down her back. They kissed, long and deeply, water swelling and swirling around them.

He carried her back to the campsite, laying her down on the blanket and himself next to her. Where the fish had been cooked, embers still glimmered, casting a red glow over sand and rocks, over naked flesh.

His hands caressed, seeking every secret part. At first shy, she responded hesitatingly. But soon ignited, she answered with a fervor, mouth and hands stroking and tasting sumptuous skin, muscled limbs.

She mounted him. Sand-matted hair cascaded down her back and haunches, over his hips beneath her. The drumming began. Not the quick staccato of the taiko, but the soft, muted throbbing of a *wolf's heart. The throbbing quickened and the beats deepened. When the rhythmic harmony of wolf's heart and drum reached a crescendo, fusing into one long quivering pulse, she felt the burst of thunder. The heavens opened and rain began falling, filling the rivers and then the ocean, burgeoning its borders to create the tsunami wave sweeping over her.*

Loyalty Oath

Manzanar, 1943

Terri is listening from behind the partition, sitting on her sister's cot. She can't believe her mother is actually talking back to her father, even raising her voice. In the past months Terri has seen a gradual change in her mother, as if she were awakening from a long, deep sleep. She's heard Carmen and Mac commenting on this odd behavior. "Mom's going through 'change of life.'"

Still, Terri is not prepared for her mother's vehemence, nor is her father. He sputters, then shouts a long string of cuss words. Terri once asked Obachan why her father swore so much. "He thinks those *hakujin* words have power, so when he's threatened he uses them like a weapon, to scare and keep people away."

Terri thinks his swearing is silly, and it sure doesn't scare her one bit. She thought her mother was always cowed by his shouting, and thus is surprised when she doesn't retreat in silence but yells back at him.

"How can you urge Mac to sign 'yes, yes'! They'll draft him into the army!"

Her father is so unsettled he at first tries to calm her, blurting, "Take it easy . . . easy." Then, frustrated, he turns to his usual arsenal of swear words. "Goddamn it! I'll tell my kid what I want! Don't give me any son-of-a-bitchin' fucking mouth about it! Who do you fucking think you are, telling me what to do!"

Terri can hardly believe her ears when her mother retorts, "He's my son, too! I don't want him going into the army. He's just a boy!"

"And how the hell are you signing the oath? 'No, no'?" He laughs, ridiculing her.

"Maybe I will. Maybe I won't sign at all!"

He laughs again. "And they'll pack you off to some other camp and then to Japan when the war's over. Don't be so goddamned stupid!"

"It's the loyalty oath that's stupid! We're Americans. You and I and the kids have never been to Japan. It's such an insult , , . just like this camp."

There is a hiatus of silence. Her father's voice sounds less angry, even tinged with some regard when he answers, "You may be right, but we can't take a chance of being deported."

"They can't deport us for the way we sign such a stupid piece of paper. Let's not sign at all!"

Her father explodes again. "Don't fucking tell me what to do!" The door slams. Terri peeks around the partition and sees her mother sitting on the bed wiping eyes with a handkerchief. She feels embarrassed for her mother. She doesn't want her to know she has overheard their battling, so she remains behind the blanket wall.

After her mother leaves the compartment, Terri meanders down to the canteen to see if any new items have arrived. Not that she has money to buy anything, but it is something to do. With the soldiers gone and the weather too snowy and cold to play outdoors, she is bored. Even daydreaming about Billy has become monotonous.

She walks through the firebreak to Block Two and spots a clump of men outside the canteen, huddling in thick army coats, white steam puffing from their mouths. She knows they're talking about the loyalty oath. Inside the canteen barrack, other men with serious faces speak loudly as if giving speeches. The whole camp seems to be at war again. Just two months away from the riot, and already another conflict is tearing them apart. Disappointed by the scarcity of goods and not interested in eavesdropping, she trudges through the snow back to Block Sixteen.

Obachan sits on a zabuton on the floor, embroidering. Terri is surprised to find her alone. Lately, her grandmother has been out attending meetings, or others have been visiting, also discussing the latest crisis. She's pleased to have Obachan to herself.

Putting the embroidery aside, Sayo begins preparing tea. She sets the heavy black kettle on the oil stove and retrieves two ceramic bowls from a cloth-covered box. She gestures for Terri to sit across from her at the low table. Terri obeys and kneels, sitting back on her haunches, flattered to be treated like one of her grandmother's guests.

"I have been neglecting you lately, Teru-chan, so, this is a good time to have *ocha* together and catch up."

"Thank you, Obachan. I have missed you."

The water hisses, indicating it is hot enough. Sayo sets it on the table, next to a canister. Using a teaspoon, she dips green-tea powder into the two bowls. She adds a bit of water from the kettle and beats the green fluid with a small bamboo whisk until it is frothy, turning the bowl slowly with meticulous precision. She fills it with more hot water.

Terri lifts the steaming bowl to her lips, savoring the earthy aroma. Although the strong caffeine sometimes jolts her senses, she always is calmed by the ritual. Obachan fills her own bowl with more water and sips.

She sets down the bowl. "You must be curious about all the excitement in camp."

Terri should have known her grandmother could read her mood. "I guess I am. What is this 'loyalty oath' anyway? Why is everyone fighting about it?" She isn't sure if she should tell about hearing the arguing between her parents.

Sayo sighs. "Another unnecessary obstacle to bother us with. But you should know so you won't be frightened by all the commotion."

Between delicate sips of the green froth, she explains the government's demand. All internees over the age of seventeen need to sign a questionnaire that is supposed to determine their loyalty to America.

"But, we are Americans," Terri says defensively. "Mom and Pop were born here."

"Of course, and even I, born in Japan, have lived longer in this country than those in the administration forcing us to sign that oath!"

"Then you're a citizen, too, living here so long."

Sayo pours hot water in her empty bowl and swishes it around. "Unfortunately, I am not."

"What!?"

"You see, there are laws that deny Asian people the right to naturalize."

"But that's unfair, Obachan. Why only Asians?"

"There are other groups, too. It is a long, sad history which I can't tell today. But I want you to understand why people are so upset about this oath."

She gets up from the table and returns with a sheet of paper. She sets it down in front of Terri. On it are a list of questions, the last two underlined in red.

27. Are you willing to serve in the Armed Forces of the United States on combat duty, wherever ordered?

    _____   _____
        (yes)   (no)

28. Will you swear unqualified allegiance to the United States of America and faithfully defend the United States from any or all attack by foreign or domestic forces, and forswear any form of allegiance or obedience to the Japanese emperor, or any other foreign government, power, or organization?

    _____   _____
        (yes)   (no)

Sayo says the last question is especially insulting because she sees it as asking her to renounce Japanese citizenship, the only citizenship she has been allowed to keep these forty years since she immigrated.

"If I sign 'yes,' I will be a person without a country. There are many others like myself. That's why there is such dissension. And there is a rumor that if you sign 'no' to both questions, you will be sent to another camp and then deported to Japan after the war. So, you see, it is very confusing, and when people are locked up together like caged animals, they cannot attack the true enemy, the ones who imprison us. They turn on each other."

Terri hears again her father's strident voice.

"So, how will you sign, Obachan?"

Sayo smiles mischievously, humor softening her intensity. "Who cares about an old lady like me? I'm not signing anything. I've been invisible to the government for forty years. I'll stay invisible!"

Terri can't imagine her grandmother being invisible to anyone. But what about her parents? And Mac? She decides to tell what she has overheard. Sayo is not shocked.

"This drama will pass . . . just like the riot. Too much crowding makes tension. Don't worry, Teru-chan, we will come to our senses soon."

"But will Mac have to go into the army if he signs 'yes, yes?' "

"Perhaps. But we will cross that bridge if we come to it."

Their small room, with its polished floors and spare furnishings, roaring oil stove, simple shrine next to Obachan's futon, becomes a cozy asylum instead of a place only for sleeping, a place where she usually feels safe. Pushing the loyalty oath question to the back of her mind, she tries to enjoy the rest of the day chatting with her grandmother. But now, more than ever, she is confused and saddened by the tumultuous change in the family since their arrival at Manzanar. Unused to thinking of the future or about the war, she wonders when it will end and what will happen to them. Would they be living in this desert forever?

Mirrors

Manzanar

As it turned out, Shimmy did not return from his military venture the night Mac reported it to Hana. A soldier had arrived for a visit with his parents, and the young men hanging around the entrance gate mistook him for Shimmy. Misinformation traveled fast around camp. Ever since the riot, anything unusual that shifted the daily routine was fodder for rumor. Again the internees were ready to explode, ready to release pent-up emotions.

Hana focused her attention on the loyalty oath, disagreeing with Tad and arguing openly with him. She had expected Shimmy to return weeks earlier, and as the days passed, waited with anticipation and growing agitation. It was a relief to shout objections, to see Tad's face redden with frustration. Sometimes her defiance had no roots in the oath crisis at all, but was simply anger at herself for so many years of remaining silent.

Today she hears again that Shimmy has come back. At lunch, her mother whispers, "He came in late last night and stopped by the *ochaya* this morning." Her eyes glitter with intrigue. "I told him you wanted to talk and offered my place for a meeting . . . this afternoon at three o'clock. I will take Terri with me to the *origami* class at Block Twelve."

"How does he look?"

Sayo chuckles. "The same. A little thinner maybe. But I think he is anxious to see you, too."

"Thank you, *Okasan*." Gratitude deepens her weak voice.

"But, remember we will be gone for only two hours."

At the latrine, she brushes her teeth. She washes her face with the sweet-smelling Lux soap she uses for special occasions—as she did before the orphanage Christmas party. Cold water stings when she rinses away the suds. She pats her face dry with a rough towel and rushes out the door, shivering in the light kimono she hurriedly had donned after returning from mess hall. Luck is with her, for Tad has gone to work at the canteen and Mac and Carmen are out and about. She is alone in the barracks.

Smoothing "vanishing cream" over cheeks and forehead, she studies her reflection in the round mirror tacked on the wall. Fine lines fan out from corners of her eyes and above her lips, lines that have appeared since coming to the desert. Sayo says it is the dryness and harsh wind. At least her eyes are not constantly red like those of many internees. She applies lipstick and smudges some of it on her cheeks. Normally she refrains from wearing makeup, but this afternoon she is another person, no longer the submissive wife and *yomei-san*. She wants to look as different as she feels.

She dresses in slacks and sweater, but remains barefoot in *getas*. One does not enter Sayo's tearoom with shoes. She puts on the navy peacoat and clatters out the door, clogs crunching over icy snow. Within seconds she enters her mother's empty room and slips off the *getas* and hangs her coat on a nail pounded in the wall.

She sits on the floor at the low table, surveying the spare room. No sign of clothes or clutter. She knows clothes are immaculately folded and tucked away in the baskets and suitcases stacked against the walls. On the shrine sits a small bronze incense-burning pot, which now emits a trail of musky-smelling smoke. She is touched by her mother's thoughtful gesture to mask the strong odor of burning oil. She sees a feather, fan, and small dish filled with rice also placed on the shrine. Noticeably missing is the wooden mirror that had always adorned her mother's sacred shelf for as long as she could remember.

She fidgets, clasping and unclasping perspiring hands, finally drying them by smoothing back her pompadoured hair. Will he notice the hairdo? As part of a new image, she now has upswept her hair, gathering it at the top and rolling it into large pompadours, somewhat like the coiffure of Japanese women at the turn of the century. At first she thought it made her appear older, but she soon grew accustomed to it, liking the feeling of air on her naked neck. Mac had voiced his approval just the other day. "Hey, Mom, you look like Betty Grable."

A light knock. She holds her breath. Exhaling, she calls out breathily, "Come in."

Snow glistens on his wool cap and thick army coat. He taps boot-clad feet against the outside threshold, shaking off ice. With the door shut behind, he turns to face her, his smile familiar and friendly.

Her nervousness disappears, and she scrambles to her feet to help remove his heavy coat. She restrains the urge to embrace him.

"Thank you."

His simple words of appreciation move her. She can't remember Tad or any of his brothers ever thanking her directly for anything. He sits on the floor and removes his boots. "I'll make some tea," she says, and sets the black water kettle on the oil stove.

Sitting across from him, she notices his army uniform, well-fitting wool khaki pants and shirt with tie. Sayo is right. He looks thinner, and with the short crewcut even younger. He is silent, smiling slightly as he gazes at her, his hands clasped on the table.

Her anxiety gone, she reaches over and covers his hands with hers. He enfolds them in his upturned palms, an intimate embrace that sends heat up her arms to her cheeks.

She says, "I'm so happy to see you."

"It's been longer than I thought it would be." His voice sounds deeper. "But I didn't have a clue what I was getting into."

"Are you involved in something dangerous?"

He laughs in his carefree way. "No. But it's pretty important for the war effort." He pauses. "I guess I can tell you what I'm doing. Just don't mention it to anyone else . . . except your mother."

With large hands clasping hers, he tells her he is training in a new intelligence unit of Japanese-American soldiers whose job will be to penetrate enemy lines in the Pacific war.

"This is where knowing Japanese comes in handy. We'll be studying how to break codes, how to interrogate prisoners."

"Prisoners!" she exclaims. "Will you go overseas?"

"That's the ultimate plan. Right now I'm training at Camp Savage in Minnesota."

"You've been in Minnesota?"

"That's right. And if you think it's cold here, you'd freeze in that state. This weather is balmy in comparison."

"Will you be going back soon?"

"Yes. In four days."

This shocks her back to the matter at hand. "You know why I wanted to see you?" she asks.

"I think I do."

"Do you think I am brazen . . . a fallen married woman?"

"Of course I don't. I wouldn't be here now if I thought of you that way. I wanted to see you, too."

"My mother believes in love, that it is the greatest force in the world, that once it is freed it cannot be stopped."

"Yes, Sayo and I talked about love." His narrow eyes have turned liquid. "I think I believe it."

"What do you mean 'think'?"

"Well, you know my history when it comes to 'love.' I sure am not an expert."

An uncomfortable silence. Could her mother have been wrong about this rendezvous? She is beginning to lose her nerve.

"What I mean is, I want to believe it," he says.

"Did Sayo tell you my marriage was arranged? That there is no love between Tad and myself?"

"She didn't have to."

Finally, the air is cleared. In four days he would be gone; no time for guessing and polite words. Impulsively she gets up from the table and kneels beside him and embraces him. Spontaneously, he pulls her close, kissing her mouth. She collapses against him, crying softly.

"Hey, I didn't come here to make you cry," he says gently.

"It's because I'm happy . . . and I'm sad, too, I guess."

"I know." He kisses her again. "I've thought about this for a long time. If I weren't going overseas . . . maybe never coming back . . . I wouldn't be acting so selfishly."

She bolts from his arms. "Don't talk like that! You're not selfish. I am. I'm the one who is married!" Her voice rises. "And you will come back!"

Both are silent, shaken by her outburst. Finally, Shimmy says in a serious tone, "I know there is no future for us, Hana."

"What do you mean?" She knows what he means, but pretends misunderstanding. She wishes they could leave the future out, savor the moments with each other solely in the present.

But he wants to be clear and honest with her. "I know you will not leave Tad and injure your family. I don't want you to. I respect you for that. But I wanted to see you before I go overseas . . . tell you how I feel." His voice is mournful, eyes soft and black. She remembers the day he spoke of his first love.

"I've always regretted holding myself back when I loved Sophia. Do you remember her? I know it sounds arrogant, but I truly believe her life would have turned out differently if I had acted on my feelings instead of being so proper. I realize she loved me. But I was a coward, a pious coward."

Quiet. Finally Hana says calmly. "Shimmy, you needn't explain why you are here with me. Sometimes people cannot help what they do. What do you want?"

He sighs, as if grieving. "I'm in love with you . . . and I want to make love to you."

The kettle begins hissing. Grateful for the interruption, she pours water into a teapot filled with tea leaves and gathers some cups. Shimmy has confessed his past cowardice and is willing to risk the pain of involvement with a married woman. Is she brave enough to unleash emotions she has caged for so many years? What would happen if this turbulent power were released with no object upon which it could be lavished? Shimmy could leave her life forever. Would she go mad?

"I don't want to rationalize my actions," he continues, "but the war has changed things, even my own sense of honor. I realize I may not come back from the Pacific. I'm selfish enough to want to taste as much as possible before I leave . . . even the fruit that is forbidden."

Hearing his words, she realizes she has no choice. Already the force of her love has been freed.

"Can you meet me tomorrow at noon? Next to the sentry tower at the south end of camp. Sayo took me to a special place. We can be alone."

He smiles. "Your mother is a true romantic."

"She is. But she is practical, too, and believes in karma. She says that people who fall deeply in love but are in situations that deny their being together have been destined to meet . . . even though their life together may not happen in his lifetime."

"Sounds like Kabuki drama to me," he says lightheartedly, and then seriously, "I believe in karma. If it's meant to be, it will happen."

Hana carries an extra wool blanket and is pleased to find the air warm inside the gorge. Shimmy, following wordlessly, never questioning the strange pathway to Sayo's secret place, is stunned as they descend down rocks bordering the frozen waterfall. "My God! It's as if spring has been trapped down here." Gazing up at the translucent roof of foliage and snow, he sucks in his breath. "How did your mother ever discover this? It's invisible from the top and outside the camp boundary."

"You should know by now Sayo has unexplainable powers."

They follow the ice-covered creek and soon reach the boulder fronting the entrance to the cave. When they enter, they are both astonished to see a dozen or more candles lining the shelf, an arrangement of dried branches and driftwood decorating one corner, and several blankets piled on the floor. Sayo's wooden mirror, wool gloves, and some *mochi,* feathers, and bones are neatly arranged on the altar. Incense permeates the air. Gratitude sweeps over Hana as she realizes her mother had come earlier to set the stage.

She remembers her first visit with Sayo, watching her untie the scarf-wrapped bundle containing the articles now lined on the shelf. Like Shimmy, she had been awed, realizing she had entered another world, mysterious to her but familiar to Sayo, whose reality, she knew, crossed the threshold of dreams and visions, prophecy and truth, resulting in an unconventional common sense.

"I feel like I'm dreaming," she had said to Sayo.

"You are," Sayo had said, laughing. "Life is a dream. We make up everything. Our life . . . dreams. Now isn't this the perfect magical place for you to dream with Shimmy?"

Watching Sayo place the articles, Hana had asked, "I know what to do with the candles and incense . . . but what about your mirror?"

"I have put it here for good karma. The person who made it was very powerful. You will be protected. But don't worry, nothing bad can happen. This is a holy place."

"If it is sacred here, wouldn't it be disrespectful to . . ." She had been embarrassed to finish the sentence.

Sayo had smiled. "Showing love is not a sign of disrespect. The spirits know who desecrates."

She had accepted her mother's words. By their crossing of the forbidden boundary circling the camp, the barriers that blocked out imagination and magic seemed to have fallen away.

"This is amazing!" says Shimmy. He examines the articles left on the shelf. He picks up the mirror, running his hand over its smoothness. "Such fine craftsmanship." He hands it to Hana.

She tries to imagine someone whittling and sanding the dark wood. An electric charge tingles up her arms. She gazes at the mirror and is taken aback by the face reflected, an image of herself, bronze-colored with long black braids. Frightened, yet drawn by its mysteriousness, she stares, feeling strangely comforted. She closes her eyes. When she opens them, she sees her pompadour-framed face.

Shimmy lights the candles, first lighting one with a match left by Sayo and then igniting the others with it. The room glows, its semi-darkness now shimmering gold. "I was an altar boy, so I'm good at lighting candles."

He spreads a blanket on the earth and beckons for her to sit down. He begins unlacing his boots, but still wears the wool cap and army coat. She removes her navy peacoat, again surprised at the balmy temperature. Before she can untie the lacings of her army boots, he stops her and takes over, gently removing them. Her feet are cold. He warms them, massaging with his large hands and strong fingers. She is uneasy receiving comfort instead of giving it, and tries to withdraw her feet. He holds them tightly.

"Let me do this, Hana. Enjoy it."

Emboldened by his words, she embraces him and takes off his cap, caressing his shorn head, stroking bony ridges behind the ears.

She helps him out of his coat. He wears a sweatshirt over a wool shirt, which he removes. She remembers how his muscles rippled and shone as he pounded *mochi* with Mac for New Year's. Bronze gods, Sayo had said.

With the deliberate sureness of a tailor's hand, he unbuttons her blouse. She wears no brassiere. As if measuring them, he cups her small breasts and kisses her neck and shoulders. She gasps when his mouth finds the erect nipples.

"Stand up," he says softly.

She rises to her feet. Kneeling before her, he removes her slacks and underpants, sliding them both down hips and legs, an artful servant ministering to his mistress. She is exquisitely naked, exposed and open to seeking lips and hands.

She is conscious of light in the cave, flickering shadows dancing on the walls, the moist air that swirls around them like fog. With arms outstretched she stands still, a tawny statue come to life, coaxed from inertness into trembling flesh. She sees rays of light beaming through the cave's entrance and hears faint sounds of singing, soprano voices chanting. She feels warm breath on her thighs, hears herself moan as she surrenders to his devotion. Ecstatic, she collapses on the blanket-covered earth and sees clusters of white gardenias floating in the air. Intoxicated by the fragrance, his velvet skin, she opens to receive him. She envelops him with orange light. The ground quakes, the cave walls tremor. The orange light explodes into a myriad of colors, a rainbow upon which they both begin to climb.

ACT V

Flight of the Lovers

A New Life

San Jose, 1904

After returning to San Jose from the beach outing, Cloud left again for Watsonville, promising to return in a few weeks. Sayo remained in seclusion, packing Hiroshi's belongings in a box to give the bachelors, except for his paintings. She found a dozen or so in one of his chests and was surprised to find the portrait of a nude Ruby. She was compelled to hang it on the faded wallpapered wall, finding a strange camaraderie in the sky-blue eyes shining forth from the white face.

Sooner than she expected, a letter from Mentor arrived. With eager hands, she opened the envelope, hoping Mentor would have advice for her future.

Dear Sayo-san,

I have just received your letter and am answering quickly, as I understand the serious crisis in your life. How unfortunate Hiroshi has fallen in such a dramatic way. One only can pray for his soul and that he has strength to somehow overcome the demon that has seduced him. But even though you must feel abandoned by the gods, do not despair. What appears to be disaster may be a gift from Heaven. I have not heard yet from the Matsubara, but it is possible they will learn of Hiroshi's problem through the gossip trail that transverses the great ocean. But that is no longer your concern.

First I will give you an interpretation of the dream you

wrote in your earlier letter. Since you are seated on top of seven zabuton, *observing the scene below, you are a teacher or one in higher authority. The number seven is an auspicious one, marking beginnings and endings, growth and success. Every seven years is a cycle of death and rebirth. The* zabuton *represent softness, tenderness, the erotic arts of the Pillow Book. The women with loose hair are courtesans, perhaps geisha, since you hold in your hand my antique fan which I acquired during my days as one. Interesting you would dream of a wolf, as that indicates you have unfulfilled desires and are struggling with honor. The color black foretells a future of mystery and unusual circumstance.*

The old person in strange clothing is yourself, as you determined. But the articles you hold in your hand—the sake cup and pitcher made from a dried gourd—are a riddle to me. The sake cup is you, but the gourd pitcher is foreign. Perhaps you will be involved with a foreign man, not the usual hakujin, *but a man of the land, of the earth, a stranger like you among the white ghosts. He will help you.*

I hope my interpretation is useful. I feel your dream guides you to a way to take care of yourself. I do not know if the Matsubara will continue sending money other than passage back to Japan. I advise you strongly to be considering a new life. Are there geisha houses in America? I do not mean the common brothel. I speak of the respected teahouses in which I have served. Is it possible for you to establish one and manage it as the okasan? *Could this not be a way to earn a livelihood as well as add some refinement and pleasure to the hard life your countrymen live? I hear their joys are confined to drinking and gambling, devoid of feminine comfort. Think about this. As I have told you, the* okasan *and geisha need not share the pillow with customers. Entertainment and social exchange can be enough, especially for lonely men isolated in a strange land.*

*In haste I send this letter on to you. Whatever happens,
it will be interesting, perhaps even thrilling. Better, in any
case, than the dullness of this village.*
        I remain your loving teacher and friend

She read the letter several times, growing more enthusiastic with
each reading. Ever since Kiyomi had suggested she work at the New
Moon, a suggestion she immediately had discarded as too humiliating for the Matsubara, the thought of establishing an ochaya had
been on her mind. Why not create her own teahouse? This was
America, after all, where preposterous ideas became reality. Why
not create a refuge for bachelors—and for women—to relax and
be entertained?

Mentor's stories of life in one of Kyoto's geisha houses were not
lost on Sayo. As a child she had been enthralled by exotic knowledge passed on, tales that may have been exaggerated or made up
to entertain. But it didn't matter in America. Things would have to
be improvised, anyway, adapted to a rougher land where nihonjin
men's souls had been deprived too long of yamato womanhood.
And she would make the ochaya available to families, too, not only
to men.

Already her mind began racing with ideas. yes, she would be
okasan, the nurturing mother who supervised everything—from the
girls' dresses and manners, to rules by which each guest must abide.
Her excitement grew as she thought of possibilities and challenges
of creating such a unique place of entertainment,

First, she must consult Kiyomi. She would need help in recruiting
other women. And what about Cloud? How would he feel about her
running a teahouse?

"A fantastic plan!" Kiyomi exclaimed. "I will help you get started
without payment. I want to learn to be genteel—like you. And entertain without having to sleep with customers! What an outrageous thought!"

Before Sayo could move forward, she realized she must find a
suitable house similar to the New Moon and also be certain she had
women willing to try their chances in such a venture.

"We must be very secretive," warned Kiyomi. "Pimp would not hesitate to injure—even kill—if his place is threatened."

"Do you think any of the girls from the New Moon would come with me?" asked Sayo.

"I can guarantee everyone will, Sayo-san."

"Then we must consider moving away from San Jose. What are your thoughts on that?"

"Absolutely. We must move to another town. Manzo can be dangerous."

What other town would be appropriate? Not San Francisco, nor the towns north of San Jose where nihonjin numbered less. Watsonville. She had not seen the town of Watsonville, but knew from Cloud many Japanese had settled there on farms. Struck by the verdant countryside and magnificent coastline backed by mountains rising gently to the north, she remembered how the landscape reminded one of Japan. The beach was an exceptional place, a magical spot in her dreamworld. Perhaps Watsonville existed in her destiny for more reasons than that unforgettable interlude on its beach.

She awaited Cloud's return with some trepidation. But she had made up her mind she would follow her plan. If he objected, it would be difficult to break with him as she was deeply in love. She had wished to write Mentor about that night on the beach. But how could words express those feelings? What words could tell how this Indian warrior with a samurai spirit had awakened her soul's deepest passion, had connected her to the earth's heart? Their union was destined, she now knew. But in what way other than igniting her female fire, she did not know.

"It sounds interesting," said Cloud after she told of her idea. Since you are planning on entertaining women as well as men, I take it you are not thinking about a brothel . . . like the New Moon." He had gotten to the point immediately.

"Yes, Cloud-san, the teahouse will be unique."

"Will you move to Watsonville?"

"How did you know that was the idea?" Cloud was steps ahead of her. She marveled how he seemed to perceive things so quickly, always deducing the wisest move.

"*Watsonville is most logical. Far away from Pimp and close to many Japanese. There are fine houses there, too.*"

"*Do you think we could rent one?*"

"*I don't see why not.*"

"*Is there a* nihonmachi?"

"*Not like San Jose, but there is a section of town where you would be able to rent. I know some people who can help you.*"

"*Cloud-san!*" *Abandoning her usual reserve, she flung her arms around him. "You have been sent by the gods!" She laughed openly, not bothering to cover her mouth with hand or kimono sleeve as a well-bred Japanese woman would do. In her joy, she allowed herself to act brazenly American.*

Cloud joined her frivolity, lifting her, twirling around with her slim body clinging against him. For a moment she was a child. Vague memories of being carried and playfully jostled by a man who must have been her father seeped up from the past. How safe it felt with Cloud. It would be so easy to let him take over her life, let him care for her, a passionate lover and ever-protective father. But as seductive as such security was, she yearned more for a chance to meet the challenge of surviving on her own. She knew she need only ask and he would move in with them. She chose not to mention it.

He embraced her and kissed her mouth in the American fashion she had grown to savor. Seppun. *Much more erotic than the neck-licking practiced in Japan. She had learned that in this country a woman's bosom and mouth were sexually arousing, just as a woman's long neck was exciting to the Japanese male. She answered his kiss wholeheartedly, knowing she could count on him to help deal with whatever the future might hold.*

Before Sayo, Cloud, and the girls were to travel to Watsonville, there was a celebration at the New Moon. Pimp was out of town, making it possible to have the party, which included Ito and the bachelors from the compound. That night Ito and two other men decided they too would move to Watsonville and continue working with Cloud there. "Life would be too lonely without you and the New Moon women, Onesan," said Ito. "You have become our family here."

Thus, Sayo, the New Moon women, and three bachelors left San Jose, making the arduous journey to Watsonville crowded aboard three wagons—Cloud's and two others borrowed from the barber and Mr. Lee, the grocer. Heaped high with trunks and small pieces of furniture, bodies spilling over the sides, the entourage looked like a caravan of Asian gypsies newly arrived from the plains of Inner Mongolia.

After camping overnight in the countryside between San Jose and Watsonville, they arrived at the rented home the next day at dusk. Cloud's friend had found an old two-story wooden house near the bridge crossing the Pajaro River at the outskirts of town.

A tall hakujin man greeted them. Lean and wiry, with brown hair and dark skin, he spoke respectfully to Cloud. When he was introduced to Sayo, she could see his eyes were as blue as the woman's in Hiroshi's painting, exuding a warmth that was politely admiring. This was a genteel hakujin, she thought as she bowed low, so different from Hiroshi's boss, Daley, who she remembered as coarse and somewhat barbaric, with a thick body and dusty complexion, hair a shock of hay.

He ushered Cloud and herself through an entryway that narrowed into a hall with archways opening to two rooms on either side. Cool and slightly damp, the rooms smelled musty. Dust covered the wooden floors like a fine veil, indicating the house had been empty for some time. After inspecting the rest of the building—large kitchen downstairs, outside toilets, four bedrooms upstairs—Cloud asked if she was satisfied.

"Very much," she said, hoping not to be rude speaking Japanese in front of his friend. But she saw the friend watching with interest, a smile on his face.

"Good. Then let's move you ladies in," said Cloud as he retreated to the waiting entourage.

She turned and held out her hand as she had seen the men do. "Arigato-gozaimasu." She made a point not to bow, feeling odd uttering the words without bowing to further emphasize her gratitude. He grasped her hand firmly and shook it with friendliness, unintelligible words tumbling from his mouth. She smiled graciously, still repressing the urge to bow deeply.

After unpacking the wagons and helping the women get settled, the men retired to a boardinghouse several blocks away where Cloud had headquartered during his sojourns in Watsonville. The women set about cleaning and decorating their new home. They painted walls, hung drapes and curtains, and even some family pictures. With the last Matsubara allotment soon to run out, Sayo knew it was crucial to open the teahouse soon. They must begin earning money.

Earlier in San Jose, Kiyomi had arranged a meeting with Sayo and the Chinese girls. Only then had Sayo discovered they were only seventeen years old and had been kidnapped and sold to a madam in Shanghai who, after exploiting their innocence, arranged to have them smuggled to San Francisco.

"Drink tea," Kiyomi had said. "Drink sake with men. Dance. Sing. But no more sleep-sleep." She tried to make it clear they could work at the teahouse and make money without pillowing with men.

Night Jasmine had smiled mischievously, tiny teeth glistening between plump lips. "Me like dance, drink, sing. But me want make much money. Buy land. Okay I sleep-sleep?"

Sayo understood Night Jasmine's desire. She wanted freedom someday, and land would give her that. More money could be made in carnal trade than companionship. This the Chinese girls knew. Beneath their giggling, childish exterior, Sayo realized they harbored a survivor's fierce wisdom, a strength that had overcome horrors beyond what she could imagine. She must allow the women to pursue their profession as they wanted. The ochaya would offer good food, conversation, entertainment and music, and importantly, an affectionate family atmosphere among the women as well as with clients. She decided pillowing would be allowable. After all, there were many lonely bachelors in Watsonville who needed female comfort of the flesh.

Within a month the combined efforts of the women and bachelors transformed the old building into a respectable-looking house. They had planted rosebushes and flowering shrubs that already had begun blooming, covering the open dirt of the front yard with colorful buds. What passerby would guess this wholesome-looking house was, in truth, a brothel? In Sayo's mind, it was not a common house of pleasure, but a training experiment to prepare for the fine teahouse she held in her imagination, a large homelike inn with space for a landscaped rock garden and communal o furo, tatami-matted floors upon which the self-styled geisha would dance Kabuki drama, transporting homesick men back to the motherland of sweet-smelling plum and jade green rice fields. This dream for the future allowed her to accept the ochaya's *mundane reality. But temporary and humble as it was, she nevertheless plunged into fashioning a place of entertainment that would attract and comfort the area's many immigrant bachelors.*

Soon the lone house at the town's outskirts was seen lit up at nights until early morning, gas lamps shimmering in windows like beacons in a lighthouse, beckoning, guiding customers to its oval-mirrored door. Dressed in clean, though mostly shabby clothes, a trail of men arrived, slicked-down hair black and gleaming like crystal globes, eager to partake of generous, if not voluptuous, offerings reputed to abound at the new teahouse. Music and tinkling laughter and sometimes boisterous booming of inebriated men filled the air. It became the gathering place, a social club for many bachelor immigrant farmhands, who toiled daily to make "the killing" that would send them back to the homelands rich and respectable. There were Japanese, Chinese, Filipino men, and even some local hakujin *farmers—"Slavonians," Cloud called them. Tall, lean, and dark-skinned, these strangers brought an exotic flavor into the otherwise totally Asian world of the teahouse. Sayo welcomed them with special graciousness. She found them extraordinarily handsome and well-mannered, observing how gently they spoke to the women even though neither party understood one word. They were never overly anxious to pillow, either, sometimes playing cards or learning mah-jong with the Chinese girls for the entire evening.*

Cloud, of course, was a frequent visitor, staying with Sayo most nights when he was in town. He was gone often, still working with farm laborers north in Santa Clara Valley and as far south as Guadalupe. But his long absences did not worry Sayo as her days were filled with managing the teahouse, leaving little time to think of af-

fairs of the heart. As if understanding her driven desire more than she did, he retreated into the background, observing from a distance, yet, she knew, available immediately if any problem should arise.

Spring swept by. Yellow daffodil–covered hills turned light green as summer air baked the land and rushing rivers dried up into trickling creeks. Sayo sat at the kitchen table, sipping tea, enjoying the morning coolness and moments of solitude before the girls arose. The house was clean, put back to order after the night's business, but still smelling of tobacco and wine, an aspect of entertainment she wished could be disposed of. Even strong incense and fragrant flower arrangements were not enough to cover the telltale residue of partying.

She heard footsteps at the front porch, a soft knock on the door. "Sayo-san?"

She recognized the voice of one of the bachelors.

"Come in," she called.

It was Jiro, the youngest. He was breathless.

"Onesan!" Have you heard about the geisha who is visiting Watsonville?"

Used to rumors circulating in the community like fruit flies, she reacted without surprise. "I haven't, Jiro-san. But do you know what part of Japan she is from?"

"She's from Sacramento, I hear. I don't know what ken. *But word is she is an elegant courtesan."*

"Really?" Her interest was piqued. She wondered why she hadn't heard of her before.

"But, Onesan, what is so fantastic, I hear she was asking about you. She called you 'Lady Matsubara.'"

Who could this mysterious geisha be? "Well, I'm flattered word of our ochaya has traveled as far as Sacramento. But I know no one there. How did you hear about this?"

"Ito met her at Kato's grocery. I think he told her where to find you." He shuffled his feet. "That's why I came to warn you."

"Thank you, Jiro-san. I appreciate your thoughtfulness." Aside from Jiro's sincere wish to keep Sayo abreast of any news relating to

the ochaya, *she knew he must have hoped to glimpse the stranger if she indeed had found Sayo and was there as a guest.*

"But, if this lady does come here, I will see to it that she meets all my friends . . . especially the gentlemen from your boardinghouse."

Jiro bowed deeply several times. "Arigato, *Sayo-san. Please do let us know." He backed out of the kitchen and then down the hall.*

"I promise," she called.

For a while Sayo sat in wonderment, but soon dismissed any more thoughts about the stranger, deciding the news was most likely just exaggerated gossip. That afternoon she sat on the front porch, enjoying the cool breeze wafting up from the river. She rarely sat outside, but for some reason she chose to that day, to sit on the wooden rocker looking out to the road from town. Cloud was still away; perhaps he would come home unexpectedly and she could greet him as he rode in.

After about an hour, she saw in the distance a horse-drawn carriage approaching. Through shimmering light, she made out a hazy outline of a man handling the reins and a woman sitting next to him. He was dressed in a black suit with black hat shading his face. After straining for some moments, Sayo could see he had hakujin *features. The carriage stopped in front of the house, several yards away from the porch. Holding a cream-colored lace parasol that hid her face from view, she alighted while the man set a large satchel on the ground next to her. He climbed back up to the seat and turned the carriage around toward town, leaving the woman standing alone with her bag. Sayo could see the long blue skirt was wrinkled, but her high-necked blouse was crisply white, trimmed in lace, with large puffed sleeves that narrowed and fitted tightly from elbow to wrist. This* hakujin *woman was well-dressed, thought Sayo. She must be rich.*

Curious, Sayo stood up and began stepping down the porch stairs to greet the unexpected guest. The woman also began walking toward her, parasol now held high enough for Sayo to discern shiny black hair swept into pompadours atop her head. Finally able to make out her face, Sayo was shocked to see she was Japanese. There was something oddly familiar about her, the tall, strong-looking body,

*the way she walked, somewhat like a young colt. The figure now
began loping toward Sayo, an angular face wreathed in a smile.
"Matsubara-san! Matsubara-san!" a childish voice called.*

*Sayo's mouth fell open. She knew that voice. But how could it be?
Then she saw the square-jawed face, apricot skin luminous in the
sun. "Chiba! Is it really you!"*

*Now running toward Sayo, parasol thrown aside and arms ex-
tended, she cried "Sayo-san! Finally I have found you!" She threw
her arms around a stunned Sayo, who, barely able to respond, patted her young friend's heaving back as she sobbed against her.*

*"I'm so happy to see you," Sayo managed to say. "Such a sur-
prise." She held her friend, studying the tear-streaked face. "You
look every bit a respectable matron. Where is Yoshio?"*

*Chiba's face clouded. "It's a long story, Sayo-san. But to be blunt,
I have run away from him . . . actually, a long time ago."*

*"We can talk about that later. As you can see, I am no longer
with Hiroshi, either. But how did you find me?"*

*"That is another long story, but I posed as your geisha friend
from Sacramento."*

*Sayo laughed, "So you are the mysterious courtesan." She re-
membered the innocent sixteen-year-old who had ingeniously
helped her pass the worm test before leaving Yokohama. Chiba had
shown even then she knew how to use her wits.*

*Sayo guided Chiba up the stairs into the house. "It's time for cele-
bration. Please stay as my guest for as long as you wish. We have
much to catch up on."*

*Indeed, after talking for hours with Chiba, Sayo heard a story ex-
ceeding the most fantastical of Kabuki dramas. It seemed that after
settling in Marysville with Yoshio, living in a small shack on his
piece of land, knowing no other* nihonjin, *Chiba had become desperately homesick. "Yoshio was a good man," she explained, "but
too old and too silent. He rarely spoke to me . . . or anyone. I tried
so hard. Truly I did, because he was kind enough to send money to
my family in Kumamoto."*

Sayo recalled meeting the balding man who had deceived the young bride's parents by sending a picture of himself taken twenty years earlier. She remembered how his hat had unexpectedly fallen off his hairless head, but observing then how Chiba had retrieved it, brushing the dust off gently with her kimono sleeve, she had figured Chiba's youthful strength would carry her through the strange marriage. She did not know how powerful that youthful strength could be when awakened by a handsome, attentive—and clever—young bachelor. The suave gambler had ridden into the small town of Marysville and called upon Kimura Yoshio, the only other Japanese in the area.

"When I first saw him, I instantly fell in love," said Chiba. "He was so handsome and dressed elegantly, like Hiroshi. So I took it for granted he was aristocratic, and honorable. I found out the one pleasure Yoshio had was gambling. So I was pleased he became friends with Manzo, who was a gambler, giving me a chance to see him.

"Manzo!" Sayo exclaimed. "Did you say Manzo?"

Chiba replied hesitatingly, "Do you know him?"

Manzo! Chiba needed to tell Sayo no more. Already she guessed what had happened. Indeed, it turned out Chiba had been seduced by the infamous gambler-pimp. They left together one night, stealing away from Yoshio's shack, taking one of his horses. First, Manzo took her to a home in Sacramento that he claimed was a boardinghouse for unhappy picture brides such as herself. Innocent, believing her handsome prince, she was not suspicious of men visiting the women in the evenings. Besides, Manzo kept her sequestered with him much of the time, taking her to taverns and restaurants, showing her a fast life glittering with gamblers and imposters. But the glamor soon wore off. Chiba yearned to return to a farm, to land like her family worked in Kumamoto.

Then the unexpected happened. Yoshio hunted them down in Sacramento and showed up at the "boardinghouse" one night. Chiba and Manzo weren't there, but the girls related with terror how he had practically destroyed the living room, throwing furniture and breaking a large mirror hanging over the couch. "Such a strong bull, that old man," they said. The couple immediately fled Sacramento on a barge down the Sacramento River to San Francisco.

Chiba was guileless, but not dumb, and seeing Manzo's person-ality change during the short time she was with him, she began to have doubts. Often sullen and irritable, he paid little attention to her except to order her around as if she were his slave. The "boarding-house" in San Francisco did not bother to maintain even a facade of a normal hostel as the Sacramento house had. Immediately ap-parent was the type of place Manzo had brought her to. He left her alone in a big strange city, without money or anyone she knew. Too ashamed to try to return to Marysville and Yoshio, she locked her-self in the room, refusing to "work." The other women were kind, bringing food, trying to help her "adjust" to what they claimed was an unalterable fate. "Manzo can make life miserable for you," they warned. "But if you work for him you can make some money so you can leave. Don't be so stubborn. He'll be coming back in a few weeks."

But Chiba was stubborn and young enough to move rashly. Told by one of the women about a home that took in women off the streets, women in trouble, she saw her way out. She secretly fled from the brothel early one morning, purposefully dressed in light cotton yukata, *with no shoes on her feet. Dressed so poorly in San Francisco's cold, wet fog, she figured someone from the home surely would spot her, or perhaps some compassionate person would di-rect her to it.*

Her assumption was right, for an older hakujin *woman, dressed in dark gray with an old-fashioned bonnet covering white hair, ap-proached her. Chiba sensed the woman's kindness and, not speak-ing the American language, began to cry, uttering in Japanese, "Please take me with you! Please, kind lady!" which, of course, was unintelligible to the woman. But seeing Chiba's cold, bare feet and foreign attire, she guessed the young girl's plight and took her arm, leading her several blocks away to a narrow, three-story Victorian-style house. Chiba's refuge was the Mercy Mission Christian Home for unwed mothers and abused and abandoned women.*

After living at the mission for a year, where she learned some English and how to cook American food and sell Bibles on the street, she decided to try to find Sayo. She knew Sayo had gone to San Jose with Hiroshi. With the mission's blessing and some money she had managed to save, she paid her way on a wagon traveling from Japantown in the city to the small town in Santa Clara Valley.

At San Jose's nihonmachi, *she learned that the beautiful "Lady Matsubara," whose husband mysteriously had disappeared two years before, was now running a successful teahouse. Ecstatic that she finally had found the only person in America with whom she felt connected—the gracious, generous lady who had befriended her on that long journey from Yokohama—she immediately found a way to Watsonville with a Mr. Walker, minister of one of San Jose's Presbyterian churches, the denomination that administered the Mercy Mission.*

When Sayo heard Chiba's story, she laughingly told of Jiro's announcement that a professional geisha had come into town from Sacramento. Giggling, Chiba confessed she had started the rumor in order to find out about Sayo's teahouse. "I bought this new outfit and parasol to look the part."

"It certainly worked," Sayo laughed. admiring Chiba's nerve.

As summer drew to an end, Cloud's work outside Watsonville slackened, allowing him more time to spend with Sayo and the inn's extended family. Hot days and nights inspired picnics in the countryside, and Ito, who since Chiba's arrival had taken on the job of party coordinator, had seemed more than enthusiastic to plan numerous outings. Sayo and Cloud relaxed together, no longer worried about family obligation or whether the teahouse would be successful. She had not been able to spend such time with him since the night on the beach. The Matsubara in Japan were absent from her dreams, and Hiroshi was a finely etched shadow disappearing into a pale landscape, two years of faded scenes in an ancient painting.

Ito's most recent and highly successful event was a pilgrimage to some hot springs a good four hours' journey from Watsonville. Hidden amidst rocks and oak scrub blanketing a flat, open valley, the undeveloped springs bubbled and gurgled, hot water jetting up through cracked rocks, occasionally spewing a hiss of steam into the air. A welcome oasis after the wagon ride.

The men set up a shelter of canvas awning, and the group was soon comfortably shaded to enjoy a picnic meal of chicken, rice balls, tsukemono, *and cucumber salad. Afterward, with the sun beginning to set, they disrobed and frolicked naked in the pool like children. Even Cloud, dropping his dignified stance, cavorted with Sayo, reminding her of that night on the beach when the wave knocked them over, her hair entangled with sand and seaweed. Gazing at the orange-purple sky, inhaling sulfurous fumes with Cloud beside her, she was overcome by her good luck, the good life she now enjoyed, her new family, and the wild beauty of untouched land. The gods had blessed her. She was content. Only one thing remained to complete her fulfillment. Cloud. She must invite him to move into the teahouse with her. Yes, she must ask him soon.*

But the gods were fickle, and before Sayo could act, catastrophe struck with a sudden ferocity that delayed all plans. A week after the hot springs picnic, Cloud had gone to San Jose for several days, and the women had returned to their usual routine: sleeping until late morning, cleaning the house, spending afternoons lounging, leisurely tending to personal grooming. They ate early dinners, usually vegetables and fish and lately, because of the heat, a bowl of soba, *buckwheat noodles swimming in ice-cold broth. They had eased into this pattern, contented and unaware of anything unusual to warn them of the tragedy that would soon befall them. In retrospect, they recalled that Chiba had commented she thought she smelled gas when they were retiring to their rooms after the teahouse had closed for the night. "It's probably tobacco," someone had said.*

If it were not for Cloud coming back in the early morning darkness, who knows if any of them still would be alive. As it happened, Cloud's early return had not been planned. He was to leave San Jose two days later. But he told Sayo he knew he had to get back to the teahouse quickly when coyote howling awakened him from a strange dream.

"Brother Coyote is a helper. He was warning me."

"And what was your dream?"

"You were lost in the forest, wandering deeper and deeper into darkness. Then the wind began blowing, and I was looking for you, but the wind was too strong. I couldn't even walk against it. Then Coyote woke me up."

Even before the house came into view, before he smelled smoke, dread had hardened the pit of his stomach. He lashed his horse mercilessly, while whispering apologies into the sweating ear. His inner legs were slick with froth from the flanks of the courageous horse, who never faltered.

He neared the river, where thick smoke seared his throat. Tying a bandanna over his nose, he galloped to the house, alarmed at the clouds pouring out of windows. He bolted off the horse and, from the corner of his eye, saw a man's figure running to the river. His immediate thought was he was going for help. He raced through the open front door and was met by flames crackling in both drawing rooms. Sparks and heat rose up the stairway whose bottom steps were beginning to burn. Where were the women?

"Sayo! Kiyomi!" he yelled, bounding up the stairs to the second-floor landing, where the air was opaque with smoke. He crashed into Sayo's room and saw her prone figure on the futon. He carried her unconscious body down the stairs and outside, where he laid her on the ground. She began coughing and sat up, pressing her soot-streaked face against him. Then she screamed, "The girls! The girls! My God, they are still in there!"

Cloud leaped through the flames and up the stairs again. "Kiyomi! Night Jasmine!" Kiyomi and Reiko were staggering from their rooms, clutching one another, and when they fell, Cloud carried them both together down the stairs and outside. Sayo was at the door.

"Cloud-san, let me help you." She held a cotton cloth to her face.

"No!" he shouted in a voice that even Sayo would not defy.

He entered again, dodging burning wood as he again climbed the now flaming stairs and landing to the Chinese girls' room. They were unconscious on their beds. On the floor lay Chiba, also unconscious. Thanking the spirits that the girls were so tiny, he slung each one over a shoulder and maneuvered down the shaky stairs, anxious to deposit them and return one more time for Chiba.

"It's too dangerous to go back!"

"Chiba is still inside!"

But just as Cloud climbed the porch stairs to reenter, there was a sudden explosion that threw him back to the ground, blowing shards of flaming wood into the sky, one striking him on the side of his head. Sayo and Kiyomi pulled his inert body away from the burning house. He had been knocked senseless and was bleeding profusely from a gash down the side of his face.

In shock, the girls gathered around Cloud's still body. Sayo was relieved to see he was breathing and was not injured other than the cut on his face. She tore off her kimono sleeve and pressed it against the wound. Then Kiyomi screamed, "My God! Where's Chiba?!" Sayo froze. What remained of the house was a burning heap of scattered wood. How could anyone have survived the explosion? Still, she jumped to her feet and began running toward the fire, but was pulled back by Kiyomi and Reiko. In horror they stood and watched the soaring flames, unable to utter any sound, unable to weep. Sayo dropped to her knees and began praying. She prayed fervently that Chiba's spirit had left her body before the blast. She believed such violence would have disoriented Chiba's soul, and would cause it to remain in the vicinity wandering forever, a haunted white-haired obake, *feared and rejected. The girls joined Sayo on their knees, praying for what they knew not.*

Soon the bachelors arrived, wide-eyed and disheveled. They had heard the explosion, as had others who now were converging on the scene. Cloud was still unconscious, tended to by Sayo and Kiyomi. It was apparent the house was lost. Attempting to put out the fire would be futile. The crowd stood stiff and speechless.

"Where is Chiba?" Ito asked Sayo, a sense of foreboding in his voice. He knew from her silence that his instinct was correct. Without another word he turned and disappeared into the dark. She was too exhausted and worried about Cloud to pursue him and offer comfort. She bathed Cloud's wound, a deep, jagged gash in front of the ear down to his chin. One of the bachelors had gone for Dr. Sakamoto, the local nihonjin *doctor who could stitch the wound.*

Cloud regained consciousness before the doctor arrived and asked immediately, "Chiba?"

Surprised by her own serenity, Sayo answered in a calm voice, "She is with the Buddha . . . in the Pure Land."

Cloud closed his eyes and grimaced. She knew he was blaming himself. "It is her karma, Cloud-san. We are the ones left to grieve her absence. It is our loss, not our fault. She is at peace."

After some moments, he broke the silence. "I saw a man running toward the river. Did any guests stay until early this morning?"

"No," answered Sayo, brow furrowed.

"I think the fire was set purposely by someone," Cloud muttered. "I could smell gasoline . . . not gas for the lamps."

Sayo gasped. Who would want to hurt the women, and in such a dreadful way? Poor Chiba. So vibrant and in love with life, and such a survivor. For the first time that night, she allowed tears to flow, both from relief for Cloud's resuscitation and deep sorrow of Chiba's death.

"Shi-kata-ganai," she repeated to herself. "Shi-kata-ganai." It can't be helped. It's karma. Despite those words, whispered gently like a holy mantra, a part of her raged against the senselessness of it all. Karma did not kill Chiba; someone evil had snuffed out Chiba's life. No amount of chanting mollified her grief or her umbrage at the unknown assailant. In Japan, such a calamity might drive a woman to commit seppuku. *But here in America, Sayo did not turn guilt on to herself; she refused to blame herself for the tragedy. Instead, she vowed to avenge her young friend somehow. Making this decision, she ceased chanting and turned her attention to Dr. Sakamoto, who had just arrived.*

Family Breakup

Carmen bursts into Obachan's compartment, crying that Mom and Pop are fighting. "They're really going at it this time," she sobs. Obachan jumps up from the futon and is out of the room in a flash. Terri follows reluctantly, already having witnessed numerous spats between her parents. She is tired of it and wishes they would divorce. But she knows it is not possible while they remain in camp.

Mac is restraining his father, who to Terri's surprise is not spouting his usual script of obscenities. His face is pale, lips trembling. She can't tell if it's from rage or shock. A thin line of blood seeps from his nose. Her mother's complexion is ashen. She stalks back and forth among the cots, holding a hand to her face. Carmen cowers on the bed.

Obachan leads Hana to her compartment, motioning for Terri to follow. Entering their room, Terri notices how fresh and light the air is compared to the heaviness of her parents' barracks. They sit on the floor around the tea table, Hana no longer frozen-looking, crying softly into a handkerchief.

Hana explains what the fight was about. After observing so many young men leaving for the army, she says she expected Mac would receive a draft notice soon. Yet when it happened, she was not prepared and had reacted with tears and remorse for signing "yes, yes" to the loyalty oath. In her view, the loyalty oath was an invitation to be inducted. She blamed herself. She blamed Tad.

"When he came home from gambling with his gang at the canteen, drunk from that home-brewed rice wine, I lost my temper," Hana says. "I screamed at him and told him we should have signed 'no, no.' Mac now has to go to war! I guess he didn't expect such an attack and was drunk enough to take a swing at me. He hit my cheekbone hard." She rubs the side of her face. "So glad he didn't get my eye." She smiles wanly. "Mac jumped in to protect me, but not before I landed a strong blow to Tad's nose!"

Her mother tells what happened in an almost matter-of-fact way, which disturbs Terri. What has the world come to? Now her parents' arguments have escalated to hitting each other, her mother even sounding proud she gave her father a bloody nose!

Obachan, too, listens solemnly. She then says, as seriously as Terri has ever heard her, "Once a man hits a woman, it is like his first taste of wine. If he likes the wine, he cannot stop drinking it."

Hana nods, still crying. Terri sees a look pass between her mother and Obachan, a look of understanding to which she is not privy. She feels left out, jealous of their intimacy. Ever since the loyalty oath, she has noticed how close Hana and Obachan have become. She wishes she had Obachan to herself, as in the past.

Then Obachan suggests Hana stay with them until things blow over. Terri feels more alone, isolated in a world gone crazy. She misses Billy. Why didn't she get his address when he asked her to write? Now she'll have to wait to hear from him—if he remembers her. He probably won't.

After Max leaves for the army, reporting to a tank division at Fort Knox, Kentucky, her parents seem to reach a truce. Hana stays a week at the "tearoom," but moves back after Tad apologizes and promises he won't drink the rotgut anymore. They no longer fight, but seem to lead their lives apart, Hana mostly gone volunteering at the Children's Village.

One day Terri finds out her father will be going to New Jersey to work at a frozen-food plant. "Relocation," her grandmother says. He will be leaving with a number of other internees—mostly young couples and single adults. Terri learns that because of the war migration from the East to the West Coast defense plants, there is a shortage of laborers, and factories have begun recruiting from the camps. "They're even taking workers from the German prisoner-of-war camps in the States," Obachan says.

"You mean there are prisons for Germans here in America?"

"There are. Some will work at Riverside Farms with your father."

No one talks about it, but Terri suspects her father's going alone to New Jersey, ostensibly to clear the way for the family to join him later, is really a separation between her parents. After he leaves, he writes to the family. He says it isn't too bad there, that at least they have toilets in their apartments. "No more latrines," he writes. Their wages are low, though—only twenty-five cents an hour. Some of the workers, insulted, take revenge by urinating on the washed vegetables before they are to be frozen!

Only the women are left. Carmen and Hana occupy the family apartment while Terri and Obachan stay in their "tearoom," all single women living in a dormitory. Carmen and Hana often visit, but things have changed drastically. For two years they haven't eaten a home-cooked meal or sat at a nicely set dinner table. She had hated doing dishes, often fighting with Carmen over who would wash or dry. Mac, of course, never lifted a finger in the kitchen. He was a guy, after all. Today she would gladly wash *and* dry dishes, and clean up a house too, a real home with stuffed furniture and carpets and an indoor bathroom.

Inside the confines of the barrack, without a beach to escape to, she has been forced to witness her parents' problems at close range. She had never admired, or even much respected her dad. He seemed so self-centered, expecting all the attention. But before Manzanar, at least he hadn't been a drunk and had worked hard to make a living. She wonders how it will all end for them, when the war is over . . . if that ever happens.

* * *

Terri is crossing the firebreak, cursing herself for getting caught outside in the sizzling afternoon heat, so hot the heat waves waver up from the ground, distorting her legs and feet into wobbly tree limbs. She had been taking art class at Block 2 and had forgotten the time. Trudging through sand, she begins to feel dizzy, mouth dry. Her barracks is another firebreak away. She hopes she doesn't get sunstroke.

Suddenly the air turns cool. She looks up to see if a cloud has passed over the sun. But its brilliance is still blinding. Gentle wafts of smoke brush across her face. She smells sage. Hears drumming. Legs heavy, she can barely move, lifting each as if a sack of rice is tied to each foot. Time stands still. A few yards away, in the firebreak's center, she sees a circle of figures, at first shadowy, but soon evolving into distinct sharp shapes. They are dancing. Feet shuffling and hopping, they sing what sounds to Terri like a mournful dirge. She recognizes the granite warrior from the Horimoto barracks—strong-looking, with smooth bronze chest and muscled arms. Next to him dances an older Indian, a chief, Terri guesses. He is extraordinarily handsome, with a high sharp nose, like a falcon's beak, and piercing green eyes.

It seems she has been watching them dance for hours when the earth begins to tremble. A mist rises up within the circle's center. Soon the translucent clouds materialize into forms, Indian figures! Ghosts! Transfixed, Terri watches, barely breathing. She stares at the apparitions until she feels dizzy. She passes out.

When she wakes up she is on her futon in the *ochaya*. Obachan is cooling her face and naked body with cold towels.

"Teru-chan, you had me worried." Obachan's voice sounds stern. "You know better than going out in this heat without a hat."

"I'm sorry, Obachan. I forgot."

"It's a good thing Buffalo happened to be going by when he saw you fallen in the break. He carried you home." She rinses another towel in the bucket of cold water. "Sunstroke can be very dangerous, you know."

Terri wanted to tell her about the warrior dancers in her vision, and that she saw many ghosts who danced with the warriors. But she decides not to, wanting to keep the memory to herself, to preserve its clarity, to see again the power of the dancers. Somehow, the memory eases her concerns for the family. She remains quiet, accepting her grandmother's gentle admonitions like a submissive child, enjoying the soft hands and cold towels cooling her body.

Cloud's Gifts

After the fire, Sayo and the women moved temporarily into the men's boardinghouse. For days they all had been paralyzed, barely able to speak to one another. Ito, especially, was remote, disappearing for two weeks to a strange area in the coastal range where clusters of needle-shaped rock formations jutted from low mountains. "Pinnacles," it was called. Sharp spires and dark, dank caves formed a perfect no-man's land in which Ito could contemplate the tragedy. It was no secret that Ito had been attracted to Chiba, perhaps even in love for the first time in his celibate life. The group honored his quiet grief, allowing him solitude, never uttering Chiba's name in his presence. When he returned from his pilgrimage, astride Cloud's horse which he had borrowed, he was noticeably tranquil, brow smooth, jaw and neck muscles relaxed. Sayo embraced him gently. She saw his eyes were steady and clear.

"Did you battle the Tiger?" she asked.

"Yes . . . and the Dragon too."

More than ever, he appeared monklike. He was thinner, and an aura of peace surrounded him.

"Did you fast and meditate?"

"Yes. There was a special cave. I felt I was on another planet, perhaps the moon."

"I'm glad you're back, Ito-san."

"I am too." He smiled wanly. "You are my family on this earth. This is home."

From that day forward, Ito's personality returned to the more ma-

ture one he had shown before Chiba's arrival. Sayo knew Chiba had touched Ito, that their short relationship would remain with him forever . . . more precious, perhaps, because of its brevity. Once he had said to Sayo, "Like the seasons, life is transient. Nothing lasts. Each drop of dew on a leaf, each tear squeezed from the eye lives its full life and is then gone in seconds, content it has fulfilled its purpose."

Sayo, on the other hand, was still not at peace. She was angry and desired vengeance. Word had circulated that Manzo had been seen in Watsonville the day before the fire and then disappeared. Kiyomi was certain Manzo was the culprit. "He's the devil," she said, "possessive of any woman who works for him. I've seen him beat women, and I know he burned down a brothel in Stockton. But there, no one was in the house!"

"How does he get away with it?!" burst Sayo.

"Because he is handsome and charming. Most of his women first fall in love with him. Then he uses them. Such a snake!"

Sayo swallowed her anger. She needed to give full attention to finding another house, to starting over again. Fortunately, although painful and unsightly, Cloud's wound was not life-threatening, but it kept him bedridden for some days. Sayo was at his side constantly, applying compresses to the long gash down the side of his face. It healed without marring his handsome features, but left a bright purplish cord that she rubbed with sesame oil. At night when they lay together on the futon, and she massaged the scar with her fingers and lips, tasting sweat mixed with oil, she imagined absorbing into herself his bravery and strength.

Sooner than expected, they found another house. Peter, one of the Slavonians, knew of a large Victorian-style home for sale farther out from town in the countryside. Without hesitation, Cloud offered to make the down payment, creating for Sayo a quandary. She had no money. The house was exactly what she wanted. But would Cloud's generosity turn to possessiveness, to unspoken control like that of the elder Matsubara? She had tasted freedom, was intoxicated by its promise of full independence. Nothing in Cloud's behavior or attitude hinted that his encouragement for her to act as his equal was false. Yet she hesitated.

"What would I do with this money I have saved?" He held her close. *"I don't need any more horses."*

"Don't you want to buy your own land?"

"No one can 'own' a part of this earth. I don't believe in it like the white ghosts. But you need a home to survive. Besides, Hiroshi gave me the wagon, worth quite a bit."

In her heart she knew his motives were pure. *"Will you live in the house with me?"*

"If you are asking me, I will, of course. But the house is yours, Sayo . . . no strings attached."

She was surprised he was so aware of her reason for hesitating; then realized, he only could know because he, too, craved to be free, unfettered by obligation.

With gratitude and a newfound respect for him and the precepts of their relationship, Sayo accepted his offer and took ownership of the grand house.

Built in 1898, the six-year-old building was immaculately clean, smelling of pinewood and equipped with the most modern conveniences of the day—a water pump in the kitchen and a flushing toilet that rose like a throne, elevated at the end of a long, narrow room. A wide porch wrapped around the exterior, with long stairs leading down to a grassy meadow.

On the first floor a large living room, sitting room, and dining area provided ample space for entertainment and festivities. After all floors were covered with tatami and low square tables and zabuton, an open expanse was left to serve as a stage for Kabuki dance and drama. A large kitchen with western-style table and chairs, shelves, a gas stove and sink, along with the toilet room, completed the first floor.

On the second floor, accessed by a sweeping spiral staircase, Sayo and Cloud occupied one room and the women two others. Desiring more privacy for Cloud and herself, she hired the bachelors to construct an addition to the house, a long Japanese-style bungalow with an outdoor platform running its length and serving as porch and entryway to the rooms—one for each woman.

*Working long hours on weekends, the men were able to complete
the project in short time.*

*While the bachelors and Cloud worked on carpentry, Sayo and
the women transformed the large backyard into a rock garden
with fishpond. They shoveled and raked the earth, planted reeds,
bushes, and dwarf trees, and arranged boulders and stones Cloud
had procured from a nearby quarry. Sayo's plans for the future included building an o furo, a luxurious outdoor tub large enough to
hold a family. It would be authentic, heated with burning wood, a
relaxing offering for clients before enjoying the massage she had
been teaching the women.*

*Upon completion of the renovations and garden, the new tea-
house was again ready for business. Past customers had not forgotten its cheerful predecessor and had been inquiring faithfully for
the reopening. Thus, the opening celebration became a gala community event, with families attending as well as their Slavonian
friends. For days before, the women prepared sushi and teriyaki
chicken and pickled vegetables, and on the morning of the party,
Ito brought fresh fish he had just caught. That night, food was sa-
vored and rice wine flowed. Shamisen music tinkled in the air, accompanied by the women's high lilting voices and sometimes the
raspy droning of the men.*

*The party lasted through the night until dawn. A great success.
Still, Sayo's ebullience did not truly reflect her inner feelings. She
missed Chiba, her innocent laughter and mischievous antics. The
evil fire and Chiba's tragic death rankled in Sayo's heart. Even
Cloud did not guess her joy was not all-consuming; only Ito knew of
her silent sadness.*

*Seated outside in the soft afternoon sun, Sayo watched a slight
breeze ripple the glistening water of the fishpond. She gazed at the
rock garden surrounding it, admiring the two stone lanterns, procured by Ito, that guarded the entrance of the arching wooden
bridge. For a moment she was transported back to Hiroshima, to
the Matsubara compound and its vast gardens and ponds. It pleased
her to realize her present view surpassed that of the one in her mem-*

ory. *Persimmon and cherry leaves of trees she herself had planted rustled, and at the property's far end, the small orchard of apple, plum, and pear gleamed with green foliage.*

"I see you are appraising your empire." It was Cloud.

She stood up and embraced him, pleased he had returned so early from San Jose.

"I finished sooner than I planned," he explained, "and was anxious to get home and bring this surprise for you." He retrieved a bucket from the porch. It was filled with water and two red-orange carp darting about within.

Her hand flew to her face, covering her open mouth.

"Do you recognize them?" he asked.

"Of course! I can think of nothing more wonderful for our garden. It's good you rescued them from that filthy pond, and I know they will bring us good karma."

She took the pail and rushed to the water. Before she released the carp, Cloud suggested they perform a ceremony "to the Great Fish Spirit." He then began chanting, strange yet familiar sounds, guttural and melodic like Shinto prayers. She was reminded how little she knew of him, how each week she seemed to learn something new, something extraordinary. So much remained a mystery. Where did he come from? When she had asked, he had said simply, "Very far away." He pointed east. Did he have a family? What provoked that somberness in his eyes, the darkening of green when he gazed at the mountains beyond the town. He seemed to love the ocean, yet she knew his soul was bound more somehow to mountains.

But she accepted this enigma, in fact, found it appealing, even sexually arousing to make love with a "stranger." She had adopted an American attitude toward what constituted fulfillment—challenge and excitement. And what did Cloud know of her? He never asked of her past, and she never volunteered to tell him. What mattered was that their hearts spoke a language both understood. As Mentor once said, "The mind lies using words. The heart has no words with which to lie. It conveys only truth."

They released the koi. *Silvery tails flitting like fans, the colorful fish explored a huge, cleaner world, freed at last from the murky ooze of the San Jose pond. Who knew how long the ancient carp had survived in that thick algae? Who knew what dark history they recorded in their gills—the annals of Chinese riots, lynchings, burning of towns, forbidden love. It was said carp lived for a thousand years and remembered everything.*

"Should we name them?" Cloud asked.

"Oh yes." She thought for a moment. "Fish symbols avert evil forces, and they signify freedom from all restraints . . . see how they move so easily in any direction? We must name them after people who are fully free, who are very powerful."

Cloud pondered and then said, "We'll call the dark orange one Wodziwob."

"Wodziwob?" She tried to pronounce the name.

"What will you name his mate?"

"Amaterasu . . . after the Japanese Goddess of the Sun who created all of Japan." She paused. "But, Cloud-san, tell me about Wodziwob." Again she stumbled pronouncing his name.

"He was an Indian prophet, like a holy man. A Ghost Dancer . . ."

"What is a Ghost Dancer?"

"Wodziwob believed by dancing the Ghost Dance, my people would be reunited with the dead, who would then rise up and expel the white eyes from the land. He healed the sick and could control weather, make rain."

"He sounds like some of our shamans. But in Japan they are usually women—and blind. Do you believe in him?"

"He lived long ago and his prophecies did not come true. But another prophet, Wovoka, lived among my people only fifteen years back. He did the Ghost Dance, and his power was very strong. Many Indians from across the land followed him." His voice became low, jaws tight. His eyes took on a faraway look. "The Lakota were dancing the Ghost Dance when they were massacred in eighteen-ninety."

"That was only fourteen years ago! Who were the Lakota, Cloud-san?"

"They were Indians who lived far away in the flatlands. They heard of Wovoka's religion and believed in it and danced the Ghost Dance in South Dakota. The whites thought they were war dancing and killed many—over two hundred and fifty. Not just warriors, but women, children, and elders, too."

Cloud's head was bowed. Tense. She realized he carried many wounds, those he suffered in his own life and those of his people. Insults and brutalities of the past, many lifetimes ago, still reverberated in his soul. She felt the weight of his sorrow and was helpless. Finally she managed to say, "With my goddess and your spirit god swimming together in such harmony, surely great power will come from them. They will bless our land, our home here."

His thoughts of the past seemed to recede, and he put his arms around her, drawing her close. His embrace tightened.

"I heard in San Jose that Manzo has been seen there recently."

Sayo stiffened. "He has such nerve! He better stay away from here."

"I am worried about that," Cloud muttered, smoothing Sayo's back with his hands.

She asked nervously, "Are you serious, Cloud-san? Do you really think he would come back here to do us harm?"

"Yes." Quietly but emphatic.

Cloud's voice was so certain, her skin prickled as if a cold wind had blown through the garden.

"Wait here a moment." He entered the house and returned with a wooden box. Setting it down, he opened it and withdrew a long knife with a bone handle. He held it in front of her, eyes studying her face. Without hesitating, she accepted the knife as she would a gift.

"Good. You're not afraid of it."

"No, I'm not. It is very beautiful." She turned it in her hands, gingerly touching the sharp blade, caressing the sleek handle. "It is old. It must be precious to you."

"My father made it. I want you to keep it by your side when I'm away." He watched while she continued examining the knife. "Do you know how to use it?"

Sayo remembered the samurai warrior dances she learned from Mentor, how she brandished swords and knives, depicting battles and even hara-kiri, all gracefully enacted in full costume. Would she be able to actually stab someone in true life?

Her voice was calm. "Other than in dance I've never been famil-

iar with knives. But I would not be afraid to use it to protect my-self . . . or anyone else."

"Good." He sounded convinced. "I'd prefer not to have to be away, but I'll feel better knowing you have this knife to defend your-self."

"With our special koi *and your father's beautiful weapon I feel secure. Besides, the women are close by in their bungalow."*

Fall had descended quickly, arriving with crisp, cool air, turning green trees into stands of orange, gold, and maroon. She had loved this time of year in Japan. Aunt Sachiko had dreaded it. "It reminds me of approaching winter, of death," she would say. But having been born in that season, having drawn her first breath with air that had filtered through golden maple trees of the surrounding countryside, Sayo loved autumn, a time of reflection, of preparing for the earth's long rest in the coming months.

It was a month since Cloud had brought the koi, *and a week since he and Ito had left Watsonville. Celery growers in Guadalupe had been refusing to pay Japanese and Filipino laborers their right-ful wages, and now the workers wanted to organize. Cloud was be-coming well known, even as far south as Santa Maria, and farming camps throughout the central coast began asking for his help. Sayo missed him during his frequent trips, but supervising the teahouse's brisk business kept her well occupied.*

Nights had grown chilly, requiring a thick futon blanket to re-place the thinner one used during hot months. Sayo readied herself for bed, locking windows and doors. Carefully, she placed Cloud's knife beside the futon near her side. For some unexplainable rea-son, she felt anxious. Perhaps it was the owl's hooting she heard ear-lier, and, too, the night seemed peculiarly darker than usual, even with the sliver of a moon glinting against its velvet backdrop. She shivered and crawled into bed, comforted somewhat by Cloud's scent wafting up from the futon. Soon she was asleep.

She dreamt. It was night, and she was in a forest, a dark and thick forest of pines, with a new moon barely visible through the dense canopy of pine needles overhead. Astride a horse, she moved with caution, uncertain where she was going, yet filled with urgency and a sense of foreboding. Ducking under hanging branches, she brushed away spiderwebs, gauze nets sticking to her face. What was that noise? She heard crying, someone moaning. Ahead floated a woman in white kimono, long sleeves billowing like sails, young beautiful face shimmering and framed by silvery white hair. It was the ghost of Chiba. Unafraid, Sayo asked, "Why are you here?" The ghost mouth opened, a dark empty hole. Sayo barely heard the word "Danger" when the horse reared up, flames shooting out from his nostrils.

"Uma no hi! Uma no hi! Fire Horse!" the ghost cried and then disappeared.

Heat surged up Sayo's body, a piercing hotness entering between her legs straddling the horse's flanks. She shook. It was as if lightning had bolted from its body through hers, vibrating in each of her cells. They no longer were separate. She was the horse. On fire!

She sat up, awake and dripping sweat. She felt hot, but the room was cold, murky black. She sensed someone was in the house, not in her room, but downstairs. She heard shuffling noises. With swift surety she grabbed Cloud's knife that lay beside her and crawled from the futon. Soundless to the door. Her heart hammered, taiko drumming in her ears. No fear. Heat of "uma no hi" still coursed through her body. She stood up and, clenching teeth, managed to unlock and open the door without a sound.

On the landing, she heard clattering in the kitchen. Intuitively, she knew it was not one of the women. Clutching the knife with slippery hand, she crept down the stairs. Another clang. Whoever it was did not seem concerned about being heard.

Finally she reached the open door to the kitchen. Hiding against the wall, she peered into the room and saw bent over some objects on the floor, the figure of a man. She smelled a strong odor. Gasoline. Manzo! It had to be him.

"You! What are you doing!"

Bolting upright, the figure turned toward the voice. Too dark. Faceless. She saw the whites of his eyes, glittering as they darted about. Eyes of a madman. She never had met Manzo but knew it was he, knew he was demented, a ghost already whose soul had

*been stolen by demons. She caught a whiff of his breath. Whiskey
smell.*

*With a growl he lunged toward Sayo. She instinctively shot her
hand out in front to protect herself, the hand holding Cloud's knife.
She heard the crunch of metal penetrating bone and felt the weight
of his chest against her hand. He groaned. She pulled the knife out.
Stabbing again higher in his neck. A hissing sound. Warm liquid
spraying her face. Blood. He fell backward and twitched. Gurgling.
He lay still.*

*Sticky hand still clutching the knife, she crept into the kitchen.
Gasoline smell strong, but floor dry. Too dark to see what damage
he may have done, but she didn't dare light a lantern. Avoiding his
body, she circled around the kitchen to the back door and ran to
Kiyomi's room in the bungalow.*

*"Kiyomi! Kiyomi!" she pounded on the door, shocked back into
her body by the sound of her own voice.*

*The door opened. "My God! Is that you, Sayo-san?" Kiyomi stared
wide-eyed at the blood-splattered woman holding a knife and
swaying before her.*

*"I've killed Manzo," she said calmly, then fainted, falling on the
wooden runway with a loud thud.*

As it turned out, Sayo had not killed the would-be arsonist,
though she would have felt no guilt if the knife had found a fatal
mark. He was wounded badly, but recovered under the competent
hands of Dr. Sakamoto, who cared for him at his own home in
town, keeping the incident "hush-hush" within the community. The
Japanese were considered to be a law-abiding, stable group—hard-
working and serious, impervious to scandal. In addition, they had
a low, "kowtowing" profile of meekness and passivity; and arson
and murder did not fit the nonthreatening image.

After Manzo's recovery, he left quietly without notice. It was later
learned he had managed to borrow money and return to Japan.
Sayo was relieved to hear this, but still felt pain in her heart when
she thought of Chiba. To memorialize her young friend, she and Ito
built a shrine at the orchard's end, a clear pebble-filled space with a
statue of Buddha in the center.

Summer 1945

Manzanar

Frank Sinatra croons "Higher and Higher" to the screaming audience in the firebreak between Blocks 20 and 21. His lean body, snappily dressed in a wide-shouldered, pegged-legged suit, sways with the microphone, sending teenage girls into swoons. Terri sits with friend Mitzi in the last row of wooden benches at the outdoor movie theater. They had come early and saved the seats, knowing from many past movie-watchings they could sit comfortably by leaning against the posts holding up the projection tower behind and above them.

"I can't figure out why those girls get so torn up over him," Mitzi shouts over the din. "So he's got a good voice. But, man, he's skinny. Look how his Adam's apple sticks out!"

They decided to go to the movie, more to watch the audience than the film itself. They are not Sinatra fans, a rarity at this time in camp when most teenagers are crazy about the popular music and movie stars that they hear about from the outside world through magazines.

"I wonder if anyone will faint, like last time," says Terri, recalling the near emergency when Bessie Ota, who has epilepsy, went into convulsions when the crowd got hysterical.

"I don't see her," says Mitzi. "Anyway, it seems everyone is not as crazy tonight. Must have scared them. Do you see Baby?"

Terri scans the crowd looking for Baby, who doesn't look like one anymore. Three years have passed since they arrived at Manzanar, and those who were adolescents then, barely out of childhood, are now close to graduating from the camp high school.

Terri spots him standing with his buddies at the crowd's edge. She still doesn't know what Mitzi sees in him. For two years, Mitzi has nursed a crush on Baby, and for the life of her, Terri doesn't know why. He's barely spoken more than a few words to Mitzie. She treasures every one, telling and retelling Terri how his eyes said more, or how he smiled without opening his mouth to show off his dimples.

Obachan and her mother have been saying Terri has grown pretty and must be attracting some nice boys. She hasn't noticed, but isn't interested, either. Ever since the school finally opened, months after the riot, she plunged herself into studying, and in the last year has been especially interested in art—drawing and painting. No time for boys. She still thinks a lot about Billy, but not with the pain she felt after the shooting. The gloves he gave her still rest in the hidden cave.

After the soldiers left, the new administration began allowing internees outside the fence, but designated only certain areas for hiking and picnics. The pool and underground ravine are still off limits, its constant water supplying the Los Angeles Water District. "Hell, we could poison the whole city of Los Angeles," Mac had exploded one day, feeling particularly frustrated as more of his friends were drafted. "And they lock us up here because they're afraid we might be traitors? How stupid can you get?"

When Terri visited the cave, which amounted to a few times in the past two years, she found it unchanged except for some candles and incense added to the altar. She figured those were Obachan's offerings. She left Billy's gloves, even though prayers had not resulted in a letter from him. The pool and covered mini-canyon remained untouched, protected from invasion by frightening rumors of ghost sightings that had circulated around camp. Adding fuel to the rumors was a dead body found near the pool, an internee who had died from a heart attack. Since he was fairly young, in his fifties, the story was that he had been scared to death by ghosts.

When the film is over, Terri and Mitzi saunter back toward their respective blocks, disappointed the evening produced nothing more entertaining than some emotional shrieks at Frankie's wide-mouthed face. Terri can't even remember the story. *But at least there are movies,* she thinks to herself. Anything to fill in long empty days that pass so slowly. She is tired of summer's suffocating heat, and of the bone-piercing cold of winter, and the ever-present wind that blows so much dust the coated barracks and ocher air look like sepia-toned photographs from some lost world. She wishes the war were over, if only to end the excruciating boredom.

"Have you heard from Mac?" Mitzi asks, trying to make conversation with her glum friend.

"Mom got a letter yesterday. He's in Italy, I think."

"I bet you folks are happy he didn't get wounded, with so many of our boys getting killed. Our neighbors both have gold-star flags hanging in the windows."

Mitzi conspicuously doesn't ask about Terri's father in New Jersey. Terri knows the gossip is that her parents do not get along and the reason Tad relocated back East was to get away from her mother. She doesn't care. She's even glad he's gone. At least there's peace in the compartment, and her mother actually looks younger, like she's finally enjoying her life, though the thought that her mother seems happier in camp than when they lived in Venice is perturbing. She tries to recall if the family had been close, like normal families she'd seen in the movies. She realizes they were not. In fact, they were odd, with her mom so withdrawn and pent-up, tiptoeing around her dad like some intruding stranger and he a slumbering wild dog. She feels a wave of gratitude for her grandmother, more a mother to her than Hana. But why is Hana, whom Obachan must have raised, so different from both of them? She decides they are not a normal Japanese family and wishes she knew what was.

They reached Block 15. "Hey, this is where I get off." Mitzi says. "Are you going to Obon practice tomorrow? It's at the firebreak near the administration building if you go." She veers toward the barracks, her white wedgie sandals scrunching over sand.

Terri doesn't feel like dancing at Obon, remembering the past years when the huge circle dances churned up dust so thick she developed bronchial asthma. But it would be something to do. Everyone congregates at Obon. Obachan says it's a time when the souls of ancestors return and must be honored and comforted by song and dance. In Japan, sacred preparations precede the dancing, and special rituals are performed for spirits of parents who died the previous year and those who died violent deaths. Terri doesn't like to think about death, and somehow Obon dancing seems more like a celebration, people of all ages—from small children to camp elders—twirling and stamping to a huge taiko's rhythm. Last year Buffalo beat the drum, standing in tall *getas*, a sumo-wrestler giant calling to the dead.

Terri arises early next morning, unable to sleep in the heat. Obachan is already gone, most likely working at the huge vegetable garden outside camp where volunteers grow premium produce for mess halls. There's even a chicken and pig farm. On hot days when wind blows from the south, their smell permeates camp, reminding everyone of where the last meals of chicken fricassee and pork stew came from.

She takes a cool shower and decides to skip breakfast. It's not too hot yet to walk across camp to the post office. After Billy left, going for the mail had provided a reason to be eager, a purpose for enduring the bleak mile hike. She used to imagine receiving a letter from him, a letter asking forgiveness for the shooting and confessing his love. But after a time, trudging the distance with no reward at the end became a chore, and the anticipation disappeared. Now she rarely makes the pilgrimage.

Inside the postal room, she notices a large poster tacked on the bulletin board next to the announcement for Obon practice. A drawing of several Indians wearing feathered headdress stare from beige-colored cardboard. A troupe from Big Pine will be coming to give an exhibition of dances at the high school playing field. The Lone Pine and Independence School football teams earlier had come to camp and played against the Manzanar team, but Indians coming to entertain is something new. She had thought those who lived in the desert were all dead.

She remembers her vision dancers in the firebreak and stares again at the poster. These dancers are dressed differently and look sad to Terri, not strong and powerful like the ones in her dream. She reminds herself to be sure to see the Indians when they come to entertain.

"Any mail for Murakami? Block Sixteen, Barrack Ten, Apartment Two?" She's hoping there will be a letter from Mac. Her mother has been worried even though the war in Europe is over. She's afraid he'll now be sent to the Pacific to fight the Japanese.

"Don't you have a sister named Carmen? The one who's such a good singer?" asks Postmaster, "And is your name Terri?"

Startled, she stammers yes.

"There's a strange letter here addressed to 'Terri,' " he reads, " 'Sister of Carmen who sings like Carmen Miranda, Japanese Internment Camp, Manzanar, California.' That's all it says." He shakes his head. "This is an old letter that's already been to about two or three other camps. Amazing it got anywhere addressed like that."

Terri's heart hammers. "Does it say who it's from?"

He looks on the back of the worn envelope. "No name, but it must be from some soldier. There's an APO number." Chuckling, he hands her the letter.

Unable to utter more than "thank you," she rushes from the barrack, shoving the letter into the pockets of her shorts. She is certain it is from Billy, but cannot bring herself to open and read it. And what if it isn't? Could it be some joke? She trots across the break, not knowing where she is going, unmindful of morning heat now rising from the sand. She keeps jogging, past the school, past her block, beyond the hospital. In a trance she continues until sweat soaks her blouse and slickens her *getas*. Finally she finds herself at the guard tower. The wood is gray and splintered, with sections of roof and deck torn away and hanging loose in odd angles. Tumbleweeds have sprouted in the no-man's land between barracks and the fence and surround the sagging structure. Sitting in its shade, she gingerly retrieves the letter from her pocket and tears it open. A waft of cigarette smell tickles her nose.

Dear Terri,

Hi, partner! I don't know if this letter will ever reach you since I'm sorry to say I forgot your last name and sure didn't have your address. Dumb of me, I know. But I

*did remember you had a sister named Carmen who
sang, and I figure with a name like that someone would
figure out where this letter is supposed to go. It's a long
shot but here goes anyway.*

*The main reason I needed to write is to say how sorry
I am about what happened at the riot. I've been living
with that memory for so long and still can't get it out of
my mind. I feel bad too that I never got the chance to say
good-bye. Man, they shipped us out of there so fast. Since
then I've seen some action in Italy and France, the real
war. But what happened at Manzanar was real war for
me, too. It was wrong. Putting you and your family in
prison is wrong. I know it now. Our company has been
hearing a lot about the 100th Infantry Battalion who are
Nisei soldiers fighting over here. We hear they're real
brave and tough. Did a fantastic job at Anzio. Some
come out of the camps. Hell, don't know if I could do that
if they locked up my folks.*

*Anyway, I've been lucky and haven't taken any bullets.
Have a lot of time to think, too. Do you still go to the pool
and Indian cave? Met any other G.I.'s guarding at the
tower? Thinking back, I sure appreciate how you came to
visit and made my days interesting. And you were just a
kid of thirteen. A real smart kid, though. You must be fifteen by now. Any boyfriends? How about your sister
Carmen? Too bad she missed her chance. Just kidding.*

*Well, partner, sure hope you get this letter somehow. If
you do, it would make one southern boy real happy if
you wrote back. Hope you found another supplier for the
movie mags, too. Thanks again for the good memories.
They were the only good ones from my stint there.*

Love,
Billy

P.S. My last name is Fordham—in case you write.

He had written an APO address at the bottom. She smoothes the
two pages of the letter and holds them to her nose. She imagines

they smell of Billy's cigarettes. She feels strangely calm, buoyant, as if a stone has lifted from her shoulders. If she had received the letter long ago, she would have been delirious with joy, running to Obachan with the news. Now she wants to keep the letter to herself, even though it may have been Obachan's magic that finally brought it to its true destination.

Reading the words, she could hear his boy/man voice of the past, the musical southern accent, his kidding chuckles. She sees his gray-speckled eyes and red dragon hair. With clear eyes, she sees he was an eighteen-year-old bored soldier, eager for fun like any teenager, but also a good person; a good person who saw with his heart and befriended a young girl who was supposed to be the enemy he was guarding.

She realizes she would not have understood if she had received the letter two years ago. He had taken risks for her, had warned her about the impending crackdown by the military. And now he asks for forgiveness, just as she had imagined he might. It doesn't matter that he didn't confess his love. She is sixteen now and realizes eighteen-year-olds don't fall in love with thirteen-year-olds. She thinks of Mac, same age as Billy, interested in someone sixteen years old today. No way.

She sits in sweltering heat, remembering the good times gambling, playing cards, swimming at the pool, talking for hours. Her time with Billy lasted only months, yet shone so bright in her memory that the years since he left seem faded, like overexposed movies filmed in slow motion.

Looking past the barbed wire, she can see the hedge of greenery marking the pool and hidden canyon. She decides she will visit the cave tomorrow and retrieve Billy's gloves. Then she will write him a letter and hope it will get to him somehow.

The still morning is whispering with wind that usually kicks up in afternoon. Clutching the letter tightly, she heads for home. Her gait is jaunty. She decides she will go to Obon tonight and dance—not only for her dead ancestors, but also for all the soldiers killed in the war and for the Indian warriors who died in this desert.

Sayo's Secret

*T*he o furo *was completed. A ghostly temple, the octagon-shaped pavilion rose through the mist-shrouded backyard. Covered by a redwood canopy, the square tub, large enough to hold seven persons, was surrounded by a deck set about four feet off the ground. Cloud and Ito were tending the fire under the tub, keeping flames crackling with redwood and oak scraps from the house's addition.*

Sayo's plan was to celebrate its completion by taking a group bath. Afterward, they, and guests invited from around the countryside, would feast on food prepared during the last two days. Then they would dance and sing until dawn.

Darkness descended quickly as soon as the sun settled beyond the horizon. The bachelors arrived early, dressed in yukata *and wearing* getas.

"Did you walk all the way in those clothes?" laughed Cloud. "You're lucky you weren't arrested for dressing like women!"

"The sheriff did stop us, but we invited him to the party."

Sayo gasped.

"Don't worry, Onesan *we're kidding. We waited until dark to walk here. Didn't want any scandal."*

They entered the wash area, a graveled space at the side of the pavilion surrounded by bamboo and covered by a corrugated tin roof. Some low stools and buckets were scattered inside. This was the "washroom" where one first cleansed away the day's grime before soaking in the tub.

The men, already naked, began dipping hot water from the tub in buckets that they poured over themselves. Cloud removed the dark blue yukata Sayo had made for him and hung it on a peg attached to one of the posts. With his broad shoulders and straight back, long hair gathered in a braid, he looked every bit the samurai warrior. She motioned for him to sit on a stool and began soaping his chest and back. Kneeling, she washed his feet, struck by the hard, callused soles, thick and smooth as leather. Noticing her interest, he explained, "For many years when I lived as an Indian, I never wore shoes. My feet grew their own soles."

He was first to enter the tub, moaning with pleasure. He called for the others to hurry so they could watch the full moon rise. Quickly, Sayo scrubbed Ito's back and washed his hair, while Kiyomi and Reiko tended to the other bachelors. Finishing with Ito, Sayo took off her kimono and hung it over Cloud's. Unpinned hair fell down her back, a black mane that reached her buttocks. She wove it into one long braid.

She stepped into the steaming tub, seating herself next to Cloud. The tin bottom was covered by a wood-slatted raft that protected the bathers from the scorching heat of the fire underneath. Soon Reiko and Kiyomi joined them. Although large, the tub had no room to spare, with seven bodies languishing side by side, arms and legs brushing against each other like flittering carp in a pond. With water reaching her neck, Sayo's tail of braided hair floated on top, a sinuous black water snake.

They were quiet, except for an occasional sigh or hiss to relieve the heat building up from the still-roaring fire beneath. It was dark and misty, as only an autumn night in the countryside could be. But it was also an extraordinary night, with a full moon expected to rise earlier than usual. The air was brittle, sharp even through the warmth rising up from the water.

"Where are Jade Young Moon and Night Jasmine?" one of the bachelors asked.

Kiyomi explained their shyness in partaking of a group bath. "O furo is not in the Chinese culture, you know. Besides, they are much younger than we. We must seem old and musty to them."

Just as she spoke, the two Chinese girls approached, one carrying a tray and the other swinging a kerosene lantern.

Night Jasmine's high tinkling voice announced, "We bring sake to celebrate!" The two girls immediately set about to serve rice wine in cups from the tray.

"Such an auspicious beginning for our o furo," said Sayo, rising up from the water like a sea goddess. She took a sake bottle from Jade Young Moon and poured its contents into the tub. She then asked Cloud to bless it with an incantation in the Indian language. Resembling a mizu kami, one of those ancient water deities that protected Japan's many hot springs, Cloud also rose up in the steam and chanted in his deep voice. The perspiring bathers listened reverently, lulled by heat and inhaled sake fumes wafting up from the water.

After the blessing, Kiyomi exclaimed, "Now we must name the ochaya! We don't have a name for it yet . . . do we?" She peered at Sayo, hoping she had not overstepped any boundary by suggesting a naming ceremony that included all of them. But Sayo was pleased, agreeing it was a good idea to name the teahouse that night. It was a special full moon, and already the luminous disk was beginning to show.

"Blow out the lantern," said Ito, pointing east above the house and beyond. Half of the yellow moon shone above oak trees.

"How about the Apple Blossom Inn," suggested one of the bachelors, "for all the apple orchards in this valley."

"I would like the name to have an aura of eternal bliss . . . of paradise," offered Sayo, "so that guests will expect an uplifting of their souls as well as comfort for their earthly bodies."

The group became quiet, reminded of how serious it was to name a place. After long contemplation, Ito spoke. "I think Heaven should be in the name. Heaven is a state of mind. It is here on earth, however we create it with our minds."

"How about the Heaven and Sun Inn?" said Cloud.

"Forgive my humble opinion," piped Ito, "but the words are too yang, too 'hot,' if you will excuse the innuendo."

Laughter. Then Sayo spoke, voice strong and reverberating with the authority she had earned in the past months of steering her vision to its completion. "The Heavenly Cloud Inn," she said simply.

A communal "aaahh."

"I think it is appropriate this ochaya *be named for our greatest patron, for it would not be possible without him." She embraced Cloud in the water. She emptied another bottle of sake into the bath.*

The full moon now glowed above them, its creamy face so close, gray shadows of unmapped craters and ravines stood out like scars marring an otherwise perfect complexion. Sayo knew this day was the most propitious of all days since her arrival from Japan. She could foresee how the Heavenly Cloud Inn would teem with activity, bringing comfort and solace to lonely countrymen—perhaps to lonely hakujin, *too. It would earn its place among the highest of respected teahouses. Mentor would be proud. But Sayo guessed her teacher already knew her success. Hadn't she, after all, suggested it? But now Sayo realized an important reality. Her destiny was not to continue the Matsubara line in the New World. She was to complete Mentor's karma. She would extend Mentor's line, the line of the Fire Horse Woman, outcasts in Japan, but heroines in America where they must realize this feminine power in order to survive and prevail.*

A year had passed since o furo's *completion. The Heavenly Cloud Inn flourished with customers traveling from as far away as San Jose to be entertained. All the original women remained, though others came seeking employment, mostly disappointed picture brides fleeing match-marriages gone wrong. Without family or money, the women were desperate, but few wanted to return to Japan. Sympathetic, but unable to take them in, Sayo gave money and advice, urging a move to Los Angeles, where a large Japanese community was growing.*

O furo *was the inn's famous offering. Many bachelors from Watsonville, and some families, too, became regular customers, bathing weekly and some staying for massage. In the beginning, men were eager to pillow with the women, but as time passed, Kabuki dances and plays became a favorite entertainment and some chose instead to spend money socializing with Sayo and the dancers in the big living room turned theater. There were several who became steady pillow partners with Reiko and the Chinese girls. Kiyomi, though,*

was not available, having made the decision to not provide her ser-
vices to anyone. Only a man who will marry me," she vowed. "A
rich man, that is."

For Sayo, the year seemed to fly by like a fierce wind. Her atten-
tion had been mostly focused on guiding the inn to its successful
fruition, and although Cloud was often gone organizing farm la-
borers, the time when he was home she devoted to him. She fell more
deeply in love. He was constant, a steady, strong beat in the rhythm
of her life. He came and he went, as free as the hawks that traversed
the skies overhead. She rarely thought of the Matsubara; Hiroshi
was a dim memory, and even Tadanoshin's memory had faded, al-
though in the few letters she had received from Mentor, she was glad
to hear the Matsubara were faring well.

Lately, she noticed Cloud seemed preoccupied. She wondered if
there was a particularly difficult job he was worried about. She didn't
ask, knowing he would tell her when the time was right. Besides, Ito
had organized a grunion-hunting party for the exceptionally high
tide expected during full moon. Tonight they all would gather at the
beach and build a fire. So romantic! What could be more cozy than
watching flames flickering in front of a backdrop of pounding
waves.

She found Cloud sitting by the fishpond, staring into the water.
Deciding not to disturb his reverie, she retired to their room up-
stairs. Several hours later he joined her, still looking pensive, almost
solemn.

"We're having a grunion party tonight. Full moon. A nice time to
relax, don't you think, Cloud-san?"

His glum countenance didn't change. He put his arms around
her. "I need to go away, Sayo-san."

"You've gone away many times, dear Cloud. Is this time any dif-
ferent?" From his manner she felt something serious was brewing.
"Is it another strike you must lead?"

"No." He tightened his arms around her as if protecting her from
a blow. She felt his heart's steady thump against her cheek, heard
his words vibrate in his chest. "I must go far away. First to San
Francisco."

She remained still, not so alarmed by the news as by his tenor in telling it, understanding he would not leave without good reason. "But you will come back soon?"

He pulled her closer. "Of course. I promise I will return as soon as I can." He released his breath. "There is big trouble where my people live. The white eyes stole the land before, and now they steal the water." Anger deepened his voice. "I am son of a chief. They do not know how to fight the white man's way. But I do. I must help them."

Despite a sinking heart, she encouraged him. "That is the honorable thing to do. You must protect your family and your people. How far is your village? And how do you know of this?"

I have known for a while . . . the mountains spoke to me." He looked to the east and pointed, "My village is far away in mountains beyond those. It is many years since I have been home. An Indian from the area confirmed what I felt when I met him in San Jose last month."

So this was the news that had been occupying Cloud's thoughts these past weeks. "Then you must go immediately so you can return soon. I will pray and light incense for every day you are gone." She tried to be cheerful. "You will come to the beach tonight, won't you?"

"I plan to. It will be a nice send-off." He walked to the closet and rummaged, returning with a tissue-wrapped parcel. "Here's a gift for you. I wanted to give it for Valentine's Day but hadn't finished it."

She unwrapped a smoothly finished wooden hand mirror. Deeply touched, she was unable to speak.

"I cut the wood from a tree myself. It's walnut."

"But how did you find time to make this? You have been so busy working." She hugged him, murmuring, "Thank you, thank you." What had she to give him? Should she reveal the secret she had kept these past two months? Could that be her gift? She had hoped to tell him at an appropriate time, a romantic moment. Now she felt this was not the right moment, either. It would worry and distract him to know she was carrying his child. He might choose even not to leave. Then he would bear the burden of his family's dishonor, per-

haps even blame her in years to come. No, she would not tell him now.

Cinders crackled out of the bonfire, red fireflies dancing around the revelers awaiting arrival of the grunion, the slender fish that migrated from deep water to sandy shores, depositing eggs during high tide. Sayo and Cloud sat apart with a blanket draped over them. Although hot during the day, the air turned sharp at night. While others chattered, sipping rice wine, some wading in the high tide's foamy water, Sayo and Cloud were restrained, concerned parents watching an unruly flock.

Her hands rested on her belly, still flat with only a hint of roundness. She was filled with awe thinking of his seed sprouting within, his seed that would grow into a human being whose veins would run with the blood of ancestors who had lived so many centuries in the New World.

She heard Kiyomi complaining, "Ito, where are these fish you say fly in with the tide? The tide's here, and no fish!"

"They'll come soon. They run all along the coast and haven't found us yet."

As he spoke, a flapping sounded in the water. "See!" he shouted, "There's a few!"

The water turned phosphorescent. Slivers of fish, tails beating frantically, leaped out of the froth. After the wave receded, they convulsed on the sand, spent from swimming through oceans to reach this end. Pails in hand, the gatherers scurried, scooping up quivering grunion from wet sand. After filling pails, they began throwing fish at each other, laughing. Sayo felt a pang of sympathy for the pregnant fish. How sad to make such an arduous journey to deposit eggs, reach the destination and then be tossed in the air like a dead twig.

"Do you think the grunion spirit is angry at the way we gather them so frivolously?" she asked Cloud.

"No," he answered thoughtfully. "They have accomplished their purpose. What matters is in the heart of the gatherers. Their joy is better than greed, and they take only what they need."

At the inn, Ito and Kiyomi fried the grunion and served a late-night meal. After eating, Sayo and Cloud retired. He hadn't told them of his departure.

"Will you tell them before you leave?"

"No. I shouldn't be gone too long. It's best for them to see my absence as part of work. Then everything will remain as usual."

But this was not a "usual" trip, she thought. An urge to reveal the pregnancy pressed upon her, but she pushed it away. She opened his suitcase and helped him pack.

Halfway through packing, he stopped and sat on the floor, motioning for her to join him. He began speaking, and Sayo listened intently, knowing what he had to say was very important. He was a man of few words and rarely offered more than a few sentences at a time. But on this occasion he talked for a long while, telling her his deepest thoughts.

He talked of his people who lived for centuries high in the mountains. He told how they had lived off the earth where game and fowl teemed in woods and streams and lakes. Then the white man came and took the land and soon soldiers arrived to protect those white men and their families from Indians fighting to regain the land. "Thirty years ago, they imprisoned a thousand of my people and force-marched them a hundred and seventy-five miles away to another fort prison," Cloud said bitterly. "Feet bleeding, hungry and dying of thirst, they were driven like maimed horses by the white eyes." He sighed. "I was an infant then, but we have not forgotten. I left as a young man, discouraged, wanting to leave that life behind, travel the world. But now the spirits are calling me back. I must go."

She helped him finish packing, grateful he had talked of his pain. Now she understood the wound that festered in his soul; she hoped this journey would help to heal him.

They made love. He was gentle. Yet a desperation underlay his passion, as if he was trying to absorb her very essence. She surrendered wholly, succoring and nourishing him, a river feeding the ocean.

Initiation

*C*loud had been gone for three days. In the kitchen, Sayo and Kiyomi prepared dinner, discussing the day's strangeness. First of all, the weather: hot and muggy, it seemed more like the last days of summer than the first days of spring. An odd haze hung over the valley, the air heavy. Stillness before a storm. Yet there was no sign of clouds. And dogs barking in the neighboring farms sounded like a pack of arguing wild wolves.

"Such a din!" said Kiyomi. "But have you noticed they're quiet now?" She washed some celery at the pump.

Sayo stopped chopping onions, then shrugged her shoulders as if shaking off flies. "It's very quiet . . . too quiet. Another strange thing: when I went to feed the carp, they were swimming in crazy circles."

Changing the subject, Kiyomi asked, "When will Cloud come back?"

"I'm not sure. He couldn't say."

"Well, I'm sure he will be back soon," Kiyomi said comfortingly. "He will know what makes the carp swim in circles."

Sayo wanted to tell her of the pregnancy, but decided to wait, at least until Cloud returned. "I think he will be home in time to see the cherry blossoms," added Kiyomi.

Sayo retired early, feeling tired and strangely anxious. What was this heaviness she felt in her belly? Shaking off an ominous feeling, she got up and opened a window, hoping fresh air would lighten her mood. But it was still muggy. She returned to bed and lay down without covers. Before she dropped off to sleep, she thought she heard a *hototogisu,* the cuckoo, calling spirits of the next world in its melancholy voice.

Sometime in the early morning darkness a tremor awakened her. Sitting up, she knew instinctively it was an earthquake. Living in Japan, where quakes struck as commonly as thunderstorms, she had learned to react quickly. She ran down the stairs, jostling against walls and banisters as the tremors increased. She heard sounds of falling pots and pans and breaking glass above a deep rumble coming up from the earth. Outside, she joined the women, huddled together away from the building. As the ground swayed, rolling like a wave, she heard water lapping out of the o furo and carp pond. She ran and discovered the fish flopping on the ground. She threw them back into water.

Within minutes, the shaking and rolling ceased, the tremors leaving an eerie pall. Kiyomi broke the silence. "The earthquake kami *is very strong in America, and angry too! I could hear him roaring!"*

The Chinese girls began to cry. Unacquainted with such tremors, they wailed loudly when an aftershock jolted the ground. Sayo tried to calm them. "It's over. We'll stay outside for a while longer, just to be safe. But this is not a very big quake . . . I've felt much bigger in Japan."

They remained huddled in the yard until dawn, when they were joined by the bachelors, breathless from running. Ito guessed Watsonville was not the quake's center. "I have a feeling it was concentrated farther north, perhaps San Francisco."

"San Francisco!" Sayo cried, "Are you sure, Ito?"

"I just have a feeling, Sayo-san. Why?"

"Cloud may be there!"

Ito was silent a moment. "Don't worry, Sayo-san. Cloud can take care of himself."

The bachelors stayed and helped clean up broken glass and collapsed shelves. Soon things returned to normal, and the women went about business as usual. But Sayo felt a sense of foreboding throughout the day. She stayed in her room, meditating, willing her mind to empty itself of worry. When Kiyomi tried to comfort her, she sent her away.

The next day, they received word that San Francisco indeed had suffered the worst damage. The quake had toppled buildings and cracked streets. Fires raged from broken gas lines. The estimate was over five hundred killed and scores injured, and there was still great danger of further gas explosions. Devastated by the news, Sayo held hope Cloud had passed through the city before the quake hit. If he had escaped injury, she was sure he would return to Watsonville without traveling further. And, if he had been lucky enough to miss the catastrophe altogether and had reached his family, she need only wait until he completed his mission. Either he would be back in a few days or in a month or so.

For the next week she kept busy planting vegetables and flowers, rearranging her room, practicing the shamisen *as if nothing had happened. Now and then the earth would shudder, aftershocks reminding her of the disaster and plunging her into despair. She walked a dozen times a day to the road, anxious eyes searching its length to the horizon.*

Sympathetic to her suffering, Ito decided to travel to San Francisco and try to find out what he could. Sayo wanted to go with him, but he persuaded her to stay, in case Cloud returned. He went to the Asia Hotel and learned it had been demolished, with several inside killed, though no one knew who they were. Crestfallen, he returned to Watsonville and broke the news to Sayo.

But Sayo did not give up. She desperately held on to the hope he had made it to his destination before the quake hit, that he was in the mountains with his people and would come back in May or early June, at least in time to smell the apple blossoms of the valley's many orchards.

When after three months, Cloud had not returned, she began to prepare herself for the inevitable. She prayed and meditated for hours, welcoming prayer offerings from the women and bachelors, who had watched with helplessness as the realization of what must have happened to Cloud sank in. No one considered for one moment that Cloud had abandoned them. He was honorable, a true leader among men. Only death or something close to it would have prevented his coming back. With Sayo, they mourned, comforted they had named the inn for him.

Her grief was so deep that in its darkest moment she had contemplated seppuku. *But the growing mound of her belly gave a reason to live. She wrote to Mentor, lamenting her fate. "Is this what it means to be a Fire Horse Woman? First Hiroshi left, now Cloud is gone. Do we outlive our men?"*

Mentor's answer consoled her somewhat. "Your fate is not your destiny. There is much more to live before you will discover your purpose. When you know your purpose, you will know your destiny. Being a Fire Horse Woman means you are powerful. You can be strong without a man. Besides, you don't know if Cloud is truly gone. And you carry his seed within you, so he lives on anyway. Do not despair."

When six months had gone by, she resigned herself to a life without Cloud. She directed energy toward the unborn child and to greater success for the Heavenly Cloud Inn. She held the mirror he had given her and studied the reflection gazing back. Brows drooping with sadness, lips drawn and dry. She had aged. Yet a light still gleamed in the dark eyes, a light that acknowledged she had survived one initiation and now was prepared for what others life had to offer.

Secret Uncovered

Manzanar, 1945

Hana visits Sayo every day, discussing matters both mundane and momentous. The war is over in Europe and appears to be ending in the Pacific, a good time to take stock of their situation. Hana has decided not to join Tad at the frozen-food plant in New Jersey.

"Divorce?" asks Sayo.

"Yes, but not now. There are enough things to think about and do when the war is over and we leave this place."

"I'm glad you made your decision," says Sayo, pouring another cup of tea for her daughter. "What finally did it? Have you heard from Shimmy?"

"I have." She sips the pungent tea slowly. "But that is not the only reason. I want to go to college and become a teacher. That could never happen being with Tad." She has been teaching at the orphanage—small crafts at first, but later arithmetic and beginning reading. She enjoys working with children and knows she is a good teacher.

"And Shimmy?"

"I'm not sure. But I'm leaving the door open. He wants to get together when he returns from overseas."

"Then he knows of your decision to divorce."

"I've told him. But he never urged me to in any way." Hana now pours her mother a cup of tea. "Did I tell you Shimmy may stay in the army? He wants to become a minister, a chaplain."

"No! Really?"

Hana nods, smiling.

"Actually, it's not surprising—in fact, perfect for his inclination," says Sayo. "Destiny reveals itself in life's most crushing moments. Who knows what tragic incidents he lived through as interpreter for military intelligence." She solemnly adds, "He may not be the same Shimmy."

"I'm not the same Hana." She remembers how she had shocked herself when she assailed Tad, blaming him for forcing the family to sign "yes, yes," making Mac vulnerable for the draft. All her suppressed rage had exploded—against him, against his family, against herself. She blamed him for being the tyrant, the warden of her self-imposed prison, and she hated herself for having given him that power. But after she hit him in the face, bloodying his nose, her anger ceased. She knew another life existed for her and must be strong to claim it. And it might or might not include Shimmy.

"I'm happy for you, Hana. Tad was not the right person for you. And, again, I apologize for arranging your marriage. Life cannot be undone, but you do have three beautiful children from that union. And now you have another chance. You are young."

"Yes, I am."

"And the war will soon be over."

Hana realized the war within herself had been over for some time.

Today the Obon dance is finished, marking perhaps the camp's last communal event. Hana sips cold tea with Sayo. She notices her mother is different. An intensity sharpens her features, as if the flesh has melted away beneath the skin of her face. Her eyes glitter.

"The days of our time in this prison are coming to an end," Sayo says. "Soon we move off in our separate ways."

Hana worries. "What are you talking about, Mama? Just because the camp closes doesn't mean we separate. We still stick together."

"There are some things you need to know, and this may be the last time I have a chance to tell you."

Worried by the ominous tone of the conversation, Hana asks gently, "Why do you say that?"

"Don't argue with me about 'why.' I am about to tell you something. Just listen." Sayo's voice is sharp.

Subdued by her mother's unusual edginess, Hana is silent as Sayo begins to talk. "Now that you are splitting with Tad, I can tell you the truth." She pauses and takes a deep breath. "I lied to the *baishakunin* that your father was Hiroshi, so the arranged marriage with Tad could go through."

The words sink in. "You mean . . . Hiroshi isn't my father?"

"No, he isn't." Another deep breath. "Your father was a man named Cloud . . . John MacCloud. He was an Indian."

Stunned silence. Hana remembers the face reflected in Sayo's hand mirror, the long black braids. Sayo's words are a revelation, yet in a way, she had sensed it. Now things fall into place. She understands why she looks different from other Japanese, why her bones are long, and she is tall. She understands her skin's amber tones, the high-bridged nose, eagle-wing eyebrows. My God! She is half-Indian! Numbed by this truth, she sits frozen as Sayo talks about her past, filling in the blank spaces about which Hana had been reluctant to ask. Sayo tells the story of her aunt lying to the *baishakunin* in Hiroshima, giving her wrong birth sign and age. "So you see, it was not hard to lie again about your background when Tad's family sent a *baishakunin*."

"She met Cloud the day she arrived in America," Sayo told Hana. "He was her husband Hiroshi's best friend."

"Did you love him immediately?" asks Hana, now recovered and immersed in the drama of her mother's life.

"No, but there was great attraction between us. I was married, after all. But in truth, I was in love with my husband's father at that time."

As Sayo reveals her past, Hana sees through her mother's eyes a colorful pageantry—people and events cloaked in drama, betrayal, and redemption, all accepted by Sayo without judgment. She always guessed Sayo's life never could have been dull, but she is unprepared for the sensational scenes her mother describes. Weeping, Sayo describes her last moments with Cloud as if they occurred yesterday. The hand mirror he gave. His promise to return.

"Your father was a man of integrity. He was a leader, a strong leader willing to take a stand for his beliefs. That is why he left to help his people in the mountains. But, unfortunately, he was killed in San Francisco.

To learn Cloud died in the quake, tragically ending their idyllic love, wrenches Hana, and she too cries—for her mother, for the Indian father she never knew.

"But what about Yoshio, the man who raised me?"

"That is another story," says Sayo, and she relates how Chiba, Yoshio's *shashin kekkon*, had run away from him and found Sayo in Watsonville, joining the teahouse.

"So how did Yoshio get into the picture?"

"Well, one day, when you were still an infant, he came knocking at the inn's door, looking for Chiba. Poor man, he had been searching for two years, it seems."

"Did he love her that much?"

"I think he did love her . . . like a father. And he was concerned for her. You see, she had run away with a pimp." She chuckles. "In fact, we were quite frightened he might become violent, having heard of his bull-like strength and temper. I put him off from coming inside that first day and invited him to a party the next night, where I had to tell him of Chiba's death. He was shocked and sad, of course, but mainly very lonely. I don't know what got into me, but I felt sorry for him and invited him to stay with us at the inn. He was pleased to do so, and, as you know, stayed for years until he died."

Hana sighs. "Then he wasn't my stepfather?"

"No. We were never more than friends . . . good friends. He was very good to you."

"Yes, I remember him as someone kind and considerate, a fine friend to all the women." Hana speculates, "That's why it was so shocking to move in with Tad's family of men. The only man I knew was Yoshio, who was quiet and gentle."

Hana is tired, emotionally spent. So many revelations to digest. *Where is the mirror Cloud made for Sayo?* She remembers it was left in the cave. She wishes she could hold it now, look into it and perhaps see her father's face or her own mixed-blood one. She thinks of the hapa children at the orphanage, some abandoned because they are "half-breed," causing them to think of themselves with shame and self-deprecation. Yet they are exquisitely beautiful, with exotic almond-shaped eyes—sometimes green, gray, or hazel colored—and rose-hued complexions, some with delicate, high-bridged noses.

Hana realizes how her mother and the Heavenly Cloud women kept the secret of her bloodline, how they protected her from an ostracizing society that fears differences.

She feels a strength never before felt. Instead of the tall, gangly outsider she thought she was, she is a cross between two bloods, a hybrid person with a soul both Japanese and Indian.

It seems they have been sitting for hours when Terri enters, lugging a large cardboard portfolio. She is in good spirits, a welcome change from the depression she has displayed for so many months. Hana looks at her with new eyes. She sees the tawny skin, long limbs, high cheekbones. *Yes, of course, she looks like me—mixed blood,* Hana thinks.

"What have you been painting, Terri-chan?" asks Sayo.

"Some Indian dancers down at the school."

Eyebrows raised, Sayo asks, "Dancers? From where?"

"Oh, I don't know. Probably from around Lone Pine or Bishop. There's a whole band of them. Really interesting. You know, they look like us."

"Are they gone now?"

"Yeah, but they'll be back tomorrow. Why don't you come see them, Obachan?"

"Maybe I will," says Sayo.

"Let me know when they'll be dancing," says Hana. "I'd like to see them."

Terri looks at her mother with questioning eyes, but realizes she is serious. *Wow, things really are changing,* she thinks.

Ghost Dancer

When Sayo awakens in the morning, a current of excitement runs through her. Something amazing will happen today. Maybe the war is over. She is buoyant and tickles Terri awake.

"Obachan, what's the matter? Haven't seen you so chipper . . . anything wrong?"

"I have a good idea. Let's go to the cave and get our offerings we left there. I think we will be leaving this place soon."

Terri stretches, sits up. "But I want to go see the Indians dance again today."

Sayo has forgotten about the dancers. How could she have forgotten such a momentous event? She wonders if age is catching up and she is losing her memory.

"Oh yes. What time will they be here?"

"Late in the afternoon, around sunset when it cools off, I think."

"Good. We can go to the cave tomorrow."

But later in the morning, Sayo feels compelled to visit the grotto herself. The morning already hot, she doesn't want to putter around the compartment, even though the electric fan ordered from the Sears and Roebuck catalog whirs, stirring up a small breeze in the oppressive room. She puts on boots and a light cotton kimono. On her head she ties a bonnet, a heavily starched conelike hat she has made—along with many other women in camp—to shade her face from the relentless sun.

She doesn't quite know why she feels this need to go to the cave this morning. It's been months since she last went. Perhaps it's the inevitable ending of the war, the possibility the internees will be rushed from camp as ruthlessly as they were hurried in. She wants to retrieve the mirror, Cloud's last gift to her, which she had left for the spirits.

Trudging through the dry sagebrush, the desert scent now a familiar perfume, she feels strangely at peace. The ocher sand, dotted with small pebbles and round rocks of black, white, lavender, and maroon, seems to stretch for miles in every direction, a huge carpet sweeping clear up to the mountains' base. *How beautiful it is,* Sayo thinks. Why hasn't she noticed this breathtaking panorama before?

Inside the cave, she sees everything remains as it was—bones, feathers, driftwood, dried flowers, even the candle shards. The mirror lies on the altar, gray with dust and sheathed by delicate cobwebs. Carefully she wipes it clean with her kimono sleeve, blowing breath on the glass. She looks at her reflection. Yes, she is old. But she still sees light in the black pools of her eyes. Slowly, the reflection begins to fade, finally disappearing altogether. An ominous feeling tightens her belly. Is this a sign? Is she soon to vanish from this earth? No, she is not ready to leave yet.

The mirror is filled with another image . . . an image of a man! He is old, too, long hair streaked with white. His face is handsome, although the cheeks are lined with wrinkles. His nose is hawklike, proud. Her breath quickens. The image is gone.

She returns to her room and wanders aimlessly about. Then she decides to refold her kimonos and *obi,* layering them in wicker baskets. Not knowing why, she begins packing away the cups and teapot into a box. She leaves her shrine intact, adding the wooden mirror.

After lunch, which Sayo skips, knowing the mess hall will be unbearably hot, Terri crashes into the room, flopping down on her futon bed.

"That was the worst lunch . . . pigs feet in some tomato sauce! They must be butchering all the pigs at the farm."

"Could be. I think they'll be closing down the whole camp soon."

"Really? Where will we go?"

"I don't know." Noticing Terri's stricken face, she adds, "But maybe we can look at it like a new adventure. You can choose anyplace in America."

"Can we? That's great. I don't want to go back to Venice."

At that moment, Hana enters. She's dressed in shorts and yellow shirt, her long legs girlish and tan. It pleases Sayo to see her daughter looking so happy, years younger than her age. And all this happening in the last two years—after meeting Shimmy and after the talk about true heritage.

"Say, Mom," spouts Terri immediately, "I want to go to North Carolina when we leave this place."

"What are you talking about?"

"We've been discussing what we'll do when the camp closes," explains Sayo.

"Yeah, and I don't want to go back to Venice."

"But why North Carolina?" To Hana, North Carolina is some swampy outpost in the South where people chew tobacco and lynch black men. "They're prejudiced there."

"No they're not!" says Terri defensively. "Not everyone."

"Well, I don't think we need to make any decision today. But you're right about one thing. We won't be going back to Venice."

Hana's agreement is enough to appease Terri, which closes further discussion of their destination after the war.

Hana and Terri leave. Sayo decides to shower in the afternoon, a departure from her nightly routine. But, sensing big changes are coming, she figures she might as well begin with small ones. While showering in the cool cement room, she thinks about rumors of Japan's imminent surrender. How could Japan ever have imagined it could defeat America? The stupid military leaders, deluded by their despotic powers, never had even glimpsed the vast raw resources of this country. Japan is ancient compared to America and should have known better. Couldn't they see they were fighting adolescents, volatile teenagers whose awesome strength was still unbridled? She wishes growing old made one more ignorant of men's cruelty to one another. But she brushes away the depressing thoughts, for she understands one does not grow up when there are no mountains to climb, no mistakes to rectify, no sins to forgive.

She decides to wear a red-and-white kimono, colors too young for her, but fitting in the orange-ish light of late afternoon. Arranging her long hair into pompadours, she sticks two ebony combs by the thick rolls.

* * *

She wears high *getas* and carries a black umbrella. Sauntering toward the high school playing field, she is a figure out of a Hiroshige woodcut. Missing from the picture are snow-capped Mount Fujii and rain, replaced instead by craggy Mount Williamson and a setting sun. As she nears the eastern edge of camp, she hears drumming. The sound is muted, the beat soft and rhythmically slow. Like warm wind blowing from the east, deep voices chant. She stops, remembering an old incantation, a blessing on all living things, the land, the ocean, even *o furo*! The sound is familiar, not very different from Buddhist and Shinto prayers.

She makes out Terri sitting in the shade of a barrack, drawing on her large cardboard easel. About a dozen Indians, dressed in buckskins, beaded ornaments, and feathers adorning black hair and hanging around their necks, shuffle and hop in a circle. Standing outside the circle, two men beat drums and sing. Already a crowd has gathered, but she is struck by a lone figure who stands above the shorter Japanese. Even from a distance, she sees his hair is gray beneath a black cowboy hat.

She approaches slowly, *getas* dragging on the road. He seems to have noticed her and walks out of the crowd. His broad shoulders and erect stance sear her heart. Since Cloud's death so many years ago, she never again met an Indian.

She stops, stunned by how he moves. She sees he is old, older than she, yet his gait is lithe, noiseless. She trembles, not knowing why. He nears and seems to quicken his steps as if recognizing her. She feels dizzy, his figure melting into wavering lines. Could she be having a stroke? In slow motion he seems to run, arms outstretched. She sees his face now, lined copper, hawklike nose, a scar down the side of his jaw. The deep-set eyes are jade green. Are those tears? Is she dreaming? Or have the dancing Indians conjured up Cloud's soul? She remembers he said years ago the Ghost Dance raised spirits of the dead!

"Sayo! Sayo!" he calls. Still in slow motion, he waves.

Unable to absorb the miracle that Cloud's ghost now runs toward her in the road, her senses fade. The rose light grows dim, and deep silence fills her ears. She sways and feels strong arms catch her—living flesh! Before she passes out, she smells a familiar scent, the smell of fresh earth and pine, alderwood and sage.

She opens her eyes and sees his face. Has she died and become a ghost, too? He smiles, stained teeth visible between brown lips. He removes a cold, wet cloth from her forehead. "You scared us there. You've been out quite a while." His voice is real. She looks up and sees Hana and Terri hovering behind him.

"Obachan, you're okay, aren't you?" Terri's voice quavers.

She stares at Cloud, realizing he is not an apparition. But how could this be? She is in her barrack compartment, lying on the futon.

"Cloud carried you here, Mama," says Hana. "You fainted, and they brought you home. Terri came next door and fetched me." Hana speaks slowly, worried Sayo is in such shock she can't understand.

Shaking, she grasps his hand, which also trembles. "Are you truly Cloud?" Unable to speak, he nods, familiar green eyes drinking in her face. "But you died in the earthquake!"

Still unable to talk, he shakes his head from side to side.

She bolts up and screams with joy, embracing him. Locked together, they both weep, oblivious to Hana and Terri watching dumbfounded. Terri is especially mystified as Hana discreetly leads her from the room.

In the next moments, more feelings are exposed than in all the intense few years they had spent together. She caresses his worn face, the ridged scar along his jaw. They both cry. Long moments of silence. Laughter of disbelief. To be reunited after all these years. To have her great love return from the dead! They try to piece the past together. How can one relate thirty-nine years of life? What happened that fateful day? Cloud's story unfolds.

Anxious to reach his destination, he had passed through San Francisco without stopping. He was in the Sierra foothills, traveling east toward the mountains, where he would turn south when he felt the quake. But he had no idea of the destruction it would bring. A day later, he finally reached the Owens Valley.

"My people are Paiutes," he says. "Our ancestors have lived in this valley for thousands of years. When the water-thieves tried to take our water, that was the reason I left—to help my people resist them."

"Why did you not return after you won the battle?"

Cloud turns glum. "We didn't win." He sighs. She sees pain in his still handsome face. "I organized a Ghost Dance, hoping to unite the Indians, give them back inspiration and power stolen from their souls by the whites. We danced and danced. It was powerful medicine and the people became strong. So strong, we resisted and fought back. Then the federal agents came and arrested us."

"Arrested you?"

"Yes . . . and put me in prison at Fort Tejon."

Shocked, Sayo asks, "For how long?"

"Twelve years."

"Oh my God!" She feels her heart breaking. She cannot speak. More than thirty years ago . . . still he is the same Cloud, her samurai warrior, defender of people.

"Twelve years is so long . . ." she managed to say.

"I tried to escape several times, but was caught and sentenced to more years each time. I was a crazy man." He laughs. "They called me Captain Mad Cloud."

He tells how he couldn't get word to her from prison. Even his own people were kept from knowing where he was. For some years it was rumored he was dead, and he was forgotten, left to fade into oblivion, isolated from other Indians, his family, the world. Then he was transferred to another federal prison in North Dakota. After his release, he tried to return to Watsonville. He got as far as San Jose, where he learned Sayo had married, had a daughter, and was still running a thriving teahouse.

"What could I expect after twelve years of silence? It was the hardest thing I ever did in my life . . . forcing myself not to cross the mountains to see you. But I couldn't intrude in your new life. I knew that."

She weeps. How can she tell him she never married Yoshio, and the daughter was his own! Would the tragedy of misinformation be too crushing to bear after all his years of suffering, of thinking she had not waited for him? What can she say?

She tries to comfort him by telling how she and the women and bachelors never recovered from the loss of his presence, how they had mourned his death, even erecting a gravestone for him next to the fishpond. "I never stopped loving you, to this very moment. I did not marry Yoshio. He was a good friend, much older, who helped me." She pauses, her throat stuck. "He helped raise my daughter . . . yours and mine."

The words sink in. Cloud looks like he's going to pass out. Pain etches deeper lines in his wrinkled face. He closes his eyes, fists clenched. She sees he is used to grief, knows how to endure it.

Finally he speaks, unclenching his fists. "In my old age, I thought I no longer could be shocked. But I admit that this news is almost more than I can take." For a moment he covers his face with his hands, but soon recovers. "Then the woman next door who called you 'Mama' . . ."

"Her name is Hana."

"And the young one . . . is my granddaughter?"

"Yes."

She asks him the inevitable question. "Did you ever marry? Do you have children?"

A smile creases the weathered skin around his mouth. "No. You are my only love. The thought of you kept me alive during those long years of imprisonment. I never could have made it without hoping I would see you again."

He tells how after thinking she had married, he traveled for months hiking alone through mountain trails until he reached Canada. He lived at an Indian reservation north of Montana for many years, returning to the Owens Valley several months ago when he heard there was a Ghost Dance revival.

"You mean the Indians dancing in camp were doing the Ghost Dance?"

"That's right," he says. "We see this internment camp as another reservation, a way to take away your power. That's why we've come to dance."

Next door Terri and Hana sit silently on the cot-sofa. Terri knows something very strange is going on. Her mother sobs into her handkerchief, barely able to answer Terri's urgent questions. Who is the old Indian? How is it that *Obachan* seems to know him? Even hugging him like an old lover. Did her grandmother suffer a stroke? Was she going crazy like old people do?

Terri sweats with anxiety. Unused to intimacy with her mother, she is uncomfortable trying to comfort her, but moves close and puts an arm around her. Hana melts and lays her head on Terri's shoulder. Finally, she is able to talk.

"I know you will be shocked with what I have to tell you," she sniffles. "I only have just learned . . . some things about our family."

"What do you mean? About Dad?" Terri is becoming more confused.

"Well, no . . . about *Obachan* . . . and me."

Feeling a twinge of jealousy at being left out, Terri nevertheless patiently listens.

"It's so hard to tell you." She unexpectedly hugs Terri. "But, the Indian with *Obachan* is my father . . . your grandfather."

"What?"

"His name is Cloud, and he was Sayo's great love. She thought he died in the San Francisco earthquake many years ago."

Terri barely registers what Hana has said. Yet the anxious feeling in her stomach begins to immediately subside; an odd warmth moves throughout her body like liquid gold. "He's my grandfather?"

"Yes. And I understand from Sayo he is a great man, a man of integrity and courage."

Terri remembers the granite warrior, her visions of Indians battling in the firebreak. She understands somehow those spirits—spirits of her ancestors—had been speaking to her. "So, that makes me part Indian, too," she says with pride, "and Mac and Carmen, too."

"That's right."

"Woweee!" yells Terri. "Now don't you really feel like you're somebody? Not just some plain ol' Japanese!"

Hana laughs, buoyed by Terri's infectious glee.

The door opens and Sayo enters, followed by Cloud. Her grandmother is radiant, looking very young. Terri stares at her grandfather, impressed by his strong face and tall, erect figure. She doesn't even feel excluded when he approaches Hana and embraces her, his large hands stroking her hair and patting her back. She sees how rugged his hands are, yet gentle and without awkwardness.

When he turns to Terri, his eyes twinkle. She feels completely at ease, as if she has known him forever. Suddenly she realizes the granite warrior in the Horimoto compound looks exactly like a young replica of her grandfather. She watches him inspect the room, taking in the knotholed walls, hanging blanket curtains, and box furniture. He saddens, and she recognizes Hana's taciturnity, her reserve in his face. She wonders if she resembles him, too.

"So, you are Terri, my granddaughter."

Uninhibitedly, she hugs him, burying her face in his buckskin-covered chest, smelling leather and tobacco.

"I guess the Great Creator allowed me to survive so I could see you three."

Hana says, "Your gift to Sayo . . . the beautiful hand mirror . . . I looked at it once and thought I saw your face."

"You did." He sounds like Sayo, mystery surrounding his words.

Sayo interjects, "Cloud says he came to this desert because his people were again dancing the Ghost Dance, to help us in camp."

"Really?" Terri smiles at him. "Thank you . . . I mean you and your tribe for dancing."

"No need to thank us," says Cloud. "We're all of the same tribe."

Terri remembers those very same words spoken by the granite warrior.

They visit until Pot-Banger's clanging sounds from the mess hall. Cloud rises to leave, saying he will return the next day. "We will dance one more time," he promises.

Together Again

That night Sayo sleeps alone in the compartment. She told Terri to spend the night with Hana and Carmen, wanting to ponder alone all the day's incredible happenings. She thinks about the next day when Cloud should return and he will meet Carmen. It will be difficult explaining things, as Carmen's life has revolved around music and song and friends outside the family. She never stays at Hana's apartment during the day and often sleeps at her friends' places at night. Sayo wonders if she even knows about Indians, and is quite certain she is not interested. But she realizes she cannot worry about her other granddaughter now.

She is restless, forcing herself to not think of what might have been. She sighs. Perhaps this is all a dream, or perhaps she truly has died and has met Cloud in heaven. It is karma. *Shi kata ganai*—it can't be helped.

Dozing off, she is awakened by gentle jostling. It's Cloud. "I thought you would be returning tomorrow," she says, now fully awake.

"It is tomorrow. It will soon be dawn." He embraces her and lifts her off the futon. He has brought a bundle, which he unties, revealing a pair of boots and some woman's Indian dress.

"Quick, put these on . . . before it gets light." His soft voice is urgent.

Without questions, she dresses and slips on the boots, which he ties, bending on knee before her. The dress fits loosely, and smells of sage. "What are we doing?"

"I am taking you out of this prison."

Sayo giggles. "Have you permission?"

"I need only yours. But we must leave now, before the sun comes up."

Realizing he is serious, she asks soberly, "Won't you get into trouble? They could put you in prison again."

"They'll never find us. I know this country like the palm of my hand, every creek, ravine, and boulder."

"But what about my daughter . . . our daughter and grandchildren?"

He holds her firmly by the shoulders. She barely can see his jade eyes but feels their intensity. "Sayo-san . . ." Her heart twinges hearing him speak her name with such endearment. "I don't dare think of the last thirty years as wasted. I would have to kill myself. But we have some years remaining. Let's live it for each other. Are you willing?"

Without hesitation, she answers "Yes."

"Then we leave right now."

"Now? Without saying good-bye to them?"

"I assure you, they'll understand."

She trusts him. They slip silently out the door and quickly walk past the latrines and laundry room. They pass the mess hall and cross the firebreak. Finally they reach the barbed-wire fence. The sky is purple, lavender at the eastern horizon where the sun will soon rise. For one last look, she turns to scan the camp—bleak, tar-papered shacks, empty acres of sand and dirt. She sees a vision of Hana going to college, teaching school, and later together with Shimmy. Mac is home safely from Italy and relocates to Chicago. Carmen is a famous singer, recording songs for movies. Terri is an artist, married to a tall *hakujin* man with red hair.

She is satisfied, and, feeling no remorse or trepidation, she turns away from the view. She looks to the west, to Cloud waiting at the fence.

Sayo is young again, her sagging flesh now smoothly succulent, breath fresh as spring. Cloud's leathery skin is moist, stained teeth brilliant white. They cavort in the ocean, naked limbs full and firm, bodies agile. They ride curling waves to the shore, through tunnels of turquoise. On the beach, they dance. Indian drums sound the beat, and they sway and bend, stepping high in a Ghost Dance. They dance and dance, breathing life into their souls left wounded so many years. They dance for the wolf and deer, coyote and bear, buffalo and elk, for all the parts of souls wandering in the Land of Ghosts, where hatred, greed, guns, and barbed wire have rendered a barren world. They dance to the Goddess of the Sun, Amaterasu, to the prophets Wodziwob and Wovoka, to the Spirits of the Whirlwind and the Mountains.

Cloud holds her hand and guides her under the wire. On the other side he puts his arm around her and leads her into sagebrush and tumbleweed. The sun is now rising, a fan of gold lightening the eastern sky. She breathes deeply, exhilarated. She is free! Free again to begin and end another life.

Epilogue

If one passes by on Highway 395, only two pagoda-roofed gate-houses at the camp's entrance are visible now, sentinels to dried tumbleweeds and sage blowing about. Beyond them, if one ventured to drive west over a gullied dirt road through stunted pear and apple trees, ruins of rock gardens, concrete slab foundations tilting crazily from erosion and quakes, one would come upon a lone white obelisk upon which are engraved Japanese characters, "Memorial to the Dead." Several graves, outlined in rocks, rest within an area fenced with barbed wire to keep out wandering cattle.

This is what remains of an encampment once the biggest city between Reno and Los Angeles, a city of 10,000. The wind still howls and sudden dust storms can obliterate the view of Mount Williamson within seconds. Some say they can hear voices in the wind, in rustling leaves of elm trees planted by internees more than fifty years before. Sometimes the sounds are wails, cries, and other times, music—big-band tunes and Indian drums.

The old-timers of the valley have reported sighting ghosts who haunt the terrain between the Alabama Hills and Independence. Archaeologists have uncovered Indian relics that date back hundreds of years, buried beneath two layers of artifacts—those of white settlers who took the land from the Indians, and Japanese-Americans who revived and restored it for a period of four years. Now intermingling, spirits from three layers of existence summon up the past's ghostly vestiges. But the most memorable story told by those who remember Manzanar in 1945 was the day it snowed in summer.

The date was August 7. A huge gray mushroom cloud appeared high over Mount Williamson, smoky billows swirling and enfolding, darkening a previously blue sky. Rain began to fall, sooty black and thick, covering the desert and camp with coal-like cinders.

A brilliant sun rose above the cloud, dissipating it, and those internees who dared to look into its light swore it bore the figure of Amaterasu, the Sun Goddess. Cinders became petals, fragrant red and pink. Now stark white, the sky was an empty canvas awaiting a painter's brush strokes. Against the whiteness, at first dimly colored but soon vivid, appeared a black horse with two riders astride—a handsome warrior and a radiant woman in kimono. They streaked across the heavens, fire flaming from the horse's nostrils.

The petals turned white, turned to snow that purified the soiled land, raining down in frozen tears. The fallen tears became pebbles, which still today are scattered in the desert and lie in gurgling creeks.

Glossary

arigato-gozaimasu	thank you
bakatare	idiot
benjo	toilet
gaijin	foreigner
getas	wooden clogs
hakujin	Caucasian
hai	yes
hara	stomach
hototogisu	cuckoo
inaka	countryside
issei	first-generation Japanese
kami	god
kibei	educated in Japan
mizu-kami	water-god
mochi	rice cake
nihonjin	Japanese
nihonmachi	Japantown
nisei	second-generation Japanese
obi	wide belt
ocha	tea
o furo	bath
ohaiyo-gozaimasu	good day
onsen	hot springs
origami	paper art
seppuku	suicide
seppun	mouth-kissing
shamisen	banjo/lute

shashin-kekkon	picture bride
tokonoma	display shelf
umeboshi	pickled plum
yogore	uncouth one
yomeii-san	wife of eldest son
yukata	cotton kimono
zabuton	pillow

About the Author

JEANNE WAKATSUKI HOUSTON coauthored *Farewell to Manzanar,* the true story based upon her family's experience during and after the World War II internment. It is now a standard work in schools and colleges across the country. Her essays and short stories, first collected in *Beyond Manzanar: Views of Asian American Womanhood,* have been widely anthologized. Among her numerous honors are a U.S.–Japan Cultural Exchange Fellowship, an Arts American Traveling Lectureship in Asia, and a Rockefeller Foundation residency at Bellagio, Italy. *The Legend of Firehorse Woman* is her first novel. She lives in Santa Cruz, California.